GILLY MACMILLAN

ODD CHILD OUT

Sphere
An imprint of
Little, Brown Book Group
Carmelite House
50 Victoria Embankment
London EC4Y 0DZ

An Hachette UK Company
www.hachette.co.uk

www.littlebrown.co.uk

sphere

SPHERE

First published in Great Britain in 2017 by Sphere
This paperback edition published by Sphere in 2018

1 3 5 7 9 10 8 6 4 2

Copyright © Gilly Macmillan 2017

The moral right of the author has been asserted.

A CIP catalogue record for this book
is available from the British Library.

ISBN 978-0-349-41292-4

Typeset in Bembo by M Rules
Printed and bound in Great Britain by
Clays Ltd, St Ives plc

Papers used by Sphere are from well-managed forests
and other responsible sources.

Gilly Macmillan is the *New York Times* bestselling, Edgar-nominated author of *What She Knew* and *The Perfect Girl*.

Gilly grew up in Swindon, Wiltshire and lived in Northern California in her late teens. She studied art history and worked at *The Burlington Magazine* and the Hayward Gallery in London before starting a family. Since then, she's worked as a photography teacher and now writes full time. She lives in Bristol.

Also by Gilly Macmillan

What She Knew (first published as Burnt Paper Sky)
The Perfect Girl

To my dad. You are missed.

AUTHOR NOTE

Odd Child Out is set in my home city of Bristol. While some locations have been used as precisely as possible, others have been altered for the purposes of the story. The characters and events in this novel are entirely fictitious and any resemblance to actual persons, living or dead, or to actual events, is entirely coincidental.

THE NIGHT BEFORE

After Midnight

A black ribbon of water cuts through the city of Bristol, under a cold midnight sky. Reflections of street lighting float and warp on its surface.

On one side of the canal there's a scrapyard, where heaps of crumpled metal glisten with frost. Opposite is an abandoned red brick warehouse. Its windows are unglazed and pigeons nest on the ledges.

The silken surface of the canal water offers no clue that underneath it a current flows, more deeply than you might expect, faster and stronger.

In the scrapyard a security light comes on and a chain-link fence rattles. A fifteen-year-old boy jumps from it and lands heavily beside the broken body of a car. He gets up and begins to run across the yard, head back, arms flailing, panting. He runs a jagged path and stumbles once or twice, but he keeps going.

Behind him the fence rattles a second time, and once again there's the sound of a landing and pounding feet. It's another boy and he's moving faster, with strong, fluid strides, and he doesn't stumble. The gap between them closes as the first boy reaches the unfenced bank of the canal, and understands in that moment that he has nowhere else to go.

At the edge of the water they stand, just yards from each other. Noah Sadler, his chest heaving, turns to face his pursuer.

'Abdi,' he says. He's pleading.

Nobody who cares about them knows that they're there.

Earlier That Evening

At the end of my last session with Dr Manelli, the police psychotherapist, we kiss, awkwardly.

My mistake.

I think it's on account of the euphoria I'm feeling because the sessions I've been forced to attend with Dr Manelli are finally over. It's not personal; it's just that I don't like discussing my life with strangers.

At goodbye time she offered me a professional hand-shake – long-fingered elegance and a single silver band around a black-cuffed, slender wrist – but I forgot myself and went in for a cheek peck and that's when we found ourselves in a stiff half-clinch that was embarrassing.

'Sorry,' I say. 'Anyway. Thank you.'

'You're welcome.' She turns away and straightens some papers on her desk, two dots of colour warming her cheekbones. 'Going forward, I'm always here if you need me,' she says. 'My door is always open.'

'And your report?'

'Will recommend that you return immediately to the Criminal Investigations Department, as we discussed.'

'When do you think you'll submit that?' I don't want to sound pushy, but I don't want any unnecessary delay, either.

'As soon as you leave my office, Detective Inspector Clemo.'

She smiles, but can't resist a final lecture: 'Please don't forget that it can take a long time to recover from a period of depression. The feelings you've been having – the anger, the insomnia – don't expect them to disappear completely. And you need to be alert to them returning. If you feel as if they might swamp you, that's the moment I want to hear from you, not when it's too late.'

Before I embed my fist in a wall at work again, is what she means.

I nod and take a last look around her office. It's muted and still, a room for private conversations and troubling confidences.

It's been six months since my therapy began. The aim was to throw me a lifeline, to save me from drowning in the guilt and remorse I felt after the Ben Finch investigation, to teach me how to accept what happened and how to move on.

Ben Finch was eight years old when he disappeared in a high-profile, high-stakes case, the details of which were plastered all over the media for weeks. I agonised over him and felt personally responsible for his fate, but I shouldn't have. You have to preserve some professional distance, or you're no good to anybody.

I believe I have finally accepted what happened, sort of. I've convinced Dr Manelli that I have, anyhow.

I call my boss in the Criminal Investigations Department as I jog down the stairs in Manelli's building, my eyes fixed on the pane of glass above the front door. Slicked with daylight, it represents my freedom.

Fraser doesn't answer, so I leave her a message letting her know that I'm ready to come back to work, and ask if I can start tomorrow. 'I'll take on any case,' I tell her. I mean it. Anything will do, if it gives me a chance to rejoin the game.

As I cycle away down the tree-lined street where Dr Manelli's office is located, I think about how much hard graft it's going to take to play myself back in at work, after what happened. There are a lot of people I need to impress.

Riding a wave of optimism, as I am, that doesn't feel impossible.

I'm upbeat enough that I even notice the early blossom, and feel a surge of affection for the handsome, mercurial city I live in.

The light from the gallery spills out onto the street, brightening the dirty pavement.

Tall white letters have been stencilled on the window, smartly announcing the title of the exhibition:

EDWARD SADLER:
TRAVELS WITH REFUGEES

In italics beneath, there's a description of the work on show:

Displaced Lives & Broken Places:
Images from the Edge of Existence

The photograph on display in the window is huge, and spotlit.

It shows a boy. He walks towards the camera against a backdrop of an intense blue sky, an azure ocean speckled with whitecaps, and a panorama of bomb-ruined buildings. He looks about thirteen or fourteen. He wears long shorts, flip-flops and a football shirt with the sleeves cut off. His clothes are dirty. He gazes beyond the camera and his face and posture show strain, because looped across his shoulders is a hammerhead shark. Its bloodied mouth is exposed to the camera. That, and a red slash of blood on the shark's muscular white undercarriage are shockingly vivid against the ruined architectural backdrop: marks of life, death and violence.

On the Way to the Fishmarket. Mogadishu, 2012, reads the caption beneath it.

It's not the image that made Ed Sadler's reputation, that gave him his five minutes of fame and then some, but it was syndicated to a number of prestigious news outlets, nevertheless.

The gallery's packed with people. Everybody has a glass in hand and they're gathered around a man. He's standing on a chair at the end of the room. He wears khaki trousers, scuffed brown Oxford shoes, a weathered leather belt and a pale blue shirt that's creased in a just-bought way. He has sandy-coloured hair that's darker at the roots than the tips and thicker than you might expect for a man in his early forties. He's good-looking: broad-shouldered and square-jawed, though his wife thinks his ears protrude just a little bit far for him to be perfectly handsome.

He wipes his suntanned forehead. He's a little drunk, on the good beer, the amazing turnout, and the fact that this night represents the peak of his career but also a devastating personal low.

It's only four days since Ed Sadler his and wife, Fiona, sat down with their son, Noah, and his oncologist, and received the worst possible news about Noah's prognosis. Reeling with shock, they've so far kept it to themselves.

Somebody chinks a spoon against a glass and people fall silent.

Head and shoulders above the crowd, Ed Sadler gets a piece of paper out of his pocket and puts a pair of reading glasses on, before taking them off again.

'I don't think I need this,' he says, crumpling the paper up. 'I know what I want to say.'

He looks around the room, catching the eyes of friends and colleagues.

'Nights like this are very special because it's not often that I get to gather together so many people who are important to me. I'm very proud to show you this body of work. It's the work of a lifetime, and there are a few people that I need to acknowledge, because it wouldn't exist without them. First, is my good friend Dan Winstanley, or as I should say now, *Professor* Winstanley. Where are you, Dan?'

A man in a button-down blue shirt, and in need of a haircut, raises his hand with a sheepish smile.

'Firstly, I want to thank you for letting me copy your maths homework every week when we were at school. I think it's long enough ago that I can safely say this now!' This gets a laugh.

'But, much more importantly, I want to thank you for

9

getting me access to many different places in Somalia, and in particular to Hartisheik, the refugee camp where I took the photographs that my career's built on. It was this man Dan who took me there for the very first time when he was building SomaliaLink. For those of you who don't know about SomaliaLink, you should. Through Dan's sheer bloody-mindedness and talent it's grown into an award-winning organisation that does incredible work educating and rebuilding in projects throughout Somalia, but it was founded almost twenty years ago with the more humble objective of fostering links between our city and the Somali refugee community, many of whom came to Bristol via Hartisheik and its neighbouring camps. I'm very proud to be associated with it. Dan, you've been my fixer for as many years as I can remember, but you've also been my inspiration. I never could contribute much in the way of brains, but I hope these images can do some good in helping to spread the word about what you do. Taking these photographs is often dangerous and sometimes frightening, but I believe it's necessary.'

There's a burst of clapping and a heckle from one of his rugby friends that makes Ed smile.

'I do this for another reason, too, and that, most of all, is what I want to say tonight . . . ' He chokes up, recovers. 'Sorry. What I'm trying to say is how proud I am of my family and how I couldn't have done this without them. To Fi, and to Noah, it hasn't always been easy – understatement – but thank you, I'm nothing without you. I do all this for you, and I love you.'

Beside him, Fiona's face crumples a little, even as she works hard to hold it together.

Ed scans the room, looking for his son. He's easy to find because his friend Abdi is beside him, one of only four black faces in the room, apart from the ones in the photographs.

Ed raises his bottle of beer to his son, salutes him with it, and enjoys seeing the flush of pleasure on the boy's cheeks. Noah raises his glass of coke in return.

About half the people in the room say, 'Awww,' before somebody calls out: 'Fiona and Noah!' and everybody raises a glass. The applause that follows is loud and becomes raucous, punctuated with a couple of wolf whistles.

Ed cues the band to start playing.

He steps down from the chair and kisses his wife. Both are tearful now.

Around them, the noise of the party swells.

While Abdi Mahad is at the exhibition opening with his friend Noah, the rest of his family are spending the evening at home.

His mother, Maryam, is watching a Somali talent show on Universal TV. She thinks the performances are noisy and silly, but they're also captivating enough to hold her attention, mostly because they're so awful.

The show is her guilty pleasure. She laughs at a woman who sings painfully badly and frowns at two men who perform a hair-raising acrobatic routine.

Abdi's father, Nur, is asleep on the sofa beside his wife, head back and mouth open. Maryam glances at him now and then. She notices that he's recently gone a little greyer around the temples, and admires his profile. He doesn't have his usual air of dignity about him, though, because he's snoring loudly enough to compete in volume with the shrill presenters on the TV. A nine-hour shift in his taxi followed by a meeting of a local community group, and a heavy meal afterwards with friends, has knocked him out as effectively as a cudgel.

As the TV presenters eulogise over a rap performance that Maryam judges to be mediocre at best, Nur snorts so loudly that he wakes himself up. Maryam laughs.

'Bedtime, old man?'

'How long have I been asleep?'

'Not too long.'

'Did Abdi text?'

'No.'

They've been worried about Abdi going to the photography exhibition. They know the subject of the show is refugee journeys, and they know that some of the images that made Edward Sadler famous were taken in the refugee camp they used to live in. These things make them uneasy.

Abdi never lived in the camp. Nur and Maryam risked their lives to travel to the UK to ensure that he never had to experience a life that looked the way theirs did once everything they'd ever known had unspooled catastrophically and violently in Somalia's civil war. Both of them were torn from comfortable, educated homes, where James Brown played on the turntable some evenings, and Ernest Hemingway novels sat on the shelf amongst Italian books, where daughters were not cut, and children weren't raised to perpetrate the divisive clan politics that would soon become lethal.

Nur and Maryam tried hard to dissuade Abdi from going to the exhibition, but he wasn't having any of it.

'Don't wrap me in cotton wool,' he said, and it was difficult to argue with that. He's fifteen, confident, clever and articulate. They know he can't be sheltered for ever.

They reasoned eventually that if the extent of his curiosity about their journey as refugees was to visit an exhibition, then perhaps they would be getting off lightly, so they let him go, and told him to have a good time.

Maryam turns the TV off, and the screen flicks to black, revealing a few smudgy fingerprints that make her tut. She'll remove them in the morning.

'Are you worried?' she asks Nur.

'No. I wasn't expecting him to text anyway. Let's sleep.'

As her parents go through the familiar motions of converting their sofa into their bed, Sofia Mahad, Abdi's sister, is sitting at her desk in her bedroom next door. She's just received an email from her former headmistress, asking if she would be willing to revisit the school and give a speech to sixth-formers on careers day.

Sofia's twenty years old, and in her second year of a midwifery degree. She's never done public speaking before. She's shy, so she's avoided it like the plague. She's flattered by the invitation, though, and especially by the sentence that describes her as 'one of our star pupils'.

'Guess what?' she calls out to her parents, 'I've been asked to give a speech!'

She takes out one of her earbuds so she can catch their response, but there isn't one. They obviously haven't heard her. She'll tell them face to face later, she thinks, when she can enjoy seeing the proud smiles on their faces.

She rereads the email. 'One thing that might really interest our Year 13s,' the headmistress writes, 'is hearing about what inspired you to become a midwife.'

Sofia does what she usually does when she's considering something. She gets up and looks out of the window. Outside, she can see a small park that's empty and quiet, and a large block of flats on the other side of it. The uncurtained windows reveal other people's lives to her, lit up in all shades from warm to queasy neon, some with a TV flicker.

She knows exactly what inspired her: it was Abdi's birth. The problem she has is that she's not sure if she can write a speech about it, because nobody in her family has ever talked openly about what happened that night. Her mother tells a very short version of the story of Abdi's birth: 'Abdi was born under the stars.'

Sofia also knows that's not the whole story, because she remembers the night in vivid detail. Like all of her memories of Africa, it's intense. She sometimes thinks of that part of her life, the part before England, as a kind of hyper-reality.

Abdi was born in the desert, and Sofia can picture those stars. They roamed the sky in great cloudy masses. They looked like cells multiplying under a microscope. They cast their milky brightness down once the truck had stopped and the headlights were extinguished.

The men didn't let Maryam out of the truck until her time was very close. She had been labouring for hours, crammed into the flatbed with the others, and she continued to labour in the Saharan emptiness. There were no other women to help, so it was Sofia who knelt and cradled her mother's head, her fingers feeling the sweat on Maryam's cheeks and the clench of her jaw. Nur knelt beside them and delivered the boy with shaking hands.

Sofia remembers the feel of the stones digging into her shins, her knees and the top of her feet. She remembers how the light from the stars and the crescent moon made the shifting surfaces of the sand dunes shimmer. She thought that their brightness drew Maryam's cries up to the heavens and coaxed the baby from her body.

The smugglers spoke harshly to Maryam, telling her to be quiet and quick. Each of them had a third leg to their silhouette, made from a long stick or a gun. They leaned on them impatiently, propped up by violence, and hungering for speed and the maximum profit from their human cargo.

Sofia remembers how the blade of the knife glinted in the torchlight when the men severed Abdi's cord. 'Hurry! Get back in the truck!' the men said, and their eyes cast threats of abandoning Maryam there if she didn't obey. Minutes later she delivered the afterbirth obediently, wet and bloody onto the parched ground, and the wind speckled it with sand.

Back in the truck, the faces of the other passengers were swaddled against the sand and wind. Maryam passed out: heavy body sweat-soaked, and clutching blood-dark material between her legs. Nur held her and his breathing shuddered as the engine revved. Sofia cradled her new brother. She kept him warm. She put her face up close to the baby's and gazed at him. In the starlight she examined his sealed-up eyes, his damply soft flesh and hair, and she knew that she loved him.

As the truck swayed and skidded on the track through the desert, that thought brought her a feeling of warmth, even though she was very afraid.

Sofia breathes in suddenly – almost a gasp – and it snaps her out of her reverie. She types an email to her headmistress thanking her for the invitation and telling her she would like to give it some thought.

When that's done she lapses once again into thinking about Abdi, and how strange it could be to be born between places, as he was, under the gaze of smugglers and thugs. Where would you belong, really? How would it affect you, deep in your bones? Would you know that threats had torn you from your mother's sweaty, terrified body?

She doesn't dwell on it too hard, though, because her attention is soon diverted by the buzz of her social media notifications, and all the distractions of the present.

Sofia doesn't think about Abdi again that night. Nor do her parents, apart from a brief discussion once they're tucked under the duvet, when they sleepily debate whether Abdi should give up chess club to make more time to study exams he's due to take this summer. They have so much hope that he will get the results he needs to apply to a top-rank university.

All is quiet in the household overnight. It's in the frigid early hours of the morning that the buzzer to their flat begins to ring repeatedly, long and loud, before dying away like a deathbed rattle as the battery fails. Nur climbs out of bed to answer it. He's hardly awake enough to be on his feet.

'Hello?' he says. He can see his breath.

In response, he hears a word that he learned to dread at an early age: 'Police'.

THE INVESTIGATION

DAY 1

It's a good moment putting my ID badge back on after so many months off. 'Detective Inspector' is a title I worked hard for.

The air is crisp and cold and the traffic seems lighter than usual on my morning journey to Kenneth Steele House, the HQ of Bristol's Criminal Investigations Department. I make good time on the new road bike I bought when I had time on my hands, between therapy sessions and tedious teaching duties. The ride feels very sweet.

Here and there, I see evidence of fallout from a march that took place in the city centre a week ago: a huddle of yellow traffic cones like part-felled skittles wait for collection near the waterfront; a few boarded-up windows punctuate the reflective panes.

The march started as a small-scale problem, a nasty little anti-immigration demonstration by a neo-Nazi group, the only redeeming feature of which was that it was anticipated to be very sparsely attended. It might have petered out after a couple of hours if it had been well managed – it should have done – but things got out of hand. Medium-scale rioting and looting led to some large-scale embarrassment for the police. The whole debacle left a nasty taste in the mouths of many city residents.

I don't dwell on it as I coast down the road to work, though. I'm focused on holding my head as high as I can when I walk back through those doors into the office.

Detective Chief Inspector Corinne Fraser doesn't look any different from when I last saw her, months ago: grey eyes, frizzy slate-coloured hair only partially tamed by a severe bob cut, and a gaze as penetrating as a brain scan. She gets up from her desk and gives me a warm, two-handed handshake, but wishes me luck in a tone that makes it clear that I've got work to do to regain her trust. It's a welcome back, but an unnerving one. It's vintage Fraser.

My other colleagues greet me nicely enough. Mostly it's in a hail-fellow-well-met sort of way that feels pretty genuine, though one or two of them don't hold eye contact for as long as they might. There's no shame, Dr Manelli once said, in what happened to me, in the fact that I flipped my lid publicly, but I reckon some of my colleagues might be feeling it on my behalf. I try not to take it personally. That's their problem, I tell myself. My job is to prove how good a detective I am.

It's during 'Morning Prayers', her daily briefing meeting, that Fraser hands me the Feeder Canal case. I get the feeling she's glad to have some poor soul to allocate it to. Its priority level is made clear by the fact that it's the last item on the agenda before a housekeeping request that we make an effort to reuse the plastic cups at the water cooler.

Fraser asks a familiar face to precis the details of the case for me.

Detective Constable Justin Woodley throws a half-smile

my way and clears his throat before reading from his note-pad. I haven't had much to do with him since he witnessed me throwing up into the front garden of a major witness on the Ben Finch case. It was a humiliating reaction to a bit of bad news.

Water under the bridge, I tell myself. Hold your nerve. I nod back.

'A fifteen-year-old boy fell into the canal last night, just down the road from here by the scrapyard. He was fished out by emergency services and they took him to the Children's Hospital. He's in very bad shape currently, in intensive care and in critical condition. He was with another lad who was found canalside. Not injured, but in shock, and he's being checked over at the Royal Infirmary.'

'And they want someone from CID because . . . ?'

'There's a witness. She says she thought there was some funny business going on between the lads before the fall into the canal. She's the one who called it in. She's still at the scene.'

'What does the lad who wasn't injured say?'

'He's not spoken to anybody yet.'

'Why not?'

'He's just not speaking, apparently. Whether it's can't speak or won't speak, we don't know.'

Woodley flips his pad closed.

'I believe the victim's a white boy, and the other kid is from the Somali community so sensitivity is paramount,' Fraser chips in.

'Of course,' I say.

Fraser continues: 'I'm sure it won't surprise you to hear that budget is tight to non-existent, so I'm not going to press the investigation button on this one unless there's very good reason to. If we can put it to bed easily, then let's do that and let uniform handle it. Jim, you and Woodley will be working together on this.'

Fleeting eye contact tells me that I'm not the only one feeling nervous about that.

Woodley and I take a walk down to the scene. It's less than half a mile up Feeder Road from Kenneth Steele House, and it's not Bristol's most scenic destination.

We pass beneath a stained and graffiti-tagged concrete overpass that moves four lanes of traffic from one corner of the city to another. It's oppressive. Even on a nice day the underside is gloomy and the shadow it casts is deep.

Beyond the overpass, the properties that border the canal-side road are mostly warehouses, lock-ups and the odd automotive place, and most of them have high-visibility security in the form of spiked or barbed perimeter fences.

'Does this case sound like a hospital pass to you?' Woodley asks.

'I don't know. Depends what the witness saw. It could be something or nothing.'

'Did he jump, or was he pushed?' He makes it sound like a teaser. I forgot that Woodley had a sharp sense of humour. I find myself smiling.

'Something like that.'

Woodley clears his throat. 'Full disclosure: I cocked up really badly on a case. I lost some evidence.'

24

I take a moment to absorb that. I guess I'm not the only one who's walking wounded, then.

'What was the case?' It matters.

'Child abuse.'

'Did it cost you a result?'

'Yes. The dad was allowed back to his family. He was guilty as sin. My fault.'

It's the very worst kind of case to make a mistake on.

'Happens to the best of us,' I say, though I'm sure that doesn't reassure him at all. I'm not sure what else to say. I'm in no position to judge him, but now I understand why Fraser has us working together. We're the last kids to get picked for the team. We'll sink or swim together on this case.

'For what it's worth,' he says after we've walked on a bit, following the canal's path, 'on the Ben Finch case I thought your work was solid. Lots of people did. You went after what you believed.'

I look at him. Nose like a ski jump, a small patch of thinning hair appearing on his scalp, and those clever eyes, searching mine for a reaction. He still wants to be a player, I think. That's good for us both.

'Thanks. I . . . ' but I don't know what else to say; it feels too soon to be having this discussion with a colleague. I'm not ready. Woodley doesn't push it.

Further up, we pause at the edge of the canal to take in the scene. The water looks soupy and uninviting. Sludgy pale brown mud banks up the sides and the foliage along the water's edge looks as if the long winter has depressed it terminally. A fisherman is huddled in wet-weather gear a few hundred yards to the east.

Beside us, there's an abandoned warehouse and a modest Victorian pedestrian bridge that spans the canal. The path across it is weed-covered and trash-strewn. Underneath a layer of black paint that's peeling like a bad case of psoriasis, the structure looks rusty enough that it's unlikely to last another hundred years.

Across the water, we can see the scrapyard where the incident took place. I can't imagine what business two teenage lads would have around here. It feels like a waste-land. They must have been mucking about. Daring each other to trespass, or looking for somewhere to sneak a drink or smoke a joint.

'I think this case is a minnow,' I say. I look into the murky water. There's nothing to see except the legs of a shopping trolley that's gone beetle-up on the bank. 'Small fry. But it's better than traffic duty.'

In retrospect, I misinformed Woodley, because neither of us recognised this case for what it really was: menacing, strong and smooth, perhaps not making waves at first, but able to turn on a dime and surprise you with a razor-toothed bite. This case was actually a shark.

Of course I didn't recognise it. Nobody else had, so why should we?

Fraser would never have let us have it if she'd known better.

Darkness is dissolving over the city, lingering only in pockets, as the Mahad family arrives at the Accident and Emergency Department at Bristol Royal Infirmary. They have been given very little information, no more than a scant outline of what's happened to Abdi.

The officers accompanying the Mahads greet two colleagues outside the rear entrance to A&E. They're speaking to a man who has his back against the wall and blood matted in his hair. He's sucking hard on a cigarette. He's talking about salvation. Half of his face is in darkness, but a caged light fixture throws out just enough of a glow to show Sofia that his pupils are pin-pricks. When he catches sight of Maryam his agitation increases.

'That's what I'm talking about,' he says. 'They wear them dresses so they can hide bombs under them.' He lurches towards the Mahads. 'You can go back to your fucking country. You're ISIS, you fucking terrorists!'

The officers react instantly, containing him, but not before a gob of his spit has landed near Sofia's feet.

Nur stands between his family and the man and ushers the women into the hospital. His face is perfectly composed, though his chest heaves. He knows that these are the words of an ignorant and almost certainly crazy man, but they still wound.

Inside, the waiting area is filled with rows of chairs arranged in an airport configuration so the injured and unwell can pass the time by eyeballing each other. The police officers make sure the family bypasses the queue at the reception desk. A nurse takes them down a narrow corridor where there are bays containing beds, each with a curtain at one end that offers scant privacy.

A police officer stands at the entrance to one of the bays, mainlining takeaway coffee. He steps aside so the Mahads can slip past the drawn curtain.

Abdi lies in bed. He looks at his family, yet he seems not to see them.

His parents and sister search his face for clues as to what he's been through, and find nothing to reassure them. He hardly resembles the boy they love.

There's no animation in his face, no spark of life in his eyes, no twitching of his muscles around his mouth to hint that he's about to smile or gently tease. He's withdrawn to a place that's blank and still.

At the sight of him, Maryam feels fear flap darkly inside her. She doesn't dare look at Nur in case she sees her mounting sense of dread mirrored in his expression.

'Oh, Abdi,' she murmurs.

Sofia watches her mother lean in towards Abdi and place her cheek against his. She sees how Maryam tries to embrace him fully, but Abdi does nothing to reciprocate. Maryam withdraws and takes his hand instead. Sofia thinks there's a strange energy between them.

The space around the bed is cramped, but Sofia and Nur shuffle around each other so that they can try to embrace Abdi, too. He responds to neither of them. Both think that he feels somehow rigid yet not really there. They shuffle back, and stand awkwardly around the bed, trying not to stare, not knowing what to do or where to put themselves.

Sofia watches her mother for a cue, because Maryam often sets the emotional tone in their family. Sofia's not sure whether their mother will question Abdi, chide him, or tuck the blankets up around him and stroke his forehead. She expects Maryam to do one, if not all, of those things. She thinks of her mother's love as a soft rain. It drenches gently, and when it's warm, it's the most gorgeous feeling in the world. When it's cold, not so much. Either way, Sofia experiences Maryam's love as intense and unwavering.

Maryam stares at her son for what feels like a long time. She looks to Nur, and reading her silent request he takes her place at Abdi's bedside.

'Abdi, we're here for you. Whatever happened, you can tell us about it.'

He runs the back of his fingers gently across the boy's temple.

Abdi flinches and moves his head across the pillow.

Sofia feels the prickling of tears. She thinks she would probably rather see Abdi physically injured than in this state.

'It's OK,' Nur tells him. 'It will be OK. Nobody will be angry.'

Abdi shuts his eyes.

Nur persists. 'Abdi, can you tell me what happened?'

Nothing. Sofia can hardly bear to watch.

In the bay next door, a doctor is treating somebody, and Sofia tunes into and out of their conversation.

'Why did you do it?' the doctor asks. He gets a mumbled response from his patient that Sofia can't quite hear through the partition.

'Abdi.' Nur won't give up. It's killing him that Abdi's unresponsive. He shakes the boy's shoulder gently and Abdi rolls onto his side, turning his back.

'Why?' The doctor's voice is raised in the bay next door.

Nur looks at Maryam and she shrugs. She doesn't know what to do to get through to Abdi, either. Her hand covers her mouth.

'Why did you do it?' the doctor says again. 'Tell me why you did it.'

It must be a suicide attempt, Sofia thinks. *It's unbearable to listen to. No wonder Abdi's in such a state. He shouldn't be here.*

As Nur makes another attempt to get Abdi to talk, Sofia whisks back the curtain, surprising the police officer outside.

'Why is my brother here?' she demands, her shyness forgotten as she thinks only of getting Abdi home. 'This is the wrong place for him to be treated. He should be at the Children's Hospital. He's only fifteen.'

'The only ID we found on him was a library card, so if he won't talk to us, we can't know his age,' the officer says. A strip light flickers above them. 'We had to guess so we assumed sixteen or over because he's a big lad.'

Sofia doesn't really care what the explanation is. She wants action.

'Well, he's fifteen, and we'd like to take him home.' She's convinced that Abdi's in shock, that he'll talk to them and become a more recognisable version of himself again if they can just get him out of here.

She waits for the doctor to come out of the bay next door, and presses him for an update on Abdi.

'He checks out fine physically,' the doctor says, stripping off a pair of blood-stained gloves and binning them. 'But we think he could be suffering from shock. You can take him home, but you'll need to make sure he's warm and comfortable, and keep an eye on him.'

'Has he said anything at all since he's been here?'

She thinks of the way Abdi behaved when he came

to meet her after one of her days on placement at this hospital. There was nobody on the ward he didn't greet effusively. No hand he didn't shake and no end to the questions he asked the consultant who took the time to chat to them.

'I don't believe so. It's possible he's suffering some kind of emotional trauma relating to what he witnessed.' The doctor seems to take pity on her, throws her a bone. 'Resting up at home will certainly be better for him than being here.'

Sofia replaces Nur at the head of Abdi's bed as her parents go to complete the discharge paperwork.

'Rest, Abdi,' she whispers to him. She lays a hand tentatively on his shoulder, and he lets her leave it there for a moment, before shrugging it off.

'OK,' she says. 'I'll leave you be. We're going home soon.'

She folds her hands into her lap and remembers that when Abdi was a baby he followed her everywhere as soon as he could move, and tried to copy everything she did. If she studied his face in the minutes after he was born, he studied hers a million times in the years that followed. She remembers his gummy smile, his baby-tooth smile, his gappy smile and the smile after that, when his new adult teeth seemed too big for him. She feels that the two of them were knitted together at his birth, and always would be.

He'll be able to speak when he gets home, she tells herself, and she says this out loud to her parents when they return to the bedside.

The police escort them out and offer to drive them home.

As they exit the parking area, Sofia sees the Children's Hospital next door. They've told her that Noah's being treated there. That makes sense. There's no way they could have mistaken him for a sixteen-year-old.

Noah's condition is critical. The police have explained this to Abdi, apparently, in an effort to persuade him to talk. She wonders how wise that was.

She also wonders what Abdi saw and what he and Noah did.

When she swallows, all she tastes is fear.

'Noah,' Mum says. 'Can you open your eyes, love?'
    I can't.

She asks me to squeeze her hand, but I can't do that either. I can't move at all.

'Anything?' Dad asks.

'No.'

I think I can feel Mum's fingers tightening around mine, and then, a little louder than before, she says, 'Noah! Darling, can you hear me? Can you squeeze my hand at all, Noah, even just a little bit?'

My first response is to think, I'll be able to later, I'm sure I will. But then I'm not so sure, because everything is kind of a grey mist right now. I've no idea what's happening. There's only one thing that's clear in my mind: a very recent memory. It's the unforgettable, irreversible fact that I've had the talk, the one where they tell you that the wheels have fallen off the bike and there's no putting them back on.

'How long have we got?' Mum said to Sasha, the day we got the news. We were sitting in the room on the Paediatric Oncology ward that's supposed to be for parents to take refuge in when everything gets a bit much. Only families who are new to the ward use it, though, because everybody else knows that it's also known as the 'Bad News Room'. You learn to avoid it like the plague.

Sasha's my oncologist. Full name: Dr Sasha Mitchell, with lots of letters afterwards, but she's been treating me for years – we're firmly on first-name terms.

'I can't predict that with any accuracy,' she told Mum. 'I'm sorry.' She had a grip on Mum's hand, and I was glad because Mum looked as if she might vaporise if somebody didn't physically hold her. 'But I would hope, if we don't get any kind of unexpected event, that there might be a couple of months. We can discuss how we might alleviate Noah's symptoms, so that time can be as enjoyable as possible, but I'm afraid that's all we can do.'

Silence.

'I'm very sorry,' Sasha repeated. I didn't want her to look at me.

Dad wasn't with us that morning. He was on a plane back to Bristol from somewhere.

My favourite nurse, Sheila, was in the room, sitting in the circle of bad news. She's been treating me for years, just like Sasha.

My medical notes were on her knees, a stack of papers so thick that nobody had yet transferred them to the electronic system. They're filed in multiple cardboard folders, each bursting with paper, dog-eared and coffee-stained, and joined to the next with treasury tags. They follow me around the hospital to wherever I'm having treatment. Trolleys look as if they might sag under the weight of them, and nurses have to carry them with two arms. They document everything that's ever happened to me here. Families who haven't been in the system for as long as we have eye them with fear. One of Sheila's tears soaked into the cardboard cover. I wondered what the hospital would do with them when I'm gone. Trash them, I suppose.

I blubbed in the Bad News Room, of course I did. The three of them rallied around me, arms criss-crossing my back and Mum said, 'Noah, love, Noah.'

I said, 'But there are so many things I need to do.'

On the way back to my room, with Mum and Sheila and the rolling IV stand that I was attached to, I noticed the other nurses at the station averted their eyes. They knew. I wanted them to face me. I used my elbow to knock over a tray that one of them had left in a precarious place. Syringes and blood vials clattered across the linoleum. The fourth-floor colour scheme is blue in Bristol Children's Hospital, if you're interested. Blue floor, blue walls. The vials rolled a satisfyingly long way. I felt as if everything was happening in slow motion.

Mum's voice interrupts my thoughts. She's speaking slowly, like I'm half-witted or deaf. 'Darling, you've been in an accident. You fell into the canal and you banged your head while you were under the water. The doctors have put you in an induced coma because they think that's the best way to get you better. You're in intensive care.'

'Do you remember being by the canal last night?' Dad asks.

The canal: black water, the surface a thick, slick membrane until I hit it, and the cold clenched my chest.

'With Abdi?' he adds.

'Don't,' Mum says.

'He might remember.'

'He's not even conscious.'

'Then why are you talking to him and asking him to squeeze your hand?'

'Because I think it's good if we talk to him, but I don't think we should be asking distressing questions. We don't *know* what happened.'

'It was an accident. What else could it have been?'

'I'm not talking about it now. I've just said it might distress him.'

She has lowered her voice, but I can still recognise the tone she uses to let him know that she knows best. She does know best. Dad's never home enough to understand everything about my treatment.

My parents are quiet for a while, until Mum says she's going to the loo. Dad waits until the sound of her footsteps has faded and then he talks to me again.

'You're tough, buddy, you're going to pull through this. We have things planned, Noah, and we're going to do them. It's not going to end like this.'

He's talking about my bucket list. We made the list when he arrived at the hospital after I got the news. He lay on my bed with me all night, smelling of airports and strange places, and we handwrote the list with a stubby pencil he always carries in his shirt pocket. Together, we whittled it down to thirteen items. Thirteen is not a lucky number, I know, but at this point you can probably understand why I'm not too concerned about that.

Noah's Bucket List Item No. 1: Don't Tell Anybody Else I'm Dying. Not Even Abdi.

'Are you sure about that?' Dad asked me.

'Completely sure.' I wanted to spend my last few weeks doing things my way, and you can't do that if everybody's sobbing or being funny around you.

Dad had stubble on his chin that night. I always wanted to have stubble one day, but that wasn't going to happen now.

Cancer's a big fat thief, we agreed when we talked that night. It had taken so many things from me since my diagnosis – things I wanted to do, friends I wanted to make, experiences I didn't want to miss out on, normal stuff – and now that it had decided to ink its signature onto my death warrant, it was going to take my future away, too.

I'm aware of a weight on my hand and I think someone's holding it. It must be Dad, because he's talking to me again, or trying to. I can't feel the temperature of them today, but I know that his hands are always warmer than my mother's.

'I wish we could have taught you to swim properly,' he says. His voice cracks.

I had some swimming lessons before my diagnosis, but they put a permanent line into your chest when treatment starts. It's called a central line. It's designed so they can shoot the toxic drugs into you and drag blood out of you whenever they want without sticking you with needles.

Here's a cool thing Sasha did when I freaked out about

36

one of the drugs they were giving me, because I overheard a nurse saying it burns your skin. She showed me a photo on her phone of a little purple flower.

'Firstly,' she said, 'this drug can't burn your skin because you have a line in, so it's not possible because we'll inject it down the line. Secondly, look hard at this flower. It's called *vinca*, and it's what your chemo drug's made from. When you get home, go and look in your garden and see if you can spot some growing there. If you do, you need to give it a little salute because it might look like nothing, but it's going to do a grand job of fighting the cancer cells. It's your friend, right now.'

No-shit Sasha. That's what my dad calls her, and he's right. I liked her straight talk even when I was little.

Anyway, whatever good stuff the line did, it was also a big pain. I wasn't allowed to get it wet. Swimming lessons ended before I learned to swim strongly for more than one width of the pool. Pathetic.

Dad's repeating himself in the sort of self-flagellating way that drives my mum crazy: 'We should have made sure you could swim better.'

When he starts to cycle on the *we should have*s, it means he's going to lose it big-time, and he does.

A machine begins to beep.

'Oh, crap. I've set you off,' Dad says. He does this all the time. Mum knows how to slink carefully around my bed like a cat, but he blunders, snagging tubes or bumping machinery.

I hear the metallic swoosh of curtain rings being whisked back.

'Sorry,' Dad says. 'I think that was my fault.'

A nurse must be there. They're very quick to come on PICU. I'm impressed, though I guess it figures.

'I'm not sure it was you,' says the nurse. 'I'm going to call the registrar.'

Pressure grows and intensifies in my head.

'What's happening?' Dad asks.

'Give us some room, sir, please.' A new voice.

'Noah!' Dad shouts. 'Noah!'

'Stand back, sir!'

'Charging. Clear!'

A hammer blow to my chest.

In my mind, water closes in over me and drags me away. There's fire in my lungs. Above the surface of the water I see Abdi. He's blurred. He's no more substantial than an eliding set of shadows. He's something and nothing.

As I sink, he watches.

Detective Constable Woodley and I find the witness in one of the Portakabins at the scrapyard. She's sitting with a uniformed constable who's made himself a bit more comfortable than he should have. He gets to his feet quickly when we step in, looking like a kid caught with his hand in the biscuit tin.

A fan heater pumps sickeningly hot air into the tiny space, powered from a socket that's half hanging off the wall. Invoices and purchase orders cover a desk that fills most of the space. A stack of yellow hard hats and fluorescent tabards hang off a coat rack, alongside a row of keys on hooks, a dog lead and a calendar featuring pictures of sports cars.

The witness isn't what I expected from an industrial neighbourhood like this one. She's young, late twenties at a guess, attractive, and, apart from the dark circles under her eyes that have doubtless emerged over a long night, well groomed.

She stands up to shake my hand when we're introduced, and it's a confident gesture. Under a tailored jacket she's wearing only a thin blouse and I understand why the fan heater is on full blast. Skintight jeans and a pair of very high heels complete the outfit. I thank her for waiting around to speak to us.

'I was collecting from my lock-up, over there.' She points in the direction of some low buildings behind the scrapyard. 'It was just after midnight.' She's in control; her voice is calm.

'What were you collecting?'

'Stock. I own a lingerie shop. Upmarket, before you jump to conclusions, Detective. It's in Clifton.'

My own flat is located in a building on the edge of Clifton, and it's also the neighbourhood where the boy who nearly drowned and his parents live. Clifton's made up mostly of wide, tree-lined streets lined with Victorian mansions, many of which have chic mews houses hidden behind them. Some very pretty parkland and the city's famous suspension bridge complete the picture, making its real estate some of the most expensive in Bristol. The shops are mostly small, smart and pricey. I think I know which is hers. Only one has a window display of mannequins dressed in tiny scraps of lace with extraordinarily high price tags.

As if she can read my thoughts, the witness flashes me a

smile that's both sweet and knowing, and I have to fight to stop myself returning it instinctively. Out of the corner of my eye I notice Woodley smirking.

'Do you normally collect stock in the middle of the night?'

'Not normally, no, but I was out last night and I didn't see a text saying we needed more stock until I was on my way home.'

'Can you describe what you saw?'

'It was more what I heard. I was loading my car when I heard shouting. I wasn't too bothered at first because it sounded like somebody calling somebody else, but it got rougher.'

'Could you hear what they were saying?'

'Not exactly, but it sounded like a name, like they were calling out to somebody. It was hard to tell where it was coming from, but I thought it was probably the scrapyard.'

'Could you see anything happening at all?'

'Not at that point. I locked up because I felt a bit nervous, and got in my car. As I drove past the scrapyard I could see two figures by the edge of the canal. Looked like two young lads.'

'Did you see this from your car?'

'I was too nervous to get out.' Her gaze flickers across mine as if she's wondering whether I'll judge her for this admission. 'There was something about them.'

'Can you explain a bit more what you mean by that?'

'There was a threatening look about them.'

'Did you witness any violence between them?'

'They were pushing and shoving.'

'Was that how one of them ended up in the water?'

'I couldn't say, but it's not rocket science, is it? One of them was much bigger than the other.'

'But you didn't actually witness the fall?'

'No. I was getting my phone out of my bag so I could call you, wasn't I?'

'And the next time you looked, what did you see?'

'Just one of them, standing on the side, looking into the water.'

'Did he try to help the boy who went into the water?'

'Not that I saw.'

'Did he try to run away?'

'No.'

'Did he threaten you?'

'No. He didn't see me. I wondered if they were off their heads.'

'What makes you say that?'

Her eyes dart sideways. 'One of them, I think it was the one who fell, was weaving around a bit before.'

'In what way?'

'Sort of sideways. Like this.'

She gets up and enacts a bizarre drunken stagger. Woodley and I avert our eyes until she sits back down. It's a small space and she has a curvaceous figure.

'Did you see how they got into the scrapyard?'

'No. Climbed the fence, I expect.'

Woodley says, 'Emergency services had to cut through the chain locking the main gate, so they must have, unless there's a hole in the fence somewhere.'

The witness shivers in spite of the heat. She looks tired.

On the desk between us a mobile phone begins to buzz and dance, as if on cue. It has a glittery case. She grabs it and takes a look at the screen. Her finger hovers before she rejects the call.

'It's my partner.' She lays it down carefully.

'Do you need to call him back?'

'No, it's fine, we already spoke. He's just worried.' There's something about the way she says this that makes me keep my mouth shut for a minute, just to see if she'll elaborate. She does; they almost always do. Most people have an urge to explain.

'He doesn't think I'm in danger. He just wants me home, you know.'

I notice a small dash of lipstick on the front of her teeth as she gives me a smile that's more an exercise in muscle control than a show of emotional warmth.

'Of course,' I say. 'That's understandable.'

She squeezes her arms together awkwardly, showing me a glimpse of something lacy as her blouse parts. I look away again. The fan heater's still blasting out hot air and Woodley and I are both tugging at our collars.

'So, just to clarify, you didn't see what happened at the precise moment when one of the lads went into the canal, because you were getting your phone out of your bag?'

'I didn't see, but just as I dialled I heard a splash and when I looked again the white boy was gone. It was just the black boy standing there, looking at the water.'

'And were you able to identify the skin colour of the boys from where you were sitting?'

'No, but I saw them after.'

'After what?'

'After emergency services got there and pulled him out of the water. Honestly, I'm surprised he was still alive. I can't believe the other boy did nothing to help. If I hadn't phoned you . . .'

'You did the right thing.'

As soon as she's gone, I flick the heater off and leave the door open. Woodley and I watch her stride across the yard to retrieve her car from outside the entrance. It's a top-of-the-range small Mercedes, sporty and fast.

'What do you think?' Woodley says.

'She hasn't actually witnessed a crime.'

'She'd go down well in court, though,' he says as we watch her leave.

I agree. She's articulate, confident and well presented.

'Why would she have to fumble in her bag for her phone if she drives a motor like that?' I ask. 'Surely it would be Bluetooth connected. Can you check the paramedics' account supports her story? And I'd like to hear the recording of the emergency call she made, please, if we can arrange that.'

When the Mahad family arrives home from the hospital, Abdi walks up the stairs to the flat on his own, though Nur hovers anxiously behind him all the way. It's painfully slow progress.

Abdi takes himself straight to bed. He still hasn't uttered a word.

Sofia, Maryam and Nur have decided that the best thing

to do is let him sleep, in the hope that it will help him get through his shock. Even so, for the next couple of hours, Sofia can't stop checking on him. She reminds herself of the anxious first-time mothers she helps at the hospital.

For a while she sits beside him in a silent vigil, a textbook beside her that she can't concentrate on, but the sight of his immobile body gets to her. She fidgets, and her head snaps up sharply when her father appears in the doorway, blocking the light. He peers into the room.

Sofia loves her father deeply and knows every inch of his silhouette as well as the back of her own hand. She's noticed a stoop in his shoulders lately, which is new, and gives her a little pang of sadness.

'Sofia,' he whispers, 'can you phone Fiona Sadler? We want to ask how Noah is.'

Fiona Sadler is Noah's mum, and Sofia doesn't like her. There's nothing specific Fiona's said or done that Sofia could give as a reason for this if somebody asked, it's more that she doesn't seem to be a warm person. Sofia finds her prickly and difficult to talk to.

'Do you think we should?' she asks. 'They're probably at the hospital.'

It's a poor attempt to put off making the call, because she knows that if they're asking, her parents will have already decided. They've asked her because she's always been the one to call the Sadlers. When Noah and Abdi were younger, Maryam could never phone to make arrangements for play dates because her English wasn't good enough, so it fell to Sofia. Nur has better English, but he's not fluent like his children.

It's a language barrier that's given Sofia and Abdi plenty of opportunities for mischief over the years, just like the children of fellow immigrants they know.

Sofia dials the number, secretly praying that nobody will answer. Her shyness makes phone calls a bit of an ordeal generally, but today her sixth sense tells her that making this particular call is also a bad idea.

After just enough rings to make her hopeful that voice-mail will pick up, there's a breathy, 'Hello?'

'Mrs Sadler? It's Sofia, Abdi's sister. I'm so sorry to bother you but we were wondering how Noah is.'

She feels as if she's got wedges of lemon in her mouth.

At the other end of the line, Fi Sadler makes a sound like a gasp and then moans, long and low, and Sofia feels the sound echo at the very core of herself. She's drenched in something that feels like shame as she realises that she was right. It was entirely the wrong thing to do to make this call. Whatever's happened to Noah is very bad.

She turns her back on her parents.

'I'm so sorry . . . ' she starts to say, but another voice comes on the line.

'Who is this?'

'Mr Sadler? It's Sofia Mahad. I'm so sorry, we were just wondering how Noah is doing, but I shouldn't have called.'

'Sofia.' It sounds like a sigh. 'Fi's not up to talking. We had a very tricky moment with Noah, but he's stable again. They've put him in an induced coma because he banged his head when he was in the water. That's all I can tell you.'

Sofia, feeling out of her depth by about twenty thousand leagues, can only think of very formal words to say: 'Please know that we are thinking of him and praying for him and for your family.'

'Thank you,' and then, just as she thinks she's going to get away, he asks, 'How's Abdi?'

Silent, she thinks, *but apparently physically fine.* It feels wrong to say that when Noah's situation sounds so desperate.

'He's very traumatised. He's home, but he's in shock. He's sleeping.'

'We were wondering ... did Abdi say what happened? The police told us that he wouldn't talk to them.'

Sofia wonders if she's imagining the slightly accusatory tone in his voice. She's uncertain enough that she replies very carefully.

'It's because of the shock. He can't talk right now, but he will when he wakes up, I'm sure.'

There's a silence on the line that feels a fraction too long to Sofia, but she second guesses herself as soon as she has that thought, tells herself it's her own paranoia.

Just three nights ago Abdi struck a strongman pose in front of the TV. 'Black and Muslim,' he said, flexing his muscles, moving this way and that to show them off, laughing at himself as he did. He was modelling a new T-shirt.

Sofia laughed, because Abdi was good at making fun of himself, but the smile died on her lips quickly, because references to her family's race, creed or religion give oxygen to a fear that burns in her day in, day out. She can't ever shrug off the idea that any one of those labels is a reason for some people in Britain to hate her, and she finds that very painful to live with.

On the phone, Ed Sadler's talking again, 'Do you have any idea why the boys were down by Feeder Canal? We can't understand it.'

'No. We don't know.'

'We just can't think why they would go there. To a scrapyard apparently?'

'We don't know either.'

'Do you think they were heading to your home? Or somewhere in your neighbourhood?'

Sofia considers this, but Feeder Road isn't on any route she'd take from Clifton to Easton, though she's aware that her sense of direction isn't great.

'No, I'm sorry, I don't think so. We thought they would be with you all night. Abdi was looking forward to it.'

She regrets those words as soon as she's said them, in case they sound accusatory, but Ed Sadler's distracted.

'I'm sorry, Sofia, I have to go. The doctor's here.'

The line goes dead before she's able to say goodbye.

When she turns around her parents' faces are so eager for the news to be good that she downplays Noah's condition.

'He's stable,' is all she says.

'Was it Fiona Sadler?' Unable to communicate effectively with Fiona herself, Maryam has always been very curious about this woman.

'No, it was Ed.'

Nur stands up. The tension's so great he can't sit still. He says a silent prayer for Noah, for both boys. It takes him a second to hear that Sofia's asking him a question.

'Where's Feeder Canal, exactly?'

'Behind Temple Meads station.'

Nur carries the city in his head like a map seen from a bird's-eye point of view. He can visualise the rail lines snaking away from the train station, from where they eventually reach out into the rest of the country. A short distance away from those serpentine tracks he knows there's a dead-straight road running alongside a dead-straight stretch of water: Feeder Road and Feeder Canal.

Nur is a voracious reader and a self-taught student of everything, so he knows that the canal is part of the grand Victorian engineering project that made Bristol's floating harbour and swelled its trading coffers. He knows everything about the colourful mercantile history of his adopted city, and on the whole he admires it in spite of the deeply shameful parts of it. Nur admires it because he believes in possibility, and in hard work paying off. He believes that there's good to be found in people, and in life. He believes in hope. It's what gives him the strength to get up each day. It's what got him and his family here, all the way from Somalia.

'They asked me if we knew why the boys were there,' says Sofia.

'Abdi will tell us when he wakes up,' Maryam says.

The dishcloth she's holding is twisted tightly between her hands.

*

48

Next time I wake up, I remember that I'm in intensive care, but I don't know how much time has passed. To be more accurate, I know I'm physically present in the intensive care unit, but I feel as if I'm floating on water somewhere with a big empty sky above me. It's only the sound of my parents' voices that anchors me now and then. Mostly I spend my time drifting, experiencing my past and my present all at once.

I met Abdi on my first day at secondary school. I was nearly twelve.

I looked like a thin, ratty kind of creature that day. My hair had fallen out unevenly during treatment and begun to grow back unevenly afterwards, so my scalp resembled a badly shorn sheep with some fuzzy bits in places and some weird comb-over wisps, all a lifeless shade of pale brown, and not enhanced by the ghostly pallor of my complexion and my red-rimmed eyes. You don't take a lot of selfies when you're in treatment.

Before I went to my classroom I had to sit in a meeting with the headmistress, the special education needs coordinator from the school, my specialist learning mentor from the hospital, Molly, and my mum, and they went through my care plan which was designed to help me back into mainstream education. It was the world's most boring document.

I shut my eyes while they over-discussed every point and sub-point. When Mum picked me up on it, I said I was conserving energy so I could get through the rest of my day. It was sort of true. I felt like I would get chronically fatigued if I heard the word 'special' one more time.

'Don't feel self-conscious,' Molly said to me when we

eventually stood in the corridor outside my new form room. She was always very earnest, and more often than not she had biscuit crumbs stuck between her bottom teeth. 'Just be yourself.'

I was a bit worried, but I wasn't going to tell her that, because I was determined that I would make friends and have a good time at Medes College. I felt like people would be nice to me there. It was my dad's old school. Our family knew at least two of the governors. After my last relapse, one of them sent me a framed photograph of the Bristol City football team. It was signed by all the players. I made some good money for that on eBay.

In the classroom, everybody stared at me when I went in, and I had to stand at the front and be introduced.

The kids sat at tables in pairs, apart from one boy, who was all on his own: Abdi. I took the spare seat beside him.

By the time Mum came to collect me after school, I felt dead on my feet. I was leaning against the school fence in the spot where we agreed she would pick me up. She didn't need to ask if I'd made any friends because Abdi was standing right beside me, grinning. He stuck out his hand when I introduced them, and she shook it and complimented his backpack.

In the car, she said, 'Abdi seems nice.'

'He's really nice.'

'What are the other children like?'

'They're OK.'

'Did you talk to them?'

'A bit. It was very tiring.'

The truth was that I hadn't talked to anybody else because I'd concentrated on being Abdi's friend. He was funny, and he showed me everything I needed to know. Not many other people talked to him, so it was mostly just the two of us sitting together in class and hanging out at break and lunch. I didn't want Mum to know that, though, so a timely reminder that my stamina wasn't a hundred per cent did the job of distracting her nicely.

'You've done so well to last the whole day. I was expecting a call earlier if I'm honest.'

I rested after school and thought about my day. I made it to the table for dinner that night. Dad was home.

'To a good day,' Mum said, raising her glass of wine to her lips. I was happy to see her smile was in her eyes, too. It wasn't always.

I didn't have much appetite, but I ate a bit and pushed the rest of the noodles to the edge of my bowl where I calculated Mum couldn't see them from where she was sitting.

'Did you talk to Will Kelly?' she asked. 'At school?'

I shook my head.

'He's in your class.'

I knew that. I spotted him after I sat down with Abdi. He's the kind of boy my parents probably thought I should be: a rugby/hockey/football boy with the kind of clear skin and confident posture you only get if you play sports all summer and every weekend. At break, I noticed he was surrounded by a group of boys and girls. They jostled each other and talked loudly.

I thought about joining them, but I decided to go with

Abdi instead. He needed help moving some books for the librarian. Will Kelly could wait until we got the chance to talk when it was just us, and probably when I was a bit stronger. I didn't want him to judge me on my breadstick limbs and my voice that didn't have a hope of projecting across a canteen. I was confident this was a smart decision but I didn't think Mum would understand.

'I'll talk to Will Kelly tomorrow,' I said. 'I just didn't get a chance today.'

'Who's Will Kelly?' Dad said.

'You know, the Kellys, who live on Chantry Road?' Mum said, as if she were referring to God or the prime minister, it was so obvious.

'Oh! OK. That's nice.' I could tell Dad still didn't have a clue.

Silence. Mum topped up their wine.

Dad made an effort: 'When did we meet them?'

'Noah's sailing course. Last summer.'

Mum rewrites our history a lot. What she meant by that was the morning I sat on the side of the floating harbour and watched my peers learn to sail. They wouldn't let me take part because of my central line.

Mum loved it because she got a bit dressed up for once, and had a coffee with the other mums in the sunshine while I helped the instructor's daughter sort out lifebelts.

Dad nodded.

'I thought we might be able to share lifts with them,' Mum said, as if that explained everything.

To change the subject, I told Dad about Abdi.

'Where's he from?'

'I don't know. He doesn't walk to school. His dad brings him in his taxi.'

'I mean where is his family from?'

'I don't remember. But he said he might take the bus to school when he's older.'

'Daddy means what country are his family from originally?' Mum never speaks with her mouth full, so she did a whole load of laborious chewing before saying that. Outside, the light was fading, and I could see a magpie scaring the smaller birds off the feeder.

'I don't know.'

'What's his second name?'

'He's got two second names, but I can't remember them.'

'Somalia, maybe,' Dad said. 'Ask him if they're from Somalia.'

Mum's eyes rolled because Somalia was one of Dad's favourite subjects. He began to give us a potted history of Somali immigration to Bristol, even though we'd heard it all before: 'Lots more of them than you'd think ... over decades ... strong links between the camps and Bristol ... quite a community now ... do you remember that shop in Easton where we went to get the preserved lemons for the Nigella recipe ... most of them live there ...'

When Mum couldn't bear it any longer, she cut him off by saying, 'Anyone for dessert?'

As she went to take the ice cream out of the freezer, Dad leaned over and ate the rest of my noodles.

'You should ask Abdi where his family's from,' Dad said. 'It's interesting to know people's stories.'

'OK.'

'Guess where I'm off to next week.'

'Timbuktu?'

'Ha! Not a million miles away actually, though maybe a few thousand.'

He sucked a noodle into his mouth slurpily and raised his eyebrows as if to say: 'Keep guessing!'

'I don't know.'

'Namibia. Skeleton Coast.'

'Where the shipwrecks are?'

'Shipwrecks that stick up out of the sand like carcasses. And sand dunes that look like shallow waves when you fly over them, but when you're at ground level they're immense. They drop off into the ocean like the face of a cliff.'

'Will you go in a plane?'

'A small plane, yes, so we can fly low to get the shots.'

'You won't use a drone?'

'No. I like to hold the camera and feel the picture with my own hands, see it through the viewfinder myself. You know you're making something special that way because you connect with the scene. You're the author of it.'

'Noah!' It was Mum, back in the room, cookie dough ice cream and bowls in hand. 'You've gone white!'

Just like that I was back in the land of fatigue and fussing.

I heard my parents talking as I lay down in the next room. They were always bad at lowering their voices.

'Sounds like it went well today,' Dad said.

'I think so. The teacher gave me that impression.'

'You spoke?'

'Uh-huh.'

That made me feel upset because I didn't like being spied on or reported on. I wanted Mum to take my word for it.

'A good start, then,' Dad said.

'I just . . .'

'What?'

'I want him to fit in.'

'I know. I do, too.'

'Do you think this boy is a suitable friend?'

'I'm sure he is.'

She said something that was too quiet for me to hear, and Dad said, 'Seriously, don't do this.'

'Don't do what?'

'Don't create a negative from something that's good news. He's had a good day. He made a friend. Shouldn't we be grateful?'

A clash of cutlery and crockery and then Mum's voice: 'Sorry.'

'Talk to me, Fi.'

'It's nothing. I am grateful. I can't believe he's even made it back to school.'

'He's made a friend on his first day. That's got to be a good sign. I loved Medes College. I know he's going to.'

'I just want something to work out for him.'

'It will. I promise you, it will.'

I put a cushion over my head. Ears muffled, I imagined myself in a small aeroplane, high in the sky above the Skeleton Coast, flying into the sun until I was so close I couldn't see anything at all.

The next day when I got to school, Abdi was talking to another boy, but I tapped him on the shoulder and asked him if he could help me find the maths staffroom. I could have found it myself, obviously, but I wanted him to come with me.

On the way, I told him all about my dad's trip to Namibia, and the sand dunes that rose into the sky like cliff faces. I talked so much that I got out of breath, and Abdi helped me to a bench where we sat and rested for a few minutes. The bench was in the marble corridor, and I showed Abdi where Dad's name was printed in gold letters on a big wooden board because he was a House Captain.

It was nice.

Noah's Bucket List Item No. 2: Visit the Skeleton Coast (this one's a long shot, I know).

In addition to the recording of the emergency call, I request public CCTV footage from the city centre, along any routes that the boys might have been likely to take from Clifton to Feeder Canal. I want footage from the scrapyard and surrounding area, too, but that's going to have to be requested from any local businesses that might have private cameras, so I ask Woodley to get onto it.

Woodley and I sign out a pool car and make the short drive over to Easton. He agrees to keep a low profile during the interview. I want him to observe while I question. Some members of the Somali community have a reputation for keeping themselves to themselves. I don't know how fair that is, but it makes me wary of behaving in any way that might alienate this family.

The Mahads live on an estate that's sandwiched between Stapleton Road and the motorway. It's not the ugliest estate in the area, nor does it have the worst reputation, but it's probably somewhere you'd be plotting to get away from if you had anything about you.

There's a small, grassy area that sits between the buildings in the middle of the estate, and I park alongside it. It looks muddy and unkempt, and I don't think the swing set could pass a health and safety inspection even if it bribed somebody.

We've had no detailed briefing about the family so I'm not sure what to expect as we approach their building. In the middle of a short row of buzzers that are broken or just identifiable by number, theirs has a neat card inserted into a space beside the button with their name carefully printed in ballpoint pen.

Inside, there's no lift, and the stairwell's badly lit, though not so much that you can't see the blistered paintwork. The Mahads live on the third floor. We're greeted with a handshake by a tall man who's wearing round gold-rimmed glasses, a white shirt, grey trousers and an expression of deep concern.

'Nur Mahad,' he says, and we introduce ourselves.

Inside, seated on one end of an L-shaped sofa, are two women, both dressed in hijabs. The younger woman's headscarf is deep ruby red and draped stylishly over a soft, oatmeal-coloured sweater. She also wears slim dark jeans. She's rolling a gold bracelet around her wrist. She's slightly on the chubby side, but also strikingly pretty.

Her mother's clothing is much more conservative: a

black headscarf worn over a long, deep brown gown that covers her feet. She wears a pale blue cardigan over the top of her gown as well, but it doesn't stop her looking as if she's cold. There's no spare flesh on her face. Her cheeks are almost concave.

I nod in the direction of the women, remembering that it might not be the right thing to do to offer my hand if this family is very devout.

'My wife, my daughter,' Nur Mahad tells me. 'Maryam and Sofia.' His voice is heavily accented.

'Is Abdi here?' I ask. 'I'd like to have a word with him if possible.'

Five paces bring us to the door of a bedroom containing a single bed and a modest-sized desk. Curtains are drawn across a small window. Abdi lies with his back to us, almost completely covered by his duvet.

'Abdi!' his father says. 'The detective is here to talk to you!'

He opens the curtains and shakes his son gently by the shoulder. Greyish light filters in, but not much of it, because the view from the window is mostly of a wall opposite. Abdi's body moves as he's being shaken but falls still as soon as his dad lets go. He looks much taller than Noah Sadler, from what I can tell. He's skinny, with long limbs: the shape of an adolescent boy having his big growth spurt. His hair's cut short and neatly. He's very much a schoolboy.

Nur Mahad shrugs. 'I'm sorry,' he says. 'He's been like this since he got home. We don't know what to do.'

He goes to shake the boy again.

'Sir,' I say. 'That's OK. May I speak to him myself?'

He steps away and I squat beside the bed, but I keep a respectful distance. If the kid's suffering, I don't want an accusation of harassment.

'Abdi,' I say to the back of his head. 'I'm Detective Inspector Jim Clemo.' I think the rise and fall of his shoulders accelerates slightly. He's listening. 'I'm investigating what went on at the canal last night. Are you feeling up to talking to me about what happened?'

No change. My gut tells me that he's not putting this on. He's afraid. He's either seen something or done something that's terrified him into silence. It's got me interested.

'You're not in trouble, son,' I say, even though I'm not a hundred per cent sure of that. 'I'm here to listen to you.'

Nothing. I consider my options and settle on the only one that's realistically available.

'Abdi, I'm going to leave my card here.' I take one from my wallet. There's no bedside table so I pin it on the corner of a corkboard that hangs beside his bed. The board's covered in school certificates and commendation letters. There's also a photograph of two boys, about twelve or thirteen years old, I guess, arms slung around each other's necks and holding a trophy between them. It's shaped like a chess piece.

The caption reads: *It's a county win for Abdi and Noah!*

The happy, smiling boys celebrating their victory in the photograph couldn't be more different from the inert body in the bed in front of me.

'You can contact me at any time, Abdi. I'd really like to hear from you about what happened last night.'

I try to keep my tone even and non-threatening. It's all I can do at this point. To force an interview, even if I could, might risk anything I learned from him being thrown out of court down the line if it's considered that he wasn't well enough to talk to me.

I think about what my dad might have said about that, how he would have sent a couple of DCs around to scoop this boy up and march him down to the station to make him talk.

The women melt away from the door as I turn to leave the room but I'm acutely aware of their gaze, even as I take a seat in the living room. Woodley's been there all along, sitting quietly. He's good at that. It's an important skill for a detective, to be able to morph into a wallflower. People let down their guard around you, and you can learn a lot.

I glance around, taking in the room for the first time. Net curtains with gold-coloured trim cover the room's window. On a small shelf unit in the corner of the room there's a bowl of oranges and a few books. The mother brings a tray of tea and sets it down on the glass coffee table. Aromatic steam rises from the cups.

'Obviously we'll need to speak to Abdi himself once he's feeling better,' I say, 'but I'd like to take a few details from you in the meantime, if I may.'

Nur Mahad nods his assent. He's taken a seat on the sofa that's set at a right angle to the one I'm perched on. His knees are almost touching mine and he's leaning forward. His body language is screaming that he wants to please. It's not the nervous or unresponsive demeanour of a parent who's harbouring a teenage troublemaker.

60

'How old is Abdi?'

'He's fifteen.'

'Where does he go to school?'

'He goes to Medes College. He won a full scholarship.'

Medes College is a top-class, expensive private school located in the centre of the city. I'm impressed.

'Is it typical of him to be out late at night with his friend?'

'No! No, not at all.' It's a very vigorous denial. 'We thought he was at a sleepover with Noah. Abdi has never, ever been in trouble with the police, with school, with anybody. He's a very good boy. Always top grades, chess champion, badminton team.'

'So this is out of character?'

'Very out of character.'

His daughter's watching me closely, but his wife seems more disconnected. She's showing very little emotion, and I still haven't managed to make more than fleeting eye contact with her. I direct my next question to both of them.

'It's important that we build up as full a picture of Abdi as possible. Could you tell me about his normal routine? Who he hangs out with, where he goes?'

Nur looks as if he wants to answer, but he knows he should defer to someone else. I've been briefed that he works as a taxi driver, so I suspect he's out of the house at all hours.

Sofia answers. Her voice sounds thin. 'Abdi takes the bus to school. He leaves at seven thirty in the morning and he gets home at about five o'clock unless he has an after-school club or a chess tournament or a badminton match.

Then it's later. Noah's his best friend. He's the only friend who Abdi visits at home.'

'Can you tell me a bit about their friendship?'

'It's good. They're very close. They made friends straight away when Noah started school. It was nice for Abdi. He met one or two boys before that, but didn't have a best friend.'

'Did they ever argue?'

'I don't think so. Abdi never said.'

'No minor disagreements at all? Especially recently?'

'Not that I know of.'

'How would you describe the friendship?'

'Happy, quite competitive about schoolwork and stuff. Kind of nerdy. The boys would never do anything bad to each other. Abdi's not like that. He's really kind.'

Her father nods his agreement, and her mother puts a hand on Sofia's arm and says something in Somali.

'I'm going to translate your question for her,' Sofia says, and they have an exchange in rapid Somali before turning to look at me again.

'Did your mother have anything to add?'

'She says the boys were good for each other. They spurred each other on to study hard.'

I don't like not being able to understand what they're saying. My job is to listen to people and to read their body language at the same time. That's where you can often spot the fault lines in their stories. There's not much I can do about it now, though, so I press on.

'Did the boys ever get into trouble?'

'No. Abdi liked school. He wanted to make a good impression.'

She's sounding increasingly defensive, so I swallow my next question to give us all a breather. Into the silence Nur Mahad says, 'Abdi sometimes volunteers with his mother at the Welcome Centre.'

'I'm not familiar with it.'

'It's a drop-in centre for refugees. Only five minutes from here. Maryam volunteers there, she helps cook. Refugees can get a hot meal five days a week.'

'How often does Abdi go there?'

'Sometimes in the evenings after school, depending on homework.'

'And what does he do when he's there?'

'Anything they want him to: translate, chop vegetables, play ping-pong with the other boys, wash up. Whatever they ask him. He's a good worker.'

I look over my notes. There's enough to be following up on for now, and I'm not learning anything new. I decide to quit while I'm ahead and get onto the other interviews.

'You've been very helpful. Thank you. Please contact me immediately if Abdi improves, and feels ready to talk to us, and also if you think of anything else I might need to know.'

I leave another of my cards on their coffee table.

Once we're in the car, Woodley says, 'What do you reckon?'

'If that boy was up to no good, then I think it'll be news to his family.'

'I got up to all sorts of things at his age and my mum and dad didn't have a clue.'

It's a good point. It wouldn't be the first time a teenager

had a secret life. Though in the house I grew up in, it was different. When your dad rules with his fists, you think very carefully before you step out of line. I did, anyhow. My sister was braver or stupider, depending on your opinion.

'And the "best friends" image totally contradicts the witness,' Woodley says.

'I got the feeling that boy was scared.'

As we drive back to HQ, Woodley laughs out of the blue, as if he's just remembered something: 'I did some seriously stupid things when I was fifteen.'

'Care to share?'

'Nope. Nice try, boss.'

As I drive, I think that if there's one thing I'm going to be sure to do, it's to bring a translator with me if I visit the family again. I'm also getting a feeling that we're not going to be able to put this case away neatly or tidily, or even soon.

I want to find out what scared the hell out of that boy.

After the detectives leave, Sofia's seized by an urge to get out of the flat. She loves her family and her home, but there are times when a sense of claustrophobia overwhelms her and she feels as if she needs to be away from them, so that she can cease being a daughter and a sister and just be herself. It's the best way she knows to work out her own thoughts.

'I'm going to the library,' she says. Nobody will argue with that, because education is king in their family. 'Dad, call me if anything changes.'

On the street, she walks until her head starts to clear.

She feels bad about leaving Abdi, though she knows her parents will watch him closely. She's not sure what she thought about the detectives. DI Clemo was quite nice, but Sofia's not immune to the fear that many in her community have, that the police will judge them and suspect them because they're Somali. If you listened to the boys talk at uni, it seems that none of the white boys are ever stopped and searched by the police, but it happens to the Somali boys a lot in their neighbourhood. It makes them feel targeted and vulnerable, and sometimes angry, too.

Sofia's feeling increasingly afraid that Abdi will be discriminated against if he doesn't speak up, and maybe even if he does. She wonders what she can do for him and thinks it might be helpful if she goes to get his stuff from the Sadlers' house so he has it when he starts to feel better. The thought gives her some energy and a welcome sense of purpose.

Two bus rides later she's in Clifton Village, walking up Noah's street and thinking about how long it's been since she was last here. She knows the Sadlers will probably be at the hospital, but she hopes their housekeeper will be at the house. She rings the bell and the door opens almost immediately. Alvard, the housekeeper, is just as Sofia remembers her: a small, anxious-looking woman with short dark hair, sharp dark eyes and a deeply creased forehead. Whenever Sofia sees Alvard she remembers the time Alvard pressed a napkin full of warm cookies into her hands and told Sofia that what she most missed about Armenia was her mother's peach orchard.

'Nobody's here,' Alvard says. 'They're at the hospital. They told me I can go home but I want to straighten up the house for them.'

'Is it OK if I pick up Abdi's things?'

Alvard shows her into the hallway and asks: 'How's Abdi? Is he all right?'

Sofia finds herself losing the composure she's been fighting to maintain. 'No, not really,' she says into Alvard's shoulder. Sofia hates to cry. When new mothers cry at work she finds it beautiful and right, but when she cries she feels ugly, and weak.

Alvard holds her gently in the overheated hallway of the Sadlers' home. As she gets control of her emotions, Sofia tunes into the deep, slow ticking of a grandfather clock and thinks what a sad sort of sound it makes.

'We'll get Abdi's things,' Alvard says. 'Come.'

Sofia pauses instinctively before following her up the stairs, because she's never been further than the hallway in this house. The hallway was where she used to wait for Abdi after he'd been to play here. She would will him to hurry up because either their dad was waiting outside in his taxi or they would have a bus to catch. Fiona Sadler would stand at the bottom of the stairs, shouting up, and then showing Sofia a tight smile, neither of them knowing what to say to the other.

'Come!' says Alvard from the top of the stairs, and Sofia begins to climb, putting her hand on the gracious banister rail for the first time ever, her fingertips feeling the heft of it and the shine on it.

Noah's bedroom is on the top floor of the house, and

Sofia's impressed. It's a huge space, flooded with light from two skylights, as well as a casement window that has a view out across Clifton and towards Leigh Woods. Noah has a double bed to himself and there are shelves of books and mementos around the room, as well as a TV and an impressive computer gaming set-up. It's the kind of kid's bedroom that Sofia's only ever seen in films.

Alvard bustles over to a single put-up bed and Sofia recognises Abdi's bag lying beside it on the floor, half-open, looking like he's just slung it there, which would be typical of him. His nightwear has been dropped on the bed.

As Sofia packs up Abdi's things, Alvard rifles through the stuff on Noah's desk.

'Some of this might be Abdi's,' she says.

Sofia's momentarily distracted by the sight, through a partially closed cupboard door, of a ton of medical paraphernalia. There's a bucket for sharps, packets of syringes, dressings, flushing fluids, gloves and an oxygen tank. She sees these things every day when she does her hospital placements, but the sight of them tucked into the corner of this perfect bedroom reminds her of the fact that sits at the centre of Noah's life, which is that he has often been close to death. Sofia can't help wondering if he has ever been as close as he is today, and the thought makes her shudder.

'Sofia?' Alvard prompts.

She apologises. She hopes she hasn't appeared mawkish, staring so obviously.

Alvard hands her an iPad.

'That's not Abdi's,' Sofia says.

'I don't think it's Noah's.'

'Oh.'

Sofia takes the iPad from her and turns it over. There's a school sticker on the back. Abdi must have it on loan. She puts it in his bag.

'We'll check downstairs, too,' Alvard says, and Sofia trots behind her as they go down. She knows Alvard wouldn't have let her in if it wasn't OK, but even so, she can't help feeling as if she's snooping behind the Sadlers' backs, and prays that they won't come home suddenly.

On the first floor of the house Alvard opens a door into a room that's spacious but cosy, and leads Sofia in. It's definitely a man's room. There's a battered leather couch, a pair of running shoes discarded in front of it, a huge TV and a signed cricket bat in a case on the wall. A large modern desk faces the window. It's very different from the Buckingham Palace-style decor that's going on in the hallway and in the other formal rooms of the house that Sofia has glimpsed through doorways.

'It's worth checking in here,' Alvard says. 'Noah likes to come in here and use his dad's desk.'

'That's fine.' Sofia's desperate to get away now. This space feels like even more of a Sadler inner sanctum than Noah's room does.

It's as she's turning around to leave that she sees the folder. It would never have caught her attention if it hadn't been so boldly labelled. The word 'Hartisheik' leaps out at her. She moves closer so that she can examine it.

Alvard is plumping the cushions on the sofa – they look slept on – and Sofia takes the opportunity to flip open the folder. Inside there's an official report titled 'Living

Conditions in Hartisheik Camp'. There's also the stub of an airline ticket to Addis Ababa and some other documents, amongst them a hand-drawn map on lined A4 paper that's dog-eared and creased where it's previously been folded to pocket-size.

With one finger, Sofia eases the map out of the folder so she can see it in its entirety. It shows a bird's-eye view of the refugee camp where her family lived before they made the journey to England. Whoever drew it has worked quickly, sketchily, but has labelled each area. She runs her finger over the map, tracing along the main thoroughfares. Her memory of the camp isn't perfect because she was a little girl when she was there, but she recalls the hospital, the UNHCR buildings where food and water were distributed, the market, the cemetery and the area her family lived in.

It's all there, and more. It's very detailed. Sofia's so absorbed that she jumps when Alvard appears beside her and says: 'Mr Sadler goes to some difficult places. He does difficult work.'

'Yes,' Sofia says. She can't tear her eyes away. She was born in this place. She reacts physically. Her nostrils curl as she remembers the smell of it. She pictures the vast sky and her skin prickles as she feels the heat of the sun and the lash of the relentless wind that blew across the desert and shredded the tarpaulin that covered their shelter, day after day.

She already knew from Abdi that Ed Sadler had spent time at this camp, but didn't pay much attention to the information. Why would she? There was no nostalgic conversation to be had about what her family experienced there. Rather, Sofia would have felt a sense of shame having that conversation with Ed. She'd put the link out of her mind and kept it there, even when her parents were agonising over whether to let Abdi attend the opening of Ed Sadler's exhibition.

Actually seeing the evidence of Ed Sadler's visit there, however long ago it was, is different, though. It makes this link between their families feel much more real, and for the first time she shares her parents' deep unease about it. She tears herself away, not wanting Alvard to think that she's lingering too long, and snooping where she shouldn't be.

Downstairs, Alvard says goodbye affectionately, squeezing Sofia's hand between her own. 'I am praying for both boys,' she says.

As Sofia walks away from the house she adjusts her hijab so that it shrouds her face more than usual, partly because it's got very cold, but partly because she doesn't want anybody to see her looking upset. She regrets it a few minutes later when she gets on the bus and a woman tuts at her, shifting in her seat to put distance between them.

Sofia wants to tut back at the cross the woman is wearing around her neck, just to make a point, but she doesn't. She knows that's not how it works, and she's not that kind of person. Instead, she sits very still in her seat, Abdi's bag at her feet, and feels both afraid and angry. Next time the bus stops, she moves to a seat at the back.

*

When I was in primary school I had a friend called Matthew. He came to visit me in hospital very soon after my diagnosis. I was in the main area of the ward where there were three other beds in the same bay as mine.

'It's a bit like camping, isn't it?' Mum said when we unpacked our things into the small cabinet beside the bed. The doctor said we were going to be in for at least four days. The plan was to have an operation to put my central line in and do some more tests so they could choose the right medicines for me. It was my first operation and my first time staying in the hospital.

In the bed opposite was a bigger girl sitting up with pink headphones over her ears, watching a film on a portable DVD player. Her arms were toothpick thin and she had a tube going up her nose. Her mum sat on a chair beside her. She had a book open on her lap, but her eyes were shut.

In the bed beside me was a boy a bit younger than me with a bald head, looking at a Pokémon sticker book. He was on his own. He got out of bed and stared at me. 'My dad's getting a motorbike,' he said. He had a massive scar that went all the way over the top of his head, and one of his eyelids was droopy.

'That's nice,' Mum said.

'I'm five,' he said.

When the nurse came, she put him back under the covers and turned on the TV that was on the end of a plastic arm that swung out over his bed. It was showing a very loud cartoon.

'If you stay in bed until the end of the programme,' the nurse told him as she closed the curtain around him, 'I'll tell Mummy how good you were when she comes.'

I unpacked and checked everything out and felt excited about my friend Matthew coming to see me. I wanted to show him the controller that made my bed tilt and fold.

Matthew came to visit me two days later. His mum brought me a present. By then, I was sore from the operation to put my central line in, and it hurt to move much, but I showed Matthew the see-through dressing on my chest that covered up the place where the line came out of me, and I showed him the little fabric bag the nurses gave me to wear around my neck for storing the ends of the line in. The bag had smiley dog faces on it and a blue ribbon. The nurse told me nice ladies made them especially for the children. When Mum saw what I was doing, she said, 'Noah! Don't! Put it away!'

'It's OK,' Matthew's mum said. 'It looks very good, Noah. You've been very brave. Don't you think so, Matthew?'

Matthew stared at it and sucked his finger. I pulled down my top.

We put on the TV while the mums got tea, but we couldn't find anything we wanted to watch. Mum wouldn't let us play with the bed controller after Matthew tested it out and all my things fell off the end.

It was very cramped for us all around my bed, so we went to the playroom that was on the ward. I told Matthew a dog had come to visit us in the playroom the day before. It was a special dog that visits people when they're sick. I stroked it and when I said 'sit' it sat down, but it wouldn't roll over when I asked it to. It just licked my hand. I told Matthew about how I'd been going to get a dog but after I got my diagnosis we had to tell the breeder we couldn't have the puppy. Mum promised we would get a dog as soon as I got better. (That never happened, hence this: *Noah's Bucket List Item No. 3: Borrow a Dog.*)

The boy from the bed next door to me came to the playroom with a hospital play specialist when me and Matthew were there. They started to build a train set together. He had lines drawn in black pen on his bald head.

'Radiotherapy, I think,' my mum muttered to Matthew's mum.

Matthew stared again. His hand crept into his mum's hand, and he sat down beside her and didn't want to play.

After they went home I said to Mum, 'I don't want my friends to come any more.'

Abdi was the first friend to visit me in hospital after Matthew, and when he came he had the right attitude.

It was the end of the spring term of our second year at school. Abdi and me were best friends by then. We did everything together: we were seat buddies on the coach to the sports grounds, we did chess club and IT club together, we sat together at lunch and we hung out together at break. I helped him with English work and he helped me with maths.

Abdi arrived at the hospital one evening after I'd been there for about a week. He had a chessboard and a stack of graphic novels tucked under his arm. I was in a room of my own. You get one if you're a baby or if your treatment is very harsh.

'Don't you think chess is a bit much?' Mum said.

Abdi looked at me. 'I don't mind. We can just talk,' he said.

'I want to play,' I said.

We had to do some complicated rearranging of my tubes and machines, and it took a while to prop me up, but we got there. Abdi perched on the end of my bed and set up the chessboard on a pillow between us.

'I think this might wear you out,' Mum said.

'We can stop if it does.' Abdi laid out the chess pieces with neat movements.

'You could go and get a cup of coffee if you like?' I said to Mum.

For a moment, I thought she might refuse, because she looked so surprised. She said to Abdi: 'If he looks any more pale than this or if his breathing gets ragged . . . '

'I'll call the nurse,' Abdi said. 'I promise.'

Mum knew that Abdi was trustworthy, because I'd told her he was, loads of times, even though, ironically, I wasn't being a hundred per cent honest about that, because who is?

'OK, well, I think I'll just sit outside the door here, so you can call me if you need me.'

'Mum, I'm fine.' That wasn't totally true either, because I had some pain in my back that the morphine wasn't touching and a wee bit of visual disturbance, but I wasn't going to admit to that.

When we were alone, Abdi started the game with a move that I'd never seen him make before.

'Are you taking advantage of a sick boy?' I asked him.

'I'm not going to let you win just because you're in here.'

I made my move.

'Feisty!' he said.

He didn't once mention how sick I looked. He didn't stare. As we played, I was concentrating so hard I stopped hearing the hiss of the oxygen and the sounds of the ward.

Abdi cracked open the window after a while. The sounds of a rained-on street came into my room with the cool air. He persuaded the nurses to bring us a glass so he could put his phone in it and improvise a speaker. He'd made me a playlist and we listened to it as we plotted the destruction of each other's chess pieces. It was the most fun I'd ever had in hospital.

I lasted about forty-five minutes before the pain got to me and I had to re-dose on morphine. When I came around, Mum was back in her chair beside me and Abdi had gone, but the chessboard, with the pieces in place, had been moved to the windowsill and it stayed there until he came back the next time and we continued the game.

And the best bit? Abdi came back whenever he could. It wasn't all that often, because he needed to be collected by his dad who was fitting it in around his shifts, but he was the first and only friend to visit me regularly.

I'm aware that there's a lot of noise going on around me. Machinery noise and music, as if through headphones. I think I'm having a scan.

Scans make me panic. I've had to be sedated in the past. It's the claustrophobia. I feel it now, but I can't do anything about it apart from wait, watching the blackness, hearing the noises, feeling the fear rise. For the first time, I wonder when they're going to bring me out of this coma, and exactly how sick I am. I am desperate to be able to ask my mum. She would have the answer.

I have a sense of motion, of turning wheels and a few bumps, and then we must be back on the ward because I hear Dad: 'Did they say anything?'

'They'll speak to us after they've reviewed the scan with the consultant.'

'I got you a tea.'

'Thanks.'

I hear them drinking their tea.

Mum says, 'That Asian registrar said that if the bleeding in his brain has stabilised they might try to bring him round tomorrow.'

'And if not?'

'I don't know. Let's not go there.'

I hear Dad crick his fingers and groan as he stretches. He yawns very deeply and says, 'I still can't believe neither of us heard them leave the house.'

'Don't beat yourself up about it. There's no point.'

'I shouldn't have tied one on.'

'It was your exhibition opening. You were allowed a drink.'

Here's what I want to say to Dad: 'Boy, did you drink!' Because he did: one fancy bottled beer after another while we were at the gallery.

Woodley meets me at the entrance to the intensive care ward in the Children's Hospital.

Inside, it's as grim as you might expect. The children and babies are sicker than you ever want to see. Directed by the nurses, Woodley and I walk up the ward towards a bay at the far end. On either side of us, the beds are occupied for the most part by still bodies. Parents sit beside them, cloaked in anxiety.

Cast a cold eye, I think to myself. Dr Manelli and I share an enthusiasm for poetry by W. B. Yeats. She told me to use it if it helped. I need a cold eye to keep moving between these beds, or I'll have to turn around and walk out of there.

At the far end of the ward, a woman in scrubs pulls back a curtain just as we're approaching, and I see a woman who must be Noah Sadler's mother.

She sits in a chair on one side of his bed. She looks collapsed somehow, as if she's missing something vital. On the other side of Noah's bed there's a huddle of machinery and a knot of plastic tubes and wiring.

Noah Sadler looks very sick. His eyes are closed and he's motionless, just as Abdi was, but unlike his friend, Noah exhibits no hint of life at all. I try not to be transfixed by the small veins running across his eyelids. I already know that I'll remember this, that the sight of the prone body of Noah Sadler has worked its way under my skin.

Fiona Sadler doesn't want to talk beside Noah's bed.

'I don't know how much he can hear,' she says, 'but I don't want to be away from him for long.'

She confers with the nurses before leading us out of the main area of the ward, into a small lobby.

'There aren't any rooms available,' she tells us. 'Will this do?'

We sit on plastic chairs in a row. Opposite us, nurses prepare meds in a brightly lit room with a half-glass door. A solid door beside it is labelled 'Parents' Room'. Fiona Sadler is physically slight, as if she hasn't eaten a decent meal in a long time. Woodley and I, sitting on either side of her, dwarf her. It's not my preferred way to conduct an interview, but I dive in.

'Do you have any idea why the boys might have been out last night?'

She shakes her head. Before I can ask my next question, she has one for me. 'Do you know that my son has cancer, Detective?'

There are some sentences you hear that are an emotional body blow, and hearing that a child has cancer is definitely one of them.

'I wasn't aware. I'm so very sorry.'

'He's terminal.'

And that would be another of those sentences. I've met some families in truly awful situations, and the Sadlers just joined the ranks of the most desperate.

'I'm so very sorry.' I'm repeating myself. I want to say more, but I'm lost for words.

Sometimes you can't wait to get your teeth into a witness or a family member whom you suspect of being neglectful or complicit, but there are other times when questioning can feel cruel, even if your ulterior motive is to get to the truth. If it wasn't already, this has definitely just become one of those times.

'They told us we had a few months at best.' She raises her chin and blinks repeatedly until she recovers her composure. Her self-control is phenomenal.

I open my mouth to try to phrase a response that isn't totally inadequate, but she cuts me off with her next comment.

'I want those months, Detective.'

'I understand.'

'I want every single one of them.'

She's stopped herself from crying, but her hands are shaking so much that the takeaway cup she's holding threatens to spill.

I find her distress difficult to witness. It provokes memories of Ben Finch's mother, Rachel, that threaten to knock me off my stride. If I'd been asked to describe one professional scenario I would have liked to be able to avoid in my first day, week, month or even year back at work after the Ben Finch case, it would be this: a mother for whom everything is at stake because her child's life is in grave danger. Yet here I am, and I have to be effective.

I try to formulate a response that acknowledges and respects her grief. I have to keep a lid on my own feelings, so they don't develop into something I might not be able to manage, but I don't want to seem cold.

The door to the parents' room opposite swings open as a man exits, a mobile phone protruding from his back pocket and a cup of something hot in each hand. The door doesn't close automatically behind him, so we have a view of a cramped space containing a kitchenette with a refrigerator, a microwave, a sink and a small square dining table. On the fridge there's a big notice that reads, PLEASE LABEL YOUR FOOD CLEARLY WITH YOUR CHILD'S NAME AND WARD NUMBER. The room disgorges a strong smell of microwaved food that seems to thicken the air in the corridor. I watch a wisp of steam trail from the spout of the kettle.

Fiona Sadler saves me from coming up with an appropriate response. 'Sorry,' she says. 'It's not your fault.'

'We can do this another time, if you prefer?'

'No. I want you to find out what happened to my son. Something happened. To be out at night, without us, in some industrial place, I can't tell you how far from normal that is for Noah.'

Now that she's got her emotions under control, she's sounding steely.

'Perhaps you could start by telling us what happened yesterday evening, before the boys sneaked out?'

She describes the party they went to at her husband's gallery, and how she brought the boys home at about ten-thirty. As she talks, fatigue drips steadily into her voice, dulling it incrementally. Her final words sound beaten. Her skin looks an unhealthy shade of yellow under the lights.

'It was a special night. I wanted it to be a night that was just for family, but Noah asked us if Abdi could come to the party and for a sleepover afterwards, and we felt we couldn't refuse.'

'Was it common for Abdi to sleep over?'

'Not common, but they'd done it before once or twice.'

'Had the boys got into mischief before on sleepovers?

Sneaked out of the house, or anything like that?' I'm pretty sure I know the answer to this already, but I have to ask.

'Never, that I'm aware of. Noah wouldn't do that. I just can't imagine it. He's never been that kind of boy.'

'Did he and Abdi have a good friendship?'

She pauses before answering and picks at the edge of the plastic lid on her cup.

'Yes.'

'But you have reservations?' It's not rocket science. Her response was uncertain at best. This is the first inkling I get that Fiona Sadler's view of this friendship might deviate from the Mahad family's. It quickens my interest.

'Look, Detective, can I be frank? This is just a feeling and I've got no real basis for it, but I always thought this friendship would end up being bad for Noah.'

'Can you tell me why?'

'I don't really know. A feeling? Intuition? Call it whatever you like. And I probably shouldn't even say it at all because I expect it's not fair to Abdi, but that's my view. Ed will tell you that Abdi's a charming boy, which he is, so maybe I'm being over-protective. Noah's illness distorts things.'

'I understand.'

'Do you?'

I look away from her gaze, because there's a new edge to her now, and it's hostile. In my experience, a mother doubted can be a ferocious adversary, and I don't want to make an enemy of this one. Not unless I have to.

'I try to,' I reply.

My response softens her just enough. Her eyes flicker

across mine, as if she's searching for signs of sincerity. She nods.

'Ed strongly encouraged the friendship, and Noah always wants to please him. He worships Ed. His dad's a hero to him.'

She says this as if it's not always a good thing. For a moment I think we're done, that she's going to get up and walk away, back to her son, but I'm wrong. Instead, she opens up:

'What you have to understand about my husband is that he works with people in some of the most terrible situations you can imagine. And in some of the most terrible places. He brings that home with him, Detective, that compassion, or hunger for danger, or whatever the thing is that drives him. So when Noah met Abdi Mahad, Ed was delighted, and he encouraged the friendship. He's worked in all sorts of places but he's particularly interested in Somalia and the camps, so it was the icing on the cake when he found out that Abdi's family had come here via one of the camps he'd visited. Of course he wanted them to be friends after that. Is it a good friendship? I don't know. Maybe, but I can't deny it makes me anxious. I suppose I want, wanted, Noah to feel free to make his own friends, not hang out with people because they fit into his father's agenda. But, you know, it's irrelevant now, all of it, and Ed's going to have to stop taking responsibility for every misery that's out there in the world, and focus on his own family instead. Perhaps we're finally miserable enough for him to take a bit of bloody notice.'

Her voice is raised by the time she's finished her speech. One of the nurses hesitates beside us, but Fiona waves her on.

'Sorry,' she says.

'Please don't be. You've got nothing to apologise for. Can I ask, do you know if there's been any friction between the boys lately?'

'Not that I'm aware of, though Noah talks to me less these days. He doesn't share everything like he used to. He's fifteen, so I suppose it's inevitable, no matter what we've been through together.'

She gestures at the space around us, and I think I get what she means: the four walls, the tacky, dated, wipe-clean hospital decor, the drugs, the equipment, the swift footfalls and professionally friendly chatter of the doctors and nurses. It's the hospital as a machine, and one that she and her family have been cogs in for a very long time.

'Can I ask how the boys were during the evening? How they seemed to get on together?'

'Great, from what I saw, though I didn't have my eye on them all night, because it was a party. I suppose that makes everything I've said up until now sound stupid, doesn't it, but I can't deny they seemed to have a good time. Noah's coped far better than Ed or me since we heard his prognosis. What I will say, though, is that if they hatched a plan to sneak out together in advance, I can guarantee you that Abdi was responsible for that. Noah wouldn't know where to start.'

'Do you have a relationship with Abdi's family?'

'Ed tried, but really we only ever see the sister and she's very shy or reserved or something. She always looks as if she can't get away quickly enough. Abdi's father drives a taxi so he works all hours and the mother doesn't even speak English.'

'Would you be happy for us to take a look at Noah's computer and any other devices he might have? It could help us to see what his communications have been recently.'

'Do you really need to?'

'It might help.'

'Then OK, I suppose. It feels like an invasion of his privacy, though, I will say that.'

'At this point it's something we would only do if you're happy about it.'

'It's fine. Ed will be at the house for a couple of hours. You've only just missed him, he's popped home to get changed and get some rest. You can collect the computer while he's there if you want.'

I'll certainly be heading over there to interview him. The computer will have to be collected separately, to preserve the chain of evidence. I want everything done by the book.

'I'd like to know if Noah's ever spoken about Feeder Canal or visited the area he was found in?'

'I don't think he knows it exists. His world is home, hospital and school. That's why I think them going there has to be Abdi's doing.'

One of the nurses puts her head around the doors that lead into the ward.

'Mrs Sadler,' she says. Fiona Sadler's head snaps around to face her. 'The doctor's ready to speak to you.'

'Please, go,' I say. 'Thank you for your time.'

Her takeaway cup rolls across the floor in her wake, small dribbles of coffee trailing it.

Woodley and I find the elevators and wait beside a wall of grubby plate glass that gives us a view of the city centre. The sky is thick with rain-heavy clouds and the streets are busy. Seagulls hover against the dark grey horizon. The contrast with the artificial brightness and quiet of the intensive care unit is a relief.

'Some mixed messages, back there,' Woodley says. I can see his face partially reflected in the glass.

'She's out of her mind with grief.'

'You would be, wouldn't you?'

I nod. I watch as the people on the street below begin to put up umbrellas and rain splatters against the window like hail.

On the way down in the lift, we're joined by a man in scrubs with a thousand-yard stare and a packet of cigarettes and a lighter in his hand.

Sometimes it's hard not to let other people's misery seep into your own bones.

One thing I do know is that Noah Sadler's situation will complicate the case. He's not just any kid who's gone out for larks or a bit of petty crime that's gone terribly wrong. He's a teenager who's terminally ill. If nothing else, the cynic in me recognises that this fact makes the case very newsworthy. The cancer automatically labels Noah Sadler a victim and I want to make sure that doesn't condemn his best friend without a fair examination of the evidence.

'We need Abdi Mahad to speak,' I say.

In the corner of the bus where's she's tucked herself to minimise contact with the other passengers, Sofia thinks about the papers relating to Hartisheik camp that she saw in Ed Sadler's office, and wonders why they were out. It's a coincidence that's hard to ignore. Abdi's interest in their life before he was born has been growing recently, so she wonders if he was questioning Mr Sadler, asking things that he might not want to ask at home for fear of upsetting her or their parents.

To distract herself, she gets the iPad out of Abdi's bag and clicks the home button. It asks for a password. Sofia takes a gamble. She knows the password for the school laptop that Abdi has borrowed in the past is 'Medes' followed by the academic year so she tries that. It opens, but the battery's so dead that it won't do anything else. She rummages in Abdi's bag and finds a cable. She'll charge it when she gets home.

She pulls out the papers that she scooped up and flicks through them. It's hard to look at them properly on the bus, though, because they slip around on her knees. She admires her brother's perfect cursive handwriting, but from what she can see, the papers tell her nothing interesting. It's just school stuff, a chemistry project so far as she can tell. She stuffs them back into the bag.

She looks out the window of the bus and thinks about the life she has in Bristol. She doesn't usually dwell on her circumstances, preferring to get on with her studies and her life, but the last twenty-four hours have thrown things into focus.

Sofia's generally a happy person. She knows that her family have none of the material advantages that a family like the Sadlers have, but she doesn't mind, because she feels loved, and she remembers what true hardship felt like.

She understands why some of her peers feel conflicted about their immigrant identity – neither fully British nor fully Somali, somewhere in between – but Sofia's hard work at school and uni has rewarded her richly, and she draws huge amounts of focus and strength from that. On a good day, she creates her identity from these positives. On a bad day, she lets her fear of being a target of hatred mute her actions and worry at the edges of her confidence, and this is a bad day. She wonders if she's been complacent. Perhaps she should have listened to her fears more, instead of letting others reassure her. Perhaps it's not possible to just get your head down and start a new life here in the way she and her family thought it was. Perhaps even if you do everything right, it can all go horribly wrong.

A text pings through on her phone. It's from her dad. There's no change in Abdi, it says. It asks her what time she's getting home and if she can collect some milk on the way.

In the shop, Mrs Khan's busy monitoring three school-boys who are cruising the aisles, looking shifty. Sofia recognises one of them as a friend of Abdi's from primary school. She grabs some milk and heads out, grateful on this night to avoid small talk with Mrs Khan.

She has no such luck as she rounds the corner on the way home. Filling the pavement is Amina.

'Sofia!' Being enveloped in Amina's arms provides a sensation of total immersion in fabric and fragrance. Sofia loves Amina and thinks of her as a loosened-up version of her own mother. She wishes that Maryam would dress like Amina does: in beautiful colours and silky turbans instead of the dowdy robes and heavy headscarves that Maryam refuses to shed. She would love to see her mother in a bright lipstick, with a dab of colour on her fine cheekbones. She would like her mother to smile more.

The only thing Sofia doesn't enjoy about Amina is the mandatory visual and physical examination that she's never worked out how to avoid. Amina looks her over and squeezes her upper arm, as if testing it for ripeness, then delivers her verdict.

'Your colour's bad.'

'I'm tired.'

'You need vitamins. Did I tell you I got a NutriBullet?'

'You did.' *About ten times already*, Sofia thinks, but she doesn't say it because she believes that Amina is about as warm-hearted a person as you could hope to meet.

'First your mama is unwell, and now you!'

Sofia freezes, wondering what Amina knows, why she says that. Even though Amina's a family friend, Sofia knows her parents wouldn't want other people to know about what's happened to Abdi, not unless they had to. The shame of it would be an extra blow to the family.

'Mum hasn't been unwell,' she says.

'Didn't she tell you what happened? She fainted on

Friday evening, at the Welcome Centre. Completely collapsed when we were serving the food. One minute, ladling pasta, the next minute down. She would have hurt herself but Chef caught her.'

'She didn't tell me.'

'I expect she didn't want to worry you. Naughty! I told her she needs to look after herself. I would have brought her home myself, but Abdi said he would make sure she was OK.'

'Abdi was with her?'

'Yes, darling. It was last Friday. Don't tell me they didn't tell you about it.'

Amina's frown is fearsome. Sofia thinks back. She's been so hard at work on her coursework that she hasn't paid much attention to the comings and goings of the rest of her family recently. Her brain feels addled, so she lies.

'No, they did tell me. Sorry. But Mum's fine now.' It also occurs to Sofia that Amina might want to come and visit if she thinks Maryam's unwell, so she wants to reassure her.

'All right, darling.' Amina regards Sofia with scepticism. She can smell a rat from a hundred yards away. 'You don't look so well yourself.'

'I'm fine.'

'That's what your mother said! OK, darling, I have to go. Take care of yourself. Tell Maryam I'll call her.'

Another warm hug and Sofia's released. She thinks back to Friday as she walks on. Did her mother appear unwell that night? She doesn't think she can remember anything unusual, but Maryam's difficult to read. Loving and affectionate one moment, shut away the next, her family have learned to live with extremes, not to question them. Maryam has been that way for as long as Sofia can remember. She's long suspected that her mother suffers from some kind of depression, but knows that can never be voiced.

A sense of urgency takes over as she nears home. She wants to see Abdi, to know how he is, but she braces herself in case there's no improvement.

In the flat, Maryam watches her daughter put the milk in the fridge. She's trying to think of what she might be able to cook to tempt Abdi to eat, because nothing's passed his lips yet today, and she's caught off guard when Sofia asks, 'What's the name of the camp we lived in?'

'Hartisheik,' she says, hoping Sofia doesn't catch her swallowing as hard as if bile had risen in her throat. 'Why?'

'I was thinking about it today, but I forgot the name.'

Maryam can tell that her daughter's not being truthful. She can read Sofia like a book. But the very fact that her normally earnest and honest girl is lying drains Maryam of her courage to ask why. She resists a powerful impulse to shudder, because mention of the camp, on this day, can only be a bad portent. She wishes Nur hadn't just left the room. She needs to tell him. She wants it to be face to face.

As her mind works, she continues to potter in the kitchen as if on autopilot. She makes batter for pancakes. They're Abdi's favourite. She's not sure what else to do. As Maryam makes the mixture she endeavours to hold back memories of the camp, turning the radio on, distracting herself with music, beating the batter for far longer than she needs to. Sometimes she's successful when she uses tactics like these, sometimes she raises blisters on her hands rather than stop and think, and sometimes nothing can hold the memories at bay.

Sofia has noted her mum's reaction and the way she's trying to hide it, but she's not too surprised by this because Maryam hates to speak about their past. Sofia's too nervous to ask about the fainting incident at the Welcome Centre in case it upsets Maryam further. Perhaps she'll mention it to her father.

She finds Nur in Abdi's room, sitting by the boy's bed, gently cleaning his glasses.

'I've tried to get him to talk, but no luck,' he says. 'I have to go to work.'

'I'll try tonight,' she says.

He kisses her on the forehead, and leaves the flat before she has a chance to talk to him about the Welcome Centre.

So far as she can see there's no change in Abdi at all. His bedroom's gloomy and he doesn't seem to have moved. Rather than dump his bag in there, she takes it into her own room, thinking she might get the laundry out of it and wash it for him. She doesn't burden her mother with it. She'll do it herself. She also takes the iPad and charger out of the bag and plugs them in in her bedroom.

'Hartisheik,' she whispers, as she does so. The word rolls itself around her mouth. She was right, then: the paperwork she saw in Ed Sadler's office related to the camp they lived in. She wanted to hear confirmation of the name of the camp from her mother, but she didn't want to burden

Maryam with what she saw, not until she's thought about it some more, about what it might mean.

She has a swiftly changing kaleidoscope of memories from the camp they left when she was a little girl. She remembers the yellow jerrycans that stored water, which was the most precious commodity of all in Hartisheik, and the straw mats that covered the floor of their shelter.

All around the camp people put up their shelters in enclosures made from the branches of thorn bushes woven together. The sheep had black heads. Sometimes the camp flooded and they couldn't lie down on the ground at night. A thin red curtain hung between the living and cooking area of her family's *tukul* and she would play with its tattered edges, pulling at the threads until her mother chided her. Outside, the boys played football as the sun set, and the dust they kicked up turned golden.

Sofia takes pancakes to Abdi and sits with him.

'Abdi, can you talk to me? It's just me. You can tell me what happened. I promise I'll keep it to myself if that's what you want. Come on, Abdi.'

He doesn't reply, even when she waves the pancakes under his nose and tells him he'll feel better if he eats. The pancakes go cold on the plate on his desk and the hot tea Sofia brought with them goes undrunk. She loses heart and joins her mum.

Maryam has switched on the television and is staring at it. Sofia understands that her mother doesn't want to talk so she goes to bed early, long before her father gets home.

They're in limbo, waiting for Abdi to speak. It's all that matters. The waiting is disorientating and frightening.

Waking in the night, she checks the iPad. It's charged. She taps and scrolls, and at first she's part disappointed and part relieved because there doesn't seem to be anything on it that could offer her a clue as to what's happened. But then she notices the sound file. It's the only one in a voice memo app. It's dated from late yesterday evening.

Sofia taps the play button and watches as a thin red line tracks across the screen under an audio graphic. At first there's silence, but a second or two later Sofia hears a familiar voice.

'Where do you want me to start?' It's a man's voice and it sounds slurred and slow, like a drunken storyteller.

'What was it like being at the camp?'

Sofia recognises both voices. The first is Ed Sadler, the second her brother, Abdi. Hearing his recorded voice startles her.

'Harshek,' says Ed Sadler. He can hardly get the word out. He laughs, and tries again. 'Har-ti-sheik. I went to Hartisheik camp back in 1999. 1999 was one of my first trips I made with Dan, or was it 1998? First or second, not sure, but anyway, 1999 was good because Fi came to meet me in Addis Ababa when I had some R and R and we went to visit those underground church things, you know? The early Christian churches?'

'How did you find conditions in the camp?' Abdi sounds very earnest, as if he's aspiring to be a serious correspondent.

'Bad, very bad, so bad.' He's snapping in and out of sounding very drunk and very sober. 'They didn't want the outside world to see what it was like in the camps so visits were controlled. They did that to stop word getting out about what was happening to those people in Somalia. But you know, I'm so glad I persisted, and then Dan gave me my break. These are the sort of things you have to do and connections you have to make to get stories.'

'How long were you in the camp?' Abdi's voice sounds small but very serious.

'Just two days. I made two visits on two days. It was amazing. Amazing people. So much tragedy, but so much humanity too. I'd been in Somalia proper the previous year, front line, you know, flak jacket, helmet, the works, in the thick of it, bullets flying everywhere, very *Black Hawk Down*, so going to the camp was a continuation of that story, showing the place where people went when they'd fled that horror.'

'What was the worst thing about the visit?' Abdi says.

'The sadness, the hunger, thirst, malnutrition ... the lack of hope.'

'And the best?'

'Well, you know, I was thinking when I was hanging the exhibition that the day of that football match was a great day. We were due to leave that evening, but the aid workers had hooked up a TV screen outside their office to show the Champions League Final. Manchester United vs Bayern Munich, a huge match, so we stayed to watch it. Amazing atmosphere, all the men gathered around the screen. Incredible sense of camaraderie.'

Ed Sadler breaks off into a big yawn. 'Apologies, but I think I'm going to have to turn in. Few too many.'

'You took a photograph of the men watching the game,' Abdi says. 'I saw it at the gallery.'

'You're right, I did.'

'What's wrong with that man's mouth?'

'The man with all the teeth sticking out?'

'Yes.'

'He has a cleft palate. It's quite a common birth defect, and if you were born with it here it would get operated on within days or weeks. That doesn't happen in Somalia, especially if you're from a rural community. There are very few facilities, and even if you can access one, you probably can't afford to pay for the operation.'

'Did you talk to the people in the photo?'

'Not him, that's for sure! I had to snatch that shot. He was a man who wouldn't have wanted his picture taken. He was in a group of new arrivals and the aid workers suspected they were troublemakers. You can imagine that, right? That not everybody who arrives in the camps is a victim of the war. They said that he'd been part of a group who were responsible for many atrocities back in Somalia. It wasn't too difficult for men like him to slip in and out of the camps and across borders. Nobody had papers, and desperate people were arriving every day in huge numbers.'

'So you didn't learn their names?' Abdi asks.

'His nickname was Farurey. It means lip or harelip, or something like that. It refers to his lip. I never knew his real name, I don't know if anybody did, and I don't know the other men. It was so long ago. I only remember him because people talked about him. Anyway, I can barely remember my own name tonight! Bedtime? You should go up and I need to get a glass of water.'

'I tried to print something upstairs, and I think Noah's computer sent it down here. Do you have it?'

'Let's see. Have a look, but I think we ran out of paper. You might have to wait until the morning. Bedtime, Abdi, my mate. Come on. I don't know about you, but I'm on my last legs. I'm getting too old for this.'

The recording ends.

The nurses change shift, and my parents' voices get slower and lower, and stretch into yawns.

Sometime after Dad leaves, I hear Mum struggling with the big chair that converts into a bed. By the end of a long stay in the hospital, I wonder sometimes if her body will have been permanently bent into the shape of the hospital furniture.

Once Abdi asked me what I thought my family life would be like if I hadn't got ill. It was hard to answer the question, because when your family's one way, you can't imagine how it can be any different. I tried to remember what it was like before my diagnosis, and that gave me my answer: 'Normal.'

Abdi said, 'There's no such thing as "normal".'

'You know what I mean.'

We'd just started going to Philosophy Club, so Abdi was obsessed with dissecting the meaning behind everything we said, looking behind words and phrases, asking questions all the time. I thought it was a bit pretentious then, but since The Talk with Dr Sasha, it's probably fair to say I've been a bit like that myself.

Noah's Bucket List Item No. 4: Be Normal (or 'as normal as possible').

Dad's private view at the gallery was a chance for us to be the family we might have been without my illness. My mum looked beautiful. She got her hair and her nails done, wore a new dress, and stood tall. Dad took a family selfie and installed it as the wallpaper on his phone.

'A very proud night,' he said when he showed it to us. It made me very glad I hadn't let them cancel the party when we got the news.

Mum drove us to the gallery, which was in Stokes Croft. Usually she puts the central locking on if we pull up at a red light in that neighbourhood, because she says it can be 'edgy'. It's a description that makes Dad laugh. She was iffy about the location when Dad first told her about it, but he said, 'It's a satellite space for the Arnolfini Gallery: it's very prestigious. Frankly, I wouldn't want to show anywhere else except London.'

Abdi was already there when we arrived, standing at the door waiting for us.

'You look really nice,' I said.

'My mum got me a new shirt,' he said. It was dark blue and a little bit shiny.

I put my arm around him when we walked in, even though it was a bit difficult because he's grown so much taller than me lately. I didn't care, though, because I wanted everybody to see that he was my best friend.

Just inside the gallery a small notice was displayed on a board:

WARNING: This exhibition contains images from war and disaster zones. Some visitors may find it distressing.

Mum had wobbled about Abdi and me coming for that reason, but Dad saved the day.

'The boys are fifteen,' he said to her. 'They have to grow up some time.'

Too right.

Noah's Bucket List Item No. 5: Watch An 18 Certificate Film (Dad says me and him are going to watch Alien *together, even if Mum has a hissy fit. He says it's incredible.)*

The gallery was packed with people, so much so that it was hard for us to see the photographs properly, but people were talking about them: 'Jaw-dropping ... beautiful ... The focus falls away at just the right point ... He really does have an extraordinary eye.'

Me and Abdi had the job of helping to pass food around. Dad promised us a 'very decent' hourly wage in return.

Noah's Bucket List Item No. 6: Have a Job (yes, a few hours of paid employment counts).

We carried big silver platters around the room as it filled up even more, and offered the guests a choice of posh bits of food. Lots of people told me I'd grown (I hadn't much lately) and that I looked well (I really didn't – go figure), but it was very nice all the same. Me and Abdi made a good team.

After a while, the room got so crowded that we had to abandon our platters and somebody opened the door to let some cold air in.

Dad got on a chair and made a speech, and I liked it when we saluted each other at the end.

At about nine o'clock people began to leave and Mum and Dad stood at the door, saying goodbye, kissing everybody and shaking hands. Me and Abdi stood with them.

'Shall we go?' Mum said when the last people had left. She yawned. 'Your dad's going to get a beer with some friends.'

Outside on the pavement, three of Dad's friends were standing in a huddle, two of them smoking, and all of them laughing loudly.

'I won't go if you don't want me to,' Dad said.

'It's fine.' I hugged him super tightly, making sure to hold on for a long time, and I said, 'I'm so proud of you, Dad.'

'Thanks, mate,' he said. We held the hug for ages.

Noah's Bucket List Item No. 7: Make Sure People Know How Important They Are to You.

We waved Dad off and I said to Mum, 'Can we just look at the photographs before we go? Really quickly?' It was the first chance I'd had to see them properly, now that the gallery was empty.

'It's very late.'

'Please?'

'Five minutes. They're waiting to close up.' Well, she wasn't really going to argue with me, was she?

Abdi and I took a look round. The gallery was a neat rectangular space with photographs covering the walls. Some of them had been blown up very large, but others were smaller, and hung in groups. All the photographs were good. Some of them were very shocking. I wanted to make sure I looked at each and every one of them.

The photographs were from different areas of the world, and by far the biggest was a section with the heading HORN OF AFRICA. The first photograph in that section was of a baby crouched naked in the road outside a destroyed house. She had sand on her face and eyelids. In another, a very old woman was propped against a tree, leaning her head back against the trunk. Her eyes were open. She was alive, but probably not for long. A long trail of families walked past her, all of them loaded with possessions. It made me shudder, the sight of her waiting for death.

Another picture was a close-up of a mother and her baby. The baby's belly was swollen huge. The mother looked straight into the camera, over the baby's head. Both their eyes were dull and yellowy. It was the loneliest picture I've ever seen.

The other photographs were just as shocking.

There was a man lying in the middle of the street, dead and covered in blood. A boy with a gun in his hand was picking through the man's pockets.

There was a body hanging from a post, head slumped to one side, hands and feet limp. Behind it was a mural on the side of a shop showing cigarettes and sodas and toothpaste and other things for sale.

The worst was a photograph of somebody's feet, beaten to a pulp, with a fly resting on one of the toes. It was a horrible, sick-making picture, but the lighting in it was strangely beautiful. I could see my dad's skill.

Others weren't so bad. I liked one that was a panorama showing domed tents in a desert, hundreds or thousands of them. Behind them, above a ridge, a sandstorm was rising, and in the front of the picture bits of plastic rubbish caught on a thorny bush were being blown horizontal by the wind.

There was also a picture of a group of men and boys watching a football game on TV. They were outside, in front of a big screen, the men sitting on plastic chairs and the boys filling the gaps between and in front of them. Somebody must have just scored a goal, because the men and boys were frozen in celebration, some with arms pumping the air, others with mouths open. Only one man wasn't looking at the game but to the side, somewhere near the camera but not quite at it. He was sitting in a yellow plastic chair and his expression was really cold, even though his face was sweaty. He had no top lip, it looked like it was slashed open down the middle, and his teeth were growing through it at all crazy angles. He was scary.

Abdi looked at it with me.

'Come on, boys!' Mum said. 'Time to go.'

I was ready. I felt weak. The photographs were stressful and my adrenalin and good feelings were ebbing away. Abdi didn't seem to hear her. I tugged his arm.

'Come on.'

He couldn't take his eyes off the photo. I knew 'Horn of Africa' meant Somalia, and that's where Abdi's family was from, but I didn't know what it was about this photo that was so interesting that it would put him in a trance.

'Abdi!'

He took out his phone and took a picture of the photograph.

'OK,' he said, once he'd checked it. He came with me, but he kept glancing at the photograph as he put his coat on, and he turned around to try to look at it one last time when we walked to the car.

'You're very quiet, both of you,' Mum said as she drove us home.

'Tired,' I said, and that seemed to satisfy her. She put on the radio.

I didn't know why Abdi was so quiet. It wasn't like him. Maybe he was tired, too. I was happy to let him rest, because we had our plan for later.

I looked out of the window of the car as we drove home, and I wondered whether Dad had helped those people after he took photos of them.

Edward and Fiona Sadler's house is very tall. On a Georgian square in Clifton Village where most of the buildings are divided into flats, they have a house to themselves. The exterior is exceptionally well maintained. The Bath stone is clean and golden and the glass in the windows gleams. In the centre of the square is a locked communal garden where lush greenery is contained by decorative black wrought-iron railings.

'Bloody hell,' Woodley mutters.

We make our way up the tiled path to the front door. In the beds along the path the daffodils that have already flowered have been neatly tied up and the shiny nubs of emerging tulips are pushing up through the soil. On either side of the front door, dark pink cyclamen bloom in large pots, and ivy spills from their edges.

I ring the bell. The chime is distant.

When Edward Sadler opens the door, he looks rough as hell. He's a tall man, about my height and broad-shouldered.

The first thing he does after offering us a seat in a sitting room that's plush and formal is to break down, elbows on knees, head cupped in his hands, fingers slick with tears.

Woodley and I wait for him to get control of himself before I offer my condolences regarding Noah's prognosis. It doesn't sound any less stilted than when I said the same words to Fiona Sadler.

He nods an acknowledgement, but he's got something else on his mind: 'I tied one on last night. I keep thinking about how if I hadn't, things might have been different.'

Dodging the self-pity – the 'if only' lament of the victims or their loved ones on almost every case I've ever worked on; predictable, understandable, but not helpful – I ease him gently into the questioning.

'Can you tell us a little bit about Noah?'

'He's very clever, like my wife.' His mouth twitches. It's almost a smile. I suspect this is a joke he's told before: self-deprecation as a tool to make other people relax around him. It dilutes his alpha-male presentation. 'We had Noah when we were very young. We hadn't been together for very long at all. I was just starting out on my career and Fi was studying printmaking. She was – is – a very talented artist. We fell for each other hard, straight away, and we started going out. I was beginning to do a fair bit of travelling, but she would come and join me when she could because she had all these long holidays. It was fun, really fun. Those were good times. We didn't plan to get pregnant, but we were happy when it happened, once we got over the shock. We settled in Bristol so Fi could be near her parents, and we were lucky enough to have the money to buy a house, from her side of the family, so we settled down here happily enough. Fi set up a studio in the garden. Things were going well with my work, so I was starting to travel more and more, and she couldn't come with me any more, but she had help from her parents when I was away. We managed. We felt lucky. And Noah made it easy. He was a top baby. A really sunny little boy.'

I sense an 'until', and that their life together is defined by a 'before' and an 'after'. I don't interrupt him. If a witness starts to talk, you let them, and you listen hard.

'We decided not to have more kids, because we'd started so young and we felt complete with Noah. By the time he was six or seven, and we were through those early years, life was great. We were happy, and frankly that felt like a triumph against the odds of having the unexpected pregnancy. We proved a lot of people wrong by sticking together! But then everything fell apart, right out of the blue. Fi's parents died, within a few months of each other. She was totally destroyed for a long time, because she'd been so close to them. It took her ages to get back on her feet, and just when she had, the school contacted us to say that Noah had a nosebleed that they couldn't get under control. That was the start of it. Numerous GP and hospital trips later, we had the official cancer diagnosis.'

'How old was Noah then?'

'He was eight.'

'I'm so sorry.'

He inclines his head, raises his hands and drops them again. I wonder how often he and his wife have had to acknowledge other people's reactions over the years. It can't be easy.

'Having cancer's no life for a kid. By the time Noah was diagnosed, he was old enough to feel very deeply that it made him different from his friends. He was aware of all the things he was missing out on. He anticipated and dreaded his treatments. And now ...'

His voice cracks again and his hands tighten into fists. He looks up at the ceiling, as if he wishes he could find answers there. Woodley and I wait in silence, giving him time.

'Now, just as we've reached the place we've always dreaded – the end of it all, the thing we've tried to dodge for seven years – now this happens. But, you know, Noah's tough. He'll pull through. He has to. We have plans for the next couple of months.'

He crashes back into the sofa cushions and runs his hands through his hair. He looks from one of us to the other, and his eye contact is searching and desperate.

'Do you feel able to answer just a few more questions, Mr Sadler? If not, we can speak at a later time.'

He exhales heavily and makes an effort to adjust his

posture so he looks more attentive. From the hallway, a clock ticks dully.

'Let's do it now. Anything that'll help, though I've got to go back to the hospital soon. And please call me Ed. I can't stand formality. It's so pointless.'

'I'd like to know anything you can tell me about the boys' friendship,' I say.

'They're best friends. Absolutely thick as thieves. Abdi's a fabulous kid, and he was a godsend when Noah started secondary school. Noah'd been out of the system for so long during treatment we were worried he wouldn't fit in, but they made friends on the first day and they've been inseparable ever since.'

It's exactly what his wife predicted he would say.

'Was sneaking out of the house the kind of behaviour you might expect from either of them?'

'I'm not home as much as I should be, so Fiona's the expert on Noah, but personally I can't think of anything they're less likely to do. They're nerdy boys. They go to chess competitions. They study together. They freak out if they don't get merit cards on every bit of homework they do. So no, it was the last thing I'd have expected.'

Something about the way he says this makes me think that Ed Sadler was the opposite type of boy, and still is as a man. I'm particularly interested in his take on this because I get the impression that Noah's indulging in some mildly rebellious behaviour is something that Ed Sadler might welcome, or certainly be open to acknowledging. He doesn't seem to be as protective of Noah as his wife is.

Woodley chips in. 'Your wife told us that she felt the friendship might not have been very healthy for Noah. Do you have a view on that?'

He sighs. 'This stuff is hard to talk about. OK. Look. Here's the thing: Fiona's life has been dominated by Noah's illness for years, and you can probably imagine how that might make her feel. She longs for "normal". She thought I encouraged Noah's friendship with Abdi because of my own interests, and she resents that, because she would rather that Noah had made friends with a boy whose mother would have a coffee with her or share school runs with her. Be her friend. And between us, I think that's coloured Fiona's opinion of Abdi. She's never wholly approved of the friendship. I believe she's wrong, I think Abdi's a terrific friend for Noah, but you can understand how her feelings about her circumstances might have crept into her judgement of him. She's been under unbelievable amounts of pressure for a very long time.'

He's choosing his words very carefully. I consider how much he might have gained from Fiona's apparently comprehensive devotion to Noah's care: a large amount of freedom, certainly. It's clear that Ed Sadler loves his son very much, but at no point has he described the burden of Noah's care as something they undertake together. Nevertheless, I appreciate his forthrightness.

'That's a very honest answer.'

'Where we're at in life, I don't think there's any point in being opaque.'

I can't argue with that.

'So, just to clarify, you saw nothing last night that would

make you think that the boys might either have argued or have been planning to sneak out of the house?'

'I saw nothing. I don't know why they did it, neither of us does. We'd had a good night. This exhibition has been in the works for years. It was a big moment for me professionally, and also for us as a family. We thought long and hard about cancelling it when we got Noah's prognosis, but he insisted we go ahead.'

Tears slick his eyes once again, and he grinds his fists into his sockets as if he can rub them away.

'Would you mind if we took a look at Noah's room?' I ask. I want to get an idea of this boy outside of the grim picture I formed in the hospital.

'Of course, yes.' He gets up quickly, as if he welcomes the distraction, and shows us up two flights of stairs.

He lingers in the doorway as Woodley and I step into the room. 'I'll leave you to it,' he says. 'Abdi kipped in here with him last night.'

Once he's gone I take an initial look around and make some immediate assessments. The first is the most obvious one: Noah Sadler's room is undoubtedly testament to a privileged upbringing, until you notice the medical paraphernalia.

Woodley and I open drawers and carefully look through the items on the desk. A model of a Bristol hot air balloon twists slowly in one corner as we work.

Noah's bed is rumpled and unmade, just as you'd expect if somebody had crept out at night. A pair of pyjamas is discarded on the floor beside it. There's a put-up bed in the corner that also looks slept in, but there are no bits and pieces lying around that might obviously belong to Abdi.

'Perhaps he slept in another room,' Woodley says.

He has a poke around in the en suite bathroom. 'There's not even a toothbrush in here.'

'Perhaps Abdi decided to leave and packed up his stuff and took it with him. They could have had a row. He could have stormed off and Noah went after him?' I'm thinking aloud, running through scenarios, trying to keep an open mind.

'Maybe. We should ask Mr Sadler if he or his wife tidied up Abdi's stuff.'

'I very much doubt they did that. Probably the last thing on their minds today.'

'Fair point.' Woodley opens the closet, which is messy with Noah's clothes. Shoes are stacked in a heap in the bottom of it. Just what I'd expect to see in a teenage bedroom.

Only one thing really captures my attention. Above Noah's bed, a series of drawings have been framed and hung on the wall. Every one depicts a road and its sur-roundings, and no two are alike. They're intricate and meticulous. Each drawing must have taken hours to finish. They are all signed: 'NS'.

I ask Ed Sadler about them when we get downstairs and for the first time he displays a little embarrassment.

'Noah's in therapy,' he says. 'At the hospital. To help him deal with his disease. It mostly involves talking, but art therapy's a component, too — they say it helps with self-expression — so Noah produces those drawings every once in a while. They're about his journey through life, or something like that. Fi insists they go up on the wall, though I'm not sure how healthy that is, if I'm honest. I'm more of a "get on with it" sort of person. The thought of talking about everything ad nauseam terrifies me.'

It's the attitude to therapy that I held before I was forced to take a different view and found myself sitting in a chair opposite Dr Manelli twice a week for six months, in that dim room where the soft furnishings seemed designed to absorb sorrow. But I don't react to Ed Sadler's embarrassment about his son's therapy with the fervour of the converted, because for me the jury's still out.

'The therapist he sees is based at the hospital,' Ed adds. 'Noah quite likes him, I think. He's been seeing him for years now. His medical team say talking's good for him, so, anyway.'

'We didn't see anything belonging to Abdi in Noah's room.'

'That's because his sister came round and collected his stuff this morning. Alvard, our housekeeper, was here.'

Woodley and I leave him to get some rest. He seems to be just as broken as his wife.

'I'd like to speak to the therapist,' I say as we drive back to HQ.

'What about confidentiality issues?'

'I think it's worth a try, anyway. We've got nothing to lose.'

On my way home that night, I stop to pick up some food. Mrs Chin in my local Chinese place shouts my order at her husband as soon as she sees me pushing through the door: 'One special fried rice for special detective!'

I sit at one of her scrubbed and chipped red Formica tables while I wait for my order, thinking about the two families I've met, and how there's mostly a consensus about the boys' relationship, with the exception of Fiona Sadler. Experience has taught me not to ignore a mother's intuition, but she's not a mother in an ordinary situation. Word this evening from the hospital is that Noah Sadler's condition remains stable and comfortable, so that at least is something.

I check out the local rag that somebody's left on the table. The fallout from last week's anti-immigration march is still being discussed in an article that includes comments from many of the city's bigwigs:

> Mayor Tony Harris issued a statement to say: 'Bristol is an inclusive and diverse city. We pride ourselves on welcoming people of all faiths and backgrounds. If we had the powers to prevent the White Nation March from going ahead, we would certainly have exercised them.

The article goes on to describe the damage caused by the riots and the likely cost of repair to the city and to local business. Blame is firmly placed on what's described as an 'at best woeful, and at worst grossly incompetent' attempt by police to contain the situation. It's not good for us.

Mrs Chin makes her usual comments about my singleton lifestyle when she hands me the food. 'Not healthy for a handsome man to dine alone every night, Detective!'

'Thank you, Mrs Chin. I'm working on it.'

She pops a fortune cookie into my bag of food.

'Maybe this bring you luck in love!'

'I'll keep you posted.'

As I unlock my bike and hang the bag on my handle-bars for the last bit of my ride home, my phone rings. I check the caller display. There aren't many people I'd be surprised to hear from, but this is certainly one of them.

'Becky?'

'Jim. I didn't know if this number still worked.'

'It's been a long time.'

'Where are you?'

'I'm . . . why?'

I've hardly seen my sister at all since she walked out of our family home, and then only at family occasions when my mother applied enough emotional blackmail to get us both there. Becky would come to those only if she was sure she could avoid our dad. The last time we saw each other was at his funeral. We meant to have a drink when I moved to Bristol, because she was already living here, but we never got around to it somehow.

'I'm at your flat. I need a place to stay.'

Five minutes later I find her sitting on the front steps, and I barely recognise her. She has long dirty blonde dreadlocks with beads in them, and her cheekbones look sharp, her cheeks hollowed beneath them. One of her eyes is a bruised, swollen mess. When she sees me she gets up stiffly.

'Please don't say anything,' she says.

I obey her instruction as I lock up my bike, open the front door and beckon her in. She looks out of place in the elegant hallway of my building. I offer to carry the large rucksack she has with her, but she refuses. She hoists it onto her back and follows me up the stairs.

She's never been to my flat before and I watch her take it in with her good eye. I split the special fried rice between two bowls and give her one. She eats very quickly. I notice that her fingers are dirty and she also has bruising on her collarbone.

We both speak at the same time.

'Are you going to tell me ...'

'Can I stay with you for a while?'

On the last evening my sister and I lived in the same house, my father hit her, backhanded, and she fell against the wall of our kitchen. He put a lot of effort into that blow, so much that the spice rack fell off its hooks and hit the floor beside Becky. There was an explosion of different-coloured herbs and powders. Our mother was keen on experimenting in the kitchen.

I was eating fish fingers when he did it. My mother had gone out to the shed to get some ice cream from the chest freezer for dessert. It took Becky a long time to get up, and when she did, she was dizzy. My father turned his back on her to take a cut-glass whisky tumbler from the cupboard, and as he did, Becky left the kitchen silently and went upstairs to pack her things. She left a trail of spice-red footsteps on the carpet. My father had just heard that Becky had been in one place when she'd told him she'd been in another.

Not long afterwards, as she dragged a suitcase out of the front door, I watched from the kitchen and made sure to finish my meal even though it had gone stone cold long ago. I was a good boy. I was terrified. I saw my mother stuff banknotes that she got from a tin in the larder into Becky's pockets and try to lay a hand on her daughter's cheek, only to be rebuffed. I saw her wash the Neapolitan ice cream down the sink because it had melted. My mum's hands shook under the gushing water, and she ran the tap for a very long time.

My father's study door stayed shut that night, and for days afterwards when he got back from work. A week later, he had the paprika-stained carpet replaced, over-seeing the fitting of it personally, and the photographs of Becky that had been on the piano were removed on the same day. He never mentioned her again.

Becky doesn't talk the night she arrives at my flat. I give her my bedroom and lie on the sofa telling myself it doesn't matter that the springs are digging into my back, because I wouldn't have been able to sleep anyway.

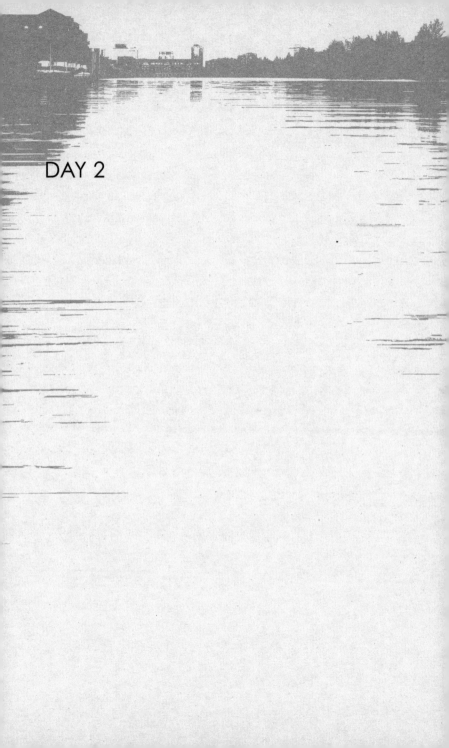

DAY 2

I'm hot.

Dad says, 'Why would this happen?'

'Most likely it's an infection that's developed very rapidly overnight. Our priority is to stabilise Noah's temperature and then we'll investigate the causes.'

That's the doctor speaking. He's a doctor I haven't met and I can't see. His voice is higher-pitched than I would like. It grates. I hear lots of shoe shuffling and squeaking. I've become hyper-aware of sound. I think there are a few people around my bedside.

'We should see the temperature drop pretty fast. That's the idea, anyway.'

'It's a lot of ice.'

'We'll keep it there for as long as we need to and replace it if necessary.'

'Will he be able to feel this?'

'I doubt it,' says the doctor, but to cover his bases he raises his voice and says, 'Noah, we're packing some ice around you because you're running a very high temperature and we need to bring it down.'

I want to say, 'Please don't.' I'm scared of the heat, but also of the cold. I don't know if I can stand it.

I still can't speak, though, so I have to just lie there. A strange thing happens. I can't physically feel the cold, but my brain reacts by taking me on a memory trip to places where I've felt cold before: a skiing holiday, an ice rink where I held onto a plastic penguin, the hospital bed I was in the time my temperature plummeted after an operation and I got uncontrollable chills, and then, of course, the canal water. I remember how hard it was to move in the water, and the pull of the current. I remember feeling powerless, the way you feel when they dose your body so full of toxic drugs that you feel as if you're as fragile as an eggshell.

The stem cell transplant was the worst and hardest treatment I had, by miles. It destroys you, strips you out. My mouth was on fire for days because it was one giant ulcer, and the morphine made me itch all over and hallucinate small creatures in the corner of the room. It was also degrading. They had to feed me with a tube and sometimes wash me like a baby.

It's hard to look people in the eye after that.

Abdi wasn't allowed to visit me, because those are the rules when you have a stem cell transplant. Because the treatment destroys your immune system, you have to be isolated for a good while, to avoid being exposed to other people's germs. It meant that by the time I got back to school I hadn't seen him for weeks. I was really looking forward to seeing him again, so what happened was a shock.

I asked Mum to drop me at school early, because Abdi always got there right at the beginning of the day. I found him at Breakfast Club, our usual meeting place. He was sitting with somebody else: a new boy. Abdi jumped up from his seat when he saw me and introduced us. The boy's name was Imran Fletcher-Kapoor. I don't think Abdi meant to shock me as badly as he did, but the truth is he could have been a lot more sensitive. He gave me no warning at all, just dumped the fact that he'd made a new friend right on top of me.

Imran was a strong boy, with thick black shiny hair. He talked fast and he was definitely a fast mover on the friendship front. I had to hand it to him on that count, actually. In just a few weeks, he'd already persuaded Abdi to drop IT club and go to badminton club with him instead.

They invited me to go with them and watch. I felt like a mongrel dog, compared to them. Unwanted, strange-looking and kicked so many times I didn't know how to do anything apart from cower. I sat on one of the benches beside the badminton court and clapped and cheered when they turned to me to celebrate after a good shot. At first I watched their high fives and fist bumps patiently, but when Abdi pumped the air with his arm and whooped I thought: *Really? Is that necessary to impress Imran?*

I thought about Imran all night after I got home from school. I told Mum about him and she said: 'Things change, Noah. Sometimes there's nothing we can do apart from learn how to deal with it.'

It made me remember a conversation I overheard her having with Dad, soon after my first round of treatment, when I'd just restarted school.

'I can't face the playground,' she said. 'The competitiveness, the people who ask me about Noah who I know don't really care, they just want something to gossip about. I find myself being really short with everybody. They're going to hate me. They probably hate me already because they think I'll infect them with our bad luck.'

Even I'd noticed her transformation from a chatty mum to a mum who kept herself separate in the playground.

'I can't even answer their questions normally.' She mimics a conversation: '"What did you do today? Oh, I took my toddler swimming and made organic cupcakes for the fundraiser, and signed a petition against the new high-street parking regulations. What did you do?", "Oh, I flushed out my son's Hickman line and returned the sharps bucket to the hospital. Then I felt really happy because he managed to eat half a chocolate bar, which frankly counts as excellent nutritional intake for us this week!" I can't have that conversation with anybody! Talking like that scares them away.'

'People will be there for you when this is over. The people who matter will, anyway.'

'That's easy for you to say.'

On the day that Imran came into my life, Mum perked up when she thought through the implications of Abdi making a new friend: 'If you don't like Imran, you could try another friendship group.'

I would never do that. It was Abdi I wanted.

The next day, when we were in French class and Imran was finally out of our way because he was in a different set, I said to Abdi, 'You don't have to show off so much for Imran, you know.'

'I'm not showing off!'

He was about to say something else, but the teacher arrived and we stood up. He held himself very stiffly when we all said, 'Bonjour, Madame.'

I didn't make it to the end of the lesson. When I told Madame Moreau that I felt really wobbly, she got Abdi to take me to the school nurse. On the way there I said to Abdi, 'Just one thing too many, you know.'

'I think you've been really strong today,' he said.

The next day, Abdi was hanging around Imran again when I arrived, along with a crowd of other boys who were impressed by a gross trick that Imran could do where he flipped his eyelids up.

I didn't think it would work to talk to Abdi about it again, because he sounded so defensive last time, so I decided to test him, secretly. All I wanted to know was whether he was a good enough friend to stick with me or if he was done with me, just like Matthew was after he came to the hospital.

The very first test happened that afternoon. When I arrived at a science lesson, Imran beckoned me over to join him at his lab table. They were designed for two students. I snubbed him, though, and he stood there in his lab coat and goggles and held out his hands, palms up, like, 'Oh well, I tried.'

I thought he looked stupid. I took another workbench, by the door.

When Abdi arrived, he looked at Imran and then at me. You could tell he felt conflicted. I said, 'I saved you a workspace.' Annoyingly, he still seemed unsure about who to work with, so I said, 'You promised we'd do the experiment together.'

'Did I?'

'You totally promised.' It wasn't true.

After he sat down beside me, I gave him a present because he passed the test. I didn't explain that to him, obviously. I just handed him a very cool, clicky pencil with thick refillable leads that Mum had given me as a 'well done for having a lumbar puncture' present a while before. It was red. Abdi was excited to get it because his parents didn't have much money so they got his pencils from the supermarket and the leads were always breaking.

I tested him lots more times after that. I tested him by not texting first, to see if he would. I tested him by leaving places without saying goodbye to see if he would notice. Sometimes I think he suspected he was being tested, sometimes not. Some of the tests he passed; some he didn't. When he chose Imran over me or forgot me I felt useless, and that could make me feel ill. When that happened, I always wanted Abdi to take me to the nurse. I made sure all the teachers knew it had to be him.

It took a while, but the testing worked eventually: Abdi saw that I was right, that he couldn't be best friends with both me and Imran. It was obvious that Imran would be fine because he'd made lots more friends by then. He spread himself thin. My final proof was when Imran easily found somebody else to play badminton with after Abdi started coming to IT club with me again. I said to Abdi, 'That sporty lot aren't our kind of people, anyway.'

We got close again, after that. We shared homework,

projects and clubs, and everything went back to how it was before my stem cell transplant.

What my parents didn't know was that before the night of Dad's gallery party, Abdi and I had made a plan. It was something we were going to do after the party.

Noah's Bucket List Item No. 8: Experience a Rite of Passage. (In my head this one could also have been titled 'Have a Beer with a Mate', but I didn't tell Dad that, because he suggested I could have a beer with him. It was a nice idea, but really, who the heck goes through a rite of passage with their dad?)

It was an imperfect plan, because I knew Abdi wouldn't drink alcohol, but I didn't really see that as a problem. The point was, we were going to sneak out of the house and do something cool together, and I was going to get to feel like a real teenager.

The sensation of heat rising in my body is becoming overwhelming. It's woozy, baking, oven-hot heat. Randomly, all I can think about is the Cat in the Hat with his fan. I would like him to fan me. I don't think the ice is working.

I'm aware that there's silence around me, where before there was talking, and I wonder why I can't hear my parents and if they're even here with me. Panic rises along with the heat. I don't want to be stuck here alone, even for five minutes. Not any more. I can't tolerate the heat. They need to make it go away. My paralysis should be over by now, my eyes should be open, I should be able to speak. I'm afraid I'm getting worse, not better. A death like this, incarcerated in my own body for who knows how long, would be awful.

I'm overwhelmed with a desire to see where I am, who's

around me, and all the familiar things that Mum brings to the hospital to make it nice. I start to list those things in my head, to calm myself down.

My old toy dog from home will be here. I know I'm too big for that kind of thing, but I like to have it with me for luck.

I want to see the tub of caramel chocolate bites on the table beside my bed. My favourites, always there in case I find my appetite. Mum will have put a bag of Pink Lady apples in the fridge in the parents' room, too, so I can have one if I ever feel like it, and it'll be crisp and cold in my mouth.

I want to see the nurses and doctors I'm familiar with, not the strange ones who are hovering around me here.

Most of all, I want to see my parents.

I feel very afraid.

I'm afraid that I'll be stuck like this for ever, and afraid that I might die. Not the way that I've imagined it would happen, but locked in my own body. With people, but not with them. Not able to say or explain anything. Alone.

'Nurse!' Mum calls. 'Nurse!'

I hear rapid footfall.

'He's crying,' Mum says. 'Look. He's crying.'

'Noah,' says the nurse gently, 'can you let us know why you're crying? Are you in pain anywhere? Can you give us any kind of sign?'

Their voices drift away like small shreds of cloud chased across the sky, and there's nothing left but a burning white sun, and its heat is everything.

*

I have to leave for work before Becky wakes up the following morning.

There's been no update from the hospital on Noah Sadler's condition overnight, so I plant a coffee on Woodley's desk and ask him to call Noah Sadler's ward for me.

'Is this bribery of some sort?' he says, lifting the lid to peer at the cup's contents.

'Absolutely. It's a key management tool, I'm told.'

'Works for me, boss.'

A note on my desk tells me that there are some CCTV clips ready for us to look at. When Woodley gets off the phone, we find the officer who's been poring over hours of footage for us.

'I could only get hold of an agency nurse,' Woodley tells me on the way, 'but she said so far as she knows he's stable, and she'll get somebody to call us if anything changes.'

The first CCTV clip the detective constable has ready for us shows Noah and Abdi walking past the cathedral, heading west across College Green towards the city centre. The boys are together, shoulder to shoulder. Noah Sadler wears a backpack, and it looks weighty. The camera has recorded them from a height so it's very hard to see their expressions, but their body language says a lot. They look like partners in whatever they're doing.

'Did we recover that backpack?' I ask.

The DC shakes his head. 'He's wearing it in every picture I've seen, so it must have disappeared nearer the scene or at it. He might have been wearing it when he went into the canal.'

'Then he'd have had to get it off in the water.'

The DC shrugs. 'Could have, I suppose. By the look of it, if he was wearing it, it would have dragged him under fast.'

Woodley's staring at the frozen image. 'They look friendly enough together there.'

'It doesn't last,' says the DC.

The next clip shows Pero's Bridge. It spans the floating harbour slap bang in the centre of the city. Fog billows over it: a result of the artist's installation that the local news has been banging on about for weeks.

'They come out from here,' says the DC, pointing at a small gap between buildings, and I see the boys emerge together and walk towards the bridge. The time gap between this clip and the last is considerable. At least twenty minutes have passed, yet the distance between the two cameras is only about five minutes' walk, if that.

The boys step onto the bridge and the fog immediately obscures them.

'Frustratingly, you can only see glimpses of them on the bridge, because the fog's so thick, but they get up to something ... here ... ' The DC forwards the tape then pauses it. 'Watch carefully,' he says. He plays the next bit of footage in very slow motion. Putting the frames together it seems as if Noah Sadler interrupts Abdi as he looks at something and then knocks it from his hand. The DC zooms in on a blurry object caught on the floor of the bridge.

'I think he knocks a phone out of Abdi Mahad's hand,' he says. 'And it goes into the water.'

We watch the clip a couple more times and I'd have to agree.

'Trouble in paradise, maybe?' Woodley asks. 'There usually is.'

The DC queries that with a look.

'They're supposed to be best of friends, these two.'

'I must have looked at it twenty times and I can't tell if it's an accidental gesture or not. The rest is obscured by fog. It's extremely annoying.'

He gets a third clip up for us.

'Next time we see them is here,' he says. 'About a quarter of a mile beyond the bridge.'

Noah Sadler's crossing a road, alone. He's walking more quickly than before, hands in pockets, head down, backpack still on. From what we can see of his expression and his gait, he's fatigued. He disappears out of frame.

'Wait for it,' the DC says. We stare at the empty crossing, and just a few seconds later, Abdi Mahad appears, following in his friend's footsteps. His hood's up, he's walking more easily than Noah, but he doesn't seem to be in a hurry to catch up. We can't see his face.

'Anything else?' I say, once Abdi's disappeared out of the frame.

The DC shakes his head.

'I'm still working on getting hold of the CCTV around the scene,' Woodley says. 'The scrapyard doesn't have any and it's a bit of a nightmare tracking down the owners of the other units.'

'We need it asap.'

I turn back to the screen.

'So what happened on the bridge,' I say, 'to separate the boys, and make Abdi start following Noah?'

We watch the clips over and over again, scouring them for clues – a bit of body language, anything that can tell us more – but we come up short. All we can say for sure is that Noah Sadler's clearly struggling physically by the last clip, and Abdi Mahad's following him as they head towards the station. Whether that's to help or harm him, and whether Noah's aware he's there, is impossible to gauge.

I run into Fraser in the canteen by the drinks machine. She's holding a packet of wasabi peas and examining it with suspicion.

'Ever tried one of these, Jim?'

'They're good.'

'I'm sceptical.' She drops the packet back onto the rack, selects a bag of crisps instead, and moves on.

I follow her to the drinks station, where she gets a coffee from the machine and puts two packets of sugar into it. I get a fizzy water and she raises her eyebrows.

'Doctor's orders,' I say. 'Because of my insomnia. I'm supposed to limit my caffeine intake.'

'And that is precisely why I avoid doctors. Sit with me a moment, Jim.'

We take a seat by the window. The sound of good-natured chatter and the smell of hot food being prepared come from the kitchen.

'Emma Zhang,' Fraser says, and coming out of the blue like that, the name almost makes me shudder. Fraser gazes at me, but her eyes are an unreadable slate grey. She

128

knew that Emma and I were involved during the Ben Finch case, and she didn't get on my back about it, even after things fell apart. I have no idea what her agenda is now.

'Yes,' is the safest answer I can think to give her. I'm wary because I don't know where she's going to go with this. I ease the cap off my water and wish I'd got a coffee.

'Have you had any contact with her since the Ben Finch case?'

'No, boss.'

'None at all?'

'None.' It's the bare-naked truth. I haven't even googled her, though I've thought about her more than once probably every single day since we parted ways. It's pride that's stopped me from trying to track her down.

Fraser nods. She slurps her coffee noisily. 'You need to know that she's popped her head back above the parapet.'

'What?'

She sighs. 'Look, I wouldn't have assigned you this case if I'd known this was going to happen but we are where we are. Have you got your phone on you?'

I hold it up.

'Google your case: "Feeder Canal teenager" or whatever.'

I feel my foot start to twitch as I wait for the results to come up. I move it away from Fraser's leg.

'See the article on *TwentyFour7 News*?'

I nod.

'That. Scroll down to the bottom of it.'

There it is: a photograph of my ex, and beside it the words, 'Emma Zhang, Crime Reporter.'

I look at Fraser and she nods. 'She's reporting on your case. First we've heard of her getting into journalism, and it's bad luck for you, it really is. I'm not inclined to move you off the case, though, so long as you think it's not going to disturb you unduly.'

I stare at Emma's picture. It's been more than a year since I last saw her so this feels like a gut punch.

'Jim?'

'Yes, of course it'll be fine. You don't need to take me off the case.'

'You're not filling me with confidence just now.'

'Sorry, boss. I do mean it: I'll be fine.'

'This makes her absolutely toxic. You understand that, I hope. Look at me, Jim.'

I place the phone on the table face down and give her my full attention even though I think I can hear the blood rushing between my ears.

'An ex police officer reporting on crime is out of bounds in every way for a personal relationship. Are your feelings for her resolved?'

'Yes, boss.'

'Are you sure?'

'I am.'

'I could turn a blind eye before, but I won't be able to again. Not now. I need to make that crystal clear.'

I stand up. 'I am absolutely past my feelings for Emma Zhang, and there is no possibility of my entering a relationship with her again.'

I know I sound stupidly formal, as if I'm translating the sentence from another language, but it's the best I can do.

'OK then.' She doesn't look one hundred per cent reassured.

I wait until I'm alone before I google Emma again.

That face. That hair. Those eyes.

My guilt.

Sofia wakes up late the following morning, overtired from being up all night and stressing about the papers in Ed Sadler's office and the recording, trying to work out if it means anything at all, and if so, what.

She has no time to try to discuss it with her parents or Abdi, because she has to run for the bus to college, but she hands the iPad over to her mother and tells her that she needs to listen to the recording. She shows her mother which button to press.

Before she leaves, she takes a moment to whisper Abdi's name from the doorway of his bedroom. He shifts a little in his bed, and hope surges in her for a second, but he falls motionless again. Frustrated with him, she enters the room and pokes at his shoulder. He shocks her by flinging his arm back towards her, almost striking her. It's sudden and violent. She backs out of the room.

At the same time as Sofia takes her seat in the lecture hall at university and wonders how she's going to be able to concentrate on a talk about neonatal care, Nur arrives home from driving the night shift. It was a slow night, so he stayed out to catch the early morning train station arrivals to make the shift worthwhile, and he's weary and worried as he arrives back at the estate.

Maryam's expression tells him everything when he

enters the flat. He knows even before he peers into Abdi's room that there's been no change.

'Whose is that?' he asks, when he sees the iPad in her hands.

'Abdi borrowed it from school. Sit down. You need to listen to something.'

She starts the recording. The volume is so low that Nur can hardly make out what's being said, but Maryam stops him from turning it up, pointing to Abdi's half-open bedroom door by way of explanation.

When he's finished listening, Nur mutters a Somali proverb under his breath. If he was to try to translate it, he might say: 'A snake-bite received at the age of six kills you at the age of sixty.' Maryam understands immediately what it means: 'Evil lingers a long time.'

She looks at her husband. 'He knows something,' she says.

Nur isn't so sure. 'He's asking questions, but we don't know what he knows.'

'Should we play it to him? Ask him about it?' The thought terrifies her.

'No.'

'Should we tell the police?'

He thinks before answering. 'I don't think it has anything to do with what's happened to Noah. We'll talk to Sofia about it when she gets home. I'll tell her that. Don't worry.'

As Nur embraces her, Maryam feels huge relief that he's taking control of this. She doesn't think she could make a single sensible decision at this moment. She's physically and mentally drained in a way that she hasn't felt for years.

It's allowing old feelings of panic to creep in and threaten to overwhelm her the way they used to after the family first arrived in the UK, when everything was so alien she thought she'd never stop feeling lonely.

Sofia drifts in and out of concentration during her lecture. The slides show incubators and tiny bodies with skin that looks as fragile as tissue paper. She thinks about how these children hover between life and death for weeks. Her mother gave birth to a baby like these ones when they lived in Hartisheik camp. Sofia glimpsed the infant's face for only a few seconds before the baby was wrapped in a cloth. It was a girl, and she lived to take only a few breaths.

Sofia walked through the camp beside her parents to the burial place, hours after the baby was born. Maryam leaned heavily on Nur's arm. She insisted on seeing her child into the ground. When they reached the place, Nur took turns with the other men to dig a hole in the ground as the women keened. In the distance, beyond the camp perimeter, where she wasn't allowed to go because there were dangerous men, Sofia saw women bent over, collecting firewood. They were there for the thornbushes whose branches grew silvery and spiky against the changing sky.

When it was done, Nur stepped into the grave and Maryam passed the baby to him so he could lay her down gently. The cloth she was wrapped in was pale blue. Sofia remembers when Nur climbed out of the grave and crouched beside it, he had dirt on his toes and sandals. She remembers the way his hands settled on his forehead, his fingertips snaking into his hair, sweat on his scalp and temples. Other men filled in the red earth over the baby's body, and the voices of the women rose and fell as Sofia clung to Maryam. The wind caught the edges of Maryam's *dirac* and whipped it against them both.

Sofia's blue-cloth sister wasn't the first baby they'd buried at the camp. She was one of many.

When her lecture's over, Sofia dodges her friends and slips away as fast as she can. She heads across campus to the library and gets out a couple of books that she needs. The librarian nods at her and smiles, and Sofia returns the greeting. Her warm smile, politeness and willingness to help others have always made her a well-liked girl, even though she keeps herself to herself.

At school, she found that some of the Muslim girls who had ignored her as they grew up through the school gravitated toward her later on, at the age when some of the non-Muslim girls began partying hard and hanging out with boys. It was difficult for cross-faith friendships to survive as lifestyles diverged when adulthood knocked on the door, but she benefited as her friendship group swelled. It kick-started a growth in confidence that's steadily increased since she started her degree.

She puts the books in her backpack and heads for the bus stop to make her way home.

After spending hours stewing about it overnight, she feels more rational about the recording now that she's had a chance to think about it in the cold light of day. Her conclusion is that it's almost certainly research material for a school project that Abdi's doing. That would also explain the printed materials Ed Sadler had got out, and it wouldn't be the first time Abdi's used his ethnic roots as the basis for study. It makes her sad that he would approach Ed Sadler instead of talking to their parents but she understands why he would, because, just like Abdi's birth, life in the camp is something that Nur and Maryam never talk about.

She feels better once she's rationalised this, much better. Even so, there's a small part of her that knows she should probably tell the detective about the iPad, in case it helps him. She'll ring him, she thinks, and tell him about the recording and her theory that it's for a project.

She gets her phone out of her bag as she walks home from the bus stop. She programmed Detective Inspector Clemo's number into it after he left his card at the flat.

He picks up quickly.

When we got back to the house I told Mum that Abdi and I were going to go to bed because I was very tired. She seemed relieved.

'I'm not surprised. It's been a big evening,' she said. 'All that socialising's worn me out, too. Thanks for your help, boys.'

Abdi went up straight away, but I stayed downstairs for just a few more minutes so I could give Mum a monster hug, just like the one I gave Dad earlier. I said, 'I love you' (see *Noah's Bucket List Item No. 7: Make Sure People Know How Important They Are to You*). I know she thinks that I love Dad more than her because he's more fun, but she's wrong. Dad's more fun but nobody else has fought for me like my mum has. Nobody.

She watched me walk up the stairs, her hand on the bottom of the banister. I thought of the hug when I got into bed: the way she felt, and all the things I hoped it said. I was so worn out that I fell asleep before Abdi finished brushing his teeth.

Abdi was fast asleep when my alarm went off at 1 a.m. My first reaction was that I was way too tired to go out, but I gave myself a talking-to (*Noah's Bucket List Item No. 9: Don't Waste Time*) and got up and put my clothes on.

By the time I was dressed, my legs felt like jelly because they were worn out after the party, but I wasn't going to let that stop me.

I shook Abdi's shoulder to wake him.

'What?' he said. He looked crumpled and tired.

'It's time.'

I expected him to leap out of bed. It had been easier than I thought it would be to persuade him to come out with me tonight, so I felt like he would be up for it when the time came, but he just looked at me. His eyes were dark pools.

'Do we have to?'

'Come on! It's going to be so good, you know it is.'

When I first suggested that we do this, Abdi said, 'No way.' I knew he would refuse at first. He's afraid to do naughty things. I said, 'Look, it's not like we're going to do anything really bad. It's just a trip out to see something very cool. Come on! Don't be so boring!'

It was hard not to tell him about my prognosis, but I stuck to my guns because if I'd told him, I wouldn't have been able to make our outing into the experience that

I wanted it to be, which was a proper rite of passage. It would have changed everything and made it all sad and weird, and I would have felt self-conscious. So I had to rely on other methods of persuasion, but I'm pretty good at that. I got to him in the end.

'OK,' he said finally. 'OK, OK, OK!' He got out of bed and pulled his clothes and shoes on, jogging around unsteadily on one foot as he did. He remembered to be quiet.

I put on my backpack – which I filled up before the party – and tried not to buckle under the weight of it. Abdi offered to carry it, but I said no because the contents were a secret. I beckoned him to follow me downstairs. The house was dark everywhere. My parents were completely peaceful. We slipped into the porch and I opened the front door. I'd been practising opening and closing it without making a sound, and I managed it perfectly. I gestured to Abdi to follow me carefully around the edge of the driveway so we didn't crunch the gravel.

When we were off the property and a decent distance away down the street, I felt psyched up. I wanted Abdi to feel the same way, but he said, 'What if your parents notice we're gone?'

'They won't!' I said. I was pretty sure of that. That's why I chose tonight to ask to have Abdi for a sleepover. Both my parents sleep deeply after they've had a drink.

The only small problem was that it had got much colder than earlier, and I forgot we might need coats. Our breath misted. It was also creepier than I thought it would be. The streets were empty apart from a fox that stood panting in the shadow underneath a hedge. Head down, ears flat, it had almost no fur, and its skin looked rough and raw.

'I think it's dying,' I said to Abdi.

We kept to the other side of the street. A hurt animal can lash out.

I felt good about how brave I was being. The only thing that wasn't right was Abdi. I felt like he should be chatting and getting into the spirit of things with me, but he was very quiet, and I was worried he might bolt back home at any second.

'It's going to be worth it, I promise,' I said to him.

'What if the police stop us?'

'Why would you even think that? Come on.'

He looked strange, sort of sick, and for a minute I felt a little bit sympathetic, because I felt scared, too, if I'm honest, but I wasn't ready to give this up.

We cut down the hill, away from the creepy dark streets to the harbour side, almost running because it was so steep, and then walked along the path at the edge of the water. The boats moored in the floating harbour looked cool lit up in the dark. All the lights were reflected on the surface of the water. Abdi looked around a lot and I reckoned he was starting to like it more.

We left the waterside near the big modern apartment buildings with balconies and headed towards College Green. On the green, the golden stone of Bristol Cathedral was lit up with floodlights, but the stained-glass windows were dark, like big blank portals to somewhere else. In the middle of the green a group of lads was sitting on the benches watching some others do skateboard tricks. They were playing music and had cans of drink.

'Come on,' Abdi said when I stopped to watch. He tugged on my sleeve. He pulled his hood up and kept his face turned away from them, as if he was afraid of them seeing him.

'What?' I said. I wanted to feel brave, not hospital get-offered-a-crappy-sticker brave, but real-life brave, so I didn't move. I stood and watched the skateboarders.

'Let's move on,' Abdi said.

'They're not going to hurt us!' I said.

'It's different if you're black,' he said – or I thought that's what he said; it was hard to hear because he kept his face turned away from them – and tugged my sleeve again. I thought he was overreacting.

'Get off!' I didn't mean to say it so loudly.

Some of the lads turned to look at us.

'What are you staring at?' one of them said.

'Nothing,' Abdi said. He started to walk away.

I stood my ground. This night was about being brave.

'What you looking at, kid?' The lad got up. He had long hair, wore low-rise jeans and held a can of drink in his hand.

'Leave him alone,' one of the others said.

The lad carried on walking slowly towards me.

'What are you, like twelve years old?' he said when he got close. His face was sweaty. He took a long drink of his beer. 'Go home, kid.'

My heart was beating, hard and fast, but I stayed still

until he got even closer. I was daring myself to. He leaned over me.

'Noah!' Abdi shouted.

The lad got his face right up close to mine.

'Boo!' he said and his beery spit flecked my face.

I screamed and Abdi grabbed me and pulled me away and we ran from them as fast as we could. They were laughing.

We pounded down the steps beside the cathedral, and we didn't stop until a doorway set into a wall offered us a shadowy place to catch our breath.

It's not easy to push back thoughts of Emma, but the call from Sofia Mahad helps. I ask Woodley to arrange for somebody to go and fetch the iPad. I want to hear the recording she's talking about, but I also want to see any other communications Abdi may have made via the device.

Face to face with Fraser, I request an underwater team to search for both the missing phone and the backpack.

'Prioritise,' she tells me when I explain that there are two locations I want to search. 'The budget hasn't miraculously increased. All-powerful as I am, I can't pull off loaves and fishes with the department's money.'

I decide that the phone's probably more important, because it might tell us something about the boys' communications. I'm beginning to think that if there was foul play, the motive lies in what passed between these two lads. Fraser signs it off.

Woodley and I take a trip to the boys' school. Medes

College occupies a tight city-centre site, and it takes us ten minutes to find a parking spot. While we wait for the headmistress to free up some time for us I read a display in the foyer, which informs me that the school will nurture my child as an individual, as well as offering state-of-the-art facilities.

The headmistress surprises me by speaking in the gravelly tones of a long-time jazz club aficionado. In a school like this, I expected more of a cut-glass accent. She wears a navy trouser suit, an elaborate enamel brooch on her lapel, pearl earrings, and reading glasses attached to a slim, gold chain. Her office is large and, in spite of a pretentious sign on the door saying HEADMISTRESS'S STUDY, it's modestly decorated. A shaft of sunlight cuts through a leaded windowpane and warms a spot on an armchair. We sit around a table where school brochures have been artfully displayed. Her assistant brings us coffee.

We've been told that the school is yet to have been informed about Noah's terminal prognosis. The Sadler family wanted to wait until they'd worked out how to handle his last few months.

'What can you tell us about the boys?' I ask. It's a general question, but I'm interested to see what springs to her mind.

'They're both very good boys and very clever boys, much valued by the school.'

'We understand that they're friends?'

'They're very good friends. They give all appearance of being inseparable when Noah's at school. You'll know that he's had a rough time of it, of course?'

'Indeed.'

'It's led to a great deal of absence, but in spite of that he's very diligent and his schoolwork remains excellent. His courage is nothing short of extraordinary.'

'When did the boys start here?'

'Both boys came to us in Year 7, though Noah was a few weeks late because of a course of treatment. He was home-schooled the year before he came to us, but he'd been in the school system previously, I believe. Abdi Mahad won a place on our Barker Scholarship programme, which is a scheme we run in conjunction with primary schools in some of Bristol's more deprived areas. He's really risen to the challenge. We're immensely proud of what he's been able to achieve.'

'Barker Scholarship, did you say?' Woodley's making notes.

'Yes! It's named after an old boy, Jolyon Barker. By co-incidence he was a contemporary of Eddie Sadler, Noah's father. I believe they're still friends. The scholarship covers uniform and travel expenses as well as fees. It's very generous.'

'Do you know whether Abdi might have been doing any kind of project or piece of work either on refugee camps or Somalia or any similar topic?' Sofia Mahad suggested this when she telephoned to tell me about the recording she found on Abdi's iPad.

The headmistress shakes her head. 'No. Both boys have GCSEs this summer. They'll be entirely focused on the syllabus. Project work would be qualification-related only.' She consults a piece of paper that's on her lap. 'I can

confirm that Abdi isn't taking Geography, which is probably the only subject I can immediately think of where that
kind of study might be relevant.'

'Can I ask whether you would describe the boys' friendship as healthy?'

'Absolutely! Very healthy. It's a lovely friendship for both
of them. It can be very beneficial for our high achievers
to bond.'

A tight smile; optimism applied to her features like
another layer of make-up.

'Are we able to speak to anybody who might have had
closer contact with the boys on a day to day basis?'

I'm not buying into the headmistress's positive spiel
entirely. In a school like this, I know her role is mostly to
be a figurehead, to sell the place to prospective parents,
and to protect it from negative press. I'd also bet money
that she doesn't know either boy very well personally.

She picks up her desk phone, hits a button. 'Could you
look at the timetable and see what Mr Jacobson is doing
currently, please?' she asks. 'He's the boys' form tutor,' she
explains to us, her hand over the receiver. There's a pause
as she listens to the response from the other end of the
line, and she hangs up. 'I'm afraid he's busy in the gym.'

'How about we go to him?' I suggest. 'We only need a
few words.'

She takes us to the gym, heels clip-clopping smartly
as we cross the campus. The grounds are manicured and
attractive.

We find Mr Jacobson overseeing some boys on the
squash courts.

'Thank you,' I say to the headmistress when she's introduced us. 'I don't think we need to take up any more of your time.'

There's a moment when she hesitates, but she takes the hint and leaves us.

We sit on a bench. Boys charge around the courts in front of us, visible through glass walls at the back of each court, and our conversation has to compete with squeaking trainers and the rhythmic thwack of the squash balls hitting rackets and walls.

I take a punt with my first question. 'The headmistress suggested that there might have been some friction between Abdi and Noah on occasion, and I wonder if you can tell us a bit more about that?'

I wait for a furrow to appear between his eyes, but it doesn't. Instead, with a sigh, he takes my bait.

'It was a bit of silliness,' he says. 'Came down to jealousy, I think. Noah was away from school for a couple of months last year, and on his return he didn't cope very well with the fact that Abdi had made a new friend while he was away.'

'How did it come to your attention? Did something happen?'

'It was drawn to my attention because the school nurse reported that Noah was unusually tearful. They worked it out, though.'

'How?'

'I had a chat with all three of the boys involved separately, and then all together. It settled down. It was a good outcome. If I'm honest we weren't sure if Noah would have the emotional maturity to make it work. With his history it's been hard for him to develop alongside the others, but Abdi's a generous boy and the new friend, Imran, is a good kid, too, so they worked it out.'

Something happening on the squash court catches his eye and he gets to his feet and yells: 'Use the corners! Don't just hit it back into the middle. Boys! You have two minutes left. Use it!'

'Is it possible to have a word with Imran?'

'You'd have to ask the head's office about that, but I don't see why not. Won't happen today, though. He's not in.'

'Did Noah or Abdi fraternise with anybody else?'

'What you've got to understand about those two is that they're nerdy boys, you know. Abdi could have been a very good badminton player, but he spent most of his time playing chess or in the IT suite with Noah. They shared a sense of humour, they were both into graphic novels, things like that.'

'Did the other kids accept that? Were either of them bullied?'

'Not that I was made aware of. We have a very strict anti-bullying policy here.'

I wonder how well Mr Jacobson actually knows these boys. He talks about them as if they're a slightly different species, and I wonder if he's one of those teachers who prefer the sporty kids. He has cauliflower ears and a rugby forward's physique. He's an alpha, like Ed Sadler. It wouldn't surprise me if this school specialises in turning them out.

A buzzer sounds, and within seconds we're standing in the middle of a flow of teenagers, boys and girls.

'Sorry!' Mr Jacobson shouts. 'Is that all?'

On the way back to the car, Woodley says, 'Almost every kid in that school is white.'

'I noticed.'

'I wonder how Abdi feels in that environment.'

'Depends how they treat him, I suppose. I think the story about the friendship issue being resolved sounds too good to be true.'

'What makes you think he was lying?'

'I think he believed what he was saying. I expect our Mr Jacobson sat the boys down, metaphorically banged their heads together, and figured that he'd done enough. They were probably smart enough to tell him everything was fine if he checked up on them again.'

'He's a big bloke.'

'Yeah. I'd tell him everything was fine if I was a nerdy fifteen-year-old.'

It's got me thinking.

'Any progress on getting an appointment to speak with Noah's therapist?'

'I'll contact the Sadlers first thing,' Woodley says.

'No. Contact the hospital directly. Let's see if we can get a conversation without the parents' involvement. A subjective opinion of Noah would be useful.'

It's a very long shot, because I expect the Sadlers will have to be notified, and I'm not even sure the therapist will tell us anything at all, but I think it's worth a try.

*

Nur Mahad needs to sleep after his night shift, but he can't. He and Maryam sit together in their kitchen at the small table. Between them is the iPad.

He knows that the recording has destabilised Maryam, and he's afraid for her.

She has two fears that overshadow all others.

The first is that their past will revisit them, and the second is that her children will become strangers to her in this country. Her fears are at the root of her complex relationship with Abdi. He delights his mother at some moments, but she finds it hard to love him at others, and it's been that way since she entered the UK with him bound to her body.

Her inability to bond with him meant that Nur and Sofia spent many hours holding the baby and playing with him, because Maryam often felt unable to. When they first settled in the UK, she took to her bed, swathed in depression for a long time and gripped by what Sofia once told Nur she thought was PTSD.

For Maryam, Abdi represented the transition from one country to another, the journey from war to peace, and all of the hope and fear. He was also an unknown quantity: the boy who shouldn't have been born after all the miscarriages, and the fact of him was too much for her to handle at first. It had got better as he got older and began to shine and to smile. He cracked open her heart, eventually, but if she's honest, a small part of Maryam has remained wary of him.

What she can't forget is that Abdi saw her faint at the Welcome Centre. He was standing just a few feet away from her when it happened.

She fainted because she looked into the face of a man she thought she knew from a long time ago. The effect of seeing him was instant. Her legs gave out, her consciousness departed. When she came round, the man was gone, and nobody else seemed to have noticed him or thought him remarkable. She thought the incident had passed, until now. Because Abdi has recorded himself talking to Ed Sadler about a man who sounds similar. But she can't understand how Abdi's made the connection that could break them apart.

'Do you think he overheard us talking last week?' Maryam asks Nur.

She's referring to the nightmare she had on the night she fainted. How the man returned to her in a dream and she woke in terror. Nur comforted her and they whispered into the night, discussing the incident, rationalising that Maryam couldn't possibly have seen the person she thought she had.

'I'm sure he was asleep,' Nur says. 'I'm sure.'

'I can't remember if we said too much. What did we say?'

'We were careful. I'm sure we were.' He can't remember exactly what they said either, only the terror in his wife's eyes when he woke her from the nightmare and reminded her that they were safe, and then the long minutes it took for her heart rate and her breathing to slow.

Maryam has a feeling they said enough, but she keeps this to herself. Nur murmurs more reassurances into the silence: 'It will be all right. Don't be spooked.'

He yawns, once, twice.

'You need to sleep,' she tells him.

Usually Nur naps in Abdi's bedroom when he's done a night shift, but as that's not possible today, he settles down on the sofa. He falls asleep quickly and Maryam places a blanket over him.

In the kitchen she looks at the iPad and then plays the recording again. When it's finished, she makes a few swipes and jabs across the screen.

She deletes it.

She doesn't want it to exist. It feels too much like a bad omen.

'What were you doing?' Abdi said as we crouched on the steps beside the cathedral. 'That was really stupid.'

Noah's Bucket List Item No. 10: Do Something Reckless. On Purpose. Dad was surprisingly OK with this one – I think because he's super reckless – and I don't think he thought I had it in me to do anything this mad.

If I'd had the strength, I would have said, 'Shut up!' to Abdi, but I was still gasping for breath.

'We shouldn't be here,' he said. 'You should be at home.'

'No! Come on. Please, let's just go. We're nearly there.'

When I finally caught my breath and stopped trembling, we carried on down the steps and crossed over the road into Millennium Square, where the lights were bright and the gigantic mirror ball that's a planetarium inside looked amazing. We sat down for a bit because I was still panting. It felt much safer there.

'Noah ...'

'I'm OK.'

'You're not.'

'Really, I am.'

I had a packet of dextrose tablets in my pocket. I ate three and offered him the packet. His fingers felt chilly when he took it from me. It was time to move.

'We should be taking photos!' I said. 'We should make a record of our expedition.'

We took selfies with my phone in front of the planet-arium, in front of the water feature even though it was turned off, and then with our arms around the Cary Grant statue.

As we walked out of the square I said to Abdi, 'Close your eyes.'

He gave me a look, but I insisted. I took his hand.

'I'll lead you,' I said. I pulled him around the corner and then got behind him and walked him forward with my hands on his shoulders until he was in just the right place to get a glimpse of it.

'Open your eyes,' I said.

Pero's Bridge didn't disappoint.

Billowing fog clouds hung over it as if by magic, lit with white lights. It was like something out of a fairy tale. Together we walked out from between the buildings on the dockside and it was awesome, just how I imagined it would be. As the tops of the clouds melted away into the night sky, more appeared from below, so when we stepped onto the bridge we were continually shrouded. Visibility was reduced to a few feet.

It was a special art installation that Mum had told me about. I'd seen pictures of it on the internet, but these didn't compare to the real thing. I hadn't been able to visit it because I'd been in treatment, and I knew it would be removed in a day or two. It made me think of how my dad described being in the mountains in Nepal. 'Shrouded' in fog, he'd said. I loved that.

'Wow,' Abdi said.

'See! Isn't it worth it?'

The fog was disorientating and I lost my balance a little. Abdi grabbed my arm and guided me to the side. We stood there together and everything drifted in and out of view, changing all the time. You could almost taste the misty particles in the air around you, and the fog looked like big puffs of smoke against the darkness.

I was so glad we hadn't just come in the day, like everybody else. This was so worth it.

Abdi got out his phone, but he said he didn't want a fog selfie.

'Then what are you doing?'

'I'm calling my dad to pick us up. You look really sick, Noah.'

'Don't!'

I had a crushing feeling of disappointment. First, because Abdi wasn't into it the way I wanted him to be, and second, because I realised this wasn't quite the right place for us to sit and have our drinks. I didn't know before that there was a nightclub on the waterfront, but I could hear the music and see people hanging around outside it. The plan wouldn't work properly if people saw us. Anybody seeing me with a beer would know I was underage. It could ruin everything.

We would have to move on, find somewhere a bit more private by the water. It wouldn't take long. Not going through with it wasn't an option at this point.

I saw Abdi tapping the screen of his phone, and I took hold of his arm to stop him. The phone fell and skittered across the floor of the bridge before dropping off the edge and into the water.

We both stared down at where it had fallen. We could glimpse the black water where the wisps of fog were lightest. The phone was gone.

'I'm really sorry!' I said. 'I'll get you a new one.'

He was blinking back tears, which wasn't like him at all.

'It's just a phone,' I said.

'Give me yours.'

'No.'

'Give it to me!'

Around us the fog kept billowing, but it didn't feel so much fun now. It was claustrophobic, and all the energy and excitement I'd felt earlier disappeared. It was time to get serious.

'Abdi,' I said. Often it worked to plead with him. I could rely on him to do the right thing.

'No! I'm tired of everything we do always being about you. I'm so tired of it. Give me your phone or call your parents yourself. I don't want to do this any more.'

I felt very angry with him.

'Phone them,' he said. 'Or I will.'

I took my phone out of my pocket, held it in front of

him, and then threw it as far as I could. There was loads of fog billowing around us, and the phone arced up high and disappeared into it. It went so far we didn't even hear it land in the water. It was an awesome throw.

'What the hell?' Abdi stared at me like I was crazy. He shook his head and started walking away, towards home.

I went the other way.

I looked back after a few seconds, but I couldn't see him through the fog. I kept walking anyway. On the other side of the bridge was a cobbled area that stretched all the way along the edge of the harbour, and coming off it, opposite the end of the bridge, was a dark alleyway. I stepped into it and leaned against the wall. The bricks felt icy cold against my back and my legs were tired, but I told myself I had to fight through it even though frustration made tears prickle my eyes. Tonight wasn't going to be perfect any more, but I was determined to salvage it as best I could. It wasn't an option to fail. We would move on, find a quiet place, and finish the night properly.

I heard Abdi shout my name. I stayed completely still and waited until his voice got closer.

When I was sure he'd be able to see me, I stepped out of the shadows and walked down the alleyway as fast as I could, away from him. It was almost black in there, but dim light from a window high above fell in a jagged rect-angle onto the cobbles ahead of me, showing me the way.

'Where are you going?' he called.

I didn't answer.

'Noah! Stop messing with me!'

It was an angry shout, and I heard his footsteps pick up pace behind me.

O n the way back from the school Woodley and I stop off at the floating harbour and watch as our dive team comes up empty-handed in their search for the phone, frustration evident in their body language even before they've stripped off the masks and wetsuits.

A small crowd of bystanders watches, phones at the ready in case anything social-media worthy gets dragged up. They're out of luck.

'Visibility's really bad, and then you've got some currents here,' one of the divers tells me. 'Plus, the frequent movements of the boats in and out could easily have dislodged a phone and allowed it to drift along the bottom and sink into the silt somewhere outside the search area.' Water drops hang from his eyelashes and the end of his nose.

When Woodley and I arrive back at HQ, he heads off down the road to revisit the scene, looking out for any CCTV that we might have missed and seeing if anybody is around.

There's a note on my desk from the tech team to say that the iPad's been collected by one of our team and they've had a look at it. They've attached a printout of Abdi's school emails.

I pick up the phone and call them. 'What about the audio recording?' I ask. 'You were supposed to retrieve that.'

'We didn't spot one.'

'Did you check if it had been deleted?'

Silence from the other end tells me they didn't. I sigh loudly enough to make sure he can hear.

'Do it asap, will you?'

I take a look at the emails. Mostly, they're straightforward communications about homework between Abdi and his teachers, nothing unusual, and some mass mailings from the school administration. Only one exchange catches my attention. It consists of four emails sent between Abdi and a teacher by the name of Alistair Hawkes. He includes three titles as part of his electronic signature: 'Barker Scholarship Coordinator', 'Head of Year 11' and 'Teacher of Biology'. It's the first that interests me most.

The first email is from the teacher to Abdi: *Please could you come and see me at lunchtime to discuss a piece of work that you haven't delivered to Mrs Griffith. I'll be in my office between 1.30 and 2.45.*

Abdi replies very quickly: *I've given the work in and Mrs Griffith is looking at it. I'm working to see if I can improve it.*

Mr Hawkes bangs back a reply: *That's not the message I've got from Mrs Griffith. Let's talk about this in person.*

A few hours pass before Abdi replies again: *I have given the work to Mrs Griffith now, but I'll come to see you. Will this affect my scholarship?*

There's no response from the teacher. I have to assume they continued the conversation in person, because Abdi sent his last message just half an hour before the proposed lunchtime meeting.

I show the emails to Woodley. His eyebrows rise as he reads. 'I'll say it again: there's always trouble in paradise.'

'Let's contact the teacher. I want to know if this was a one-off incident or a habit for Abdi.'

'You'd have thought somebody would have mentioned it when we were there.'

'Indeed.'

'I'm not surprised, though. Nobody's perfect, are they?' Woodley says.

'You mean Abdi, or the school?'

'I meant Abdi, but it could apply to both. Anyway, I was coming to tell you I've just got off the phone with Noah's therapist. He can see us in half an hour if we can make it.'

'We can make it.'

We might be on a fool's errand on this occasion, but I still get a kick out of grabbing my jacket off the back of my chair and heading out for an interview at short notice. It's the adrenalin, and the hope that if you keep plugging away and talking to people, you will uncover that crucial bit of information that can break a case open.

I never want to become that detective who's haunted by a case that he couldn't solve. I've met one or two older officers who've found it impossible to let go of a sense of failure when that happens. Some of them stay obsessed even after they retire.

We find the therapist in a ground-floor room in which the lower part of the window is frosted for privacy, but the view through the top is of the entrance to a busy ambulance bay. The decor is small-child friendly, which is to say it's hard on the eyes unless you love primary colours. It's a far cry from Dr Manelli's muted nest. I wonder how Noah felt about being in that space once he became a teenager. We sit on low-slung chairs, all knees and ankles.

The therapist is a middle-aged man with a hipster beard and hair that needs a cut. He wears an open-neck shirt and black chinos. His identity badge is tucked into his shirt pocket. He swings his foot continually in a way that I find irritating.

'I don't know what I can tell you,' he says. 'You're aware of the confidentiality code that I have to work within?'

'I'm aware of it, but Noah Sadler's fighting for his life and we need information.'

'I was very sorry to hear that.'

'What I'm hoping you can do to help me is provide some insight into Noah's friendship with a boy called Abdi Mahad. They were together when the accident took place.'

'You know I can't share Noah's confidences, not unless I have reason to believe I need to in order to protect him from serious harm.'

'How much more harm do you want him to be in?'

'That's a misinterpretation of the clause, and you know it.'

He's steely, but I'm not surprised because I'm well aware of the confidentiality rules. I pored over them when Dr Manelli first shared them with me at the start of my own course of therapy.

'I'm wondering why you thought it was appropriate to invite us to meet you in the middle of an urgent investigation, where a boy's life is at stake, when you're not willing to share information with us?'

I'm not being fair, but I want to see if it's possible to rattle him.

Woodley plays good cop. 'Cases like these are extremely sensitive, we're very aware of that. All we're trying to do is minimise the distress that Noah and his family have to go through. I'm sure you can understand.'

'I can understand that, and sympathise with it, but I can't break the confidentiality code.'

He folds his arms across his chest, hugging himself. It's Body Language 101. He's not going to spill the goods.

There's a loophole I'm aware of, though, when the client being treated is a minor. It's amazing how much you can research when you're up most of the night. 'Do you share information with Noah's parents?'

'I share a limited amount of information, things pre-agreed with Noah when he first began his therapy.'

'What sort of things do you share?'

'Detective, how many ways do you want me to say it? I can't discuss the details of my client's treatment.'

'But we could ask his parents, because they're not bound by confidentiality.'

'You could.'

'Do you usually share with both parents, or just one of them?'

I think I know the answer to this already, and I'm right.

'It tends to be his mother.'

'Thank you.' I'm not surprised to hear that, and neither am I encouraged, because I suspect she's more protective of Noah than her husband.

'Except that there was one matter that Noah allowed me to share with his father and asked me not to mention to his mother.'

He uncrosses his arms and turns a copper bracelet around his wrist.

'Which was?'

'Nice try, Detective. That's all you're getting.'

'Thank you for your time.'

As we drive back to HQ, the daylight's beginning to leach away. Headlights snap on around us and the dash in our pool car glows the kind of neon green that makes your eyeballs ache. Woodley says, 'Nicely played, boss.'

'Thanks.'

'But if you don't mind me asking, why didn't we just approach his parents and question them about it directly?'

'In the state they're in? No. This is better. Now we know who and what to ask.'

I walked as fast as I could through Queen Square and then kept going a bit randomly, because I wasn't sure where I was. I passed shops from which mannequins looked blankly at me, and big office buildings. I was trying to find another place on the water, but I must have taken a wrong turn.

Abdi followed. He stayed a little distance behind me. I wished he would catch up and walk with me properly, but he didn't. I tried not to check over my shoulder too many times. I used reflections from shop windows to see where he was. I was thinking hard as I walked, trying to work out what to do next. My breath was getting short.

We finally reached the waterside again, and there was another bridge, but the road went across it, so it was far too busy. A police car passed and slowed down beside us, but didn't stop. I noticed Abdi melted into the shadows when it did that. I got lost again, once I'd crossed the bridge, and I was starting to seriously flag by the time we reached Temple Meads station, but at least I recognised it. Beside it, I saw the entrance to a dark street that disappeared between some old railway buildings. No cars were turning down there. I cut down it. Abdi followed. I slowed my pace because it was a bit scary, and he couldn't help but catch up with me a bit.

I heard something splashing before I saw the canal. There was movement on the water's surface, but I couldn't see what it was. As I walked along the canal path, the noise of the city centre faded.

Abdi caught up with me when I reached a big overpass. We stood underneath it and stared at the water. Occasionally a car shot past overhead, but otherwise there was a feeling of stillness. Finally.

I sat down on the grass. Damp soaked through my trousers straight away, but I was too tired to care.

Abdi stood beside me, his arms wrapped around his body. 'Noah,' he said. 'What's going on?'

'Shall we have our drink here?' I started to shrug the backpack off.

'It's freezing. Are you crazy?'

I'm going to have to tell him about my prognosis, I thought. The urge to share was strong. It's not what I wanted, because the night wouldn't end up how I hoped it would, but I figured it might salvage things a bit, and it would be better than arguing. I didn't have the guts to just say it outright, though. Instead I said, 'Do you ever think about death?'

He exhaled crossly. 'Why?'

'Just, do you?'

He sat down beside me, finally. 'You're mad.'

He rubbed his eyes. He looked pretty rough himself.

'Are you tired?' I asked him.

'Yes, but probably not as tired as you. You don't look or sound good.'

I was shivering. We both were.

'We should walk back to the station and get help,' he said.

I ignored that, and asked my question again: 'Do you ever think about death?'

'Sometimes.'

'What do you think?'

'I think about a thing we talked about in philosophy class. Why?'

'I don't know. I guess I was looking at the stars and the moon. Big things that are going to carry on anyway, even if we're not here.'

Noah's Bucket List Item No. 11: Experience Something That Puts Your Life Into Perspective.

Abdi was quiet for a few moments after I said that. He often considers things before he speaks. I looked at the pinprick stars so high above us, and noticed that a shred of cloud was covering up part of the moon.

When he finally replied, Abdi said something I wasn't expecting at all: 'Did you ever find out something that made you think you'd be better off if you were dead?'

'What do you mean?' For a second I panicked and thought he'd guessed about my prognosis before I'd had a chance to tell him.

He bit his lip. His eyes were locked onto the water in front of us. 'It's the thing I was thinking about.'

'Do you think about what it would be like to actually die?' I hardly dared to ask.

'In philosophy lessons, while you were in hospital last week,' he said, 'we learned about a Greek philosopher called Epicurus. He said that fear of dying is the biggest fear we have in life, and that's why we can't be happy.'

'Huh.' I didn't really know what to say about that.

'Yeah. His solution to that is to say that death is the end of physical feelings, so it's impossible for it to be physically painful, and death is also the end of consciousness, so it also can't be emotionally painful.'

'So we shouldn't be frightened of it.'

'Exactly.'

He tore up little bits of grass and threw them down the bank. They landed invisibly.

I had a question: 'But how does he know that death is the end of those things?'

'Because he believed that our souls are made of atoms that are spread through our body, and they dissolve when we die.'

'Dissolve?'

'Yeah. It's a cool idea.'

Noah's Bucket List Item No. 12: Be Cremated. I can't stand the thought of being buried. I want to be turned into smoke and air so I can be everywhere all at once.

162

I was feeling quite a lot of discomfort in my abdomen, in the area where my spleen is. Dr Sasha warned me about that. I stood up, to try to ease it, and Abdi helped me. I had to lean on him quite heavily.

'Let's go home,' he said. 'Please.'

I was very tempted, but as I straightened up I saw, a little way up the canal, on the other side of the water, a very cool sight: heaps of twisted metal stacked up in piles that looked like pyramids, and the bodies of loads of scrap cars. They all glittered with frost. I pointed it out to Abdi.

'Can we do one last thing? Go over there and sit together and drink our drinks.'

It looked like the perfect place to end the night.

I didn't wait for an answer. I knew this was the right thing to do. I adjusted the backpack, feeling the straps bite hard into my shoulders, and set off along the towpath.

Abdi called after me. 'Noah!' he said. 'Enough! We can drink the bloody drinks on the way home.'

I ignored him. I kept going along the path and around the side of a large warehouse.

'Don't you walk away!' Abdi shouted. His voice sounded distant and echoey. 'Don't keep doing this!'

Ahead of me, there was a bridge. It had high metal edges that were peeling and rusty.

'Noah! Come on!'

My lungs were tight and the pain in my abdomen was getting more intense. As I started to cross the bridge, I kicked a can by mistake and its loud rattle startled a bird somewhere above me on a warehouse ledge. It flew so low past me that I put up my arms to protect myself.

I paused to catch my breath. I thought I heard Abdi's footsteps behind me, but I wasn't certain. He would follow me, though, I knew he would in the end. He never let me down. You can't do that when you're healthy and your friend isn't. It's not fair.

The water running underneath the bridge looked like black treacle.

Voices bring me back to my hospital room. Dad's talking to somebody.

'He hasn't always been unwell.'

'When did he get ill?'

'He was seven when we first noticed symptoms, eight at diagnosis.'

'I'm so sorry. That's tragic. And he's been in treatment since then?'

'More or less. I never remember the precise sequence of events. I have to travel for work a lot, so I'm not always here. My wife has been by his side constantly.'

'Will she be here later?'

'Yes, but I'm not sure she'll be comfortable with this conversation.'

'If it's easier, I could meet you somewhere later?'

'I don't think so.'

'I'm sorry. I wouldn't normally dream of invading your privacy like this, but it's a fact that sometimes you need press attention to get the police to take a case seriously.'

'I'm not unaware of that.'

'I believe Noah has been the victim of a crime.'

'That's your opinion.'

'I'm sorry. This is very painful for you. I'll go. Here's

my card. That's me, Emma Zhang. Please call me if you want to talk. Any time.'

A chair squeaks. She's standing. But then a sob. It's Dad.

Silence. I can sense her indecision. Comfort the big man or tiptoe away?

'Mr Sadler?'

'Please, go.'

She does.

Later, though I don't know whether it's a minute or an hour or a day later, I hear the click-crunch of a phone camera shutter. Twice.

I don't know who's in the room with me.

I appreciate the orderly moments in my life; it's why I like my work. I can follow the processes of investigation in order to succeed. It's the emotional extremes that bother me. If I can, I avoid those like a cat skirting a sprinkler. The problem is that that's not always possible.

I head into Fraser's office to update her.

'How's it going, Jim?' She seems more tense than usual, but it's hard to read why.

'We're making progress.'

'How's Woodley doing?'

'It would have been nice if you'd told me that we were both walking wounded.'

I shouldn't snap at a senior officer, especially when I'm only two days back on the job, but I'm pissed off that I'm on the D team. She doesn't flinch.

'I haven't elucidated DC Woodley on the finer points

of your leave of absence, and I don't think you need to know every detail about him, either. A sort of quid pro quo, if you like, for the "walking wounded".' She stares me down. 'Is that OK with you, DI Clemo?'

'Sorry, boss.' I strolled right into that bollocking.

'You've been in and out like a yoyo, so please tell me there's some good news.'

'To be honest, so far it's messy. Every time we get a hint that things might have played out in one way, we learn something different from somebody else, but I've got a few lines of investigation going. We're getting there.'

'Uh-huh. Did it occur to you to put some more serious pressure on this lad who won't talk?'

'I thought you wanted kid gloves.'

'I want you to work carefully, but unless I'm mistaken, you have a firm witness who alleges that there was some funny business going on in the scrapyard.'

'I don't think her account *is* very firm.'

'Why not?'

'She didn't witness the moment the lad fell into the water. That's a problem for me.'

'That's not what she's been telling the papers.'

'What?'

She has a copy of the *Bristol Echo* face down on her desk. She flips it over and pushes it towards me.

The front page is almost fully occupied with a single photograph. It shows a boy in a hospital bed. I know instantly that it's Noah Sadler. It looks like a candid shot, taken by somebody standing a few feet away. It's impossible to see his face, but it's unmistakably the scene I witnessed when we were at his bedside.

The headline screams below it: TERROR IN OUR CITY!

Noah Sadler isn't named, but the caption underneath the photograph states, *A fifteen-year-old boy fights for his life at Bristol Children's Hospital after a suspected racially motivated attack in the city centre.* The brief bit of text tells a breathy, highly speculative story about Noah's fall into the canal.

There's a statement from our witness: 'I was terrified. I saw the perpetrator hunt down the boy and push him in the canal and I thought he was going to turn on me next.'

The rest is just as damaging:

Sources indicate that police have identified the suspect but haven't questioned or arrested him. This journalist wonders if they're afraid to do so just days after the White Nation March. Could the police be putting residents of this city at risk, in order to avoid upsetting an ethnic community? Are we victims of reverse prejudice?

Now I understand why Fraser's behaving like a pit bull.

She knows every expletive it's possible to know if you grew up on a Glasgow council estate in the 1970s, and I don't think she spares me a single one as she delivers a tirade about the morals of both the witness and the press.

'And do you see who wrote it?' she asks. The article's creasing where she's stabbing it with her finger.

I don't even need to look at it to know that the reporter's almost certainly Emma Zhang, once again.

Fraser doesn't wait for me to reply before launching into a tirade: 'How could she do this? If I had a poor opinion of that woman before, it's just reached depths so unbelievably low that even Dante would struggle to imagine them. How dare she?'

I take the paper from her as she's venting, and read the article. Emma's known exactly which buttons to press. Of course she has.

'Come with me,' Fraser says when I'm done.

I follow her out of the incident room and down a corridor to the office of Janie Green, our press officer. Fraser drops the paper on her desk and Janie looks up at her with an expression that's admirably calm.

'I've just seen it,' she says. 'I was about to come and find you. It's a shit storm. They gave me no warning in spite of my repeated attempts to speak to Emma Zhang and the editor today. I think they've got an agenda on this one.'

'Who would publish a photograph like that?' Fraser says.

'I know. That's why I think there's an agenda.'

'What can we do?'

'I think the horse has well and truly bolted, but I'll do my very best to limit the damage.'

On Janie's desk there's a photograph of three pink-cheeked young children, all with red ringlets identical to hers. I'm fairly sure they won't be seeing much of their mother this evening.

As we walk back to her office Fraser says, 'Get that

Somali boy to speak. He's got the answers, so it's time to stop pussyfooting around and put some pressure on him. If he's innocent or has just done something stupid, it's his only hope of getting out of this relatively unscathed. The press are going to savage him if they get hold of his identity and find out that he's clammed up.'

'Should I see him tonight?'

'No. It's too late. First thing in the morning.'

'And if he still won't talk?'

'Play hardball. Threaten him with arrest. You know what to do. We need his story. It's the only way we can throw a bucket of water on this. And then pay a bloody visit to that bloody witness and give her a talking-to about getting cosy with the press. Threaten her with arrest, too, if you have to.'

She pauses before opening the double doors that lead into the investigation room. 'Get control of this, Jim.'

'I will.'

'How's the other kid doing?'

'Stable, but still critical.'

'Stable's something at least.'

She slams open the double doors and heads turn.

'Don't anybody bloody say the words "Emma Zhang" to me unless you want to lose your bloody job tonight,' she says as she marches between the desks.

Her office door slams behind her and the window blinds shudder.

When Sofia emerges from her bedroom, her assignment drafted, ears aching from the earbuds she pressed in them tightly to block out distractions, she finds her mother loading Abdi's bedding into the washing machine.

'He's just got up!' Maryam tells her in a whisper. 'He's washing. He drank some tea.'

'Did he say anything?' Sofia asks.

'No! But he looked much better.'

When Abdi emerges from the bathroom and flops onto the sofa, Sofia tries to act casual.

'Abdi?' She takes a seat too, but keeps her distance, wary of his reaction.

He gives her some eye contact, but it makes her uneasy because his expression is still vacant.

'Are you ready to talk?' she asks.

No reply.

Sofia knows from her training that time works differently for everyone. Some mothers find that words pour from them the instant they meet their babies, every one of them designed to express the sheer joy of the new feelings they're experiencing. Others take minutes or even hours or days to find words. Sofia's good at respecting the women's processes, but even that hasn't prepared her for the frustration she feels in the face of Abdi's silence.

'You should eat,' she tells him.

She passes him a plate of sandwiches that Maryam's prepared for him. Abdi picks one up and takes a tiny bit, chewing as if it's cardboard. From the bedroom they can hear the crack of the clean sheets as Maryam whips the folds out of them before letting them float down on to

Abdi's bed. When he swallows the bite of sandwich, Sofia feels like cheering, but she forces herself to remain calm. She's worried that if she puts a foot wrong he might withdraw completely again.

She desperately wants to ask about his conversation with Ed Sadler, as well as the other events of the evening, but she doesn't dare.

'I got your stuff from Noah's house,' she tells him instead.

Another laborious swallow. His eyes rove across the room and eventually land on Sofia again, as if he'd forgotten she was there.

Her patience is stretched as thinly as is possible. 'Abdi,' she says, 'you can talk to me, brother.'

As if she'd flicked a switch, tears start to brim from his eyes, big, fat tears, copious and unstoppable.

She's horrified, but the hopeful part of her also wonders if this means he's ready to break his silence. She moves carefully towards him and takes his hand.

From the bedroom doorway Maryam watches them. She feels exhausted to her very core by the weight of what she knows and what her children do not. For a moment she wonders if she should step into the room and take a seat between them, take each of their hands in her own and tell them the whole story, everything, from the very beginning. She won't, though, because her instinct to protect her family is greater than any other.

On the street below, Nur's parking his taxi. Even if he'd had the stamina to drive into the night, the sight of the front page of the *Bristol Echo* on the news stand at the rail station would have sent him home. A copy of the paper sits on the passenger seat beside him.

Nur climbs the stairs to the flat, feeling the usual stiffness in his lower back from the hours of driving. He wishes he could turn around and walk away. He feels proud of what his family's achieved in Bristol. That they live modestly does not concern him; that he has to work long hours to support them is hard but also satisfying. They live quietly and happily; their children are achieving everything they dreamed of. Until now.

When he opens the door to the flat, he's so upset that he doesn't remember to check whether Abdi is out of bed. He takes the newspaper into the kitchen, where he finds his wife and daughter and holds it up so they can see the front page.

'They're saying it's a hate crime,' he says. 'They're accusing Abdi.'

He doesn't notice Abdi standing in the doorway behind him, until he follows Maryam's gaze and turns around. Abdi hears what his father says, and sees the headline and the photograph of his friend on the front page. He turns his back to them. His knees buckle a little as he does, but he carries on walking away. He enters his bedroom and shuts the door behind him. They hear the key turning in the lock.

Nur's devastated that he's been so careless.

Abdi's door remains locked shut, no matter how hard they pound on it. Only when Nur threatens to break it down does Abdi unlock it, but he returns to his bed after he's done so, as unresponsive as before.

Sofia goes to bed hollow-hearted and afraid, feeling simultaneously as if the walls of the flat are closing in on her while her family members are unstoppably moving away from one another, like an exploding graphic on screen, the component parts heading out into the universe in a multitude of different directions.

Nur and Maryam go through the familiar motion of pulling out their sofa bed and settling onto it. She lies rigid on her back, eyes open. She hears Nur fall asleep swiftly and knows that he won't move until morning.

She pulls back the blanket and creeps out of bed. She retrieves her most treasured possession from the shelves in the corner of the room: a small, battered tin box containing photographs from her childhood. She takes the box into the kitchen and perches on a stool at the counter. She turns on a light and removes the photographs from the box carefully. There are only two. The first is a photograph of her at school, one in a row of nine children sitting on a bench against a pale grey wall. It's an informal picture. The girls wear lace-up blue shoes, white socks, blue skirts, white shirts. Matching sky-blue scarfs are draped over their shoulders and tied at the front with toggles, and the final touch is a white headband holding each girl's hair back from her forehead. Maryam remembers how much she loved that uniform. The boys in the photo are dressed to match in blue shorts. They sit with their arms draped around one another's shoulders.

Maryam finds it bittersweet to look at the little faces of each of her classmates in turn: their easy smiles, some looking at the camera, some chatting to one another, long healthy limbs and bright mischievous eyes. She remembers that it was OK for women not to wear the hijab during her childhood. The pressure to cover up came later, in the camps, when some clerics made it their business to preach that the civil war was a punishment from Allah for disobedience, and people took to a more extreme form of Islam through fear.

Maryam knows that she romanticises her early childhood. It wasn't perfect, and her parents bickered about money and their children's education and all the usual family stuff, but in her head it remains a time of incomparable innocence, before civil war carved Somalia up into warring territories, as effectively as the sharpest butcher's knife makes short work of a carcass.

The second photograph is of the entrance to her childhood home: a white wall punctuated by a doorway painted bright blue, clouds of bougainvillea in bloom around it. She remembers her father picking a sprig of those magenta petals for her mother when he came home from work each night, presenting it to her in the kitchen. She remembers her mother resting in the evening while her father read out loud to her. Her mother would listen, rapt, too tired to change out of her nurse's uniform, her bare feet tucked up under her, her hair cut short so it framed her face in soft curls, lamplight glancing off the side of her face.

Every time she looks at the photograph of her childhood home, Maryam wishes her parents were in it, or one of her siblings. She has to use her memory to keep them alive, and she hates that, because she struggles to remember the finer details of their faces.

Maryam witnessed the death of her younger sister. Their family stuck it out in the city of Hargeisa through the escalation of police and military presence, curfews, curtailments of freedom, and then random arrests and executions that resulted from the government turning against the north of Somalia. They stayed in their beloved home to the bitter end. It was partly a stubborn show of support for the people around them who were also hanging on, and partly a sort of vigil for friends and family who had been snatched from their homes and imprisoned and tortured, or simply made to disappear. For years before they left, Maryam's family members feared for their lives.

The day they gave up was the day that planes darkened the sky above Hargeisa and set about bombing it until it was destroyed. They left the city with the other remaining families that day, lines of them making their way out, using any available route.

From the air, it was easy to spot the columns of people fleeing. The pilots were ordered to hold onto some ammunition after bombarding the city itself and to drop it on those families. They were instructed to return to Hargeisa airport to refuel and rearm their planes after that.

Maryam remembers her mother pulling them into a maize field as the drone of engines filled the air above them. She screamed at them to crouch down and hide as the black dot in the sky above them grew larger and took on the shape of an aircraft. It was chaos. Maryam dived between the plants, and when she caught her breath and looked back she saw her sister still in the road, alone, turning, confused, looking for them, for anybody.

'Halima!' she called. 'Here!'

Halima heard her and began to run towards them, but behind her the plane loomed larger, its shadow only yards away now, its ammunition strafing the road behind it, sending clods of red earth up in a neat, efficient line of destruction that hit other stragglers first, but then caught up with Halima and felled her instantly.

They had to leave her there.

Maryam puts her photographs back in the box and stashes it away carefully. She returns to bed, the memories still making her heart pound, but she's used to that. Like her husband and daughter, she falls asleep heavily and has dreams that are vivid and nightmarish.

Abdi waits patiently until everything is completely quiet in the flat and then, for the second time that week, he dresses in the middle of the night and slips out of the house and into the darkness.

Nur wakes up to use the bathroom at 4 a.m.

On his way back to bed he looks in on Abdi and discovers that he's missing.

The family works out that Abdi probably went out in jeans, a T-shirt, a hoody and some trainers. They think he probably took his wallet, which usually contains only a library card and at most a small amount of cash, but so far as they can tell he has nothing else with him.

Maryam loses her usual control and becomes hysterical. Nur scoops her into his arms and holds her as tightly as he can without hurting her.

*

I'm hearing hospital sounds less and less. Somehow I don't seem to be present in the room as much as I was, and when I am, it's more difficult to try to work out what's happening.

I mistake the squeaking of the nurses' shoes for a mouse in the corner of my room. I know it's my mind playing tricks on me, but I can see the mouse's face really clearly: its twitching nose, arching white whiskers, pink pinhead eyes.

My parents' voices distort around me. I want to feel the pressure of their hands on mine, but there's no sensation there at all. The heat of the infection burns all over me. I feel thirsty and sick, and I want to tell somebody so they can help me, but I can't.

I'm desperate to stay in the room with my parents, desperate to keep a grip on reality, but the memories of Monday night play unstoppably.

When I got across the bridge, my heart sank, because I could see that there was no way into the yard where the heaps of metal were piled. A tall chain-link fence was between me and what I wanted. I felt tears sting my eyes. Everything was so frustrating.

Abdi was on the bridge.

'I want to get in there,' I said. 'It's the only thing I want. It's just that one thing.'

I rattled the fence.

'Stop,' he said. 'Please. Stop. Doing. This. I can't stand it any more. You're going to end up getting really sick, and we don't have a phone to get help. What am I going to do if that happens? Tell me!'

'It's just one last thing.'

'Do you ever think about anybody else apart from yourself?'

'I help other people,' I said.

'Do you? Have you asked me how I am tonight?'

'You're with me.'

'So?'

'I'm your friend,' I said. 'I help you.'

'How do you help me? Did you ask me if I wanted to end up here in the freezing cold while you do stupid things? Do you ever really ask me if I want to do anything, or do you just emotionally blackmail me?'

'I asked you to the party at the gallery! And this is for you as well as me.'

Or at least I'd thought it was, but now I felt confused. It was too late to give up, though. I'd come too far.

He was beside me now, and mist from our breath mingled as we stood face to face. He took my arm. 'Come back with me.'

'No,' I said. 'Let go!'

He dropped my arm. I was surprised to see that he was crying.

'I'm dying,' I said. 'I'm going to die.'

He stared at me. 'How should I believe you?'

'Because it's true. It's happening.'

'I'm sick of you using your illness to manipulate me.'

'I'm not, I promise I'm not.'

'Oh, come on. It's what you do. You've done it before so many times. You always need me to help you whenever I'm about to do something with one of the other kids at school. I know you do that on purpose, and I try to be a good friend to you, but think about what it's like for me when you're in hospital for ages. I have to be able to make other friends, too. It doesn't mean I'm not your friend; I'm just not *exclusively* your friend. The minute I try to spend time with anybody else, you need me to go with you to the nurse's office, and it's always me. You don't need to be so possessive. You can't own me. I can have more than one friend, and anyway, it's so pointless because I like you. I would be your friend every day anyway.'

The accusations hurt, and I knew that was because they were true, but so was what I was telling him.

'I'm not lying.'

'Oh my god, you never stop! Are you even listening to me? Do you know what? I'll tell you something else: you're not going to want me now anyway. Everything is different. You just don't realise it yet because you're not actually interested in me, just what I can do for you, so let's go home and then I'll get out of your life for ever.'

'I do want you.' I didn't know what he was talking about.

'You're unbelievably selfish.'

'I do want you, Abdi!' I yelled it because I meant it so much, but he turned away.

I grabbed the fence and willed the final bits of strength from my pathetic body. I started to climb, trying to ignore the painful bite of the cold metal on my fingers, willing the muscles in my arms and legs to work. The fence shook loudly as I climbed, metallic clanging reverberating all along it.

'Oh no, Noah, no!' Abdi shouted.

I kept climbing. At the top of the fence I clung to the post.

I looked down at him and I laughed, from the surprise of having made it all the way to the top. It felt awesome to be up there. I could see all across the scrapyard and down the canal. Abdi's face looked so angry and upset, but I didn't care.

'Come on!' I said to him. 'It's amazing.'

The top of the fence was unstable, so I had to cling to the post as I got my legs over it.

'Get down! Noah!' The mist from his breath was like a puff of smoke. He shook the fence.

'Come on! I dare you,' I shouted.

He shook the fence again, violently this time, but I kept going, finding footholds, until I was close enough to the ground to jump down into the scrapyard. Abdi started to climb. He was much faster than me. I ran across the yard and he caught up with me right at the edge of the canal. Close up, the surface of the water looked like silk. It reminded me of a dark, slippery scarf that my mum some-times wears. The air was so cold that it made time seem frozen, and next to the massive, still pile of metal, the movement of the water made the canal look like a passage to somewhere else.

Abdi and I stood facing each other beside the water, both of us out of breath. The pain in my abdomen had become very sharp. Abdi's arms hung by his sides but his fists were clenched.

'That's enough,' he said. 'It's enough. We need to go.'

'Abdi,' I said, 'please.' It was hard to get the words out, because I was so out of breath. I wanted him to feel elated, just like I did. 'Please, just let me do this, just this one thing.'

'Seriously, have you lost your mind? I am so sick of you and your fucking family. Everything revolves around you; you poke your noses into other people's lives and you don't care about the consequences so long as you get what you want. Your dad's photos made me sick, do you understand? They're sick!'

'Don't talk about my dad like that!'

I loved and hated the taste of all these cruel words on my tongue and in my ears, I must admit. It felt honest but frightening, too. It felt very real.

'Look at the stars, Abdi, and the moon and the frost. It's amazing here. Let's have our drinks now. Please.'

'No.' He was shaking. 'I won't.'

When he said that, I was so angry everything seemed to get a kind of momentum that was exhilarating and sickening all at once. I shoved him in the chest, away from the water, hard enough to make him stumble backwards.

'My time's nearly up. Gone. I'm going to be dead! Do you understand? I only wanted us to do something nice together before I die, but you want to wreck it.'

I gave him another shove, and again he stumbled backwards.

'How will you feel when I'm gone?' I said to him.

He came very close to me. His eyes were black, shiny buttons in the darkness. 'Well, my time's up, too,' he said.

'What do you mean?' That wasn't what I expected to hear. 'Stop playing games.'

'I'm not playing games.'

On the other side of the scrapyard gates I heard a car rolling to a stop. Headlights passed over us, then went off. A car door slammed shut, and this noise was followed by the sound of a metal door rolling open. Abdi didn't react. He was looking at me in a funny way. Everything went quiet again.

'Who would you have if it wasn't for me?' The pain in my side goaded me on, made me crazy, and the urge to be cruel felt unstoppable as the pain pinched harder.

'Who would I have?'

'You'd have nobody.'

'I'd rather have nobody than be somebody's puppet. Come on! Let's go. I'll help you back over the fence.'

It was time to punish him. For what he was saying and for the tests he had failed, including this one: the only one that truly mattered.

'You're pathetic,' I told him. 'Nobody likes you, nobody else wanted to be your friend. You never fitted in at school without me. People feel sorry for you and for your family.'

That did it. He shoved me, just as I'd shoved him, but harder.

My feet disappeared from beneath me; there was no hope of staying upright on the frost-shiny ground. Instinctively, I struggled to keep my balance, and as I did, there was a confusion of noise: a man's voice, and a dog barking.

Then it happened. At first it felt triumphant as I fell through the darkness towards the water. It took me in with a slap, sucking me down in a way that I knew there was no coming back from. It pressed against every part of me, accepting me, keeping me. The weight of my backpack dragged me down deep very fast. It was on so tight.

From my hospital bed, I remember very clearly that I struggled to get the backpack off. It was instinct that made me do it. Instinct, and the terrible fear of dying that arrived right at the last minute and felt bigger than anything else. Above me, the last thing I saw was Abdi's shifting silhouette, and I wondered if he would try to help me, but of course he couldn't swim.

The feeling of panic had become very intense, and my lungs felt as if they were on fire, but the memory stops there. As I got the backpack off, my head hit something hard and sharp. Blackness exploded like spilled ink across a page.

I want to tell Mum and Dad about all of this. I can hear their voices around me in the hospital, and I want to tell them I'm sorry and I made a very big mistake, because of course I know now that I should have spent my last moments with them.

I want the rising heat to stop, but it feels as if it's melting me.

I want to see my parents one more time. I desperately want that. It's all I want.

The sounds of people moving around my hospital bed are becoming more and more distant, but they're increasingly frantic. I sense that very clearly, and that's how I know I'm going now, that it's time. The atoms of my soul are fading, dissolving, disappearing.

I hear my father's moan, low and terrible, but it's my

mother's voice that pierces through the others, loudest and clearest. 'Noah!' she shrieks over and over again.

My heart burns hotter than the rest of me because I know I got it wrong at the end.

This isn't how I wanted it to be for any of us.

Noah's Bucket List Item No. 13: Be in Control When the End Comes.

Goodbye, Dad. Goodbye, Mum.

I say it in my head.

I hope they can hear me.

It's the best I can do.

When I get home it's late, and I find Becky tucked under a blanket, watching TV.

'How are you?' I ask. She looks tired but comfortable. The colour of the marks on her face has deepened and spread, showing the extent of the damage that was inflicted. There's a packet of painkillers on the floor beside her.

She pulls the blanket up to her chin.

'I know I look much worse, but I feel better. How about you?'

Her voice croaks as if she's hardly spoken all day.

'I've got a couple of calls to catch up on, then I'll join you. Can I get you anything?'

She shakes her head.

A few messages have backed up on my phone during the ride back. The first is from Ed Sadler:

'Hi, Detective Inspector, it's Edward Sadler. Re the conversation with Abdi, I do recall chatting with him, but it was very late and as you know I'd had quite a few drinks. We might have talked about Hartisheik camp but I can't remember the detail, I'm afraid. I certainly wasn't aware he was recording the conversation. But he's a curious boy, so perhaps he was following up on things that he wanted to know after seeing the exhibition. I'm at the hospital now for a few hours, but you can try me on my mobile if you want to discuss it further.'

I mull over that and park it on my to-do list for the following day. It's very late to be disturbing him at the hospital, and I'd like to see him face to face anyhow, to follow up on what the therapist told us.

I call Sofia Mahad just to double-check what she said the recording contained. She insists it was on the iPad and describes it once again in detail.

I click onto my second voicemail after that, and in timing that would be comic if it wasn't so annoying, it's from one of our tech team. He apologises for not finding the audio recording this morning and tells me they've emailed it across.

I listen to it immediately. It's exactly as Sofia Mahad described it, and I think worth having a chat to Ed Sadler about. I'm also wondering whether the message was deleted on purpose or whether it could have been a mistake.

The remaining message is from Woodley. He's made appointments for us to speak to Abdi and Noah's friend Imran at the school tomorrow. Good news.

I get changed out of my work clothes into some jogging bottoms and a T-shirt, and when I'm done Becky shifts to make a space for me on the end of the sofa.

'Did you eat?' I ask.

Her hand appears from under the blanket, a chocolate bar wrapper clutched in her fingers.

'I found it in the cupboard,' she said. 'Hope you don't mind.'

It's a cheeky question because it's a Mars Bar wrapper. It was my favourite chocolate bar when we were kids. I didn't get to have one often, but when I did, I guarded it fiercely and ate it in little bits, rationing it to make it last as long as possible. She used to tease me about it.

'You don't change much, then,' she says.

'Nor do you! You know I have powers of arrest for stealing, don't you?'

She laughs, though it makes her wince a little. Even so, it's a sight that warms me. I haven't thought about that stuff for so long, and it's nice to know that we can have a laugh. The relationship I might have had with my sister was one of the more depressing casualties of our father's bullying.

'Do you want to eat some proper food?'

'What do you have?'

'Some takeaway menus.'

'I don't have any money.'

'Don't worry about that. It's on me.'

I order generously, and when the food arrives, we eat it from plates balanced on our knees in front of the TV. It reminds me of how we used to watch the box on weekend afternoons when we were kids. I'll admit it feels a long time since I've had company here in the evening, and I've missed it.

Emma and I used to sit here drinking wine and talking. I remember massaging her stockinged feet when we lay together on the sofa after a long day at work. I remember where that led. I know what I told Fraser, but the truth is that I still miss Emma, every single day.

Becky prods me with her foot. 'Thousand-yard stare,' she says.

'Sorry. Just thinking about work.' There are some things I'm not ready to share with her yet. 'I've got a tricky case on the go.'

'Can you talk about it?'

I give her some details.

'Surely they were out drinking or doing drugs?' she says. 'They must have been. It sounds like a night out gone wrong.'

'I don't know. I wish I did. I've got a feeling it might be more complicated than that.'

'What will happen to the Somali boy if he keeps refusing to talk?'

'We would have to decide whether there's enough evidence to bring charges of some sort against him.'

'What a nightmare.'

On the TV a drone camera soars over a desert where antelope are migrating in hordes, a swarm of living creatures against a hostile backdrop. The scene is both beautiful and harsh.

'I don't want to pry,' I say carefully, 'but would you like to tell me what happened?'

Instantly, she looks guarded. I'm about to back down and apologise for asking because I can see that I shouldn't have, that I've pushed her too soon, when she says, 'What will you do if I tell you?'

'What do you mean?'

'Last time I looked, you were a police officer.'

'I'll listen.'

'Is that all?'

'If that's what you want.'

She chooses her next words carefully. 'I've been in a relationship that hasn't always been ... healthy. But it's over now.'

The abuse is all there in the subtext and the understatement, in her expression, and in the way her fingers flutter near the bruising that I can't see but know is on her neck. I'm not surprised, and I'm pleased she's being honest with me, but it's still shocking to hear it from her.

'Are you sure? Sometimes abusive men find it hard to—'

'Jim! I don't need you to babysit me. I need a place to stay.'

'OK!'

I know when to back off. Telling me what happened is progress. I clear away the debris from our meal and pour us both some whisky.

'Constitutional,' I say when I hand her a glass.

Becky takes the drink and watches me with a level gaze, the blanket still pulled up under her chin, like a barricade between us. We sit in silence until she says, 'This is a nice flat, little brother.'

'Thanks.'

'We made very different choices in life, didn't we?'

'Becky ...'

'It's OK. It wasn't your fault. You were too young to stop him.'

I swallow some whisky. The reference to our father turns it into a mouthful of pins. She goes to bed soon afterwards, the blanket wrapped around her as she walks out of the room, the end of it trailing in her wake.

The long day I've had and the whisky both help me get off to sleep unexpectedly quickly, in spite of the crappy springs in my sofa, but there's no escaping the insomnia. I wake up long before dawn to find that the dark hours have been patiently waiting to wrap tendrils of anxiety around me.

I throw open the sash window and clamber out onto the parapet outside. I know it's not recommended to start your day with a cigarette, but I'm so short on vices that I excuse myself the odd smoke. A cigarette can be good company when the texture of your mind turns rough and dark, and when the paths through it feel labyrinthine.

The stone parapet is cold against my back and the tree-tops look etched against the street lights, motionless under the low broiling clouds that capture the sickly tones of the city's night glow and reflect them back down to street level. Opposite, Cabot Tower is illuminated, and the red light flashing on the spire is hypnotic.

I relish the thump of the smoke in my lungs. As I exhale, the smoke hazes the view and dims the lights momentarily. From the street below I hear drunken shouting that passes by soon enough, on its way to rouse some other unfortunate from their dreams.

I sit there for a long time, thinking.

I think about the lowlife who photographed Noah Sadler in his hospital bed and the editor who thought it was a good idea to publish that photograph on the front page of the paper.

I think about Emma, who wrote such an inflammatory article, stoking the embers of racial tension in our city and putting our case under scrutiny. And in the safety of the darkness and my solitude, I allow myself, fleetingly, to admit that there's a stubborn part of me that still has feelings for her.

I think about my sister, and how my job is to help people like her, but I don't know if she's going to let me.

I think about the witness who thought it was OK to spill all to a journalist and embellish the story she told us. I should have spent more time with her, seen her a second time to get her on side. I wonder whether I should have worked harder when I interviewed her, tried to get more out of her.

I ask myself if I've lost something while I've been away. I wonder if I've hit this case stuck in second gear when I should have been in fifth. Did I lose my edge during all the time I spent in therapy?

I don't know.

What I do know is that in spite of everything I still feel fiercely grateful to be back in the game. I'm going to continue this investigation as carefully as I can, and I will be on my game. The case needs to be put to bed swiftly, and on the QT, just like Fraser wanted.

My phone rings as I stub out the last cigarette in my pack.

It's Fraser. It's 5 a.m. My blood runs cold.

'I'm sorry to wake you.'

She sounds only partly with it herself, sleep still lurking in the deeper pockets of her voice.

'What's happened?' Something must have.

'Noah Sadler died an hour ago. He developed an infection yesterday.'

I experience vertigo for the first time in my life: a slow lurching of the cityscape around me, the nauseating certainty that I'm going to fall.

'They said he was stable,' is all I manage to say, though my mind is racing to process the news, thinking first of Noah's parents, and then how this investigation has just got a whole lot more serious for everybody involved in it.

'See you at the office, asap,' she says.

I hit the streets on my bike at a speed that's probably not recommended. I don't bother reminding myself to be careful when rain begins to slick the roads.

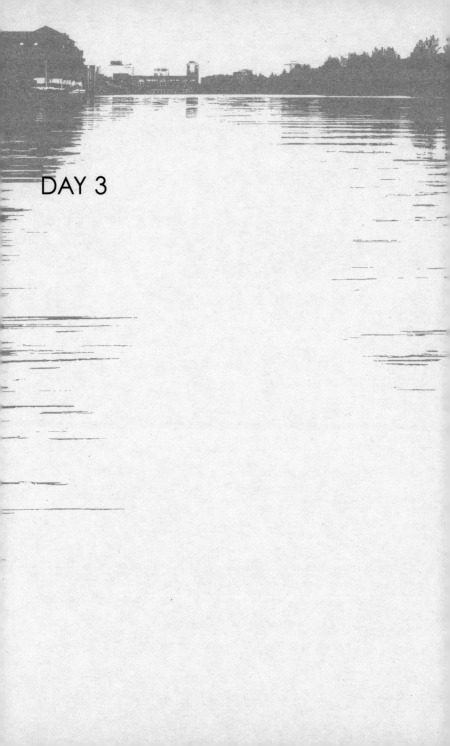

DAY 3

At seven in the morning, the buzzer in Abdi Mahad's family's flat rings long and hard before fading, just as it did the first time the police visited them.

Nur is already out, driving around the streets of Easton and further, to see if he can spot Abdi. He slows beside every darkened doorway. He leaves the car to walk the patches of wasteland beneath concrete pillars supporting raised sections of the motorway, and stares into the dampest, darkest corners underneath the railway arches. The night shifts, fear for Abdi, and his guilt about his carelessness with the newspaper all conspire to make him feel dizzy with exhaustion.

The Mahads have decided to try to look for Abdi themselves before letting the police know he has vanished. They're afraid that his disappearance will make it look as if he's guilty of something. Sofia's contacted everybody she can think of to ask if they've seen her brother, but nobody's replied yet. It's too early.

Sofia answers the intercom, but not before she and her mother have exchanged fearful glances.

'It's Detective Inspector Jim Clemo and Detective Constable Woodley. May we come up and speak to you?'

She buzzes them in.

Clemo's brought a translator with them this time: a

Somali woman who introduces herself as Ifrah Adan Faruur and says she usually translates for social services. She looks as if she's been dragged out of bed in a hurry, which she has.

Sofia texts her father to let him know that he needs to come home, that the police are at the flat.

Maryam offers no hospitality. She eyes Ifrah suspiciously even though the woman smiles at her. She remembers the neighbours who informed on her father when she was a child. She knows that other Somalis can be both friends and foes, even this far from their homeland.

They sit. Sofia keeps her eyes on Clemo, waiting for him to speak. She notices everything about him: the hazel eyes that are kind but also calculating, the dark smudges beneath them, the way his mouth seems sticky this morning. When he clears his throat, the sound of it gets under her skin.

'Is your father here?' Clemo asks her.

'He's out.'

The translator repeats everything in Somali for Maryam's benefit.

'Do you know when he'll be back?'

'Soon.'

'Has Abdi spoken to you about what happened yet?'

Sofia shakes her head and tries to keep her breathing under control. She knows she should tell Clemo right away that Abdi's gone, but she's terrified he'll be angry that they didn't phone the police when they first discovered it.

Maryam hasn't said a word.

Clemo leans forward. He's much more tense than last

time they came. 'I'm very sorry to tell you that Noah Sadler died a few hours ago in hospital.'

The translator repeats his words in Somali.

Sofia and Maryam both experience an intense moment of shock. Sofia retches and runs to the bathroom. She isn't sick, but she feels dizzy and clammy. For a few minutes she stands with her back against the bathroom wall and tries to breathe normally.

When she returns to the room, she sits beside her mother and their fingers link as tightly as a dovetail joint. Sofia weeps softly, but Maryam remains in control. Her emotions burn as fiercely as Sofia's, but she learned long ago to keep them packed away deep inside her.

The translator puts a hand out as if to comfort the women, but withdraws it when neither of them reacts.

'I appreciate that is going to be very difficult news for Abdi, and for you, especially because it changes the nature of our investigation.'

Clemo glances from Sofia to Maryam as the translator speaks. Neither of them replies. He looks at the translator. She shrugs.

'I have another question for you, if I may?' He doesn't wait for permission to ask it. 'We have now found the audio recording on the iPad we collected from you, but it had been deleted, so it took a bit of tracking down. Do you know how that could have happened?'

'I didn't delete it,' Sofia says.

When the interpreter has translated, Maryam shakes her head, as if confused by this.

'Perhaps it got deleted by mistake,' Sofia suggests.

She glances at her mother, wondering if Maryam could have done that somehow.

Clemo makes a note and moves on. 'It's very important that I talk to Abdi now. But I wonder if you would prefer to break the news of Noah's death to him yourselves, before I do that?'

Sofia opens her mouth. How to say it? She's silently scrabbling for words and for the courage to say them, eyes fixed on Clemo, when Nur arrives home.

A small cry of pain escapes Maryam – she was holding out hope that he would have Abdi with him – and she finally speaks: 'They want to talk to Abdi,' she says to her husband in Somali. 'Noah's dead.'

The translator repeats her words for Clemo.

In the beat of silence that follows, Sofia says: 'Abdi's gone.'

The energy in the room changes instantly.

Clemo fires questions at them, jaw clenched as he barely suppresses his anger that they didn't phone the police as soon as they discovered Abdi was missing. The detective with him takes a note of everything they say.

By the time they leave, the family are under no illusion that they're obliged to turn any relevant information about Abdi and/or his whereabouts over to the police or risk consequences to themselves.

'Let me make this as clear to you as possible,' Clemo tells them: 'Your son is now a person of interest in what may become a murder investigation.'

Nur speaks up as the detective inspector pulls his coat on. He isn't cowed. He has a family to protect. 'Abdi is an innocent boy. What will you do to find him and bring him home safely?'

Clemo pauses.

Be kind to my father, Sofia thinks, *he's a good man.*

'We'll do everything we can, sir. Of course.'

Woodley, his face as white as mine, jogs to catch up with me as we get back to the car, and doesn't flinch when I curse.

'I've got to call Fraser,' I say.

I slam my palm on the roof of the car. I'm already regretting not putting more pressure on Abdi Mahad to talk earlier, and I'm sure I'll be regretting it even more after I've spoken to Fraser. The look on his face tells me that Woodley feels the same way. It's the sort of expression you'd make if you'd been invited to pet a venomous snake.

When I make the call, Fraser reacts to my news with silence at first, which is almost worse than a verbal tirade. Then she gives me instructions in curt tones.

'Get over to the witness now, as planned, and make sure she doesn't breathe another word to the press. I'll speak to Janie. I don't want word of Noah Sadler's death getting out if we can help it. It might make Abdi Mahad even less willing to come home, because I'm assuming he didn't know about it before he did his disappearing act. I'm afraid we're going to lose him to the streets if we're not careful. Once you've read the riot act to the witness, and I've had a chance to put some things in motion to find this boy, we'll finalise a plan for what we do going forward.'

'Boss ...' I want to talk it through with her now, because I've got some ideas about what we should do, but she's not having any of it. It's out of my hands.

'Not now, Jim. Call me after you've spoken to the witness. Though this is *not* looking too rosy for Abdi Mahad, I'll tell you that.'

On our way to Clifton Village, Woodley and I get through the city quickly on a string of green lights. As we pass the Children's Hospital I feel my heart clench at the thought of Noah Sadler's body: lifeless, machines withdrawn.

We find the witness's shop easily. In an elaborately looped and curlicued font her name, 'Janet Pritchard,' is all over the lilac signage. As I suspected, the shop is one of the boutiques that line a street in the heart of the Village, where the glass shines and the clientele is mostly very well heeled.

Inside we find a bored shop girl behind the cash desk. When we ask where we can find the owner, she poses her answers like questions. 'Janet's at the Albion?' she says. 'Having a meeting?'

I know where the Albion is. A short walk takes us down a pedestrian street packed with cafe seating and a fruit and veg stall. Just in front of a Georgian carriage arch, which gives us a glimpse of an elegant garden square beyond, there's a cobbled courtyard where the pub's located.

Janet Pritchard's inside, having coffee with a man who wears a crisp white shirt, blazer and jeans with an elaborate metal buckle. He stands when we make our presence known. The place is empty otherwise, apart from a staff member who's lighting a wood-burning stove. A tang of beer is in the air.

'This is a surprise, Detectives,' Janet says. 'Don't you ever phone first?'

I don't like the edge to her voice. It's a change from the trying-to-please attitude she had at the scrapyard two days ago. I force a smile.

'We need a quick word with you, if possible.'

'This is my business partner, Ian,' Janet says.

'Nice to meet you.' He has a firm handshake, and the edge of a tattoo emerges from underneath a pristine cuff.

'Alone would be preferable,' I add.

Her partner gets the hint. 'I'll leave you to it. See you later, darling.' It's said with a wink. Not just a business partner, then. I wonder if he was the man who tried to call while I was interviewing her in the cabin.

Janet clears away paperwork as Woodley and I sit down.

'What can I help you with?' she asks.

'At what point did you feel that it was appropriate to speak to the press about the disturbing incident concerning two teenage boys whose families are distraught?' I ask her.

Woodley sucks in his breath. *Careful,* I can tell he's thinking, *we need her on side.*

Janet Pritchard gives me a level gaze. 'To be fair,' she says, 'I didn't know I was talking to the press. That lady came into my shop. I thought she was a customer at first, but she said she was a support staff person for witnesses and victims of crime. We went for a cup of tea.'

'And you believed her?'

'How was I to know any different?'

'Did you tell her that you witnessed a racially motivated attack?'

'No. I told her what I told you. She made the rest up.'

I'm not sure if I believe her or not, but her pout tells me that this is her story and she's sticking to it.

'Can you describe her to me?'

'Gorgeous. She had thick dark hair and lovely eyes. Bit of a foreign name, though she didn't look it. She gave me her card.'

As she roots around in her bag I already know it was Emma, and when I take the card from her I see that I'm right.

'May I keep this?' I ask.

'Sure. I won't need it now anyway, will I? Now that I know not to talk to her again.' She raises her eyebrows in a sarcastic way that I don't like.

'There could be legal consequences if you do.'

'Understood.'

'One more thing. Was one of the boys wearing a back-pack when you saw them?'

'Might have been. Yes, I think he was. The boy who went in the water was.'

'Thank you.'

As we're about to leave, I remember a detail that bothered me after her first interview. 'When we last spoke, you said you made the 999 call from your car.'

'That's right.'

'And you said you had to root through your bag to find your phone, which is why you didn't see exactly what happened as the boy fell into the canal?'

'Yes.'

'Was your phone not Bluetooth connected to your car? A nice motor like that, I'd have thought it would have been.'

She pauses only momentarily before answering: 'That's because the system in the car's broken. The Bluetooth connection doesn't work.'

As we leave, her phone starts ringing. She's obviously a lady who's in demand. She answers it in a businesslike way as the door swings shut behind us.

Out in the courtyard, Woodley yawns, feeling the early rise.

'What's happening about the recording of the 999 call she made?' I ask. 'I think we need to hear it as soon as we can.'

'I've requested it. I'll chase it up.'

Woodley looks longingly back at the pub as we walk away. 'Bit early for a pint do you think, boss?'

'Can we take a break from the wisecracks, maybe?'

On the way back to HQ, Woodley takes the wheel. I get Emma's card out of my pocket and examine it. It's simple and stylish, as I'd expect. There's no job description, just her name and there's also a phone number on it.

I'm sure Dr Manelli would warn me against it in the strongest possible terms, but I know I'm going to call Emma. I want to warn her off interfering in the case and give her a piece of my mind. I'm so cross with her right now that I can't believe it was only a few hours ago that I sat on my parapet and thought I felt something tender for her. That's a call I want to make in private, though. There's no way I'm going to do it with Woodley earwigging.

Instead I phone Fraser from the car, because there's something I do want her permission for, and I want it this morning. I request another dive search, focusing on the area of the canal beside the scrapyard, and things have got serious enough for her to authorise it on the spot. I want to find Noah Sadler's backpack. At this stage, it might be one of our best bets for getting some clues as to what the boys were up to.

Nur takes the taxi back out to look for Abdi, and this time Maryam goes with him.

'You keep phoning everybody,' Nur instructs Sofia before he leaves. 'Everybody you can think of. We have to find him.'

She works the phone, contacting everyone she can think of. By now it's pinging constantly with a series of texts and messages from friends and old school mates promising to look out for Abdi and spread the word on social media.

She doesn't take any calls. She can't face talking to anybody. She feels the shame of the situation just as her parents do, but they can't keep this to themselves any longer. Finding Abdi is the most important thing.

When she's done everything she can think of, she finds herself sitting with her thoughts. She thinks again about the recording of Abdi and Ed Sadler, and the way it disappeared. She struggles to believe her mother would have purposely deleted it, because she's not even sure Maryam would know how to, but she can't help feeling a tiny bit of suspicion that she did.

Whether her mother tampered with the recording or not, she realises that its existence is enough to convince her that the key to all of this lies in what Abdi's been doing over the past few days. It's all she has to go on, anyway.

She feels a twinge of guilt that she's been so preoccupied with her course that she hasn't paid much attention to her family in the past few weeks. She wonders where to start. She obviously can't go to Noah's school asking questions, but she remembers that Amina mentioned Abdi being at the Welcome Centre with Maryam on Friday evening, and that it was an unusual night because Maryam fainted. Sofia marches over there, looking out for her brother with every step taken.

At the Welcome Centre they're unloading boxes of food at the back entrance. Somebody's inside the van, picking over the food surplus items that have been collected from local businesses that morning.

'Got a ton of rice and peppers, tomatoes. There's chicken! And meringues.'

Chef Sami is standing at the back door, arms folded.

'Hey, Sofia,' he says, 'do you think people will like chicken meringue surprise for lunch?'

He can always make her smile, even today.

'Is Amina in?'

'She's sorting out the donation cupboard.'

Inside, the centre is busy, as usual. The English language teachers are setting out materials in the temporary classrooms, and a solicitor who offers free advice is smoothing plastic tablecloths over the trestle tables to be used at lunch. The kitchen volunteers are setting up tea and coffee urns and unwrapping packets of biscuits. The room's warm and bright, and Sofia knows that soon it will start to fill with the smell of cooking as the team gets to work making a hot meal out of whatever comes from the van.

She finds Amina on an upstairs landing. She's sitting beside an empty cupboard and a fusty-smelling pile of clothing.

Amina holds up a stained women's vest top. 'Why do people think it's OK to donate things like this?' She shakes her head. 'Coats and sweaters are what we need. Warm clothes for grown men.'

Sofia tells her what happened, feeling her composure wobble as tears fill Amina's eyes. It's actually a relief to tell somebody outside the family.

'But Abdi's such a good boy,' Amina says. 'He's the last boy I would think would be in a situation like this.'

'When you saw him here last time, when Mum fainted, did you see what he was doing?'

'You think he fell in with some bad boys?'

'I don't know what to think. I'm trying to find out anything I can.'

'I probably saw him once or twice that evening, but it was very busy – it was a cold night – and I wasn't paying attention until your mother fainted. I think Abdi helped with food prep. They had a nice young crowd of volunteers in. He didn't do serving with us, but I think he was clearing plates from the hatch. When your mum fainted, a few of us helped her to sit down and I sat with her. Abdi disappeared for a bit, but he came back to look after her and one of the volunteers drove them home early.'

'Do you know why my mother fainted?'

'No. She said the feeling came on suddenly. One minute she felt sick and dizzy and the next she was falling. I'm sorry I'm not being more helpful, darling, it was crazy busy that night. Somebody else might remember more. Why don't you ask Tim?'

Sofia finds Tim at the entrance desk, signing in the refugees who are starting to arrive. He has a friendly face and big hands that dwarf his mug of tea.

'Yes, Abdi was here on Friday,' he says. 'It was really busy. We saw a lot of new faces.'

'Do you know what he did?' Sofia asks.

'Kitchen, I think. He was buzzing around there for most of the evening. And he was asking around about somebody after your mum fainted.'

Sofia feels her pulse quicken. 'Do you know who?'

'It was a Somali man, but that's all I know.'

He checks the book where the volunteers sign in. 'Kate and Jacob were in with him that night. He chats with them a lot. They might know more.'

'Do you have their contact details?'

'I'm not allowed to give those out – sorry, darling – but I can talk to them and ask them to call you.'

'And please, would you ask all the volunteers to look out for Abdi and phone us if you see him?'

'Of course. Anything we can do. We're all very fond of him here. He's one of our most popular volunteers.'

Sofia writes her number down on a piece of paper and gives it to Tim.

'Please feel free to get a tea before you go, if you like. You look as if you could do with it,' he says.

Sofia's shyness means that her first instinct is to say 'no', but she checks herself. She hasn't eaten anything all morning, and she's feeling weak.

She helps herself to tea and biscuits and says 'hello' to the volunteers she recognises. Just as the refugee faces are always in flux here, so too are many of the volunteers. She withdraws to a table in the corner of the room and watches as refugees begin to arrive. Some are cheerful, looking forward to lessons, to a chat with friends. Others wear their experiences less lightly. There's hot tea in this bright, welcoming room and warm support for the vulnerable, but Sofia feels their collective suffering as if it were a separate entity in the room. It becomes unbearable. She tidies up her empty mug and plate after just a few minutes, and leaves.

Maryam's also thinking about the Welcome Centre as she sits beside Nur in the taxi and they drive circuits around their neighbourhood, and beyond.

In the moment before she fainted, she saw a ghost from her past, a version of a face not seen in the flesh for a very long time, but a regular visitor to her nightmares.

Nur takes a turn towards the train station and the Feeder Canal.

'I want to see where they were,' he says.

Maryam makes no reply.

As the taxi moves past the shopping centre where Sofia

and her friends love to hang out, Maryam glances at Nur. He's concentrating on the traffic. He's a good driver, very careful. How she loves him.

He calls Bristol a new beginning – it makes the children laugh that he's been calling it that for fifteen years now – but no matter how often he says it, for Maryam it feels different here. She thinks of Bristol as the place where she waits for the end, for the circle to close, because too many of the things that happened in Somalia and in the camp still sit stubbornly in her memory like unanswered questions.

If Abdi is gone or guilty of something terrible, she knows that it will break her husband.

She thinks of the man she saw at the refugee centre. Of the moment her legs buckled. She thinks of her missing son and of what he might have done or be planning to do. She knows there's a connection between all things. How could there not be?

As Nur takes the turn onto Feeder Road, her fingers move to touch a scar on her forearm.

Ed Sadler answers the door, looking as haggard and disorientated as I would expect.

We follow him inside. This time he takes us through the hallway into the kitchen, a spacious room that runs across the back of the house. A wall of glass displays the garden like a panorama.

Fiona Sadler sits at the kitchen table. She wears a pale pink sweater, and looks about as vulnerable as it's possible to look.

'I'm so very sorry for your loss,' I say.

The look she gives me is hard to return.

'Has that boy talked yet?' she says. She spits the words out like bitter pips.

'Fi.' Ed Sadler moves to stand behind her, hands on her shoulders, massaging them.

'Do you know what, Detective? We've been cheated,' she says. 'We were always playing for time, ever since Noah's diagnosis. How does it happen that we only just discovered that he had months to live, if we were lucky, and now we've been robbed of that? Cheated.'

It's the same message she delivered in the hospital, but this time she's not holding back. The filters have been removed and she's very angry. She lays clenched fists on the table in front of her. Her knuckles have a pearly shine.

'I'm afraid I need to talk to you about something difficult.' I keep my tone even, because I can't sugarcoat this too much, however much sympathy I feel. Abdi Mahad's reputation and possibly his safety are at stake now more than ever, and my duty has to be to him, too.

They look at me as if they cannot believe there's anything else I can possibly throw at them.

'Did either of you see yesterday's *Bristol Echo*?'

Both shake their heads. I console myself that it's better if this comes from me, at least. It means we can attempt to inform and control their response, rather than risk their finding out by themselves and potentially doing something reckless.

'I'm very sorry to say that they ran an article on the

front page that featured a photograph of Noah in intensive care.'

Fi Sadler begins to weep.

'It looks as if it was taken candidly, so we'll be interviewing hospital staff. Do you have any idea who might have snatched a photograph of Noah?'

'No.' The word is little more than a whisper.

'I'm sorry. I understand this is very painful for you. The article also pointed to a racial attack, which we can't speculate about until we have some firm evidence. I understand that once you've thought about this, you might feel tempted to speak to the press in order to put your own version of the story across, but we strongly recommend that you have no contact with them at all. I can't stress how important this is while the investigation's ongoing.'

'Do they know Noah's dead?' Fiona asks.

'No. Not yet. And I'd like to keep it that way for as long as we can so we can get on with our work without being in the public eye. We can't withhold that information for ever, but I'd also like to give you both the privacy to grieve without press attention for as long as I'm able to.'

'How have they got the right to publish a photograph of our son?' Fiona says. 'How do they justify that? It's disgusting.'

'Well, whether they have the right to or not is certainly something we'll be looking into, and if there's an offence there, you can be sure we'll be looking to charge somebody.'

'Does that boy know that Noah is dead?'

'Abdi has, unfortunately, gone missing.'

She stares at me, as if this is one too many pieces of information for her to absorb, and it probably is. Ed Sadler turns his back and looks out of the window. His shoulders shake.

She says, 'Abdi's responsible for this, I know he is.'

He swings around.

'Fi! You don't know that! Stop talking like that.'

But any scraps of rationality she may have been hanging on to previously have been obliterated by grief: 'Abdi was healthy. He should have protected Noah. How could he have let this happen? Noah would never have been able to walk that far or climb a fence on his own. He must have had help. Abdi has to take responsibility for this. Why has he disappeared if he's not responsible in some way?'

'You don't mean that.'

'Don't I?'

Her eyes are bloodshot and her face is slick with tears.

I stand up. It's time we left.

'Please phone me if you think of anything else we should know about the boys or about Monday. Feel free to contact me at any time. My mobile number's on here.'

I lay my card down on the table, beside a messy stack of flyers advertising an exhibition by Ed Sadler.

He follows my gaze. 'That's where we were on Monday night. It was the opening. The boys came with us.'

I pick one up.

'I wish we'd never let Abdi come on Monday.' Fi Sadler's not finished with the recriminations. Her voice rises in volume. 'It should have been our family. Just us!'

'I'll show you out, Detectives.' Ed Sadler walks to the door.

Outside the sharp air is welcome. I feel as if I can breathe.

On the doorstep, I take advantage of having Ed Sadler on his own.

'We spoke with Noah's therapist at the hospital. He couldn't tell us anything that Noah discussed with him, but he did say that he had been able to share details of some of the conversations he and Noah had with you. Is that right?'

'Not with me, with Fiona. You'll have to ask her, but maybe not today.'

'The therapist mentioned one specific thing that Noah wanted to share with you, but not with your wife. Do you have any recollection of that?'

He hesitates. I feel bad about putting him through this now, but I don't think the next few days are going to get any easier for this couple, so I want to take my chance.

'There was a thing he emailed me about, I can't remember when, maybe last year. It was when I was abroad, I think. It seemed trivial to me, if I'm honest. I didn't pay it too much attention. It was about an essay that Noah helped Abdi with.'

'In what way?'

The sound of Fiona Sadler calling him makes him glance over his shoulder.

'I'll be there in a minute,' he shouts, and then to us, 'Wait here.' He pounds up the stairs.

Woodley and I cool our heels on the doorstep for a few

minutes before he reappears. He's holding a couple of journals.

'These are Noah's therapy notebooks. I think pretty much everything he discussed with the therapist is in here, but I warn you, they make pretty boring reading. And please don't tell Fi I've given them to you. Noah didn't want her to see them. I think he feared she would pore over them and wind herself up even more. She was bad enough when the therapist reported verbally. Noah and I would have built a bonfire and burnt them if we could, but the therapist insisted we keep them, so I've kept them hidden in my office at Noah's request. He felt ashamed of them. Seems stupid now, to worry about small stuff like that.'

'We'll be sure to return them.'

'I don't care if I never see them again. It's not what I want to remember about him.'

He glances over his shoulder in response to another call from Fiona. 'Anyway, the thing Noah's therapist told me, it's in there somewhere. I wouldn't put too much store in it, though. It's just typical boy stuff. I got up to far worse at their age.'

'Thank you.'

As he closes the front door and returns to his wife, I wonder if their relationship will survive this or if they'll tear each other apart.

Sofia knows there's no way she can concentrate on her course today. She decides to visit the gallery. She wants to see Ed Sadler's exhibition for herself, and look for the photograph that Abdi mentioned in the recording. She's pretty sure neither Ed nor Fiona will be there, not under the circumstances, so she won't have to face them.

She makes her way to Montpelier on the train. It's only two stops. She could easily walk it, but she's anxious about walking through unfamiliar areas in the city. Her hijab attracts more attention than she'd like. She feels safer on the train, especially in the aftermath of the rioting. She gets a window seat and watches the familiar landscape slip past: council estates and a few lonely high rises give way to rows and rows of Victorian terraces, some industrial sites and allotments that patchwork a steep hillside. Montpelier is home to rows of Georgian houses, many painted in pastel colours, others their original golden stone. Only about half of them are well cared for. On the others the stone looks weather-beaten and stained. Rogue weeds grow from gaps in slate rooftops and graffiti tags lurk in corners.

She walks to Cheltenham Road from Montpelier station and heads down the road towards Stokes Croft. Sofia loves this area. It has an artsy vibe, cafes and street life, a mix of people.

The buildings beyond the railway arches on Cheltenham Road belong to the graffiti artists. Somebody sleeps on a cold porch under a filthy sleeping bag, and a man with pinprick pupils paces the street, castigating everybody and nobody. Sofia crosses the road to avoid him, and keeps her head down to avoid a conversation with the sociable drunks gathered on a tiny triangular piece of grass that's sandwiched between a road junction and the blind end of a red-brick building.

THE PEOPLE'S REPUBLIC OF STOKES CROFT, proclaims a large painting on the wall. It's not a no-go area, though. Hipster cafes and bars fill the gaps between strip clubs, charity shops and restaurants serving food from every corner of the earth, and the shell of a multi-storeyed, abandoned building looms behind the shop fronts, every single surface, seemingly impossibly, covered in graffiti. Behind it the Salvation Army is building a new head-quarters. A crane looms, and cars are backed up behind temporary traffic lights.

A few hundred yards down the road, Sofia's sense of unease intensifies when she catches sight of the gallery.

EDWARD SADLER: TRAVELS WITH REFUGEES has been smartly printed in white letters on the inside of the glass.

Sofia crosses the road. She barely checks for traffic. She looks at a large photograph in the window. It's of a boy who has a dead hammerhead shark slung over his shoulders.

When she enters the gallery, a girl stands up from behind a desk at the back of the room. She has long tresses of blonde hair tied up in a way that looks designed to be untidy. She wears a leather skirt and a roll-neck top.

'Can I help you?'

'I'm just looking.'

'If you're interested in buying, I have a price list and an explanation of the works written by the photographer. Not all of them are for sale. Enjoy! They're *very real*.'

Sofia needs to take only a cursory glance around the room to experience an even tighter clutch of fear.

The images from the refugee camp speak to her instantly, evoking sensory memories: smells, sensations, noises and voices from the camp all fight for her attention.

She examines the photographs of Somalia and these have a different effect on her, because she's never been there. If she googles Somalia, she sees many pictures like these. They're often images of violence, hardship and destruction. And if not that, they show camels, or nomads posed decoratively in the desert, or some other cliché of Africa. What's missing, and this is true of Ed Sadler's photographs as well, are ordinary lives. The photographs here are extreme. They're focused on shocking things. They tell a story that's incomplete and sensationalist.

Where are the mothers and daughters, fathers and sons and brothers and sisters who are the living, breathing heart of these places? Who aren't violent, and who wish only for things to be improved? Sofia can answer her own question even before she's posed it: ordinary stories are boring. They won't sell papers or encourage donations.

She misses the ordinary folk, though, in this room that depicts horror. She misses their warmth and courage and the boredom they went through and the small things they did every day to try to survive. Her parents were those people, and so were many of their friends and neighbours in the camp. The unsensational things they did are, in Sofia's mind, the true acts of heroism. In contrast, she finds these photographs to be heartless and part of the problem, but she shakes herself out of these thoughts. They're not why she's here.

In the middle of one wall she sees what she's looking for: an image from the camp of men watching football. It's the photograph Abdi asked about in the recording. She sees the man he mentioned. He's right in the middle of the picture, the only face turned towards the camera, though he's not looking directly into it. This is a candid shot. His uncorrected cleft palate is a shocking deformity. She looks hard at the picture, but finds no clue as to why this one in particular caught Abdi's attention. She wonders if she should ask her parents. She uses her phone to take a picture of the photograph.

The gallery girl approaches her, startling Sofia when she says, too brightly: 'That's one of my favourite images, too. What do you think of the show as a whole?'

'Horrific,' Sofia says. Hearing her own voice as she articulates what she's really feeling unexpectedly brings her close to tears.

'But so necessary, don't you think—'

'No. Just horrific.'

'They're shocking at first sight, yes, but if you think of the meta-meaning . . .'

Sofia speaks quietly, but very firmly: 'There is no "meta-meaning". These photographs glamorise and sensationalise suffering.'

'He's not selling the shocking ones.'

Sofia doesn't dignify that with an answer.

When she steps out onto the pavement she takes a few deep breaths to steady herself and quell a feeling of nausea. She can only imagine how Abdi must have felt, being at a party to celebrate pictures like those.

*

Back at HQ, I get stuck into Noah Sadler's therapy journals while I wait for Fraser to finish a meeting.

I feel as if I'm starting to chafe against the short leash she has me on, what with the twice-daily briefings she's asked for, but as it's only my third day back at work, I don't think I have any choice but to put up with it for now.

I try to suppress my fatigue as I read. My lack of sleep is catching up with me, and the journals are, as Ed Sadler warned me, pretty boring. In the first few journals – which are actually just slim school exercise books, labelled by year – the handwriting is immature. They contain dated lists of the topics that Noah and his therapist discussed, and nothing more. The earliest of these journals must have been started when Noah was only about eleven years old, so I'm not at all surprised that they're so bare. I can't help thinking what a sad catalogue of subjects the books contain, though. A typical entry reads: 'Talked about chemo, friendships, school.'

It's not until I get to the fifth book, the most recent, that things get more interesting as Noah begins to add personal comment to his entries. Mostly they're all variations on a theme: 'School friendships: hard work, sometimes lonely, work on asking people how they feel.'

Here and there he adds something a bit more personal: 'Need to try not to think of Imran as a threat. Think about friendship circles.'

The only place he goes into more detail is in one very recent entry, where it seems to me that a sense of injustice might have provoked him into writing more: 'School friendships: talked about getting Imran to write the essay for Abdi, and all the fuss that happened after. Don't see why it should be a problem. Imran was desperate for GTA5 and he got it for £20 in the end, from one of the sixth-formers he knows in badminton club, so everybody's happy. A never got the blame in the end. Told Dad, who thought it was a good deed!'

The entry's a bit of an anomaly in terms of the amount of detail he provides. I flick ahead in the journal. He writes some fuller entries later on, but none of them piques my interest like this one. I show it to Woodley.

'GTA5 is *Grand Theft Auto*, the computer game,' he says. 'It's very much an 18 certificate.'

I reread the passage.

'So am I right in thinking this sounds as if Noah and Abdi bought an essay from Imran for £20, because Abdi needed it, and Imran was happy to make the deal because he spent the money on a copy of *Grand Theft Auto*, which is a computer game?'

'*Grand Theft Auto 5*. It's important. It's better than the other versions. Better optimisation, gameplay, graphics.'

'Speak English, Woodley.'

'I'm just teasing you, boss. It's gaming geek-speak.'

'I understood "graphics".'

'One out of three. Could be worse.'

'You're making me feel old. Haven't you got something better to be getting on with?'

He leaves me with a small salute.

Fraser takes for ever to finish her meeting. As I wait, I toy again with Emma's card. Each new bit of information we get about these boys colours in a little bit more of their lives for me, and makes me feel as if I know them better, but it also increases my anger about the lowlife tactics she's used to get her story.

I find an empty meeting room and call her. I want to make it clear how I feel. Whether she'll listen or not, I don't know, but I'm going to try. The phone rings and rings until I'm certain that I'm going to get her voicemail, and it's only as I'm clearing my throat and wondering whether I'll leave a message, and what I want to say if I do, that she answers.

'Jim.'

So she didn't delete my number, then, and that fact whitewashes my brain momentarily, leaving nothing there apart from regret that I thought that I could handle this call. I push on anyway. I've got no choice now. I can't panic hang-up. It would be too humiliating.

'Hi,' I say.

'It's you.'

'Yes.'

I want to read her the riot act. I intended to. I want to tell her that what she's doing is wrong and unethical and to ask how could she? How could she report on crime in our city so recklessly when she knows what that can do to an investigation, to her former colleagues, and most important of all, to people who are guilty of nothing?

'How are you?'

She floors me once again with that innocuous question, her tone difficult to read, loading those three words with just enough meaning to bring them beyond the level of small talk, but not enough for me to be sure that she cares.

'I'm working the case,' I say. 'The incident by the canal.'

Silence.

'I want you to stop speaking to my witnesses.'

'You have absolutely no right to tell me what to do.'

'What you're doing is wrong. You know it.'

'How dare you?'

I don't even have time to draw breath before she unloads eighteen months' worth of resentment about how badly I treated her, how she deserved more, how I have no right, *absolutely no right at all*, to involve myself in her life now.

'Are you finished?' I ask when she finally runs out of words, because I'm ready to give a piece of my mind right back to her, but I'm saying it to myself because she's hung up.

I'm still staring at my phone, working hard to resist the impulse to throw it across the room, when Woodley pokes his head around the door.

'There you are! The 999 recording's just been emailed to us. Are you all right, boss?'

'I'm fine. Have you listened to it?'

'Are you sure you're all right?'

'If I say I'm fine, I'm sure I'm fine. Have you listened to the recording?'

'No. They only just sent it, and I was thinking about something else. When we were with Janet Pritchard in the Portakabin, she had a phone with a glittery cover. Do you remember?'

'I do.'

'But the phone that rang when we were with her at her shop was an iPhone. It had that distinctive ring tone.'

'New phone?'

'Or she's using two phones. One might be a pay-as-you-go. Explains why she didn't use the Bluetooth in her car if she didn't want to leave a trace of a pay-as-you-go phone.'

'Meaning?'

'I don't know. I'm just thinking out loud. It could be nothing, but there's something that's not sitting quite right with me about her and her partner.'

'Agreed.'

We go back to the incident room where Woodley has the link to the recording up on his screen. It sounds just as Janet Pritchard reported it.

'Hello, emergency services operator, which service do you require?'

'Ambulance.'

'I'll just connect you now.'

A new operator comes on the line.

'What's the nature of your emergency?'

'Somebody's fallen in the canal and I don't know if he can get out.'

'Where is this happening?'

'I'm down at Feeder Canal, at the lock-ups behind Herapath Street.'

'Are there any distinctive features around you?'

'They're in the scrapyard. Hurry!'

'Thank you. I'll send somebody along immediately.'

'The gates are locked.'

'Thank you I'll pass that information on. What is your name, address and your own phone number?'

After Janet Pritchard provides her details, I click stop.

By then it's already possible to hear sirens in the distance as she's speaking. Noah Sadler was lucky the emergency services were so close.

'Did you hear that at the end?' Woodley says. 'Play it again.'

We listen again, taking turns using headphones to drown out the background noise of the office, and both of us clearly hear that there's something else there.

'It sounds like a third party,' Woodley says when he takes the headphones off, 'unless one of the lads has a very deep voice. But I can't make out what they're saying.'

'Do you recall the witness mentioning anybody else?'

He shakes his head. 'She specifically said nobody else was around.'

'Can you ask somebody to try and isolate it so we can hear it better?'

'On it.'

'And tell them I want it today.'

He's already on the phone. A raised finger tells me that's he's heard and understood.

Fraser's door opens and she shakes the hands of the two men who were meeting with her. Once they've gone, she beckons me in.

'A missing persons alert for Abdi Mahad has gone out as widely as possible,' she tells me as I settle down. 'We've made no mention of the fact that he's wanted for question-ing. Priority is to treat him as a vulnerable minor.'

'I think he's been pretty sheltered.'

Her expression's grim. A child at risk will do that to you, and she and I have been in this situation before.

'We'll do a televised appeal as well.'

'I've asked Noah Sadler's family to keep quiet about his death.'

'Can we trust them to do that?'

'I think so. I hope so. The mother's very angry, she wants someone to blame, but she knows it's in her interest to keep quiet because it means Abdi's more likely to come home and give us some answers.'

'Or she could get angry enough to vent all her emotions in the press and screw the case in the process.' Fraser's mood is one of dark pessimism. I need to tread carefully.

'I don't think she will.'

'But you think she holds this Somali kid responsible?'

'I think she might do, but it's a first reaction. It's her grief speaking. Her husband disagrees with her.'

'You should have leaned on the boy to talk, Jim.'

'I know. I played it safe because I didn't want to be accused of putting too much pressure on him. Every time I saw him he was prostrate and mute. I didn't know what else to do. And he comes from a loving home. He hasn't got the profile of a troublemaker.'

'You could have leaned harder.'

I try to distract her. 'I've got my hands on a therapy journal that Noah Sadler wrote. There's a couple of things in it that might be of interest, and I'll keep digging.'

'Dig into his family and the community also, but discreetly, and let's see if that turns anything up. I don't think we can avoid it any longer. Witness?'

'I've spoken to her. She said Emma posed as some kind of victim support worker to get her to talk.'

225

Fraser's nostrils flare.

'The witness said she wouldn't speak to any more journalists.'

'Do you believe her?'

'I'm not a hundred per cent confident, but I'm hopeful. Any news from Janie?' I don't tell Fraser that I've just spoken to Emma. It would be an understatement to say that I don't think she'd appreciate the outcome of that call.

'She's spoken to the paper, but I gather that was something of a dead end. She's pulling together a press release that we hope they'll publish some of. We have to hope they don't link that story and the appeal to find Abdi. I don't want a manhunt on my hands.' She stops banging things around on her desk and points the end of her pen at me. 'I'm very worried about the welfare of this missing lad, just as you are, and I want him found safely, but don't avoid taking him seriously as a suspect because you think his mum and dad are nice. Remember, we're under close scrutiny from all quarters now.'

'That's not what I mean.'

Woodley knocks on the door. 'Sorry to interrupt, but they can deal with the recording now, if we want to go up.'

Fraser flicks her fingers at me in a gesture of dismissal. 'Go.'

I'm expecting a technology den, just like the cliché – a windowless space with overflowing bins and enough wiring to knit a scarf out of. In reality, we find a young, athletic-looking woman in a quiet space on the top floor of the building. She looks very much in control of the tidy suite of monitors in front of her and a healthy pot plant that's in flower on her desk. If she swivelled her chair around, she'd enjoy a view of some of Bristol's painted terraces stacked up on a hill in Bedminster like a row of multicoloured Monopoly houses.

First off, she listens to the recording, and then works her keyboard until she's isolated the sound that we're interested in. At first it's a noise like two deep coughs in a row, more of an outburst of noise than anything else. More tweaking and she's turned it into two words. She plays it repeatedly and screws up her nose as she concentrates.

'Sounds like "Roger Platts",' she says. 'Any idea who Roger Platts is?'

'No.' Woodley shakes his head and looks at me, but I don't know either.

'Can you send it to me?' I say. 'That bit of it.'

'Sure.'

As we leave she starts work on another recording, a phone conversation with contents so immediately sickening that I wonder how many years anybody can last in that job.

By late afternoon, Sofia has a ton of responses to her posts about Abdi. Every single person expresses shock and concern. They all promise to keep an eye out for him and to contact others to ask them to do the same. None of them has heard from him since before the weekend.

One friend writes a long post on Sofia's Facebook page about a former classmate of theirs who disappeared overnight and travelled to Syria to join the jihad. She had been carefully, comprehensively, and secretly radicalised, and nobody had realised until it was too late.

Sofia logs off. She knows this isn't what's happened to Abdi, or at least she's 99 per cent certain. In her family, they would surely have noticed. Nevertheless, she can't help googling the news report on her old school mate, and that inevitably leads to others. She delves into one story after another about good kids around the world who were radicalised and persuaded to flee their new countries to join the jihad, leaving behind desolate loved ones who are reduced to making statements to cameras imploring them to come home, and to hiring mediators to try to extract them from war zones.

It's something every parent and sibling in their community fears: a return of a family member to the violence they risked their lives to flee from. It's an immigrant nightmare. But it's also very rare, Sofia knows that. Most of her friends have too much sense. It's the vulnerable kids who get targeted. Though that thought leads her to ask herself, *Was Abdi vulnerable to such things?*

She's grateful for the distraction when her phone rings.

It's Tim, from the Welcome Centre. 'It's a bit of a long shot,' he says. 'But I asked around and one of my other volunteers, a guy called Dan who was working with Abdi on Friday night, mentioned that Abdi was agitated after your mum fainted and he was asking about a man. Dan hasn't got a phone at the moment but apparently he works at Hamilton House on a Thursday, so you might find him there if you want to talk to him.'

Sofia takes the train again. Hamilton House is only a few minutes' walk from the gallery where Ed Sadler's exhibition is showing. When she gets there, she climbs the steps at the front of the building and skirts around a Staffordshire terrier that's tethered to a railing beside a bowl of water. A couple are having a coffee and a cigarette on the narrow outdoor terrace, wrapped up warmly in colourful layers.

A large Banksy graffiti mural, *The Mild, Mild West* – one of her favourites – is on the side of an adjoining building. The wall opposite has been entirely spray-painted in gold, and a vast mural of Jesus in a loincloth, doing a one-handed handstand, has been painted on it. Sofia has no idea if it's supposed to mean anything.

A woman in the ground-floor cafe directs her to where she can find Dan. On her way she passes yoga classes and artists' studios and finally finds herself in a large space where chairs have been set up in rows facing a screen. Dan's in there, fiddling with a projector. Bursts of sound and motion fill the screen for a few seconds before it dies. It's a black and white film.

He recognises her. It's a relief, because she doesn't know him very well.

'Hey,' he says. 'Sofia?'

They sit on two chairs at the back of the space.

'Can you tell me what Abdi said on Friday?'

'Yeah, I'm really sorry, by the way, that he's disappeared. I'm sure he'll be back. He always seems close to you guys, and he's friends with, like, everyone.'

Sofia feels herself welling up.

'Sorry,' he says. 'I don't mean to upset you. After your mum fainted, everybody got her sitting down and brought her stuff. Amina was all over it, making sure she was OK. Your mum was all sort of glazed and nervous and we were thinking about calling for an ambulance but she totally refused. While she was sitting down, Abdi started looking around the room and asking people if they'd seen a man who had a scar on his top lip. Apparently he was the bloke who was by your mum when she fainted. I don't know if Abdi felt like the man said something horrible or insulting to her and he wanted to have a go at him. But the man was gone. A couple of people remembered him, but nobody knew who he was. We were so busy that night, it was mad. But I remembered Abdi asking, because it wasn't like him to be agitated like that. He calmed down pretty quickly after, and Daniella gave them a lift home. Sounds a bit silly now I say it like that. And you came all the way here. But Abdi *was* looking for a guy, and he didn't seem like himself.'

'It's very helpful, thank you,' Sofia says. 'I'm very grateful.'

'Do you mind if I . . . ' Dan gestures to the screen. 'The film's supposed to start in half an hour.'

He gets up and begins to fiddle with the projector once again. As Sofia stands, it comes to life and she finds herself standing in its glare, black and white images playing out over the front of her coat. She puts up a hand so she can see her way out of the shaft of light.

'Thank you,' she says.

'I don't suppose you want to stay, do you?' he asks.

'No. I need to go home.'

'Of course. But come any time. We do film club every Thursday. You're very welcome. And I hope you find Abdi. I know you will soon. If there's anything else I can do to help ...'

Downstairs she buys a cup of jasmine tea and takes a table where she has a view of the street life. She gets out her phone and looks again at the photo she snapped of the image of the man with the harelip watching football that was on display in the gallery. It's surely too much of a coincidence, she thinks, that the man who caused her mother to faint had a scarred top lip. Does this mean that the man in the photograph is in Bristol? Could that be why Abdi was asking about the photo on the recording? Or is she seeing impossible connections?

She opens Facebook Messenger. The cafe has good WiFi. She clicks on Abdi's name and attaches the photograph to a message.

'What does this mean?' she types below it, and presses 'send'.

She has no idea if it will get to him, but she prays that somehow it will.

It's 6 p.m. when Woodley and I arrive at the boys' school to interview Imran Fletcher-Kapoor about his friendship with Noah and Abdi. We're able to kill two birds with one stone because Alistair Hawkes, the teacher Abdi emailed about his essay and his scholarship concerns, will also be present.

We meet with the headmistress first, to inform her of Noah's death, but ask her to keep the news to herself for the time being. Once she's composed herself, she shows us into a meeting room just off the school's foyer, where Imran's waiting with his mother and the teacher.

'Sarah Fletcher-Kapoor,' says his mother, standing to shake our hands, and adding, 'I'm a solicitor,' as if we were planning to charge her son, instead of chat.

A man in chinos, a dark jacket, and a club tie introduces himself as Alistair Hawkes.

Imran's a fairly slight boy, though I expect he would have dwarfed Noah Sadler. He smiles nicely at us when we're introduced, but bites his fingernails continuously, except when his mother lays a warning hand on his arm. He wears trendy black-rimmed glasses and glances out of the window frequently and longingly.

Before I can begin to ask questions, Sarah Fletcher-Kapoor gets in there: 'Do you want to tell them in your own words, Imran?'

He looks at Woodley and me. It's an assessing glance, which makes me curious as to whether he's going to cough up about the essay he sold. I think he's wondering how much we know.

'You can tell us anything,' I say. 'Everything helps.'

He looks at his mother. She nods encouragement.

'Noah Sadler stopped Abdi from being friends with me.'

The headmistress draws her chin back into her neck, and inhales audibly through her nose. It's a reaction either to the slighting of a boy who can no longer tell his side of the story or to something she considers untrue, or perhaps exaggerated. I'm not sure which.

Sarah Fletcher-Kapoor notices and counter-strikes. 'We complained about it at the time, but nothing was done.'

'Can you tell us a bit more?' I ask.

Imran describes a series of small but slightly unpleasant behaviours that Noah Sadler engaged in when he returned to school after a spell in hospital. They all seemed designed to put an end to a friendship that had developed between Abdi and Imran in Noah's absence.

'If you take each incident separately,' his mother says, 'they're little more than a bit of wrangling over friendships, but taken together there's no question that they constitute low-level bullying.'

Alistair Hawkes shifts in his seat but says nothing. The headmistress remains tight-lipped and still. I'm not too worried about how these things affected Imran, because he looks like a pretty resilient kid to me, but it's interesting to hear more about the power play that was going on between Noah and Imran for Abdi's affections. It's a complicated little triangle.

'How do you think Abdi felt about it?' I ask.

'He really hated it, but he felt like he had to look after Noah.'

'Do you know why he felt that way?'

'Because nobody else likes Noah.'

'Why do you say that?'

'He's quite arrogant. He's all right if you do what he wants, but he tells his mum if you don't and she rings school and says you're bullying him.'

Alistair Hawkes clears his throat and interjects. 'This did happen on one or two occasions.'

'Did you investigate?'

'We looked into it, but the behaviour was more what we would consider high jinks than bullying. Some parents can be very sensitive to that kind of thing, though, and especially with Noah's medical history, I think his mother felt that he might suffer more than some of our more robust students. Mr Jacobson spoke to the boys involved.'

The big man we interviewed previously, by the squash courts.

I catch Imran's eye. 'How did Abdi feel about his friendship with Noah? Did he talk about it?'

He shrugs. 'Not really. A bit.'

'Can you remember what he said?'

'He said it was intense sometimes.'

'In what way?'

'Because Noah was clingy.'

'Anything else?'

'Maybe Noah was competitive sometimes.'

'Competitive over what?'

'Chess, and sometimes schoolwork.' He looks at his mum. 'I didn't get involved in that.'

'Were they good friends to each other as well, or was it all competition?'

'They're best friends. They make each other laugh. It's kind of annoying sometimes.'

'Are you jealous of their friendship?' I'm having to make a conscious effort not to refer to Noah in the past tense.

Imran shakes his head. 'When I started at this school I wanted to be friends with Abdi, but it wasn't really worth it when Noah got back from hospital because he made it difficult.'

'Did you feel cross about that?'

'A bit, at first, but I made new friends.'

He smiles, and I believe him. He gives the impression of being pretty socially adept. I'm guessing he finds it fairly easy to make friends.

His mother looks from me to Woodley and back again, and straightens her back. 'Is that everything? Imran has a karate lesson to get to.'

'There's just one more thing I wanted to ask you about, Imran,' I say. 'It won't take a minute and then you can go. You've been a brilliant help so far.'

He relaxes into a Cheshire cat smile, pleased that he's aced it, sensing freedom.

'It's about an essay.'

The smile falls from his face.

'Do you know what I'm talking about?'

'No.'

'Did you ever write an essay and sell it to either Abdi or Noah?'

A shake of his head, but he's not an accomplished liar. His eyes dart around the room as he tries to assemble an explanation. His mother slumps back in her seat, looking as if she's sucking a lemon. There's no surprise on her face or the faces of the teachers in the room. They all know about this already, just as I thought.

'I helped Abdi with an essay,' is what he comes up with.

'Can you explain exactly what you mean by "helped"?' I want details.

'Abdi was behind with his work and he didn't have time to do the essay.' Imran glances at the staff. 'So I helped him.'

'Once again, how exactly did you help him?'

He chews a nail. 'I wrote the essay for him.'

'And you were aware of this?' I ask the headmistress.

'Indeed. We dealt with it according to our procedures, and Imran's mother was informed.'

Sarah Fletcher-Kapoor confirms this with a curt nod.

'Did you do that often?' I ask.

'Just one time. Abdi was really stressed.'

'Abdi was offered support with his organisation. The incident was dealt with appropriately for each of the boys concerned.' Alistair Hawkes sticks his oar in. With thumb and forefinger, he worries at the corner of a piece of paper that's protruding from a file on his knee. Discomfort or boredom, it's hard to tell.

'Did you inform his parents?' I'm wondering why they didn't mention it to us.

'We wrote to them. It was their preferred method of communication because of the language issues.'

I nod, and think how easy it would have been for Abdi to intercept a letter or mistranslate it for his mother.

Sarah Fletcher-Kapoor raises her eyebrows at me and draws her handbag onto her knee, signalling that we've taken up enough of her time and her son's. 'Are we done here? I don't think Imran has anything else to add.'

Imran looks at me intently, and for the first time he doesn't fidget. He knows we're not finished yet.

'How much money did you get for the essay, Imran?'

'What?' his mother says, and the staff sit up straighter, tenser, too. They obviously weren't aware that Imran was profiting financially from his essay writing.

'Twenty pounds, thirty pounds? Forty?'

Imran shakes his head vigorously, but I need him to admit to this. It's important to know whether Noah was buying favours for Abdi or Abdi was doing it himself. It will tell me where the power lay in the relationship between them.

Woodley says: 'A copy of *Grand Theft Auto 5* costs forty quid if you buy it new, I'm guessing, so it had to be in that region. Though if you buy it second hand from a friend or maybe a sixth-former, it could be less.'

'What do you think, Imran?' I say.

I think I can spy a little bit of temper behind his eyes, though he's containing it very effectively. He knows he's busted, but he gives it one last go anyway.

'I don't know,' he says.

'Imran doesn't play violent games,' his mother says. 'We would never let him have a game like that.' But as she says the words, I can see the pieces slotting together in her mind. 'You sold that essay? You sold an essay so you could buy a copy of a violent computer game without us knowing? Imran! Answer me!'

I feel a bit sorry for Imran. It wasn't the nicest thing to do, to catch him out like that, but I get the feeling that he'll bounce back.

He's hanging his head while his mother berates him and the frowns deepen on the teachers' foreheads, but I bet his brain is working at a hundred miles an hour to work out how to minimise the damage, and he comes up with a response impressively quickly.

'I'm really sorry, Mum,' he says. 'I did do it, but I hated the game when I tried it. I gave it away. It was horrible. I promise you, I threw it away. I felt ashamed.'

'Who paid for the essay?' I ask him. 'Noah or Abdi?'

'It was Noah. He bought it for Abdi because Abdi didn't have the money.'

Woodley and I leave them in the meeting room shortly afterwards.

'I don't think Imran's going to make it to karate tonight,' Woodley says.

'Very entrepreneurial kid.' I'll admit I feel a small amount of respect for him. I would never have dared to do anything like that at school.

'Makes me very glad I didn't become a teacher,' Woodley says. 'Can you imagine listening to all those excuses and lies over and over again?'

'Sounds a bit like policing.'

'OK, yeah, fair point. But at least we can slap a pair of cuffs on them if we catch them, and their mothers don't get involved. Honestly, what was she like? "I'm a solicitor."' He mimics Sarah Fletcher-Kapoor very well.

It makes me laugh, so I don't remind him of Ben Finch's mother, Rachel, or of Fiona Sadler and Maryam Mahad: all mothers who couldn't avoid being involved in their sons' misfortune.

Brake lights flare around us as we join rush-hour traffic on the way back to HQ. I feel as if my picture of Noah Sadler's personality is sharpening. He was very unwell, desperate for friendship, and smart enough to use all of his resources to keep it. But I wonder if he alienated Abdi with his efforts, or if Abdi enjoyed the attention and the academic help.

It's Abdi who I find to be the more elusive character. I'm interested to know that he struggled with his studies sometimes, in spite of being very capable. I wonder how much the pressure of achieving got to him or if, as Imran said, this essay incident was a one-off. Either way, it doesn't shed a great deal of clarity on the case. An over-protective friendship could give Abdi a motive to hurt Noah if things had got so intense that he snapped and lost his temper with Noah. But it would be odd for this to happen by the canal, as the location implies a fair amount of planning by the boys to get there. My instinct tells me that there was no premeditation here, just an accident. But then what about the witness . . . ?

My frustration is building as each bit of information we find seems to put weight on a different side of the scales, balancing the probabilities that either one of the boys was more likely to cause trouble for the other. I also know we have only a small window to gather information discreetly. We can't keep Noah's death from the public for much longer, and there's the possibility that when it comes out all hell will break loose.

'Do you know what?' I say to Woodley. He's tapping his fingers on the wheel to a tune from the nineties. 'It's just our bloody luck that this case is a media magnet.'

He glances at me. 'You mean after the Ben Finch case?'

'It's the last thing I need. They're going to be crawling

all over us as soon as they find out that Noah Sadler's died. You know that if they can, they're going to politicise this case because of the boys' backgrounds, and that includes every bloody move we make. I don't want to be working in a goldfish bowl again.'

'Media up every orifice,' he says.

'Well, I wouldn't put it quite like that.'

'We're making progress, boss. It's all we can do.'

He's right. I must hold my nerve. This case is my chance to prove myself again but I can't make a silk purse out of a sow's ear. 'It is,' as my mother would have said, 'what it is.' That expression of pragmatism got her up every morning and sent her to bed every night, with everything around her in its rightful place, as she thought it should be. Except for her confidence in herself, which was destroyed so comprehensively by my father that she was never able to put it back together.

When I finally get home my sister's plate-eyed in front of the TV again, although the swelling on her face looks better and she's cooked us a casserole. The only thing ringing alarm bells is that she's developed a furtive addiction to her phone.

'Is that him?' I ask as our meal is interrupted for the fourth time by a text arriving.

'Are you my babysitter now?'

'I thought you cut contact with him.'

'It's complicated.'

She and I inherited my father's eyes. Brown-gold. A compelling, evasive colour. For a second, I feel like I'm looking at him.

'Becky.'

'You're not my babysitter. Let me handle this my own way.'

She snatches up our empty plates and leaves the room, taking her phone with her.

I tune into the late edition of the local news and I'm pleased to see they're rerunning the TV appeal that went out live at six. Fraser taped it from the steps of Kenneth Steele House while Woodley and I were at the school. It's another echo of the Ben Finch case, though I was beside her that night.

She describes Abdi Mahal as 'a fifteen-year-old school-boy of Somali origin'.

'This behaviour is very out of character for Abdi, and we're very concerned about his well-being,' she adds, looking directly into the camera. 'If you know where Abdi is, please contact us. We want to stress that Abdi is *not* in trouble.' The number to call scrolls along the bottom of the screen. Fraser's done a good job: firm but friendly; concerned but not panicky.

Becky's back, watching from the doorway. 'Is that your case?'

'It is.'

She sits down beside me. She's left her phone in the other room.

'How long's he been missing?'

'Nearly twenty-four hours. His friend died last night.'

'Oh god, that's terrible. Is that why he's run away?'

'We don't think he knows.'

'You look tired.'

'Why are you being so nice all of a sudden?' I'm trying to lighten the mood. I don't want to go over and over the case.

'You think that's insulting? Rephrasing: you look like shit.'

'Not as bad as you.'

'You got me there.' She touches her eye gingerly with the tips of her fingers. 'Can I ask a nosy question?'

'No.'

'Do you have a girlfriend? I wasn't prying, but I noticed some stuff in the bathroom cupboard.'

'We broke up.'

'When?'

'A long time ago. I forgot her stuff was there.'

'Did you love her?'

'Get straight to the point, why don't you?'

'Are you embarrassed?'

'No.'

'Then answer.'

'Yes, I loved her.'

'Then you know how it feels for me.'

So that's what she's playing at. She's justifying herself.

'The big difference is that neither of us was abusing the other.'

'He can't help himself,' she says, and I can't believe my own clever, resourceful sister is spouting this clichéd stuff about a violent partner. 'The things he's been through, he never had a chance to grow up normally. He's trying, but it's what he knew.'

'That's not an excuse.'

'I'm not excusing him, I'm trying to explain.'

I'm angry now. 'He's an adult. He's responsible for his own behaviour. It's a choice, Becky.'

'It's not always a choice for him!'

'That's the kind of attitude that starts by letting him off the hook if he says pretty-please-I'm-sorry-have-a-five-quid-bunch-of-flowers-to-make-up-for-your-broken-skin-and-oops!-the-broken-bones, and ends with you in hospital! I've seen it happen. More than once!'

She stares at me. 'I thought you'd understand.'

'I thought you were smarter than this. People have to be accountable for what they do, even if you love them.'

'I'm your sister, Jim, not some bugger you've just arrested who needs the riot act read. I told you, it's complicated!'

'Becky—'

'I don't need to listen to this. I'll be out of your hair tomorrow night.'

'You don't need to be.'

'Good night.'

She slams the door of my bedroom and shuts herself in there for the rest of the night.

When the clock tells me it's time to sleep, I don't even try. I throw open the window again, longing to feel the outside air, wondering not for the first time if my insomnia is a form of claustrophobia: a fear of spending time with my own thoughts, a fear that they'll box me in.

My bedroom door is still firmly shut, so I can't get any stuff. I lie down on the sofa in my clothes. Through the window I have a perfect view of the night sky, which is clear tonight, and a smattering of stars is visible. I think of the Sadlers rattling around that big house with only their grief for company. I think of Becky and her boyfriend and all the ways we can feel trapped by our circumstances. I think of the boy who is missing, and hope that he's resourceful and safe, and say a prayer to a god I don't believe in that Abdi Mahad doesn't have blood on his hands.

DAY 4

Nur Mahad can't sleep. He lies awake and his mind roams through his past, searching for things that might help him to understand his present. Just as Maryam does, Nur cherishes a store of warm memories of his childhood in Hargeisa. It was a chaotic and happy time of his life that revolved around his mother and father, his father's second wife who lived next door, and his many siblings and half-siblings.

Nur also remembers in detail the day his childhood ended.

When he woke that morning, the sky was a clear pale blue, and outside his bedroom window a flock of small birds filled the branches of a tree. They called to one another in a non-stop chatter that sounded sweet and sharp all at once. Nur was nine years old and a primary school pupil. He worshipped his big brother Farah, who was stirring in the bed next to his. Nur opened his window to hear the birds better, but the sound of the latch startled them and they rose swiftly all at once, like a handful of sand thrown into the air.

On the way to school Farah told Nur they couldn't walk together because Farah had to be somewhere. 'Don't follow me,' he said.

Nur kicked a stone as he walked, stuck with their

half-sister Fatima, who had a fear of stray dogs and peered cautiously around every corner in search of them.

They heard the chanting a few minutes later.

'We want to see our teachers, and we want to see them now!'

Bigger boys and girls were gathered outside June 26 School in a large crowd. Farah was amongst them. The children formed a column and began to march from the school towards the centre of town, fists pumping the air in time with their words. Some banged drums.

'What are they doing?' Fatima asked.

'The government put their teachers in prison,' Nur told her. 'They want them to be set free.' He feels grand telling her this, because he's heard the grown-ups talking about it. 'The teachers have barristers from Mogadishu,' he added, even though he didn't know what a barrister was.

Fatima took Nur's hand as the older children marched past, and they followed, sucked in by the strangeness and the energy of the sight. Children from other schools joined as the march continued through the city, all their different coloured uniforms mingling. They walked past the tuberculosis hospital and didn't stop until they reached the space in front of the National Security Court. Some of the children had picked up stones along the way. Nur and Fatima hung back, watching from a junction with a side street. They leaned against a shop wall, where pictures of the goods on sale were painted boldly. On the steps of the Security Court, Nur could see soldiers wearing red berets standing with their legs apart. The sun licked their hard-set faces and the barrels of their guns. The berets cast shadows over their eyes.

More children arrived, packing the space, and the chanting grew louder. A portrait of the president hung on the front of the court building. In the morning air the children's shirts looked bright, clean white. A red beret stepped forward with a megaphone and commanded the children to leave.

Beside Nur, Fatima shrank back. 'I want to go home,' she said.

'Go then,' Nur told her.

He was transfixed by the scene. As she scampered away, the sky above Nur exploded with noise. The red berets were firing their guns over the children's heads. The shots were followed by thuds, a series of them. The children were throwing stones in return. They smashed the windows of the courthouse, and the soldiers took cover to avoid the flying splinters of glass. The gunfire ceased momentarily, like a breath held, before the red berets regrouped, aimed their guns directly into the mob of children and fired.

The crackling of gunfire froze Nur to the spot, but a hand grabbed his elbow from behind and pulled him roughly into the shop, where a man held him tightly behind the doorframe. 'Stay still,' he commanded. Nur could feel their hearts beating.

Outside, vehicles began to arrive, engines growling. The children who'd stood their ground scattered now, wild-eyed and fearful.

'What's happening?' A woman's voice issued from behind the shop counter.

'They've sent in the military,' the man told her. 'Against children.'

She beckoned to them from her hiding spot. 'Bring the boy here.'

Nur and the man scuttled across the floor of the shop like lizards, and the woman pulled Nur towards her, shielding him with her body. The sounds of shouting and running and gunfire persisted. The couple threw themselves flat, pulling Nur with them so all three were lying in a tangle of clothing, faces pressed onto the gritty floor amongst little spills of maize and rice and sugar. In the doorway, a silhouette appeared: a boy, in school uniform, about the same age as Nur's brother.

'Here!' Nur cried, reaching out towards him.

'Come on!' the woman called, 'Come on, boy!'

He didn't move quickly enough.

There was another crack of gunfire and his body buckled, but it didn't fall at first. He exhaled with a gasp. His hand went to his chest just before his knees gave way and he collapsed.

The shots were still coming. Cans and bottles tumbled from the shelves above, punctured by bullets, their contents exploding. The boy landed on a sack of flour and his blood soaked into the hessian. Nur saw that the boy's eyes were open, but he wasn't living behind them any longer, and he saw that the boy's blood was so eager to flee his body that it even ran from the corner of his gaping mouth.

Nur began to scream. It felt as if he had only just stopped when he heard news that evening that his brother, Farah, had lost his life to the guns, too.

After that, Nur hated to be in Hargeisa.

The police didn't just take the life of his brother; they took his father, too. He was arrested one night by three men who knocked politely at the door at two in the morning. Nur's mother screamed as they marched him to their Land Rover. One of the soldiers returned to the house and drove the end of his rifle into her stomach.

The charge against Nur's father was never clear. Nur's mother took food to the prison for him every day for weeks until a guard took pity on her and explained that her husband had died many days ago. 'Of illness,' the guard said.

Nur's father had been healthy when he was arrested.

The two widows bereaved by Nur's father's death pooled their resources and made covert arrangements for transport the next day. The second wife had cousins in Yemen, so she travelled to the coast. Nur's mother went north, towards Djibouti, in the hope that relatives could help her settle there. Nur travelled with her and his baby brother, and on the way, in the back of the car, his mother told her sons stories about their father. She told them how he was an intelligent man and a good man, and Nur made a silent vow that he would try to be the same.

Somebody hammers on the window of his cab. A businessman. Nur rolls the window down. He's parked outside Temple Meads station.

'I'm not working,' he says.

'Then why the fuck are you parked here?'

'The queue for the taxi rank is over there.'

Once the businessman has gone, Nur walks along the

row of waiting taxis at the rank and stops at the driver's window of each one. He asks his colleagues to look out for Abdi. He hands each of them a photograph of the boy. To a man, they promise to help.

Fiona Sadler's been prepared for many years for the fact that her son Noah might die. She's a person who likes to try to face up to things. On the sly, she's even read books about bereavement, though she hid them from her husband and son. The books didn't prepare her for how it feels, though. She knows that the first stage of grief is denial, but she hadn't expected her sense of injustice to be so crushingly strong. She feels robbed of her child. She wants somebody to pay for what's happened, and she's never felt so lonely, even in all the years when she had to care for Noah by herself because Ed was away.

She bitterly resents the fact that Abdi Mahad was the last person to be with Noah. After everything, Fiona can't stand the thought that Noah's last moments of consciousness didn't belong to her. The thought eats away at her. Until now Fiona's always felt guilty that she didn't like Abdi. She's examined her motives for disliking him over and over again, because she knows that Abdi's a nice boy. He gives every appearance of being nice, anyhow. But she resented the spell he cast on her son, the way that Noah seemed almost obsessed with the friendship and clung to it as if it were a lifeline. She resented the fact that Abdi was healthy, too, that he was able to come and go at the hospital, perching on the end of Noah's bed, all alert, all clever, while her son winced and her fingers curled as she witnessed how much pain he put himself through to be better able to talk to his friend.

She's not so foolish that she wasn't aware of these emotions, and she was afraid to admit them to Ed, because he would have had no tolerance for them. Her awareness didn't erase the feelings, though. Far from it. They were deeply felt but furtive, and because of that, they were never debated or hung out to air, so they grew stronger.

She lies in bed and stares out of the window. She returns time and time again to the same idea: if Noah hadn't been friendly with Abdi, this wouldn't have happened. Noah came to harm because of Abdi.

The house is cold and she's burrowed almost entirely under her bed linen. Her hair is greasy. She can't be bothered to shower. She feels as empty as a husk. Through the window, she can see clouds hanging motionless, in layers of pale yellow and grey blue. One band glows paler than the rest, so bright it makes her blink. They're spring clouds. It feels impossible to Fiona that it can remain a season of growth and new life outside, when her whole world has petrified.

On her bedside table, the landline starts to ring. She stares at it, wondering that she never noticed before how piercing the sound it makes is. Then she reaches for it. The call screening shows an unknown number.

Fiona answers because she wants the chance to make somebody else's life hell, to hurt a stranger because she herself is hurting. 'How dare you cold-call me when my son died yesterday?' she imagines herself saying. 'How could you?' It will be a small and random hurt she inflicts, but it will make her feel better.

'Yes.' Fiona's voice croaks when she speaks, surprising her. It's not the strident, self-righteous tone she was imagining herself using.

'Mrs Sadler? This is Emma Zhang. I'm a journalist for the *Bristol Echo*. I spoke to your husband the other day at the hospital, and I wrote a short article about the case. I was wondering if you would care to talk to me a little more about what's happened to your son, Noah? I believe he may have been the victim of a crime and I'm keen to help you get the justice he deserves. How is he doing?'

Oh! Fiona thinks. *She doesn't know he died.*

Downstairs Ed Sadler is roused from a heavy, nightmare-ridden sleep by the ringing of the landline. He's stretched out on the sofa in his study, stiff and uncomfortable. Cold. He's still wearing yesterday's clothes.

It was hard to be near Fiona last night. He's always suspected that it would be like this when Noah finally died, that they would deal with it separately, just as they've dealt with the illness itself. He feels scraped out, nauseous and disorientated, as if time isn't behaving normally, but warping around him, emphasising the fact that where he once had a son, there's now a void.

Another part of him feels relief, though he'd never admit that to anybody.

He found it unbearably difficult to watch his son go through treatment. He feared more than anything else that the cancer would drag Noah to his death slowly and painfully. He knew he couldn't stand to watch the tubes being removed from his son's body when the time came to let him go; he couldn't count the breaths that would be so painful for Noah to take in his last days and hours. He couldn't swab his parched lips.

Ed lost his mother to cancer, so he knows how it goes at the end. They have at least been spared that. He knows he can't say this to Fiona, though. She's always been touchy with him when they discuss Noah, and quick to accuse him of not suffering as much as she has as the illness progressed. It's not true, it's just that Ed internalises his pain rather than displays it. It means it sometimes emerges in flashes of anger or reckless behaviour, often on location. But he knows that Fiona wanted to see him hurt more right in front of her eyes, so she could be sure that the depth of his response matched her own, and that she wasn't suffering alone.

He never could do it, though. It felt more important to be strong in front of Noah, to bring some lightness to the boy's life, until the next time Ed packed his bag and set off for the airport.

He groans softly as he manoeuvres himself into a sitting position. The bureaucracy of death looms. There will be things they have to do, a funeral to arrange. He stands, opens the shutters, and squints into the wash of tepid morning light, and he too notices the stripes the clouds have made in the sky.

When he turns away from the window, he sees the papers on his office table that relate to Hartisheik refugee camp. Once again, his mind fights its way back through the past few days, until he reaches the evening of his private view, and the conversation he had with Abdi late that night. He was home, he was drunk, and he was sitting in his office at the end of the most bittersweet night of his life. Abdi knocked on the door.

'Mr Sadler?'

'Come on in!' Ed had been glad to see somebody. He wasn't quite ready to let go of the night yet. He'd been disappointed to find all the lights out in the house when he got home, even though it wasn't very late.

He poured himself a nightcap.

'Do you want one?' he asked Abdi.

'No, thank you.' The boy was embarrassed. Always such a modest, polite boy.

'Sorry! I forgot. You're Muslim.'

'I'm too young, Mr Sadler.'

'Too young. Of course. Though at your age I'd already drunk my fair share of beers.'

Ed winces at the memory of his insensitivity. Did he really say that? He has a very bad habit of losing polite filters when he's had a beer or two. He's got into more than one or two fights at hotel bars around the world as a result. But he's also managed to bed one or two women he wouldn't have dared to proposition otherwise.

He shakes his head. That's a terrible thought to have on this day of all days. What's wrong with him?

Ed remembers that Abdi sat down beside him and asked him about Hartisheik camp and what it was like there. He remembers that he showed Abdi all the paperwork and the map he had in his files. So it wasn't much, then, the conversation, Ed thinks. Just a chat, stimulated by what Abdi had seen in the exhibition. Of course the boy was bound to be interested. It was his heritage, after all.

Nothing else about the conversation comes back to Ed, although he has a niggling feeling there's something he's not remembering. He shrugs it off quickly, though. The past few days have been mind-blowingly difficult, he tells himself. It's nothing. Ed just hopes he didn't tell the boy how shit-scared he felt most of the time he was there. How he dreaded the thought of being kidnapped. Couldn't wait to get back to Addis Ababa.

From upstairs, he can hear her voice. She must have answered that phone call. He's about to go to her when he finds he can't face it. He sinks back down onto the sofa.

'Noah!' he says, and his voice cracks.

It's a long time before he's able to stop sobbing. The feeling of missing his child is like hearing a shrill, high note on a violin that's never going to stop.

News first thing in the morning is that Noah Sadler's computer has thrown up some interesting internet search history results from late on Monday night, during the hours we believe that he and Abdi were at home after the exhibition opening and before they left the house. One of the tech team talks Woodley and me through their findings.

'We obviously don't know for certain which of the boys used this computer on Monday night, because it's not password protected, so it could have been anybody in the house,' he says. 'But we can have a good guess from the results. There's a little bit of internet activity from earlier in the day on Monday. It's fairly typical of all the other days that we looked at in the week preceding, so I think it's safe to assume that this usage is Noah Sadler's. On Monday afternoon he looked up images of Pero's Bridge, and Google Maps of Bristol city centre, and then he looked up the film *Alien* on IMDb, which he'd done before, and followed the links to some of the cast and articles about it. That activity ceases at five p.m. and the next time somebody uses the computer to go online is at eleven-thirty p.m. At that time somebody logs onto Abdi Mahad's personal email account and downloads a photograph.'

'So we think it was Abdi?'

'Unless Noah Sadler knew how to log on to his account.'

'Do we have access to those emails?'

'Not yet. We're working on the password. But we can see that Abdi or somebody else accessed them, downloaded this picture and sent it to print. He logged off after that.'

'There was a printer in Noah's room,' Woodley says, 'but nothing in it.'

'The computer's linked to two printers,' the tech officer says, 'so it could have gone to another location. A home office, maybe?'

'Do you know what the photograph was of?'

'Here.'

The tech officer extracts an A4-sized image from a document folder and hands it to me. The photograph is of a group of men and boys gathered around a television watching a football match. They look African. It's got to be the photograph that Abdi was asking Ed Sadler about in the audio recording.

I hand it to Woodley. 'What else does this person look at online?'

'They look at Ed Sadler's website: every page and every photograph. It's very thorough.'

'Is that photograph on the site?'

'No. And it looks to be a photograph of a photograph, as if it was taken with a phone.'

'Abdi might have snapped it at the exhibition,' Woodley says.

That's what I'm thinking, but I'm trying to be cautious and methodical, too. 'If we assume it was Abdi who downloaded it, that is.'

'It's got to be. Why would Noah Sadler be looking at his dad's website or going on Abdi's personal email?'

Woodley sounds frustrated with me, and I might feel the same, if I were him, but I don't want to make assumptions that might blind us to a different version of events. Even so, I'm getting a feeling that's part excitement and part unease. We're finally starting to put together pieces. The only problem is that so far they seem to be for the wrong puzzle, because I can't yet see how any of this relates to the boys' movements on Monday night.

'Anything else?'

'He searched for "facial reconstruction", and that throws up all sorts of links, some of which he follows. Then he refines it to "cleft palate surgery", and also "cleft palate surgery Somalia".'

'So he could be looking for a way this man might have corrected his appearance?'

'Exactly.'

'There's one more thing. He also looks up a football website, a history of the Champions League.'

Woodley looks at the printed-out photograph. He taps it with two fingers. 'Because that's a Champions League game,' he says. 'He was trying to find out about the game the men are watching in the picture.'

'Why would he do that?'

'I don't know. To find out which game it was? He's a proper little Google-sleuth, isn't he?'

'But what the hell takes him from a bit of cosy internet searching all the way across the city to the scrapyard just a couple of hours later?'

Woodley shrugs. 'I don't know, boss.'

'That's everything,' the tech officer says. 'There's no activity after eleven-thirty-seven.'

I phone Sofia Mahad while the tech officer takes Woodley through the internet activity one more time. I want to talk to her about the photograph that Abdi discussed with Ed Sadler in the recording.

'I went to look at that photograph,' she says. 'In the gallery. I wanted to see it for myself.'

'Did you recognise any of the men in it? In particular, the man with the cleft palate, in the middle of the picture?'

'I don't recognise him, but this is the man Abdi was interested in. Abdi was looking for a man with a scar on his lip at the Welcome Centre. He thought the man upset my mother. I was going to phone you this morning and tell you.'

'Have your parents seen the photograph?'

'Not yet. I'll show them.'

'Please can you ask them if they recognise that man?'

'Of course.'

I don't give her any details about the internet searches we've uncovered. I want to keep it on a need-to-know basis for now, but everything she's telling me is adding up with what we've discovered.

When I hang up, I relay everything to Woodley.

Woodley says: 'We should show the photograph to Kirsty Harris. She's the liaison officer for the Somali community. She might have come across this man if he's been in Bristol for a while, or know someone in the community we could talk to. But I was thinking maybe we should send it to Jamie Silva, too.'

'Who's he?'

'He's a PC. He was tapped last year by a brand new unit in London called the Super-Recognisers. They asked him to join them.'

'Super-Recognisers?' It's a new one to me.

'It's a really small unit, only six or seven officers, and they all have exceptional abilities to remember faces and recognise suspects. They wanted Jamie to join them, but he said no because he didn't want to leave Bristol.'

'Because it's the best city in the UK,' says the tech officer, who's listening as he packs up his laptop.

'You think he can recognise this man?'

'He can if we have a picture of this guy on a database

already. Jamie will probably remember seeing him before, and if he doesn't, he'll search through them.'

'What makes him a better bet for that than one of our DCs?'

'The Super-Recognisers are the opposite of people who have face blindness. Face-blind people can't remember faces. It affects more people than you might think. In contrast, the officers in the Super-Recogniser Unit have almost total recall of every face they've ever seen.'

'How do you know all this?'

'Jamie's a mate. We joined the force at the same time. He was bragging about it after he got tapped. And if you go out for a drink with him, he'll happily wreck your evening by identifying every criminal in the room. There's no such thing as off-duty for him.'

'OK. Definitely worth a try. Send it over to him now.'

The call from DI Clemo puts Sofia even more on edge. She checks Facebook every five minutes to see if Abdi's replied, but there's nothing. She can see that he hasn't even looked at the message she sent him yet.

She decides to show her mum the photograph, as she promised the detective she would. She finds it on her phone. She's also desperate to ask her mum if she deleted the recording on purpose. She's been waiting for the right moment, but her nerve fails her. She breathes deeply before leaving her bedroom. She requires courage to approach her mum.

Maryam's cooking. She's embarked on a laborious recipe for a sweet Somali treat that her own mother used to make on special occasions. Maryam didn't learn the recipe from her mother. They left Hargeisa when she was too young. She was taught it by Amina, who discovered that Maryam yearned to taste it again. They worked together one morning in Amina's kitchen soon after they met. Abdi slept peacefully, bound to Maryam's back as they worked, and when the *balbalow* were finished and she bit into one, she did something rare. She cried. She has no idea why she's making *balbalow* now, in the midst of this crisis, but she doesn't know what else to do.

Sofia arrives in the kitchen almost silently, startling Maryam. '*Balbalow*?' she asks.

Maryam nods, and continues to knead the white dough that she's made. The sensation of it underneath her fingers helps her to feel steady, as if her world isn't spiralling out of control.

'Will you look at something for me?' Sofia asks. She's holding her phone.

'In a minute.'

Sofia steps out of the room and Maryam keeps kneading. She feels as if she can't break her rhythm as if to do so would be bad luck. When the dough's formed and smooth, she puts it back into the bowl where she mixed it with her fingers, and leaves it to rest.

She wipes her hands and goes to find her daughter.

When Sofia shows her the photograph, Maryam has an instant reaction, just as she did at the Welcome Centre. It's physical, visceral and overwhelming. She grips the back of a chair and tries to stay upright, but a strong rush of nausea makes the world around her tilt.

When she comes around, she's prostrate on the sofa. Sofia's hovering beside her, staring at her anxiously.

'*Hooyo*,' Sofia says, using the Somali word for mother that softens Maryam, softens them both. 'Are you all right? What happened?'

'I don't feel so well.'

'Was it the photograph?'

'I think I need to shut my eyes for a while.'

Behind her closed eyelids Maryam fights to quell a flow of memories from the camp. She arrived there as a girl, grew up there, got a rudimentary education there, married there and gave birth to all of her children there, except one. Many of her memories feel as if they've been stamped into her mind. They are vivid imprints. She cannot erase them.

Sofia's voice interrupts her. 'Mum. Please don't sleep. I need you to tell me why Abdi was obsessed with this photo. I think he was, but I don't know why. Please, Mum.'

Maryam feels her daughter's slight hand shaking her shoulder and forces herself to open her eyes. 'Where did you get this photo?' she asks.

'I went to Ed Sadler's exhibition. I wanted to see the picture Abdi talked about in the recording. You remember? This is it. The detective phoned me to ask if any of us recognise this man.'

'Show it to me again.'

Maryam's glad she's already lying down when another look at the photograph confirms what she already knew. It is him: the man with the split lip and the teeth like a scatter of broken rocks. She'd almost missed making the connection at the Welcome Centre. She knew the man standing opposite her was familiar; she'd spotted the scar on his upper lip. But it wasn't until she heard him speaking to somebody beside him in a thick, slurred voice, a voice that she last heard so many years ago and could never forget, that she knew who he was, and the skin on the back of her neck began to crawl.

'Abdi doesn't know this man,' she tells Sofia. 'This man is nothing to do with him.'

'What else, then? What could he have seen in the picture?'

Maryam studies it. There are other familiar faces amongst the men, one in particular.

'There it is,' she tells Sofia. She points at a profile buried in the shadows of the photo, at the end of a row of boys. 'It's Hassan Omar Mohammed.' She names a family friend, another Somali who came to Bristol via Hartisheik.

Sofia zooms in and frowns as she looks at the face her mum is pointing to. She would never have recognised Hassan.

'Are you sure?' she asks.

'Completely sure! You don't believe me? Look! It's even football he's got his eyes glued to.'

Hassan's known to be football mad. His prized possession nowadays is a season ticket for Bristol City football club. Sofia looks at the face again, seeing more familiarity in it this time, but she's not buying into her mother's certainty that this is Hassan. The boy could be anybody.

Maryam is looking at her expectantly, so Sofia feels

obliged to reply, 'OK, yes, I guess that looks like Hassan,' even though she doesn't believe it.

Maryam unexpectedly takes her daughter in her arms, surprising her. Sofia clasps her back and finds an extraordinary comfort in the ferocity of her mother's embrace. In fact, Maryam's not sure if it is a younger Hassan in the photograph, though it's not impossible.

'I think the dough has rested,' she says when she's released Sofia. 'Will you help me make the *balbalow*?'

It will be a distraction, she thinks, and Sofia's glad of the chance to feel normal for just a few minutes. The recording has slipped from her mind. Side by side they roll out squares of the dough until it's thin enough to see through. They share Maryam's serrated cutting tool and each drives lines through their piece of dough so that it separates into small rectangles. Maryam shapes her rectangles into a butterfly, nipping the sides of each one together in the middle, so the wings fan out on either side. Sofia bends a ridge up the centre of hers and then brings up each side, pinching them together at either end, to make the shape of a boat.

They work in silence, each thinking. Maryam's trying to work out whether her suspicions about Abdi are one step closer to being true, now that she's seen this photograph. She tries to imagine Ed Sadler at the camp. She never saw him there, but it was a very big place. Foreigners came in and out, doling out aid, setting up facilities, medical, educational, or something other, their numbers in flux depending on the political situation. Some would give gifts to the children – sweets, mostly. Others kept a distance or left almost as soon as they had arrived. Unlike the families, they had that freedom.

Sofia feels the relief of spending a few minutes being a child, under the wing of her mother, but she remains very uneasy. By the time the *balbalow* are arranged in neat rows, none of them touching, Sofia can't hold back any longer, because there's something else she's desperate to tell Maryam.

'But Abdi was looking for somebody at the Welcome Centre,' she blurts out. 'A man with a scar on his top lip.'

Maryam catches her breath. Holds it. Composes herself. 'So what?' she says, 'It could have been anybody.'

But her eyes cloud, and Sofia sees it. Maryam leans heavily on the kitchen counter, and bows her head.

'You should lie down again, *Hooyo*,' Sofia says. 'I think we might need to take you to the doctor.'

Maryam refuses. She starts to wash up. She hopes she's managed to divert Sofia from the truth. When she glances up at her reflection in the kitchen window she doesn't see her own face, but that of the man she fears. He doesn't have his new face, the one she saw at the refugee centre, with the sewn-up lip and corrected teeth, but the old one: gashed and ugly. His eyes were the same, though, both times she saw him. They're the kind of eyes where evil pools.

She's absolutely certain now that Abdi knows more than he should.

Emma Zhang and Fiona Sadler meet at the Avon Gorge Hotel. The morning's sunny and almost warm. A waiter mops water off two chairs and a table so the women can talk on the terrace that overlooks the gorge and the Clifton Suspension Bridge.

At the bottom of the gorge, the tide's in and the River Avon runs high, obscuring the muddy banks. The gorge's rocky walls rise nearly a hundred metres to the point where the hotel terrace is built into the rock. The sunshine gleams weakly on the metal girders that suspend the bridge. In the far distance, clouds are moving, and a sharp wind threatens to bring them swiftly downriver.

Fiona Sadler takes a rug from the back of her chair and pulls it around her shoulders. She cups her hands around a mug of tea.

Emma Zhang puts her phone on the table between them and says, 'Do you mind if I record this?'

Fiona nods her agreement. *Why not?* she thinks.

Emma sets up the phone to record, and checks it twice. She's worried that the wind will interfere with the recording, but Fiona Sadler was adamant about sitting outside, wanting privacy and looking as if she felt like the walls of the dark hotel interior were closing in on her. Better an interview with some noise interference than no interview at all.

Emma's been weighing up how much mileage there is in this story. The phone call from Jim warning her off reporting on the case enraged her, but it also made her think there might be more of a story here than she'd thought. She knows she needs to exercise caution, though. She aspires to be a serious crime reporter, so she doesn't want to write something that's purely sensationalist. She'll need a good human story and a good angle. Seeing the photo of Noah Sadler on the front page freaked her out more than she'd care to admit. She'd argued that it was too much, but her editor overruled her. 'We've kept their names out of it,' he said. 'We're not breaking any laws.'

The fact that he huddled with the paper's lawyer before making that statement wasn't lost on Emma, but neither was the advice he gave her when he hired her: 'If you want to make it as a reporter, you've got to get the best stories out there, and sometimes that means you've got to do what you've got to do.'

Hearing Jim's voice on the phone, however angry, had also reminded Emma how much she missed him and how much he'd hurt her. She zips her coat up to her neck and wishes she'd worn her winter boots. She puts her game face on.

'Thank you for taking the time away from the hospital to meet me,' she says.

Fiona Sadler's gaze is that of a lioness with her prey in her sights. Her lips move, but Emma's taking a nervous slurp of her over-frothy coffee so she doesn't catch what the other woman says.

'I'm sorry?' She inches the recording device towards Fiona. 'Could you repeat that?'

'My son is dead.'

'I'm sorry, what?'

'Noah died last night. He's dead.' Fiona Sadler looks hard at Emma. It's an almost forensic study of her reaction to the news.

'I'm so very sorry,' Emma says, and she is. Unexpectedly, tears glaze her eyes and the sunshine seems too bright, the view of the bridge too vivid, its beauty something that produces not pleasure but a sharp ache.

Fiona Sadler feels a moment of triumph as she watches the shock and then the emotion on Emma's face. It's the reaction she wanted. It's a punishment for writing the article.

Aware that she's under scrutiny, Emma thinks, *Pull yourself together, take control.* As her shock dissipates, she feels a quickening of excitement, a sense that this is a bigger story now, that a death means it needs to be told.

'Can you tell me what happened?' she asks. 'In your own time.'

Fiona's slightly wrong-footed by Emma's gentle tone, but she makes an effort to stay strong, and to keep this combative. 'When you write an article like that, with a photograph like that . . . ' she begins.

'The photograph—'

'No! Please don't interrupt me. Please listen to me. An article like that hurts. You have to take responsibility for what you print. There are real people behind the stories. Real people. My son is real. Was real.'

Fiona feels the purpose of what she's trying to say slip away a little, as her own emotions well up. She tries to harness her concentration, and stay on track. 'We were robbed of time with him,' she says. 'We never knew how much time we were going to have with him, but every second was precious. Every single second.' It's becoming so hard to fight back the tears.

'I'm so, so sorry,' Emma murmurs. She's wondering if she should reach across the table and take Fiona's hand but decides not to yet.

'Do you understand you have to take responsibility?' Fiona asks.

'I do understand.'

'It's so painful for the people you use. For us.'

Emma takes a gamble and goes for a semi-honest approach. 'I'm just starting out,' she says, 'and I want to tell stories that matter, because I want to get to the truth. I know those stories sometimes hurt feelings, and I'm sorry you felt that way, but I think Noah's story is important. He's been the victim of a crime, potentially. In this political climate I think this could be buried by the police because they don't want any more trouble with the immigrant communities.'

'It could have been an accident.' Fiona didn't think she'd be playing devil's advocate, but she dislikes the journalist's certainty. She's starting to wish she hadn't come here, thinking that the best place for her would have been in bed with her grief.

'I spoke to the witness personally,' Emma says. 'I don't think it was an accident.'

'Is that what your article said?' Though she knows Emma's its author, Fiona hasn't actually read the piece. She's had far too much else to deal with.

Emma nods.

'The detective didn't tell us there was a witness,' Fiona says.

'Is that Detective Inspector Clemo?'

'Yes.'

'The police can be economical with the information they share when it suits them,' Emma says. 'That's why I wrote the article.'

She knows she's just put a stiletto in Jim's back, but she feels she exercised a bit of restraint. She could have pushed it in much harder.

'What did the witness say?' Fiona asks.

'She said that there might have been foul play, with the emphasis on *might*. But where there's smoke, there's fire.'

'Oh my god,' Fiona says. 'Noah was so vulnerable.'

Emma can't help flicking her eyes across to her phone, and is reassured by the sight of the timer counting the seconds as it records. She senses that Fiona's restraint might be about to crack, and she doesn't want to miss a word of it, but neither does she want to remind Fiona that she's recording their conversation by picking up the device to check it.

'He was so desperate for a friend,' Fiona says. 'He clung to that boy.'

'What's the name of his friend?' Emma asks. She makes good use of her police training to make sure her manner is appropriate and non-threatening. She softens her voice, is sure not to interrupt.

'Abdi Mahad. He's a Somali boy. At school on a scholarship.'

'Which school?'

'Medes College.'

Emma's pulse quickens again, though she's careful not to show it. She hadn't got around to finding out where the boys were studying, and that's one of Bristol's top private schools. This has all the elements of a big story, and if they can get hold of some more photographs . . .

Fiona Sadler feels as if she's been released from all of the social niceties that bound her to speak carefully about Noah, and brought her here to hold this journalist to account. The dam has burst, the shackles are off, the filters removed. It's been just thirty-six hours since her son died, her mind is addled with grief, and the fact that she's been lied to by the police feels like a low blow. She no longer cares about being reasonable or fair – as Ed would encourage her to be – because she's not as confident as him, and never has been. She doesn't share his certainties and his assumptions that people are good. She doesn't admit this to him, and it makes her feel inadequate, but now she's ready to say what she thinks, because in a world where her son gets cancer, and the disease eats away at him relentlessly, and the police are lying to her for political reasons, what place is there for 'reasonable'?

She puts her mug down and talks and talks, and when she next picks it up the drink is cold and a skin has formed on top of it. She realises she's shivering and the journalist is looking at her with concern.

Fiona looks properly at Emma Zhang for the first time. *She doesn't look Chinese,* she thinks. *Or maybe a bit around the eyes. She must have a white mother.* Fiona doesn't have a problem with Chinese immigrants. She feels they've generally been in the UK long enough to have integrated. They're part of the furniture now. It's the new arrivals that make her feel uncomfortable, and she puts Abdi Mahad and his family in that category.

'I'm not racist,' she says to Emma. 'It's just that you can't deny that these people have had experiences that make them different. My husband's work reveals that time and time again. They're traumatised, and do we want people with PTSD roaming through our society?'

Even though Emma has her own strong suspicions about Abdi Mahad and his motives, she recoils internally at this comment and has to muster her professionalism. Only her desire to tell this story stops her from lecturing Fiona Sadler on how anybody suffering from PTSD must have lived through hell and deserves support, whoever they are. She thinks of her own father's military experiences, how damaged they left him. She wonders if a change of subject might be in order, so she doesn't let her feelings show, and risk alienating this woman.

'Two things,' she says. 'Firstly, there may be an opportunity to go on local TV news and tell Noah's story. I'm talking with them about a slot at the moment, so I'll keep you posted. It would be wonderful if we could go on together. Secondly, what I'm thinking is that this story would be so much more powerful if we could publish it with a series of photographs that show Noah growing up, and if you have one of the boys together, that could be our headline photograph. We can blank out faces.'

'I can look through our pictures,' Fiona replies.

'Your husband said he'd done a series,' Emma tells her. 'When he provided the hospital photograph, he told me it was the latest in a series of shots. Perhaps we could use those? Only if you're comfortable with that, of course?'

Fiona stands up slowly. The blanket that was on her

knees falls to the floor. She watches a red car cross the suspension bridge, shrunk to the size of a toy. It makes her think of a bead of blood, bright red on her son's white skin. The product of the first needle they stuck in him. The first blood test. She feels as if she's been talking to the journalist in a dream and now reality has bitten its way back in.

'Ed gave you that photo?' she asks.

'I thought you knew.'

'I didn't know.'

She walks away, her footsteps increasing in pace. She pushes her way through the door that leads into the hotel, crosses the lobby and continues out onto the street. She ignores the calls of Emma Zhang behind her and the tug of the journalist's hand on her sleeve.

When she arrives home, she finds Ed in the kitchen.

'How could you?' She slaps his face as hard as she can.

'What about a reconstruction?' I suggest to Fraser. 'Of the route the boys took through town. It might jog memories.'

We've learned a lot today, but I want to focus on the events of Monday night and try to work out what the boys did minute by minute as they went through town. I'm still struggling to connect all the dots. A reconstruction could throw up something new.

She sits down at her desk and pulls off a pair of heels.

'God help women, Jim,' she says, massaging a bunion through her tights. 'We suffer for our beauty.'

Keeping a straight face is one of the biggest tests I've

faced today. Sometimes I love this woman, no matter how much of a short leash she has me on. I look down at my hands while she pulls on a pair of battered trainers and sighs with relief. When her feet are tucked out of sight behind her desk, it's straight back to business.

'If we stage a reconstruction it'll attract attention to Noah Sadler and people will ask questions about him. If he was still alive, maybe I'd do it, but I'd like to see what we can discover without it for now. Footfall, Jim. Get back out there yourself if you need to, revisit every detail until something clicks. But top tip from me: don't do it in high heels!'

I allow myself to laugh this time.

Woodley and I take another walk to the scrapyard, where a vehicle hoists clawfuls of twisted metal high against the blue sky and swivels to drop them onto a growing pile. Every time they land, it sounds like something shattering. A plane passes overhead and its vapour trails expand and dissipate in its wake. We stand by the gates to the yard. I take hold of a big padlock that's attached to a heavy-duty metal bolt.

'It's not adding up to me that there's no CCTV when this is the extent of the physical security,' I say.

Woodley surveys the scene like a builder, hands on hips, squinting a little. 'They told me they don't leave anything in the cabins overnight.'

'But this stuff's got to be worth something to somebody. Why fence it in so securely otherwise?' I know he's already been here and made inquiries about how they protect their business, but the answers he got don't feel right to me. 'Shall we have a word?'

The yard foreman who let us in is overseeing the unloading of the scrap.

'Is this all the security you have?' I ask him.

'Yep.'

'Nothing else at all?'

'No.'

The machine begins to reverse, and the beeping means Woodley has to shout to make himself heard. 'Anything else in the area?'

'I wouldn't know. You'd have to ask Ian.'

'Ian?'

'Ian Shawcross. He owns all the units around here.'

I remember a man in a crisp white shirt and an elaborate belt buckle: Janet Pritchard's partner.

'Do you have a number for him?'

'Not on me. They might do down the garage. That's Ian's place, too.'

Woodley and I leave the yard and walk past the row of lock-ups behind it where Janet Pritchard's unit is located. At the end of the lane there's a repair shop where two men are working on the bodywork of a Volkswagen Scirocco that's had its plates removed.

That's when I spot it: on the corner of the one-storey building that contains the mechanics there's a small circular patch of paintwork lighter than the rest, and three empty holes where some screws and a cable might have been. If a camera had been there, it would have had a sight line down past the lock-ups and might have caught the scrapyard gate.

A bell attached to the office door rings when we enter.

The customer welcome area consists of a pair of seats that have been ripped out of the back of a vehicle and set down facing a desk. Behind the desk sits a lad who looks barely old enough to be out of school. He's manning the landline and a large appointment book in which the heavily marked pages are swollen with ink and indentations, doubtless made by a ballpoint pen like the one he's scratching his acne with.

The radio's broadcasting the weather forecast at top volume: 'Winter temperatures have gone, but April showers have arrived a week early. We expect it to be wet overnight but clearing by the morning, and spring temperatures are on their way later this week.'

'All right?' says the lad.

'Do you have a phone number for Ian Shawcross? We need to talk to him.'

'Who's asking?'

He sits up straighter when we show him our badges.

'My aunty has his number,' he says. 'She's popped out for a minute.'

Woodley and I take a seat on the makeshift sofa. It tilts us so far back that the seats can only have come out of a sports vehicle. I get up as soon as I've sat down.

'Do you have CCTV on the premises?' I ask the lad.

'No.'

'I heard you had it taken down.' I'm working on a hunch.

'Yeah, we did.'

'That would be this week, would it? Yesterday, or the day before?'

'Yeah.'

'Why did it come down, then?'

'Broken. We had to get rid of the whole system.'

'You wouldn't have kept the latest footage from it, would you?'

He's chewing gum and he masticates stickily as he thinks about this. 'Don't think so. They burnt it all.'

'Is the CCTV the only security you had?' Woodley asks.

'No, we've Ian's brother-in-law. He does a patrol at night.'

'Do you know what his name is?'

'Jason Wright.'

A woman appears in the doorway.

'Can I help you?' she says.

'Police. Asking after Ian,' the boy tells her. 'You have his number, don't you?'

Her seen-it-all face and the way she looks at her nephew makes me think that we wouldn't have got any answers if she'd been at the desk when we arrived.

'I haven't got his number on me,' she says.

'Not to worry,' I say. 'I can ask Janet.'

She holds eye contact pretty steadily when I say that, but there's a muscle twitching on her face that tells me she's aware of whatever's being covered up.

'Your nephew's been very helpful,' I tell her. 'Very helpful indeed.'

We walk back to HQ quickly, and I ask Woodley to get hold of an address and number for Jason Wright. We need to pay him a visit. I don't tell Woodley he's an idiot for missing the trace of the CCTV camera while we're in the incident room. I wait until we're in the car on the way to see the security guard to do that.

It's not the first time Ed Sadler's been slapped by a woman, but it's the first time his wife has raised a hand to him. He doesn't slap her back, though there's a fleeting moment when he sorely wants to, when his grief over Noah creates a violent impulse. He backs away from her, and the sting on his cheek brings back the memory of the last time it happened: in a hotel room, beside a half-opened shutter, by a woman who'd only just stopped being a girl, a sheet wrapped around her. The discovery that he was married loaded the blow with more force than he'd have thought she could muster.

Fiona doesn't just slap him; she flies at him. Her fists pound his chest and his upper arms until he catches her by the wrists.

'What the hell?' he says.

'You took that photograph of Noah and sent it to a journalist?'

'Every time he's in hospital I take a photograph, you know that. We agreed we wanted to document his journey.'

Fiona once started a blog about Noah's illness. It was at the beginning when people advised her it might help her if she shared their story, but Noah was ill for so long that she ran out of steam to update it. She'd noticed that people were visiting and commenting on her posts in fewer numbers as time passed. It felt to Fiona that nobody had the stamina for Noah's cancer except her and Noah.

'This is different. You can't compare this to my blog.'

'Why not?'

'Oh, come on, Ed!'

They've separated, and stand apart. He's angry now, too.

'Tell me why this is different,' he says.

'Because you got the photograph published in the newspaper.'

'I get all my photographs published. That's what pays our bills.'

'This was our son! In a paper that our friends read.'

'How is that different?'

'Stop asking me that when the answer is bloody obvious!'

'Then explain it to me. Explain how my documentary process is a worthy thing when it's other people's children I photograph, but it's cheap when it's our own?'

Ed almost never speaks to his wife like this. He almost always backs her up, smooths her feathers, lets her make the decisions, and brings her tea in the mornings when he's home and she's not at the hospital. In return, he gets his freedom when he needs it.

He knows what her argument's going to be – that they and Noah deserve privacy – and the hypocrisy of it enrages him. He also knows it's probably not wise to pick her up on it, but he's so tired of being blamed for everything. If he's brutally honest, he also feels as if he's trapped in a domestic set-up whose sole objective has come to be the nursing of Noah, and the preservation of his life, at all costs, and rightly so, but now that Noah's gone, the domestic framework that Ed and Fiona are left with is sparse and unlovely. With Noah gone, Ed also knows he's no longer a hero to anybody, and this thought destabilises him almost as much as anything else.

'I don't know if I can ever forgive you,' Fiona says. 'I didn't even know you talked to a journalist.'

'I forgot to tell you! I just forgot. She came to the hospital. It was an honest mistake. I had a few other things on my mind, as you might imagine.' Ed catches himself before he shouts, calms himself down. 'I did it because I thought it might help to get people's attention so we can try to find out what happened. I regretted it afterwards, believe me, because I didn't mean for it to draw attention to Abdi or cast blame on him. I didn't know the journalist would do that.'

'That's the only bloody good thing that's come out of it! Did you know there was a witness who saw Abdi push Noah? The detective hid that from us. Hid it! How is that good for Noah?'

Fiona mothers like an animal: all instinct and ferocity. It astounded Ed from the very first few hours of his son's life, when he sat in the hospital room and watched the focus of Fiona's being shift from him to their son. Now it alarms him. All of that energy has turned outwards as Fiona seeks a scapegoat, somebody to blame for ruining the biggest project of her life before its natural time was up. Ed's not surprised the scapegoat's Abdi, though it makes him angry. He believes Abdi's a good kid, and he feels he's seen enough of the world to trust his own judgement. He relies on that ability to assess people quickly and accurately when he's working.

'We mustn't turn on Abdi. Don't believe everything you read. I'm sure the police will clarify if we ask them.'

'So one minute you're offering a photograph of our son to the press and the next you tell me we can't trust them?'

'Did it ever occur to you that whatever the boys were getting up to might have been Noah's idea? Noah's fault? Remember why we took him out of primary school?'

'We lost him yesterday and you bring that up?'

'Don't rewrite history, that's all I'm asking.' Ed's run out of energy for the fight. He hasn't got the appetite for ugly words any longer. 'Noah was the most important thing in my life, too,' he tells her, 'but he wasn't always perfect, particularly where friendships were concerned, so let's be careful what we say or do.'

'How careful were you being when you shared that photograph? You didn't even ask me before you did it.'

'OK,' he says. 'OK, you're right. I should have. I'm sorry. I'm very fucking sorry.' He holds up a hand, signalling that he's done with this fight. He leaves the room.

Later Fiona finds herself standing in Noah's bedroom. She takes a deep breath. She can sense and smell her son in every object and every bit of fabric, and she fancies that if she stays very still she can hear him breathing and the accompanying hiss of his oxygen mask. She thinks of his red cheeks at the party on Monday night, and how much he seemed to enjoy it. He didn't deserve this, whatever Ed says.

She sits down on Noah's bed and thinks about the unfortunate incident at primary school. Noah reacted badly with that other child, it's true, but he was under

283

such exceptional stress. It was the head teacher's attitude that Fiona hated.

'We have to look at this from both sides,' she said, 'and although Noah's been gravely ill and all of our sympathies are with him, we can't ignore the fact that he harmed another child.'

'Why did you push him?' Fi had asked Noah that night, after they'd learned that the child had broken his collarbone in the fall caused by Noah.

'He wasn't my friend any more.'

The next day she decided to home-school him. She couldn't stand the thought that friendship issues would pile up on top of everything he had to go through with his treatment. It was too much for one kid to bear.

'He'll probably be fine,' was Ed's view. 'He'll settle back in really quickly. Are you sure it's not *you* that's finding it very difficult, more than Noah maybe? That would be understandable.'

Fiona hated being called out on that. It always was Ed's way to breeze in, just off a plane, the smell of travel and other women hanging off him, and openly judge her like that. He had no idea what it was like during the hard yards of Noah's treatment, his education, his everything.

Fiona doesn't touch anything in Noah's room. She wants to keep every single thing in there, even the rumples in the bedding, just how Noah left it.

Woodley and I are standing outside a property on an aspirational housing estate that I estimate is ten years old. It's a small house. The developer of the estate's mixed property styles and sizes in an ill-conceived and ill-executed attempt to create a village feel. The door's freshly painted and the front garden's aggressively well tended. A small red car sits on the driveway. It's polished to a shine. We're at the address where Jason Wright and his wife are registered as owner-occupiers.

'Somebody doesn't mind dusting, then,' Woodley says. The windowsill of the front room has been used as a display area for china figurines of wedding-cake princesses in dresses with more crevasses and folds than a glacier.

The woman who opens the door is small and neat, wearing a housecoat and slippers with a heel and an explosion of fluff on the toe.

'Rita Wright?' I ask. 'We're hoping to speak to your husband.'

'He's out.'

We didn't call ahead because we wanted to surprise him, but I wonder if somebody's told him we were asking questions at the garage.

'When will he be back?'

'I'm not sure. Could be ages.'

'Do you mind if we come in anyway? It would be very helpful if you could answer one or two questions for us.'

She examines our IDs hawkishly before beckoning us in. She asks us to remove our shoes and leads us through to a tiny conservatory at the back of the house with a view of a paved yard that contains a painted shed and a washing line where cleaning rags are neatly pegged. Beyond it, there's a patch of lawn.

'I'd like to ask about Jason's employment,' I say.

'He doesn't work. He's on disability benefits. His back's knackered.'

'When did that happen?'

'About six years ago. He had an accident at work.'

'Where did he work?'

'Worked for the council. Housing officer.'

'So how did he hurt his back?'

'Lifting boxes, wasn't it? He ruptured a disc.'

Rita Wright gnaws at a fingernail between answers, leaving flecks of red polish on her teeth.

'So he doesn't work at all now?'

She shakes her head.

Outside, the patio stones are becoming speckled with rain. In the corner of the yard I see a large dog turd.

'I don't think I can help you much more than that,' Rita Wright says. 'If you don't mind, I'd like to get my washing in.'

She wants rid of us, and I'm willing to let her because I've had a thought.

'You've been very helpful indeed,' I say, standing with her. 'We'll call back later to see if Jason's here.'

'You could ring ahead next time,' she says.

'We'll do that, thank you.'

She hovers around us as we put our shoes back on in the hallway.

'We'll see ourselves out, Mrs Wright,' Woodley tells her. 'You get that washing in.'

The rain's worsened quickly. It's pelting down. Woodley and I jog across the road.

'I'll bet Wright's out walking the dog,' I say, when we're both in the car. 'He won't last long in this.'

We move the car a distance from the house so Rita Wright won't be able to see it, but we have a view of anybody arriving at the property.

Woodley pulls a piece of laminated card from his pocket. 'Look what I found on the floor by the door.'

He hands it to me. PLEASE DON'T RING THE DOORBELL BETWEEN 9AM AND 5PM, it says, and provides a number to text instead.

'Only somebody who works night shifts would have that.'

On the back of it there's a worn nub of Blu-Tack where it could have been fixed to the door.

'He's been claiming benefit and working on the sly.'

We don't have to wait long for the man himself.

'She must have phoned him as soon as we left,' Woodley says as a man appears at the far end of the street, hunched against the rain, holding two big German shepherd dogs on leads.

'They don't look like the kind of dogs you'd choose if you had a back injury,' Woodley says.

We get out of the car to intercept Wright. As we approach, he notices us. From the way he pauses, it's obvious that he considers taking off but thinks better of it. When we're still a good few metres away from him, the dogs start to bark. He settles them with a command. Rain drips off the peak of his cap. He's wearing a raincoat but underneath it only lightweight trainers and jogging bottoms. Both are soaked through. It's pretty obvious he went out in a hurry.

'You'd better come in, then,' he says. 'Let me get the dogs settled first.'

He lets himself into the back yard via a side gate and we follow him through. The dogs have lost interest in us now, and we watch as he puts them into a large wooden kennel, where they shake thoroughly.

'Not house dogs, then?' Woodley asks.

Jason Wright can't resist showing off. 'They're specialist dogs. Bred and trained in Germany. They're not supposed to live inside.'

'Security dogs?'

'Yeah. My wife suffers from nerves.'

'On this estate?' Woodley asks, and he's right to. The only crime we've had a whiff of here is bad architecture. Everything else looks shipshape.

'You can't be too careful, officer.' He's got a good poker face, I'll give him that, because what he's saying is non-sense, especially given that Mrs Wright's demeanour was distinctly steely. No nerves detectable there.

'Bella!'

One of the dogs stops drinking at the sound of his voice and comes to the wire fence. She's athletic and bright-eyed. Her ears and snout look like black velvet. The other dog watches, its head on its paws. The inside of the pen is as immaculate as the house.

'She's been poorly this one, haven't you, Bella?' His voice has gone gooey, and at the sound of her name the dog's tail wags, but she holds herself very still. 'Good as gold, they are, but if you give them the command they'll defend you.'

He digs in his pocket and then offers Bella a treat through the wire. The other dog gets up and approaches.

I don't give Wright any warning. I take two handfuls of his wet coat in my fist and push him back against the wire surrounding the dogs' pen. I don't push him hard, but the noise is jarring. The dogs' reaction is instant. Both of them hurl themselves against the other side of the wire, teeth and gums bared, snarling and barking. I have no doubt their jaws would be closing around my arm or even my neck if they could get to me. I let go of Jason Wright.

'What the fuck are you doing?' he says. 'Jesus!'

The dogs are still going crazy.

'Bella! Roger!' he shouts, and they back off, but reluctantly, the male dog baring his teeth.

'I think we need to have a word inside, Mr Wright,' I say.

If these dogs are just in use to guard this house, I'll eat my hat. I strongly suspect Wright was at the scrapyard on Monday night and had one or both of them with him. I think it's him we can hear on the recording giving a command to the dog called Roger, and I want to know exactly what went on.

When Sofia goes into her bedroom to lie down, to check Facebook and to try to consider what else she can do to find her brother, Maryam sits in the darkness of the room next door.

When Nur gets home he unlocks the door, clicks on the light and finds Maryam has been sitting alone in the dark.

She holds her finger to her lips. 'Sofia's sleeping.'

He sits down beside her and she takes his hand. They love each other very much and have done since the day they met at the camp, both working at the school there. They've had their differences, of course, over the years, but they've come so far together that the bond they share is very strong.

'I gave out all the photographs,' he tells her. 'Everybody says they'll look out for Abdi.'

He's saying that to fill the silence. He can tell she has something she wants to say.

Earlier, she looked in on her daughter and saw that Sofia was asleep on her bed. Sofia's phone was lying out on her desk and Maryam took it. She knows her daughter's pin code so it was easy enough to access the photograph that Sofia took earlier.

Maryam shows it to Nur.

'Sofia says she thinks that Abdi got obsessed with this photograph when he went to Ed Sadler's exhibition,' she tells him. 'You see it's the one he was talking about in the recording.'

Nur sees a scene from Hartisheik camp. He sees a few faces he recognises amongst the men and boys. He sees the man who was known as Farurey because of his damaged lip, and he sees the football game that's on the television: red shirts versus burgundy and white shirts. Without looking any closer he knows exactly when this was, and which match they're watching.

'Abdi knows,' Maryam says. They've failed to protect their deepest secret.

Nur was living in the Eastleigh district of Nairobi in

1999, the year Manchester United played Bayern Munich in a historic final. The night of the Champions League match was one of the few occasions he risked arrest by the Kenyan police by venturing out of his accommodation to join a crowd watching the game at an open-air screening. He'd been overjoyed to have some time off. The distance from his family gnawed at him every day, but he was there to make money so they could get away from the camp, where Maryam was becoming more and more withdrawn and depressed, and the prospects for his children's education were pathetic. Nur wanted to rejoin them, but knew he had to be strong and keep to his goal. He was just over halfway through a six-month trip. He was sleeping on a mattress in a room he had to share with seven other men.

That night, watching the football match was his treat: a rare few hours of pleasure. He was a Manchester United fan. The game and its noise and excitement totally absorbed him for the whole ninety-three minutes. He remembers the red flares the fans lit pitch-side, the delight of the Manchester players that verged on ecstatic when they stole the game in the last three minutes, and the desolation of the Munich team who lay flat on the grass, disbelieving the result.

The guilt that he enjoyed himself on that night when his wife suffered so much still feels like a pinch in his heart.

Maryam says, 'I don't want Sofia to know.'

'Nobody has to know.'

'We have to tell the police.'

'Why?'

'Because Abdi's looking for this man. He knows he's

here in Bristol. He saw him at the Welcome Centre, and must have overheard us talking about him that night. If he recognised *him* in the photograph –' she stabs at the face of the man with the split lip '– he could have put it all together because the football match gave him the date. It wouldn't have been too hard to work it out.'

'He can't have,' Nur says, but as he says it he's thinking about how hard it is to keep secrets, especially one this big.

'He can. He saw me faint. He's perceptive, he's clever, he's everything we wanted him to be.'

'Don't worry at your scar,' Nur tells her. Gently, he pulls her hand away from her arm. She's been known to pick at it until it bleeds.

'Whatever happened at the canal, it's worse now. Abdi isn't safe,' Maryam says.

She's assaulted by the memory of the man with the gashed lip from that night. She grips Nur's hand and tries to eradicate it, but the slap of that man's flesh on hers is something she's never been able to forget.

Maryam was helping a friend that night. Her friend was sick, and her son had sneaked out to watch the football game against her instructions. Her friend was furious but also afraid. Boys who ran loose at night in the camp were unsafe. They should have been at home in the shelter, where they could study. Many of the women Maryam knew guarded the kerosene supplies like tigresses to ensure that there was enough light for their children to do homework after dark. Nobody wanted their kids to be roaming the camp, mixing with anybody. Many of them still held out hope for the future, in spite of everything. But the promise of a football game screened in public had driven the boys a bit crazy. Maryam left Sofia sleeping in her friend's shelter with her friend, and walked up a long straight path to the area where the aid workers sometimes relaxed.

On that night they'd set up a TV so anybody who wanted to could watch the football game, but when Maryam got there, the game was over and the boy she was seeking was nowhere to be seen. The aid workers were climbing into trucks for the drive home, jolly and laughing. She wondered if the boy had gone to the hut of another family friend. She set off there but got confused. She was disorientated by the darkness. Some of the shelters glowed with torch or lamplight, but most were dark.

She realised she was lost when she found herself at the outskirts of the camp, where the women gathered firewood in groups for protection. She extinguished her lamp, afraid that it would draw unwelcome attention to her, but it was too late. There were men. Three of them, but only one had a wide gash on his upper lip. Two of them manhandled her out into the deep darkness, away from the camp where nobody could hear her or help her. Her heels dragged in the dirt as they pulled her, and all the way she watched the man who followed them, saw his deformed face and the way he walked so casually and pointed his torch ahead of them, indicating where he wanted them to take her, running the beam over her body once they got there.

His deformity meant that his speech was slurred. She's never forgotten that, either, the distinctive sound of him.

When the rape was over, Maryam cowered in the

darkness alone as the men picked their way back to the camp across the desert, and she heard their laughter. She pulled her clothing back around her and lay there because the fear of the pain and of the rest of her life was greater than her fear of scorpions or hyenas.

She felt the warmth of blood between her legs and on her arm, where he cut her with his knife. That wound would become infected before it healed, leaving an ugly scar.

Even after everything she'd endured already, that was the night that her life became defined by shame, and it was the night that Abdi was conceived.

Ed takes a call from the hospital confirming that Noah's death has been referred to the coroner for a post-mortem. The expectation, the doctor on the phone tells him, is that this will take place over the next few days and then the body will be released for the funeral, but Ed and Fiona will have to be in touch with the coroner's office to confirm this. The thought of a post-mortem sickens Ed. What he would most like, after years of medical intervention, is for them to leave Noah alone.

When he tells Fiona, she barely reacts. She went to bed after their argument, and she's still there, grey-faced.

'Shall we talk about the funeral?' he asks.

'No.'

Ed knows what Noah wanted; they talked about it the same night they discussed his bucket list, and Ed wrote notes. Noah knew more about funerals than Ed would have thought healthy in any other circumstances. He wanted a certain drawing on the cover of the Order of Service, and he wanted it to be non-denominational. He had three pieces of music in mind, one that Fi liked, one that Ed liked and one that was his own favourite. There would also be a reading from *The Little Prince* that Noah chose, and he wanted each of his parents to select another.

'I don't mind who reads them, though it would be nice if Abdi did one.'

Ed wondered how the hell he had managed to leave it until his son was in the last months of his life to have a conversation with him that was so adult. He couldn't restrain himself from resenting Fiona for that. *She kept our son from me*, he thought. Her levels of anxiety around Noah were so high that she drove me away from him. I thought of him as a patient more often than not. I didn't get to know him as well as I could have.

'I'm going to cancel my exhibition,' he said to Noah in the days after the final talk.

'No! I want to go to it and to the party. I've got months, Dad, not days. We need to do good things.'

'Good things?'

'Well, it would be stupid to do bad things. I want to see your exhibition.'

Ed broke down then.

Noah wasn't the first dying child he'd seen, but this was the first time he could truly empathise with the parents of those little souls and their families that he'd met and photographed abroad. The way Noah was that evening shattered the barriers Ed had erected to keep himself sane in the face of what he'd seen. It made a mockery of the bravado he and his colleagues enacted day after day as they waited in the comfort of hotels for stories that they could safely record, journalists and photographers alike always looking for the most sellable angle. They had employers, after all. They were there for money.

Ed goes downstairs and finds the notes he took. He takes his time reading through all of Noah's wishes. When he's done, he folds the paper up carefully and places it back in his desk drawer. He hopes with all his heart that the police will discover what happened by the canal. He wants Abdi to be at the funeral with a clear conscience, to be able to say goodbye to his friend properly. Noah would want that, too.

Ed goes upstairs again and sits on the end of their bed.

'Fi,' he whispers. He lies on top of the bed beside her and fits his body around hers. Her pillow is damp. He buries his head into her hair.

She doesn't move, and that angers him a little, because he wants to beg her, just for once, not to own this, not to make her sorrow greater than his. After a few minutes he feels that she's trying to ease him away.

'Too hot,' she says, but the skin on her neck is clammy cold.

Ed gets up. He gets his travel bag out of the wardrobe and unzips it. He packs the usual gear. Not much, just the essentials.

'What are you doing?' Fi's up on her elbows, watching him.

'I need to get away.'

'Now?'

He can only stare at her in reply.

'What about the funeral?'

'I'll be home as soon as the autopsy is done. We can't organise anything until then.'

'You can't leave now. Is it work?'

He shakes his head. She gets it, finally. That he's dreadfully lonely, and has been for years. That both of them are now Noah is gone.

'Oh, Ed.'

'I can't be here.'

'Where are you going to go?'

He's not really sure, but there's a place on the coast in Ireland where they went once, before Noah was born. No electricity, just a beautiful view and total seclusion. He wants to be somewhere like that.

'I'll let you know.'

'Please don't go.'

'I think I have to.'

So they continue in the cycle they've always been in, where Ed leaves and Fiona can't make him stay because she's not 100 per cent sure she wants him to. Both of them wonder if they ever had a true connection, or if it was parenting that bound them.

When he arrives at the airport, he sees a text from her: **I talked to the journalist, too. You never even asked how I found out you gave her the photograph.**

Woodley and I play the 999 recording to Fraser and tell her about the security guard and his dogs. We've taken a statement from him. In our conversation with him at his home, he eventually admitted to being at the scrapyard, but claimed to have arrived as Janet made the emergency call.

'He's lying,' I say. 'And I'd bet my badge that Janet Pritchard is, too. I think we should bring them both in for formal interviews.'

I'm not the only one with news. One of the admin staff knocks on the window of the meeting room and points at me, making the sign for a phone call. Ed Sadler's on the end of the line.

'Detective Inspector Clemo,' he says. 'I'm going away for a couple of days. Fiona will know how to reach me. I wanted to let you know in person.'

'Thank you. I appreciate it.'

'You might not appreciate what I'm going to say next.'

'Go ahead.' The skin on the back of my neck prickles. He sounds more formal than usual. Tense.

'Fiona's given an interview to a journalist. I'm afraid it may be somewhat – how shall I say this? – somewhat imbalanced and possibly accusatory. Detective?'

'Yes. I'm here.'

'Please don't blame her too much. Under the circumstances, she's not herself . . .'

I'm smart enough not to be destructive in front of my colleagues these days, so when the call's over, I resist the urge to punch the wall beside Fraser's office and take the stairs down and out of the building instead.

At the far end of the car park, where the noise of the overpass traffic will ensure my conversation is private, I phone Emma. She doesn't pick up, and at first I don't leave her a message, because I know I'm going to shout. I hang up and compose myself. It occurs to me that telling her to back off might be much more effective if I do it face to face. I redial.

'Emma,' I say, 'I was wondering if you'd like to meet for a drink tonight? I'm off in half an hour. It would be nice to see you.'

Back upstairs, the meeting's over and Woodley's in conference with another bod from the tech department. The bad news is that they haven't managed to crack Abdi's personal email account yet, but there's good news, too.

'Our boy's just used his social media account,' he says.

On a laptop they show me a string of messages sent between Abdi and his sister Sofia. They're totally mundane until the very last two.

'She sends him the photograph of the men watching a football game with the message, "What does this mean?" He replies, twelve minutes ago.'

Abdi's reply says: 'It means nothing. It's best if you forget me. I'm not coming home. Sorry.'

'Fuck.'

'I know,' Woodley says.

I read Sofia's reply: *Please come home, Abdi, or tell us where you are! We love you xxxxx.* A string of heart emojis follows.

'He's read that last message she sent, but not reacted to it,' Woodley says.

'Where did he log on?'

'We're working on it.'

'How long until you know?'

'Hours.'

'How many?'

'Depends on the service provider.'

'We need to get to him. Let's not waste this.'

My phone pings: a text from Emma.

Could meet now? At Berkeley Lounge Bar. Tied up later.

Putting her story to bed, no doubt. I text back, **See you there.**

'Contact me the instant you hear anything,' I tell Woodley.

The venue Emma suggested takes a bit of finding. I park on Berkeley Square near the Triangle in the city centre. A short walk away, past kebab shops, an American-style diner and an Indian restaurant, I find an alleyway where the tarmac's pocked with puddles and seems to lead nowhere. A cat sits in a lit second-floor window and stares down at me. Otherwise, there are no signs of life. I wonder if Emma's sent me to a dead end to make a point, and I'm about to leave when two punters, looking well dressed and well watered, emerge from an unmarked black door. I knock on it.

Inside, I find Emma sitting at the bar. It's a classy place but dark. Tasselled table lamps keep faces in shadow. Bottles of spirits are stacked up behind the bar in staggered rows like stadium seats, glinting dimly where they can catch some light. Emma's nursing a tall drink. A young barman in a white shirt and waistcoat is polishing glasses. He's wearing silver cufflinks.

This is a posh venue masquerading as a speakeasy, and it's an ironic place for a detective and a crime reporter to meet, as if we're characters who've been cast, not real people. I'm sure that's not lost on Emma, and I wonder what she's trying to say about us.

I get a sparkling water. She doesn't look at me until I take a seat beside her and then the eye contact is electrifying and terrifying all at once, just like it used to be. I have to look away, to focus on a pair of gloves she's put neatly on the bar, and not her slender forearm that rests there, fingertips on the rim of her glass, nails painted and glossy.

'Hello, Jim,' she says.

'You spoke to Fiona Sadler?'

'Not here for a personal chat, then?'

'Sorry.' The way I say it makes it plain it's not an apology.

'Don't be.' She puts her chin up defiantly, but I notice that she swallows, too. Nerves. So it's not just me. There's no sign of them in her voice, though. 'Yes, I've spoken to Fiona Sadler. At her invitation.'

'Are you going to publish her story?'

She stirs her drink. It looks like a cocktail and I'm sure it's for show. Unless she's changed a lot since we were together, Emma's far too focused to drink on the job, even if she's chosen a career where that's the cliché.

'We are,' she says.

'Don't.'

She shakes her head, lets out a small snort of laughter. I reach for her hand. The movement takes her by surprise. She lets me hold it for a moment, just long enough for us both to feel the warmth of the other, then pulls it away and rests it in her lap, amongst the folds of her skirt.

'You don't want to do this. It's not who you are. Think of the other boy and his family.'

'Don't tell me what I do and don't want to do. I'm publishing because I believe there's a story that needs to be told. I think Fraser and you and the CID department are trying to bury this because you're afraid of backlash after the almighty cock-up managing the White Nation March. How many injuries were there? How many arrested? Can you remind me? How much was the cost to the city in damages?'

'You're bitter.'

'I wonder why.'

'Is this some kind of revenge? You weren't the only casualty on that case.'

'From where I'm sitting, only one of us is still wearing a CID badge.'

The barman glances at us and she lowers her voice.

'You're unbelievable, Jim. Unbelievable.'

'The Somali boy doesn't deserve this. He's innocent.'

'Really? Can I quote you on that?'

I shake my head.

'Can you point me to some evidence of his innocence?'

'Not without compromising the investigation.'

'Then I publish.'

'I thought you were better than this.'

'You thought nothing of the sort. You're the one who destroyed my career.'

'You did that all on your own.' I stand. I'm ready to leave. I'm flogging a dead horse and it's time to stop.

She puts her hand on my arm as I turn to go. 'Look at me, Jim.'

How do you hide feelings that are so strong they threaten to destroy your rationality and make a mockery of your loyalties? When I look at her, I can't help seeing the future that we could have had. It's painful and tempting, and I wonder how you can hate somebody and desire them so very much.

She stares back at me. Her nostrils flare minutely as she breathes. Something hard sets behind her eyes. 'Never mind,' she says, letting go.

She drinks, draining her glass, and scoops up her belongings in a fluid movement that I'd forgotten was her habit. I watch as she walks away from me. She's dressed up to the nines. I wonder if that was for my benefit.

After making my way out a few minutes later I stand in the dismal alleyway and call Janie Green.

'CID Press Office,' she answers.

'How are you for problems today?'

'I have more than enough, thank you.'

'Room for one more?'

It was worth a try, seeing Emma. I thought I'd get the upper hand, but I guess she's more in need of a victory than I thought, after the way things ended between us. I'm not done with her yet, though. I can be patient. I can regroup. If there's one thing Dr Manelli taught me, it's that.

Sofia wakes up to find her father at her bedroom door, holding her phone. It's confusing. She doesn't know why he's got it.

'Abdi is contacting you!' he says.

Her mother and father gather around Sofia's phone with her, deeply dismayed by Abdi's message. They watch as she types her reply and sends it.

'He's read it!' Sofia says as the tiny icon beside her message displays Abdi's profile picture, and collectively they hold their breath as the sign that Abdi is typing appears, but all of a sudden it disappears and doesn't reappear.

'No!' Sofia shouts. 'Come on!'

In an internet cafe in the St Paul's area Abdi Mahad logs out of Facebook. He wanted to reply to his sister, but he just didn't know what to say. He thinks it's better if they're not in contact any more.

He's also been staring at the photograph of the man whom he believes is his father. He knows that this man no longer has a broken lip and crazy teeth, but a surgically repaired mouth, and he knows that this photograph is fifteen years old, but he still stares. He's looking for a trace of himself in the other man's face.

The trail he's followed to learn that this man is his real father started last week. He was working in the kitchen at the Welcome Centre when he saw his mother staring at a man who was queueing up for food. She had an expression on her face that he'd never seen before. She couldn't take her eyes off the man, and her eyes were filled with fear. A second later, she fainted. If it hadn't been for Chef Sami catching her, she would have hit her head.

In the chaos that followed, the man melted away into the crowded dining room, but Abdi had seen him and noticed the scar on his upper lip. Maryam told everybody that she just felt unwell, but Abdi knew that wasn't true. He tried to find the man and ask him what he said or did to Maryam to frighten her, because Abdi was sure there must have been something, and he would defend his mother to the end.

A friend gave him and Maryam a lift home shortly afterwards and Maryam made him swear he wouldn't mention to Sofia that she'd fainted. Sofia had important schoolwork to concentrate on, and Maryam didn't want her to worry.

'You promise to tell Dad, though,' he said. 'Or I will.'

It was very late that same night that Abdi was woken. At first he thought it was the sound of his father creeping in from a night shift but then he heard sounds that chilled him. His mother was crying out, almost screaming. She was in terrible distress. He got out of bed, ready to rush to her. As he was about to open his bedroom door, he heard Nur's voice.

'Maryam, Maryam.' The voice was lilting, calm, hushed, bringing her back from a terrible place. Abdi was transfixed.

What he overheard next told him that Maryam had, that evening, found herself face to face with a man who had raped her in the months before their family left Hartisheik camp. What followed felt strangely logical and fated, because Abdi has always felt as if his parents treated him differently from Sofia. It was the way they always seemed so afraid if he strayed even a tiny bit from the path of being the perfect son. They didn't put that pressure on Sofia, not to the same extent. And they're not unlike some other families they know, they don't have lower expectations of

Sofia because she's a girl. If Sofia messed up, they encouraged her to try again, to get past her mistake. If Abdi messed up, they seemed fearful, and now he understands why. It was because they didn't know who he would grow up to be.

Abdi didn't dare talk to his parents about what he overheard, but he thought a lot about the man with the scar on his lip, and how he was the child of a rapist. He might have found the right time and the courage to talk to his parents or Sofia about this, if it hadn't been for Ed Sadler's exhibition opening.

Abdi knew immediately that he was looking at the same man when he saw the photograph. More evidence stacked up when Ed Sadler told him about the man's violent reputation. When he researched the football match the men in the photograph were watching, he discovered it took place nine months before his birthday. That's when he understood that the man with the cleft palate and the hard eyes was almost certainly his father. It explained so much.

Now Abdi Mahad intends to confront this man, because he knows where he is. How exactly he's going to confront him, he isn't sure. One minute he wants to kill him for what he did to Maryam. The next minute he wants to say, 'I am your son,' to see how the man will react. *Then again,* he thinks, *perhaps I'll just take a look at him, and then disappear, because if this man is half of me, I want to see with my own eyes what I might become.*

He's desperately afraid for Noah, too. Abdi knew the fall into the canal was bad. He stood helplessly by as Noah fell, and then he froze, because he couldn't swim. He'd assumed that Noah was getting better in the hospital, though, so to see the photograph of him in the newspaper was shocking. He'd like to find out how Noah is, but he can't think of a way. He knows he won't be able to sneak into the hospital without being noticed. He should have sent him a Facebook message, he thinks, but it's too late now. His WiFi time is up.

Abdi gets up and leaves the cafe. With his hoody up and his head down, he heads into a Subway. He has only £20 left, and nowhere to stay, so he knows he should probably spend his money more wisely, but his growing body is craving food. He eats the sandwich on the street, walking. He knows he mustn't stay still too long because somebody might spot him. To avoid being seen, he ducks into the side streets as soon as he's able to.

It takes him fifteen minutes to walk to the place where he's been sleeping. In the cover of a large shrub, its ever-green leaves shiny and thick, he's made a sort of nest. He chose that place because it looks out on the row of terraced cottages that Ed Sadler told him about.

'Really crazy coincidence,' Ed Sadler said in his study on the night of the exhibition, after Abdi stopped record-ing. 'I swear I saw that man with the harelip the other day when I went with a mate to the Climbing Centre in St Werburgh's. I could have sworn it was him. Looks good now, his face all fixed up, teeth all in place, on the NHS, no doubt, but it made me do a double-take because of course I'd just been selecting photographs for the show, so his face was fresh in my mind. He was just coming out of one of the cottages opposite. He had the scar on his upper lip.'

Abdi knew the place. He'd once been on a school trip to the converted church with the climbing wall inside it. He remembered the row of houses opposite it, and remembered that at one end of them there was a dark tunnel where the railway passed overhead, and beside it was a steeply sloped park area he might be able to hide in.

He's observed lots of people on the street: climbers arriving at the centre, and drinkers coming and going from a pub. As he passes it now, he can't help feeling a tug of desire for the warmth and camaraderie he sees through the windows. He keeps his head down as he passes a group of youths. They don't give him a second glance, though.

Last night he found a blanket left out on a skip and brought it to his den. He's pleased to find it's still there when he gets back. In the middle of the bush he's snapped some twigs and small branches off to make a space he can just sit in. He crawls in and curls up with the blanket around him. He wishes he'd thought to bring a bottle of water with him. He knows he should keep an eye on the houses, but it's dark and he's bone weary, so he shuts his eyes.

He wakes suddenly out of a deep sleep some time later, sensing danger, though he's unsure why. Even the sound of his own breathing alarms him before he realises what it is and calms himself. The smell of earth is strong, and he understands as he dares to move for the first time that it's rain that's woken him. It's trickling down through the leaves of the shrub in small cascades that are wetting him and his blanket. He's shaking from the cold.

He clambers out from under the shrub and finds that it's even wetter without its protective shelter. He shudders. On the railway line a train shuttles past, just three carriages, windows lit, people visible in them. Abdi considers getting a ticket and riding for as long as they'll let him. He wonders what it would be like to throw yourself under a train, but knows he would never do that to a driver. He relieves himself against a tree and decides he's going to climb down the slope and find some shelter under the railway arch. It frightens him to be there, but he's so cold he can't stand to stay in the rain.

The slope's covered in long grass and Abdi loses his footing, sliding down, bumping hard at the bottom. He wants to cry out in discomfort and frustration, from hatred of himself that he's reduced so quickly to this. He thinks of his school uniform and his schoolbooks, and how much pride he felt in them. He thinks of the first clean page of a fresh new exercise book, and all the hope he used to feel, all the excitement at the possibility it contained. He wonders if he should go home, and he starts to stand, trying not to slip again in the muddy slick he's landed in, when he notices activity in one of the houses opposite.

A door has opened, revealing two men standing in the doorway. There's no light on in the house, but the windows of the pub opposite cast enough of a glow that Abdi is pretty sure he knows who he's looking at. The sound of violins comes from the pub, the fast rise and fall of live reel music, and in the doorway opposite, as if they occupy a different world, the men exchange just a few words through slowly moving lips, before one leaves and the man whom Abdi thinks he recognises as his father steps back into the house and shuts the door behind him.

It focuses Abdi. He clambers back up the slope and withdraws into the shelter of the shrub. The blanket is soaking by now, but he draws it around his shoulders and he sits, hunched, in such a way that he can see the house. He watches all night. A light stays on in the house until the early hours, when it snaps off and then stays dark. Still Abdi doesn't move, even though his body feels stiff and numb.

He begins to understand what it is he wants to do, and he's surprised to find that he no longer feels afraid.

Fiona Sadler listens to the sounds of her house after Ed has gone. What she hears most loudly is the absence of Noah. Even when he was at school she used to have a sense of him in the home. It could be the anticipation of his return, the trail of belongings he left in his wake, the turning around in her mind of all the conversations they had had and would have. Now there is nothing except the roaring emptiness of her loss.

Words from Noah's oncologist have been cycling around her head for a week now, and they return.

'I'm so sorry. There are signs that the disease has returned.'

These were the words Fiona had been dreading for seven years, and the worst thing about them, the very worst thing, was Noah's reaction. There was shock at first, of course, but in the aftermath, she thought he behaved as if he was relieved. Only a tiny bit, and only for an instant, but relieved nonetheless. It hurt her terribly. She wasn't ready to let him go; she knew she never would be.

'It's not impossible to understand that he'd feel relief,' Ed said when he arrived at the hospital, hours later. He was unshaven and unkempt. They were in the hospital cafe buying Noah a chocolate croissant, snatching a moment to talk privately. Upstairs in the ward Ed's travel bag and cameras were occupying a large amount of the floor space in Noah's room. Ed had arrived with a bag full of kitsch airport gifts as well as duty-free bottles for the nurses and chocolates for everybody on the ward, and she'd envied his ability to sit with Noah and laugh as they examined the tat together. Noah declared a puffin soft toy to be his new favourite possession.

'I can't bear it,' Fiona told him.

'It's OK,' he said. They held up the queue behind them as he took her in his arms. Nobody complained.

Now that Ed's gone again, Fiona has nothing to stabilise her, nobody in her immediate orbit to rage against and cry upon.

Her impotence creates a sort of fury in her. She rages against the unfairness of the situation. How is it, she thinks, that Noah is dead and she and Ed are facing intrusive questions and visits from the police, while Abdi Mahad, who by the sound of it could have been responsible, is the subject of an appeal on television that emphasises his vulnerability? Fiona has watched the appeal over and over again, rewinding it, allowing herself to get more distressed by it on every viewing.

How is it that nobody's talking about what Noah must have gone through, about the fact that his life has been snatched from him, after everything he and they have been through? How is it that she has to hear from a journalist that there was a witness, and the police don't seem to be paying this fact any attention? And she has nobody to tell. Nobody who will listen and say to her, 'Yes, it's unfair.' Nobody who will say, 'I'm sorry,' and 'I understand,' and 'I love you.' Nobody to persuade her to be reasonable, or that it would be better to ride her grief, and not lash out with it.

Fiona's face hurts, she's cried so much, but her tears have dried out for now. She reaches for her phone and calls the one person who's listened to her in the last few days without judging her, and who might be able to give a voice to Noah's side of the story.

When Emma Zhang replies, Fiona says, 'I've changed my mind. Is it too late?'

'No,' Emma replies. 'Not at all. I'm leaving for the studio shortly. I can pick you up on the way.'

After they've spoken, Fiona goes to her wardrobe and scans the outfits. She chooses to wear a black dress and a black jacket. She takes a shower, dries her hair and applies some make-up, paying particular attention to the dark marks beneath her eyes. Around her neck she fastens a necklace that Noah gave her. It's a silver chain with a small silver circle hanging from it. She looks in the mirrors, fingers the pendant.

'I love you,' she says to her reflection, but really she's addressing the boy she's lost.

Fifteen minutes later her doorbell rings.

The driver holds open the back door of a sleek car and she climbs in. In the back seat Emma Zhang's waiting, and she takes Fiona's hand.

'OK?' she asks.

Fiona nods.

Woodley seems to be the only person smiling when I get to the office.

'What's that on your face?' I ask him.

'It's a bit of good news, boss.'

'Let's hear it, then.'

'You remember what we heard on the 999 recording: someone saying what we thought was "Roger Platts"? I think I've worked out what it means.'

He beckons me to come and look at his monitor, where he's got a website up on the screen with a big German shepherd dog as its main picture.

'This is a specialist website for "*schutzhund*" training. The type of training I'm pretty sure his dogs have undergone. If you look here —' he clicks around the site '— they have a set of specific, specialised commands they respond to. In German.'

A list of words comes up with translations in English beside them, and a button to press if you want to hear the correct pronunciation.

Woodley clicks on the word for 'Down' and the computer says, '*Platz.*' He clicks again, and once more.

'I got it,' I say.

'The dog wasn't just there. It was being commanded to get down by Jason Wright – it's got to be him on the recording – which suggests that the dog was doing something it shouldn't be doing.'

'Like scaring the hell out of the boys.'

'Exactly. I think Wright was telling the truth about not having access to the scrapyard, but those dogs could have terrified the boys and made them feel trapped if they were throwing themselves against the fence and making a racket like they did with us.'

'And caused Noah to fall into the water?'

'It's not an impossible scenario,' Woodley says. 'The only thing I was wondering was why Janet Pritchard phoned if it was going to land her and Wright in trouble?'

'She was probably genuinely worried. You'd have to be hard as nails not to be, if you saw a kid go into the water and not come out.'

'I'm just surprised she didn't phone anonymously.'

'From where? I didn't see any payphones at the location, so she was stuck with her mobile. No way to be anonymous if your number's flashing up on the operator's screen.'

'So she's a Good Samaritan, then,' he says. 'Shall I update Fraser about the dog?'

Fraser's conspicuous by her absence, which works for me because I want to be on more solid ground with this before I talk to her.

'Let's speak to the witnesses again first.'

'One bit of less good news,' Woodley says. 'The

Underwater Unit can't get back out to the canal until tomorrow.'

'Why not?'

'They're fishing for a body in the river in Bath.'

I can't argue with that, though I'd like to. Tomorrow's better than next week, at least.

We find Janet Pritchard in her shop. She locks the door behind us when she understands that we're not there to congratulate her on being a good citizen, and leads us to a private office in the back. The office is a cramped, windowless space so small that Woodley has to stand in the doorway. The deep-pile carpet is dark pink. Thick white gloss paint has been slapped on every available surface. It feels airless. That might work in our favour, though. Witnesses don't always fare too well when they're boxed up with you. It gets very intense. I adjust my chair, easing it just a little closer to her.

'Would you like to tell us why you lied?' I ask her.

'I didn't lie.'

'Would you like to tell us why you lied?'

She purses her brightly painted lips. 'I'm curious as to why you're repeating yourself, Detective?'

'You weren't alone on Monday night at the canal, were you?'

She blinks.

'We've been informed that there was somebody else at the scene, another witness.'

'I don't know anything about that.'

'I think you do, and if you don't start telling us the truth you might find yourself in trouble. Perverting the course of justice is a very serious charge.'

'It carries jail time,' Woodley adds.

'All right,' she says. 'I wasn't alone. Jason was there, he does the security patrol, but he didn't arrive until I was phoning.'

'Why didn't you mention this before?'

'Because I forgot.'

'Funny you should feel so threatened by the boys when he was there with you.'

Her eyes cut from me to Woodley and back again. 'I wasn't frightened when he got there, but I'd already phoned.'

'Neither of you tried to help the boy?'

'We couldn't get into the yard. Jason didn't have keys.'

'Even though he does security?'

She shrugs.

'When did Jason leave the scene?'

'When the emergency services arrived. He had to get on with his job.'

'He didn't think it would be helpful to give a statement?'

'You'd have to ask him that.'

'I expect you understand why we're surprised that you didn't mention this earlier.'

A part of me admires the way she keeps her mouth shut and still looks defiant, but I also wonder where she gets her guts.

'I think we're going to need you to come down to the station and make a new statement.'

'And I suppose I don't have a choice about that, do I?'

Neither Woodley nor I answer.

'Can I at least call someone to man the shop?'

'I'm not sure there's time for that.'

Back at HQ we put her in an interview room.

'I want you to go and chase up the background checks on Ian Shawcross,' I tell Woodley. 'Everything dotted and crossed as it should be. And then get her statement. It won't do her any harm to sit there for a few minutes.'

I hand the witness's typed-up statement to Fraser when I see her early evening. Her frown deepens as she reads it.

'OK. Get the security guard in here for a formal statement too, and let's see if the stories match up.'

'I plan to do that first thing tomorrow. Are you all right, boss?'

'I will be when this case is put to bed. I've got so many eyes on me from above that I feel like I'm splayed out on a bloody dissection table with a class of spotty teenagers hovering over me. Why do you ask? Do I look as bloody overworked and underfunded as I feel?'

I know better than to answer that.

When I get home, I find Becky's got herself dressed up. She's covered the bruises on her face with foundation so they look purplish and beige all at once, and licks of black liner taper to suggestive points at the corner of each eye. She's sitting on my sofa painting her fingernails dark blue. She's wrapped her dreads up in a colourful scarf. Her lips are painted, too.

'What's the occasion?'

'I'm meeting someone for a drink.'

Her expression warns me not to ask who, so I don't. If I don't want to risk losing her company, I'm going to need a softly, softly approach.

'You made it home just in time, then,' she says.

'For what?'

'They're interviewing somebody on TV about your case. In a minute.'

My gut takes a swan dive. This can't be good. If it was official, I'd know about it already. I sit down beside my sister to watch with a mounting sense of dread. When the screen cuts from the newsreader on our local channel to a studio in which three women are sitting, I understand that it probably couldn't get any worse.

Emma Zhang and Fiona Sadler are side by side on a velvet-covered sofa. It's immediately obvious that when we met at the bar, Emma wasn't dressed up or partaking of some Dutch courage to help her get through our meeting. She already knew exactly where she was going afterwards. I could not have misjudged that more completely. It was an own goal. I feel my jaw clenching, a dull throb in the gums around my back teeth. Both are familiar companions to my rising anger.

Opposite Emma and Fiona Sadler, in a matching chair, is a local newsreader who specialises in making even the blandest everyday report sound emotionally turbulent. Between them there's a low table with a box of tissues on it. The newsreader looks deep into the camera and begins to speak.

'We have a very special interview for you this evening, with crime reporter Emma Zhang and Fiona Sadler, the mother of Noah, a fifteen-year-old boy who tragically died earlier this week as a result of an incident in our city. Thank you both so much for being with us tonight.'

Fiona Sadler looks like a deer in headlights, but a

determined one. Her voice is croaky at first, but she pauses to take a sip of water and then the words flow from her. She describes Noah's personality as flawless, and talks about her husband, milking his credentials as a war photographer. Then she embarks on the tale of Noah's illness. The newsreader's head bobs encouragement.

All of that is just a prologue for the main event, though. Prompted by the newsreader, Fiona Sadler begins to describe the genesis of what the scroll along the bottom of my TV screen calls 'a doomed friendship'. Emma remains very still throughout, her hands folded on her lap, focused on Fiona Sadler, and nodding whenever sympathy is required, which means that her head, as well as the newsreader's, is bouncing up and down for most of the interview.

It's a coup for her. I can see that. A coup and a scoop. I'm furious.

Emma's flagrant bending of the rules has got her here, to this: a moment of pure professional triumph. I believe what she's done is wrong, to its core, but I can't deny that it's also making me question the approach I've taken to this case. Should I have bent the rules a bit, put more pressure on Abdi, questioned whether being methodical is the best way to get a result? Has the Ben Finch case scared me so completely that I've become nothing more than a detective-by-numbers? A dull plodder?

My phone starts buzzing. It's Fraser. I ignore it. I don't want to miss a word of this interview, and nor am I ready to get a bollocking for somehow allowing it to happen.

'We've heard how they met, but how would you

describe the essence of the boys' relationship?' the interviewer asks Fiona Sadler.

'I would say that the boys had things in common, shared interests and hobbies, and they enjoyed each other's company for the most part, but I would also say that there might have been a fundamental clash of cultures at the heart of their relationship.'

'Can you give us an example?'

Fiona Sadler begins to get tearful, fighting it every step of the way. It's a live meltdown: television gold. 'No. Not really, no. Actually, I'm not sure that's what I want to say.'

The newsreader offers her a tissue.

'But would it be true to say that you feel this clash of cultures might have led this boy to harm your son?'

'I'm just saying that you don't know who people are. You don't always understand them.' She begins to cry, and the newsreader turns to Emma, who manages to talk while rubbing Fiona Sadler's back ostentatiously.

Please salvage this, I think, please.

'Perhaps you could answer this for us, Emma Zhang. You feel a crime may have been committed here, don't you, and that the police aren't doing their job properly?'

'I do. I think that political correctness hampers us. This is a sensitive case, involving minors, but I wonder if it's being pursued as assiduously as it might be because the boy in question is a Somali immigrant.'

'And you say this as somebody who considers themselves a minority?'

'I'm half Chinese and half English, so I think I can talk from both sides of the fence.'

I wonder how she can stoop so low. I'm not sure she has a single thing in common with Abdi Mahad's family.

'So you think a kind of reverse prejudice might be taking place?'

'It's a possibility.'

'But why do you think that this boy might have hurt Noah?'

Fiona Sadler doesn't respond. She's weeping, and she looks as if she doesn't want to be there any longer. The camera closes in on Emma, who's ready to seize her moment.

'This is speculation, but I wonder if it could have been some kind of initiation.'

'What kind of initiation?'

'I don't know. Maybe for membership to a group, to show that he would be capable of perpetrating a bigger act.'

'An act of terror?'

'Why not?'

'Isn't that rather speculative?' Even the newsreader looks shocked at how far Emma's pushed this. Fiona Sadler is aghast.

My phone rings again. This time I answer it.

'Did I say "toxic"?' It's Fraser. 'I meant something worse but frankly I'm struggling to think of the words just now.'

'I don't know what to say. I had no idea about this.'

'I need to talk to Janie about how we handle this. I'll speak to you first thing in the morning.'

She hangs up, and I can't shake the feeling that she's cutting me out of whatever's going to happen next.

When the doorbell to my flat rings, Becky says, 'I'll get it.'

She speaks quietly into the buzzer and then calls, 'I'm going out for a bit.'

'Who with?'

She stops with her hand on the door handle.

'Who with, Becky?'

'That's none of your business. What's got into you?'

'Are you meeting the man who hurt you?'

She leaves, slamming the door behind her, but I follow. We clatter down the stairs together and I arrive at the front door before she does.

Outside, standing on the top of the steps, is a man with longish hair and a bunch of red roses.

That's all I register before I swing my fist into his midriff.

Maryam's sipping tea in her friend Amina's kitchen when she notices Fiona Sadler on the TV. Nur's out searching for Abdi again, and Maryam's left the flat to try to clear her head. She's determined that Sofia must not know about Abdi, but she doesn't trust herself to hold it together around her daughter tonight.

Maryam and Amina watch the interview in horror. Amina has no choice but to translate the bits that Maryam doesn't understand. She feels dirtied by the ugly words she has to pass on.

'I need to go home,' Maryam says.

'I'll come with you.'

'No.'

Maryam hurries through Easton, trying to reach Nur

by phone as she goes, but he's not answering. She sees that Sofia's tried to call her. She's rushed away from Amina because instinct told her that she must be home, to support her daughter in the aftermath of the TV interview, but she's suddenly overwhelmed by the terrible burden of continuing to try to protect Sofia from all of this, and she doesn't know if she can do it any longer. Maryam stops in the street and sits down on a low wall. Her handbag slips to her feet. *It's time*, she thinks. *Time to tell everything. To protect Abdi.*

A passing young man asks her if she's all right and she says, 'Please could you help me?' At her request he walks her to a taxi rank on Stapleton Road and sees her into a car. She asks the driver to take her to the police station.

'Which one?' he asks. Behind him, neon lights in a shop front advertise money-shipping services, and reflected in the taxi's side mirror a bus approaches, its headlights dazzling her momentarily. The car stereo is tuned to a lively Asian music station and there's a stink of air freshener in the car. Maryam finds it overwhelming. She doesn't know which police station. It never occurred to her that there might be a choice.

She repeats, 'Police station, please.'

The driver meets her eye briefly in the rear-view mirror and swings out into the traffic. 'OK, lady,' he says.

Maryam sits with her back straight as a rod, clutching the arm rest as he swings too fast around the corners and joins the dual carriageway, alongside which a handful of tower blocks make rectangular silhouettes against the black-orange sky. She thinks of all the lives stacked up on top of one another inside them, all the love and all the ugly.

The police station the driver takes her to is the local one, a red-brick building on an island of tarmac by a busy intersection, near the place where her neighbourhood meets the city centre proper. She pays him with the small amount of cash she has and wonders how she'll get home if she can't get hold of Nur. She wonders if her driver knows Nur but she's too shy to ask.

Inside the station, Maryam's intimidated by the reception area, but she steels herself and approaches the desk. In her head, she knows exactly what she wants to say, but as soon as she tries to speak to the officer at the desk, the words become muddled and she finds herself blurting out two- or three-word phrases that make the officer's brow crinkle.

'Say that again for me, darling,' the officer says once Maryam has fallen silent. She's a middle-aged woman with a pencil behind her ear and a coffee stain on her shirt that's wet where she's tried to wash it out.

Maryam tries, gasping for the right words, but not finding them, like a fish drowning in oxygen.

'Your son is gone, but he's on the telly?' the officer repeats very slowly.

'Please. Help us,' is all Maryam manages in response, and she begins to weep, defeated, as ever, by her foreignness.

'Take a seat, darling, let's see if we can get a translator here, shall we?'

The officer emerges from behind the desk and settles Maryam on a hard wooden bench that's designed to discourage comfort. She offers Maryam a cup of water.

'Where are you from? What's your language?' she asks.

'Somalia,' Maryam replies.

Maryam sits and stares at her toes against the beige linoleum floor. She looks up at the ceiling where textured white tiles are interspersed with smooth rectangular light panels. She checks her phone and sees that the battery's run down to red. Her stomach begins to complain and she realises she can't remember when she last ate something.

After half an hour the officer calls out to her. 'Sorry, love, we're working on it, but it's a busy night.' Maryam nods.

She wants to say: 'You must find my son. He's missing because his life fell apart on Monday night when he discovered that he was the child of a rapist and a war criminal, and a terrible thing happened to his friend. He's alone and seeking out a man who will hurt him.'

When she realised she was pregnant, weeks after the assault, Maryam hoped that she would miscarry the child. She'd lost three babies to miscarriage or stillbirth by then, but this one was strong. As her belly thickened, so did her sense that this child would not die. She feared the baby. She had been forced to look into the mocking, sadistic face of its father and she was afraid of what it could become.

When Nur returned from Eastleigh she dreaded the moment when he would discover her secret.

It didn't take long.

That night, after Sofia was asleep, and the kerosene lamp was extinguished, its smoke dispersed, he began to explore her body, and she stopped him and whispered her story to him and knew that he might leave and never return, leaving her only with her shame and mouths to feed. Other men had done this, their pride too great to stay with a woman who had been defiled by another man. Nur placed his hands on her taut belly as if trying to get a sense of the baby. They stayed like that for a long time, both very afraid.

By morning he'd made a decision. 'We'll leave here,' he said, 'before you have the baby. We have nearly enough money.'

'Where will we go?'

'Europe. If the baby lives, I'll raise it as my son or daughter. Nobody will know any different.'

Nur promised her that they would make a home that was safe for both children, and that Abdi would never know whose blood ran in his veins. England, he promised her, would offer them a refuge. Nur never mentioned the shame, but she knew he was trying to protect her from that as well. If people had known, some of them would have shunned her and Abdi both. The children born of rape were called terrible things; their mothers, too. Maryam kept her bump covered so the eagle eyes of her friends couldn't judge its size, but she admitted to the pregnancy.

In the police station, she takes a sip of her water. One and a half hours have now passed since she arrived. Her phone is dead. A man bursts through the doors into reception. His face is covered in blood. Dark drops of it land on the linoleum. He reeks of alcohol. He walks up to the desk and tries to explain that he was attacked, but he's too drunk to get his story straight. Maryam understands that he's not any more articulate than she was.

The desk officer calls for backup, and in the chaos Maryam slips away. She's lost her nerve.

She starts to walk home in the rain. She feels frightened by her own shadow.

Fiona Sadler watches as Emma Zhang shakes the hand of the TV anchor, and they exchange smiles.

Somebody touches Fiona's shoulder and asks if they can help her take her microphone off and she lets them dig around her clothing and draw out the wire. She experiences all of this as if she's not really present. She has a sense that she was carried somewhere on a tide of anger and now she's washed up in a place where she doesn't want to be.

In the car on the way home she puts as much distance between herself and Emma as possible and stares out of the windows, whose tinted glass casts a pall on the city. She doesn't respond to Emma, whose mood is adrenalin-pumped, and her attempts to chat are amped up and self-congratulatory. It reminds Fiona of Ed when he's telling stories about his work. It's the thrill of the kill.

When they reach her house, she gets out of the car before it's completely stopped, and stumbles but doesn't look back. Inside, she retches in the hallway; the grotesque sound of it feels like a rebuke.

She crawls into bed. She feels utter mortification. She thinks, *What have I done?*

Ed Sadler is sitting in an airport lounge. When he passed

through security, he found that a copy of one of his photographs had printed out along with his boarding pass. He looked at it for a while, remembering Abdi asking about it, before putting it in a bin.

He gets another text. This time it's from a friend telling him that they've just seen Fiona on TV. He battles with slow WiFi but manages to watch the footage. It horrifies him. As it finishes, his flight is called. He gathers up his bag and thinks, *I should have stayed with her.*

Every step he takes towards the gate feels more wrong than the last, but he continues nevertheless. There's no seating when he arrives, so he's standing looking out over the airfield when his phone rings. It's Sofia Mahad's number. Ed is tempted to ignore her call, but he knows his family isn't the only one suffering here.

'Hello, Sofia,' he says.

Outside the window everything is lit up in the darkness. Ed can see lights on the runways, the planes and the busy service vehicles. They remind him of a hundred other trips, and lure him to somewhere, anywhere else.

'I'm so sorry,' he tells Sofia. 'Fiona's suffering very badly. I think she's made a mistake. Her judgement isn't what it should be at this moment, as I'm sure you'll understand. It's very difficult . . . '

He expects to get an earful from her, but Sofia's not calling about the interview. There's something else on her mind.

'Please, can you tell me exactly what Abdi asked you about when you talked about Hartisheik camp? The night of the accident?'

Ed's plane is beginning to board. He can hear his seat number being called.

'Sofia, I'm so sorry, can I call you back in a couple of hours? I promise I will, it's just that I'm at the airport, and didn't Abdi record our conversation anyway?'

'Please,' she says. 'I need to hear it from you. In case he recorded only part of your conversation. I don't think Abdi ran away because of Noah. Something else is happening, and I'm sure it's to do with the photograph. He sent us a message on Facebook and I'm scared he's not coming home. I'm so scared.'

He might have hung up if Sofia had been confrontational, but she sounds so very vulnerable, and he hasn't the heart to tell her 'no'. Part of him knows that on this occasion he probably can't walk away from everything quite as easily as he's done in the past. He thinks of the photo he put in the bin earlier. You can destroy a single copy of something, he thinks, but nowadays the life of an image never ends there.

'One minute.'

Ed approaches the check-in desk and tells the stewardess that he won't be boarding the flight, and that he didn't check in a bag. He hands her his boarding card, puts his passport in his pocket and sits down on one of the many vacated chairs.

'Sofia?' he says.

'I'm here.'

'Abdi asked me about a man.'

The conversation comes back to him in more detail than before. Sofia's distress has jolted his memory.

'A man with a cleft palate?' she asks.

329

'Yes. Abdi was very curious about him. I told him everything I know, which is that this man was known to be very dangerous. He was newly arrived in the camp at the time, and some of the families reported that they knew he'd previously been involved in some atrocities. That he was a militia soldier disguising himself as a refugee. He wasn't the only one.'

'Did Abdi say why he wanted to know?'

'No, I don't think he did.' Ed's pretty sure of this. 'I just assumed it was his natural curiosity. You know, he wanted to know about everything, didn't he? I assumed the exhibition had piqued his curiosity.' Ed is suddenly aware as he says the words of how arrogant he must sound and how he's been looking at this the wrong way. 'This isn't about me, is it?' he says to Sofia. 'It's about what Abdi saw. Is there anything I can do? To help?'

'Just tell me if you remember anything else at all.'

'There is one thing.' Another detail has come back to him. 'I told Abdi that I thought I'd seen this man in Bristol.'

Sofia's silent for a few moments, before saying, 'How?'

Ed misunderstands her. 'If he was in Hartisheik at any point, it's not surprising he could have come here. Bristol's one of the destinations in the UK that many refugees make their way to from Hartisheik.'

'I mean how did you see him? Where?'

'I was at the Climbing Centre with a mate, just last week. When we left, I saw a man who looked the image of him coming out of one of the houses opposite. Might have been mistaken, but I'd been looking at the photo for the exhibition, so his face was fresh in my mind.'

'For real?'

'Absolutely for real.'

He hears a doorbell ring where she is, an exchange of voices.

'Sofia?' he asks.

'I have to go,' she says.

She hangs up and Ed picks up his pace as he leaves the airport, only pausing to text Fiona to say he's on his way home.

Becky screams at me to get back in the house and sinks down beside her boyfriend. I pull her off him and drag him up onto his feet. The stink of his aftershave is an insult.

'If you ever lay a finger on my sister again I'll make sure you go down for a very long time, or I'll come and deal with you myself. Do you understand?'

He nods.

'Say it.'

'I understand.'

The coward can't meet my eye. The impulse to keep beating him up is frighteningly strong, but after a few seconds in which I'm breathing into his face, watching the flicker of his cowardice in a muscle on his cheek, I shove him backwards. Not as hard as I'd like to. He scuttles away, arms wrapped around his belly where I hit him. The roses are scattered across the pavement.

Becky takes off down the street after him, and I call out after her.

'Fuck off!' she shouts.

I watch her go. I hope I've made my point. I've got a feeling it's not going to be that easy, though.

Upstairs, I splash water on my face in the bathroom and avoid looking at my reflection in the mirror, in case I'm reminded of my father. Woodley phones me just as I'm towelling dry and asks me to join a video call with Jamie Silva, the so-called 'Super-Recogniser'.

I sign onto my laptop, put my game face on, and find a young bald guy with a cheerful grin on the other end of the call. He's in an office.

'I've got your man,' he says. 'Name of Maxamud Abshir Garaar.'

'Bloody hell, that was quick. How? Have you seen him before?'

'No, I haven't, so I didn't recognise him straight away, nor did the central database throw anything up. I got a break when I looked at the IND database – that's Immigration and Nationality Directorate. It's complicated getting access, and I won't bore you with specifics, but I was able to search names and faces of immigrants whose applications for asylum have failed and who have subsequently disappeared. That's where I found him. I'm about to email you everything we know about this man, but briefly, he's extremely dangerous. He had his first asylum application turned down because it was felt that he was exaggerating the threat to himself, so he appealed, and the appeal will be turned down because they've been tipped off that he was very likely a perpetrator of war crimes in Somalia himself. Not a victim, as he claimed. However, that's a moot point at this stage, because since then he's disappeared, and on top of that, he's become a person of interest to police because of possible involvement in people trafficking here, using illegal immigrants as slave labour. That could explain why he was at the Welcome Centre.'

'Recruiting?'

'Yes. Because our lovely government has a policy of destitution for refugees who are waiting for applications or appeals to be decided, there are a lot of extremely vulnerable people to be found in places like that. It could be very fertile ground for somebody like him.'

'I really appreciate this, Jamie.'

'One more thing: Maxamud Abshir Garaar has been associated with another man involved in people trafficking. He's called Rob Summers. He's already on our radar here in Bristol because of a fairly recent disturbance at a property in Montpelier. We think there's a possibility that one or both men might be there. There's more detail in the email I'm sending.'

Once the email's landed in my inbox, I forward it to Fraser and then call her to request permission to set up surveillance on the house in Montpelier. If we can find Maxamud Garaar there, it's possible we might find Abdi Mahad, and bag a wanted man as a bonus.

My adrenalin's pumping. I'm so wired I don't even want to sit down. The chances of my sleeping are zero. I'd try to wangle my way onto the surveillance team if I thought Fraser would let me, but I know she won't. My hand aches from the punch I threw. My anger levels this evening have been high, and my ability to control my actions definitely patchy. It's exactly the moment when I should call Dr Manelli. I start to dial her number, and a recording of her voice asks me to leave a message before I realise that I don't want to speak to her, so I don't have to. I hang up.

I find half a pack of cigarettes in the box that lives on my bookshelves, between a volume of Yeats poetry and a complete set of James Lee Burke novels. I throw open the window. A sharp wind gusts in, carrying bitterly cold rain that spatters my face and shirt. I stand there for a few moments before I shut the window again. I fetch an ashtray and turn out the lights before settling onto the sofa. I leave my bed free in case Becky comes home.

I turn on the TV and begin the long countdown to morning.

Nur spends a few minutes that evening sitting in his parked taxi in a favourite spot of his, a place he sometimes goes when he feels as if he needs to breathe.

He never spends long there – he's too hard-working for that – but sometimes he can't resist it because he loves seeing the city laid out beneath him: its hilly folds, its shifting perspectives, the mix of old and new buildings. Looking down on Bristol from a height reminds him of when he was a child and his uncle would take him for a drive in his Land Rover out of Hargeisa, through the scrubby plains around it and up into the hills that ringed it. Together they would look down on the scatter of white buildings in the basin below.

On this night Nur's been thinking about Abdi. He's not immune to the fear that Abdi's paternity might have created his fate before he was born, in spite of their best efforts. Over the years, it's taken all of Nur's strength to keep the faith that violence isn't embedded in Abdi's DNA. The last few days have been the biggest challenge to his faith in the boy and his decision to raise him as his own that he's faced so far.

He watches the blinking lights of a plane as it crosses the city and heads out into the world. Nur isn't immune to a fantasy that he could flee from his difficulties here and find a different path elsewhere. Many men in his position have left their families. They returned to Somalia or went elsewhere to seek more money, and sometimes another wife.

He arrives home just minutes after Maryam, who's shedding her wet clothes in the bathroom, shivering with cold. When she emerges, Nur looks at his wife and daughter and feels a pang of loss for Abdi. They are three, and they should be four.

This was the way things were in Somalia, where family members disappeared or died in ways that were at first beyond the imagination of the ordinary man and then became normalised, with neighbours informing on neighbours, and nobody you could trust. It was never supposed to be like this here.

When Maryam says, 'I went to the police,' he finds himself sitting down, as if bracing himself for another piece of crushing news. When she tells her story of not being understood and returning home frustrated, he aches for her.

Sofia says, 'What did you want to tell them?' and her

parents both hold their breath for an instant. 'What?' she insists.

'Sit with us,' Maryam says, and Nur knows that Maryam's made the decision to tell Sofia everything. He won't fight it.

They talk through the night.

For Sofia, it's as if the world she's created here, the one that contains her family and all her bright successes, has developed a crack, which widens and gapes as her parents speak. Beyond the crack is darkness, and it's seeping in, licking at the edges of their world. She tries to process everything she's learning about Abdi and her mother and to find a way to maintain her idea of their lives as a bright, pure thing, but it's impossible. Eventually she asks the only question she can think of – the one that makes her feel like a child, not the independent young adult she's become.

'What does it mean?'

It's a question that Maryam and Nur have never been able to respond to fully. They've looked to religion for the answer, and looked into their hearts. They've found partial answers, but nothing that can entirely ease or explain the pain, or predict the outcome of Abdi's life. They hoped he would never have to know the whole truth.

'It means what we want it to mean,' Nur tells Sofia eventually. 'For me, it means that I gained a son.'

'It means that Abdi is looking for this man because he wants to meet his father,' Maryam says.

'He wants to know who he is,' Nur adds.

'Do you know St Werburgh's climbing church?'

'Of course.'

Sofia tells her parents what Ed Sadler told her, and told Abdi, about seeing the man who is Abdi's father in St Werburgh's.

They arrive at the church fifteen minutes later. Nur drives and the women peer out through the car's rain-spattered windows, but it's 2 a.m. and the street's completely quiet. After a few minutes they see a light extinguished in one of the houses; otherwise there are no signs of life. The spire of the church that houses the Climbing Centre looms high above the street, a dark obelisk. They drive past the church and see that there's a tunnel and some parkland, but nothing else.

'We need to come back in the morning,' Maryam says, 'as soon as it's light. If we start knocking on doors now, somebody will call the police.'

Later she'll wish she hadn't said this. She'll wish she'd got out of the car and shouted for her son. Found him and brought him home. Before any of the rest happened.

Abdi isn't aware that his family is close by.

DAY 5

No surprise that I lay awake for most of the night. Once my insomnia had unsheathed its claws, it refused to let me drift away from consciousness for more than a few minutes at a time. Sleep came in snippets, and even then it gave me no respite from the thoughts that circulated and tightened around me, noose-like, during the small hours.

When I did manage to sleep, those thoughts simply transformed into darker, looser things that made me feel even more disorientated when I woke afterwards. All I remember from those dream shards are faces swimming in and out of focus, and that I couldn't recognise a single one of them.

By 5 a.m. I'm sweaty and exhausted and the city's unnaturally quiet, as if it doesn't want to keep me company.

It's a relief to get up. We will find Abdi Mahad today; I'm determined that we will. I head to the office at 6 a.m., even though Fraser hasn't asked us to be there until 7.30. I review the evidence until it's time to gather in a meeting room.

Fraser's in bullish mode. 'The officers watching the property in Montpelier overnight have sighted two Somali men and a British man coming and going. We're confident that one of them is Maxamud Abshir Garaar, and one is

Robert Summers, his accomplice. Armed backup's been authorised because Summers is known to have a history of possessing firearms. We believe from the limited enquiries we've been able to make that the suspect Maxamud Garaar may be resident at the property at least part of the time, with Summers. We're concerned, however, that another flat in the building is occupied by a family, and there may be young children living there. We don't have more intelligence than that at the present because we've not been able to conduct many enquiries overnight, which means we haven't been able to establish if Abdi Mahad has visited the premises. But I don't want to waste time. I want to get in there now.'

I've got the security guard coming in this morning after his night shift, so we can nail down what happened to the boys, but that interview will have to be managed by someone else. This is too important. I put in a call to a sergeant I trust, asking him to stand in for me.

I'm standing in the car park with the rest of the team Fraser's gathered, getting organised for departure, when I see a taxi pull into a parking area. Abdi Mahad's family climbs out. I curse under my breath. I can't ignore them.

'Go on without me,' I tell Woodley. 'I'll join you as soon as I can.'

I show the family into an interview room and try not to display my impatience to get away.

Sofia Mahad acts as spokeswoman. 'We have something to tell you,' she says. 'It's a very difficult thing.' Her voice is so soft that I can hardly hear her.

'I'm listening,' I say.

'My brother, Abdi, we think he's gone to look for a very dangerous man because he discovered that man is his father.'

Sofia Mahad and her father watch me carefully. Maryam Mahad's eyes remain cast down.

'My mother was raped,' Sofia says. 'In the refugee camp, fifteen years ago.' She's having to make a big effort to keep her voice steady.

'I'm so sorry.'

'By a very bad man. It's the man in the photograph, with the cleft palate. We think Abdi found out that this man is his father, and he knows where this man is. We think he's gone to try to meet him.'

'Do you know *how* Abdi might have found out where this man is?'

'Noah's dad, Mr Sadler, told Abdi that he saw this man coming out of a house opposite the Climbing Centre in St Werburgh's. He recognised the man because he took his photograph before and he noticed the scar on his lip.'

'How do you know this, Sofia?'

'Noah's dad told me. I talked to him last night. He was at the airport.'

'OK.'

My mind's racing: Sofia and her family have come to the same conclusion as us – that Abdi's gone to look for Maxamud Garaar – but they have a different location for him. And theirs is backed up by an eyewitness who's also given the information to Abdi.

'This man raped my mother violently. Please, Detective, you need to go and find him before Abdi does. He will hurt Abdi.'

Three pairs of eyes watch me intently.

'Wait here,' I tell them.

I step outside the room and call Fraser.

'I have a possible alternative location for the suspect,' I tell her. 'The Mahad family turned up at the office as we were leaving. The intelligence is strong.'

'This operation's already under way. I'm not calling it off now. Get yourself over here.'

'Boss, the Mahad family—'

'Tell me when you get here, Jim, and get here now. That's an order.'

'Can I at least get some officers sent over to the other location?'

I'm speaking into the ether, because she's hung up. I can feel my cheeks burning when I put down the phone, with frustration, and not a small amount of anger, too. I'm tired of having my wings clipped.

Through a small window in the door I can see the Mahad family in the interview room. I can hardly imagine what it must have taken for them to come here today and tell me their story. I step back into the room and take the time to sit down with them, even though I'm dying to be out of the door.

'Your information's extremely helpful, and you have my word that we'll follow up on it this morning.'

'Do you have a son, Detective?' Nur Mahad asks.

'No.'

'Abdi's my son. I'm asking you to find him and protect him.'

'I understand.'

He clasps my hands between his briefly, as if sealing a pact. It's a gesture that's human and desperate and dignified. I know what I'm going to do.

'Thank you,' he says.

I get to my feet. I'm struggling to maintain a professional demeanour, but I just about pull it off. 'I think it would be best if you go home. I promise to be in touch the minute we have any news.'

'Will you go there?' Sofia says. She's astute. She wants confirmation that they're going to get some action in return for their information.

I will act, and I will do it immediately. I wasn't going to. I was going to do it Fraser's way. Right up until that moment, when Nur Mahad entrusted me with his son's life and clasped his hands around mine. Man to man.

'Yes,' I say. 'You have my word. Please, go home now.'

As I leave the building, I think, *I've done this before. I've followed my instinct and set out on my own and I remember how that turned out*. I pack the thought away. I'm going to do this, and I owe it to Fraser to call her and tell her. She doesn't pick up, so I call Woodley instead and explain. I can tell he thinks it's a bad idea from the sharp intake of breath, but he holds back. My funeral, I suppose.

'What's happening there?' I ask him.

'We're about to start getting into position to close in on the front and back of the property. I'm with Fraser a street or two away watching the video, but she's stepped out for a moment.' He means the video cameras our teams have attached to their helmets.

'I'm going to St Werburgh's.' I give him the name of

345

the street. 'I need to check it out based on the intelligence from the Mahad family. If Fraser asks, tell her I'll be on my way asap.'

Before I leave I ask one of the officers on duty to contact Ed Sadler and confirm what Sofia's told me is true.

I take my bike and I'm in St Werburgh's in twenty minutes. The centre of the city's only half a mile away, but this is a sleepy residential neighbourhood that's retained a bit of a gentle rural feel, even though it's been hemmed in incrementally by city sprawl for more than a hundred years. The row of houses opposite the Climbing Centre looks quiet. The Centre's located inside a centuries-old church whose tall spire dominates the view down the street. The small Victorian cottages front almost right onto the road.

I knock on the door of a pub opposite and get a bit of luck. The landlady's mopping floors and she lets me in. From the look she gives my badge I don't think she's a fan of the police, but she lets me peer out through her windows. I have a good view.

I ask if I can stay there for a short while and she responds with, 'I'm not serving you.'

'That's not why I'm here, ma'am,' I tell her.

I sit and wait.

Abdi wakes up stiff and sore. His clothes are damp and muddy. He experiences a moment of blankness before he remembers why he's there and what he's planning to do. When his eyes fully open, he's surprised to find that it's already light. He creeps out of his bush to relieve himself behind a tree. He's thirsty and cold, although the day promises to be a fine one, the blue sky losing its dawn yellow wash and darkening to cobalt.

He wonders what time the pub opens and if he might be able to sneak in and get a drink of water and dry off his clothes with the hand dryer. He tells himself not to be stupid. He's here to do something, and he knows it's time. Why wait? What's the point of looking nice or doing the right thing any more?

He clambers down the slope, carefully this time. His trainers squelch. Once he's on the street his nerve threatens to fail him. The house where he saw his real father is only about seventy-five yards away, but he knows that this man is dangerous. In the end, it's only because the daylight reveals that the house is painted pink, a non-threatening pale pink, that he gets the courage to approach it. As he walks towards it, a dog trots past on the pavement, a small terrier, and Abdi moves aside to let it pass, keeping his head down as the owner follows, noting only the newspapers under her arm and her sparkly rubber boots.

Abdi allows himself a quick glance at the pub as he crosses the street. He sees the shape of a man in the window. It looks as if the man is watching him. He ducks his head again.

At the door to the house Abdi raps three times loudly. For a moment, he thinks he hears banging in the pub window behind him, but he ignores it. He's concentrating on trying to breathe. The door opens.

'Mohammed Asad Muse?' the man Abdi suspects is his father says. He doesn't enunciate the words very well, but

Abdi understands that he's expecting somebody else. Abdi is thrown off his guard, but only for a moment. He decides to lie, because it will get him into the house.

'Yes,' he says. 'That's me.'

The door widens just enough to admit him.

If the pub landlady hadn't made a comment to me at that moment I might have been looking out of the window and seen Abdi Mahad sooner. I might have been able to stop him entering the house.

I only get a quick glimpse of his face, but I recognise him from the CCTV footage, and his height and build are correct. I'm sure it's him. I hammer on the pub window to try to get his attention but he doesn't hear me and by the time I get out of the door and onto the street he's gone in, and I didn't see who opened the door.

I call Fraser. 'I just had eyes on Abdi Mahad, and I think he might be with our target. I need manpower here.'

'Did you get eyes on the target?'

'No.'

'Then I'm not going to abort at this end. We're too far in.'

'Can you send me anybody? We're only a quarter of a mile away.' I could call for backup via HQ, but a trained and armed response team would be preferable, and quicker to arrive from Fraser's location.

'I'll see what I can do. Keep your eyes on the building. Take in the boy if he comes out. What's your exact location?'

I give it to her.

348

I walk down to the end of the street to see if I can get an idea of what's going on at the back of the houses, but it's impossible to get a good view without losing sight of the front. I cross the road to the Climbing Centre and wait in the old graveyard that surrounds it. The church spire looms above me. It's tall, and pierced by four large Gothic windows from the ground level all the way to the top. I try to get a map up on my phone, so I can get a sense of the overall layout of the neighbourhood, but my signal's too poor for it to download. The Climbing Centre's shut. I bang on the door and catch some luck when an early-bird worker lets me in.

'Can you stay here?' I ask him. 'Watch the street, don't take your eyes off it, and tell me immediately if anybody leaves that house.'

I explain what else I want, and he points me to a stair-well: a steep, narrow set of stone steps with the sign STAFF ACCESS ONLY. They're worn and slippery and they lead up into the spire. I climb as high as I need to get a lookout over Mina Road through a section of clear glass in one of the windows. It gives me a perfect bird's-eye view of the location.

Abdi Mahad has entered a terraced cottage that's painted pink. The tiny gap between the bay window and the boundary wall has been planted with bamboo that's tall enough to obscure most of the window. PVC doors and windows have been installed at some point. They're grubby but intact, unlike the roof, where tiles have come away in an area around the chimney stack. The property's on one side of a block of similar terraced cottages, most of them red brick. The back gardens all meet in an enclosed area behind. I can identify only one or two easy exit points, though it would be possible to escape through any of the houses if you could gain access.

I call Woodley. 'What's happening?'

'They're in position,' he says, 'about to go in. Fraser's asked for backup to go to you, but they're not going to be quick.'

I look out of the window. Everything seems quiet at the property, except that there's a man walking down the street towards it. He looks Somali.

'They're entering the building,' Woodley reports from his end.

Abdi enters the house and closes the front door behind him. Inside, the tiny front room's furnished with two stained armchairs and a futon mattress that has a sleeping bag on it.

The man whom he thinks is his father looks him over, as if Abdi's not what he was expecting. He offers Abdi a hand and they shake perfunctorily before he gestures for him to sit in one of the chairs. Abdi finds the skin contact electric. He stares at the man, sees the line of his scar. What makes Abdi feel very afraid is the quality of menace the man exudes. It's in the way he carries himself and in the way he looks at Abdi: part contempt, part challenge.

He speaks Somali when he asks Abdi, 'So did you bring it?'

Abdi finds he can't reply at first. Everything he rehearsed

in his head in advance of this moment has dissolved into a feeling that he's made a terrible mistake. Part of him had hoped that this man would know him for who he is, that they could experience some kind of mutual recognition, but now he sees how stupid he was. Abdi knew that this man was violent, but he hadn't thought that it would be an almost palpable quality, or that he would feel such a powerful sense of danger in his presence.

Abdi makes a break for the hallway, but the man's quick on his feet and slams the door shut before Abdi makes it out of the room. He pushes Abdi back into his chair with just the palm of his hand on Abdi's chest.

'Sit,' he says.

Abdi has no choice.

'I'm not who you think I am,' Abdi tells him in Somali. He blurts it out, as if he's been challenged by a teacher. He doesn't know what else to say. He just wants to leave.

'Then who are you?' Every word he says sounds thickened. Abdi can only just understand him.

'Abdi Nur Mahad.'

'How old are you, Abdi Nur Mahad?'

'Fifteen.'

'And why are you here?'

'I came to the wrong house.'

Abdi's sweating. He knows it's obvious that he's lying.

'Try again.'

Abdi swallows. 'I have some business with you.'

The man laughs. 'I'm a busy man today, Abdi, but I'm curious. What's your business?'

'You're my father.'

Whatever Abdi hoped might happen at this moment of revelation, it wasn't what followed. He'd imagined all different kinds of emotions, but not an absence of them entirely.

The man sighs, as if he's contemplating doing something that he doesn't want to do. 'Then I should have you beaten,' he says eventually. 'Because you do not know your place.'

He stands, and Abdi recoils back into his chair.

The man grabs him, pulls him up, and shoves him against a wall.

Abdi cries out and feels the man's hand clamp over his mouth, pushing his head back painfully. With his other hand he pats Abdi's pockets. The expression on his face is one of distaste.

'If I'm your father, then it must have been a sorry whore who mothered you.'

His face is so close to Abdi's that Abdi can see the open pores on his nose and the bloodshot veins in his eyes.

'I'll go,' he tries to say, his lips smearing against the palm of the man's hand.

Somebody knocks on the door.

The man puts his other hand on Abdi's neck and applies pressure.

'Not a sound,' he says. 'Don't move.'

He lets go and Abdi's back slides down the wall until he's kneeling. He gasps for air.

The man leaves the room and a key turns in the lock behind him.

Abdi hears the front door opening.

'Who is it?' he says.

'Mohammed Asad Muse.'

'Come in.'

Woodley stays on the line as I clatter back down the steps to the bottom of the church spire.

'Ground floor clear,' he says. 'It's very dark in there.'

'Abdi Mahad's still in the house,' I say. 'I think I need to go in.'

'Don't,' he says. 'Don't be hasty.'

'I think Abdi's in danger. Another man's just entered the property.'

'Be patient. Support will be with you soon.'

'It's not soon enough!'

'They're going upstairs,' Woodley reports from the raid footage. 'It's grim. Rubbish and drug debris everywhere. Staircase treads broken.'

'I'm going in,' I say.

'Don't, boss. Remember.'

He doesn't have to say more. I know what he means. I remember a foggy dawn when he and I drove deep into the countryside to interview a suspect and I ended up puking in their front garden, facing the fact that the choice I'd made had the potential to be very destructive and to cost a child his life.

'First floor clear,' Woodley adds. 'One more floor. Oh, fuck!'

'What's happening?' I ask, though I recognise immediately that what I can hear on the other end of the line is the sound of gunfire.

*

Sofia, Maryam and Nur are left at Kenneth Steele House feeling uncertain.

Detective Inspector Clemo reassured them and told them to go home, then departed in a hurry, but he didn't explain precisely what his actions would be. Nur and Maryam are worried he's fobbed them off.

As they leave the building, a man arrives with his wife and both report at reception. The man stares openly at the Mahad family, but they barely give him a glance. He wears jogging bottoms and trainers, but his wife's in kitten heels that clack as she walks. He has a hand on his lower back, as if he's in pain.

As Nur parks outside their flat, Maryam says, 'I want to go back to St Werburgh's.'

Sofia says, 'I think we have to trust the police. We told them where we think Abdi is.'

Maryam and Nur exchange a glance. They know they should trust the police here, but what if Clemo hasn't taken their information about Abdi seriously?

'Abdi could do something stupid,' Maryam says. 'We don't know what he thinks he's going to do if he finds ...' She can't bear to describe the man. 'He won't understand the danger.'

'We'll drive there and have a look, and if we can see the police, we'll leave,' Nur says.

They don't talk much on the way there. All three feel strung out with fear.

Woodley hasn't been on the line since the gunfire. The last words he said were, 'I'll have to call you back.' I wait in the entrance to the Climbing Centre, and decide to give it five more minutes before taking action. I'm not willing to risk Abdi Mahad's safety any longer than that.

A few pedestrians have appeared on the street: one or two climbers arriving for a session in the church building, and an elderly woman who inches along, pulling a lightweight shopping trolley behind her. It's making me anxious. I need to keep the area clear, but there are far too many access points for me to do that alone. I stand aside to let the climbers in. I'm glad I'm in my Saturday civvies today otherwise I'd stand out a mile in this crowd.

Three minutes left to wait. Nothing else on the street.

I try to call Woodley, but he doesn't answer. The elderly lady has made it only about fifty yards up the road.

Two minutes.

The door of the house opens. The man who arrived earlier steps out. I take a photograph of him with my phone. One of his pockets is bulging in a way I don't think it was before. He walks away up the street, overtaking the old lady and moving on and out of sight swiftly. There's still no movement detectable in the house.

I try Woodley again.

'It's a fucking car crash,' he says. 'Shots fired, but no sign of the target.'

'Tell them to get over here!' I tell him. 'I need somebody, anybody. We need men on Mina Road at the Climbing Centre, and on Lynmouth Road, St Werburgh's Road and Seddon Road watching all exits. I need armed men before it's too late!'

'I hear you, boss. I'll pass it on.'

I call Fraser and get voicemail. I leave the same message.

I call dispatch and repeat the message again, and tell them to get anybody here that they can. I try not to shout.

On the street a mother with a child in football kit exit a house a few doors up.

Woodley texts: **Armed response on their way to you.**

I have a quick word with one of the Climbing Centre staff before I walk down the street and knock on the door of the property that occupies the corner plot at the far end of the block. I show my ID to the first householder and put my finger to my lips when he opens his mouth to respond.

'I need you to exit your property, make sure all doors and windows are locked, and go to the Climbing Centre, without talking,' I tell him. 'Wait there until you hear otherwise. Do not leave.' One by one, I call at each house in the row leading up to the target property and repeat the message. It's a slow process. I can't risk them all leaving at once and attracting the attention of the occupants of the pink house.

I have to pass in front of the pink house to alert the householders on the other side, but I hope the foliage obscuring the window will mean I can do it without being noticed. I direct those residents to the shop at the opposite end of the road. I don't want any of them to traipse past the front of the target house either.

By the time I'm done, I'm regretting the fact that I can't do the same for the side streets without losing eyes on the front of the house.

I call Woodley again.

'We're a street away, boss,' he says. 'Me and Fraser, two armed officers.'

'Where are the fucking others?'

'Still at the scene. Medical attention needed.'

That doesn't sound good, but we'll have to make do with what we've got.

Abdi stays in the room and listens as his father and the man who arrived have a conversation that he can't hear properly, and then the front door closes again. His neck feels bruised and he hasn't moved from the spot he was told to stay in. He's very afraid.

He hears the door to the room being unlocked and his father comes back in. He sits on the edge of a chair, as if they're having a casual conversation, and says, 'Now, Abdi, I need to know how you found me.'

Abdi blurts out his story.

'Does anybody else know you're here?'

Abdi desperately tries to calculate the best answer. His first instinct is to say 'my family' but he knows that might endanger them.

'The police,' he says.

'The police. Are you a truthful boy, Abdi?'

Abdi nods. Think about the general rightness of that statement, he tells himself, not the fact that you've just told a specific lie, and he might believe you.

'You've been very stupid.'

He moves so quickly that Abdi's taken by surprise once again. His father pulls Abdi up and locks his head under his arm, dragging him into a squalid kitchen at the back of the property. Abdi can see only the filthy floor tiles. Abdi hears a drawer open and glimpses the glint of a blade as his father removes it.

'On your knees,' he says.

Abdi's shaking, from both the physical weakness that a few days on the run has caused and the disbelief that he's in this situation, that violence comes so easily to this man, as if it's second nature for him, but he's also overcome by a surge of anger. When his father loosens his grip slightly to encourage Abdi to kneel, Abdi throws himself at the man's legs, barrelling into him and knocking him aside. His father crashes into the kitchen units and regains his balance quickly. Abdi stands opposite him, panting. His father is between him and the door.

He smiles at Abdi, as if acknowledging that Abdi did quite well, but it won't last. He takes a small gun from his pocket and points it at Abdi. 'I wanted to avoid a gunshot,' he says, 'but needs must.'

As he raises the gun, Abdi stares into his eyes defiantly, wanting him to know that he hasn't cowed Abdi, that he's a monster whom Abdi isn't afraid to challenge. Abdi does it for his mother and for Nur.

As they face each other and his father's finger moves fractionally against the trigger of the gun, a shadow passes across the back window. Somebody's out there.

His father makes a calculation. 'To the front,' he says. 'Now.'

They walk the few paces to the front door. His father wraps his arm around Abdi's neck from behind and puts the gun to the side of his temple.

'Open the door,' he says.

*

'The rear of the property's secured,' is the information I get over the radio, only a few seconds before the front door of the house opens.

We've sent one of our armed officers to the back and the other's setting up in the spire where a small pane of glass has been removed to give him a clear sight line to the front of the property.

Seconds later, Abdi Mahad and the man called Maxamud Abshir Garaar both emerge. Garaar has a gun to Abdi's head. They pause in front of the property and Maxamud Garaar shouts, in a heavily accented and slurred voice: 'I want safe passage out of here and I'll let this boy go if you give it to me.'

Garaar looks around, trying to see us. He knows we're watching him, but he doesn't know where from. He spots Fraser's unmarked car, which has been drawn up to partly block the road. Fraser and Woodley are stationed behind it. We don't have enough vehicles here yet to obstruct every side street.

Abdi's grimacing. The barrel of the gun is pressed hard into the skin on his temple.

In the spire, we're in radio contact with Fraser and Woodley down below. A couple more officers have been mustered and are stationed at either end of the section of Mina Road that we're on.

'I can't get a clear sight line,' says the officer beside me. He's still as a cat waiting to pounce, making only minute adjustments to the weapon he has braced against his shoulder.

'I'm going to walk slowly and you are going to let me. If you don't, I will shoot the boy,' Maxamud Garaar shouts.

He moves sideways, crablike, his body and head pressed against Abdi's as much as possible. He travels away from us and towards the closest side street, in plain sight, in spite of Fraser's position just beyond it. I suspect he knows the neighbourhood and has an exit plan in mind.

Fraser calls to Garaar. 'Release the boy and we'll give you safe passage.'

He ignores her.

At the end of the street, beyond Fraser, I see three people advancing.

I radio Woodley. 'Pedestrians coming, please make sure they're held back.'

'I have an officer doing that,' he says. 'They must have got past him.'

From the spire I see Woodley, crouching low, approach the three incomers. Garaar and Abdi are moving very slowly towards them too. My sniper still has his barrel trained on them.

'Do you have a shot?' I ask him.

'I'll take it if I do.'

Woodley gestures to the three to crouch and gets close enough to talk to them. As I watch, my stomach turns when I work out that they're Abdi's parents and sister.

'I'm going to have to let him go,' the sniper says, 'He'll be out of range in seconds. Better to move position?'

'It's not safe past the squad car,' I say. 'Too many civilians. I think he's going to break to the side.'

He radios his colleague, directing him to move from the back to take up a position in the side street.

Garaar is within fifty yards of Fraser's car when he sees

two squad cars arrive at the end of the street beyond her. It's our backup. Their timing could not be worse. He stops, taking stock. As he does, one of the people with Woodley gets to their feet.

It's Maryam Mahad.

'Shit!' I say. I can hear Fraser shouting at Woodley through my earpiece.

Maryam Mahad, apparently oblivious to everything else, walks boldly up the street towards her son and the man who raped her. At first she takes fast strides and then, as Maxamud Garaar notices her, she breaks into a run and she screams at him. It's in Somali, I don't know what she's saying, but it sounds like a lifetime of words.

It's enough.

Maxamud Garaar's concentration is broken just for a second, almost as if he simply can't believe the coincidence of what he's seeing and hearing around him, and in that second Abdi Mahad twists away and I hear the gun beside me go off. The recoil thumps into my colleague's shoulder.

Garaar falls to the pavement. Abdi runs towards his mother.

'Get them off the street!' I shout into the radio. 'Get them off!'

Garaar's wounded in the shoulder, and his gun's fallen a short distance from him. I see him reach for it.

'Get them off the street!'

Fraser steps out from behind her car and intercepts Abdi just as Garaar fires. She and Abdi fall to the ground behind her car, out of my sight. I think I hear the bullet ricochet, and Maryam falls too, after a beat. Woodley breaks out of cover and runs to her.

Woodley's bent over Maryam, applying pressure to a wound on her arm. Nur and Sofia have been contained with a group of rubberneckers at the end of the street, and Fraser has taken off after Garaar, who's disappeared down the side street. I can't see Abdi, but I hope to god he's safely in the car. The sniper next to me is talking urgently to his colleague, instructing him to intercept Garaar.

The sniper and I run up the stairs until we find a window with a better view down the side street. Garaar's visible making his way along it.

'He's out of my range,' the gunman tells me.

Garaar's holding his left arm across his stomach and blood has bloomed across the fabric of his shirt on the back of his shoulder. In his right hand he holds the gun. He's walking on the narrow pavement between the parked cars and the foliage that overhangs the low walls at the front of each property. Just as he's about to disappear from view once again, he stops, staring at the end of the street.

Via the radio, we hear the command shouted by the sniper on the street. He orders Garaar to drop his weapon. There's a moment when the tension falls from Garaar's body, as if he doesn't feel any pain, as if he's realised that it's over, but then he raises his gun arm.

There's another shout from the sniper, who has him in his sights, but it does nothing to prevent the movement. The sniper fires and Garaar's knee explodes. We're too high up to hear him, but he twists as he goes down and I can see that he's roaring, with pain, and anger. His gun lands yards from him, as before, but this time, no matter how hard he tries, he can't reach it. He's folded over his shattered knee, blood soaking his shirt and his trousers and pooling onto the street. We see the sniper appear from behind a car and remove the gun that's skittered across the road. His colleague takes off down the stairs beside me to assist.

Before I follow him I turn to get a final bird's-eye view of the scene. I want to get eyes on Abdi Mahad so I can extract him safely. I see Woodley helping Maryam at the side of the street, and as he does, Abdi stands. There's no sign of Fraser. I try her on the radio. No response.

Abdi stands in the road on shaky legs, like a young deer. He leans on the car door and gazes around him as if he's there just as an observer, not a participant. He can't see his mother and Woodley from where he stands. He doesn't hear his sister even though I can see her mouth opening and shutting, forming his name at the far end of the street. It's possible the gunshot is still ringing in his ears, or perhaps it's the emotional cacophony of everything he's been through.

I pound down the stairs and run up the street. When I reach him, he gapes at me. I arrive at his side just as another officer does. He looks at us both as if all his worst nightmares have come to pass.

I catch him as his legs give way.

'Abdi, you're all right,' I say as I stagger under his weight. 'I've got you.'

The other officer helps us. Abdi's unconscious: a dead-weight. I'm searching for signs of blood on him, but I don't see any.

'This is Abdi Nur Mahad,' I say to the officer who is helping me. 'He's a missing child.'

I'm breathing so hard I might have just run a marathon.

THE DAY AFTER

In a private room in the Bristol Royal Infirmary, Maryam Mahad lies in a hospital bed. Sofia sits beside her, holding her hand.

Maryam was stabilised on arrival at the hospital yesterday, and was the first on the surgeon's emergency list that evening. The wound she sustained was to the arm that already bears a scar.

'You're going to have another scar, I'm afraid,' the surgeon said when he explained the procedure to the family, 'but it should be quite a bit tidier.' Sofia translated. Then she added something that made Maryam smile in spite of the pain.

'It's nice to see a smile,' said the nurse as she unwrapped the blood pressure cuff from Maryam's arm.

'I told her this new scar is a badge of courage,' Sofia said.

The surgery went well.

When Nur lets himself into the room, Maryam puts a finger to her lips.

'He's still sleeping,' she says.

Abdi is lying on the relative's bed underneath the window. He looks thin. Last night it fell to Nur and Sofia to tell him that Noah had died. He took the news very hard.

Nur embraces his wife and daughter, and then

approaches Abdi. He shakes the boy's shoulder gently and Abdi opens his eyes. He fell asleep in the midst of his grief and has woken up in its grip, too. Nur sits down beside him and opens his arms. Abdi lets himself be held, and returns the embrace. It takes long minutes for him to stop shaking. When he does, Nur hands him a hot drink and something to eat, and passes food to the women as well.

The family know that they'll have to face the world once again in a heartbeat's time. They know that Abdi may have to face charges over whatever happened to Noah, and they also know that things have changed for them all.

But for now they eat together. The rest can wait.

Hours later, Sofia arrives at home to get some rest. Alone in the flat, she tidies up. She wants everything to be nice in advance of her mother and brother's return. They don't yet know when they'll be able to be at home together again, but they hope in the next day or two.

She finds Abdi's bag in her room, the one he took to the sleepover. She empties it out so that she can wash Abdi's clothes. Amongst the clothing is the paperwork she took from Noah's desk. She sits on the kitchen floor beside the washing machine as its cycle gets under way. She's bone tired and she can't be bothered to get up. She sifts idly through the papers. At the very bottom of the pile, there are two A5 envelopes that she didn't notice when she first looked through this stuff on the bus. On the first, 'Mum and Dad' is printed in neat, slanting writing; the second, by the same hand, says, 'Abdi'. Underneath each of the names, a sentence is carefully printed: 'To be opened when I'm gone.'

The handwriting isn't Abdi's, and Sofia understands immediately that these have been written by Noah, and she must deliver them.

Abdi reads his letter at the hospital, surrounded by his family.

Dear Abdi,

It's weird to be writing this, because if you're reading it, I'm dead and gone. But you know that anyway, because if all went to plan you were with me when it happened.

I wanted you there so much, and I'm so glad you were.

I got the news from my doctor that I was terminal about a week ago, and the idea of dying slowly has been too much for me to bear. I've seen it happen in the hospital, seen what it does to the patient and to the parents. That wasn't for me. I didn't want to fade away under the sheets until I was just skin and bones.

Suicide is a big thing, but not so much if you're on your way out anyway.

My only problem was that I couldn't do it alone, but I also couldn't inflict the spectacle of it on my parents.

I chose you, Abdi, to be there, because you're my best friend.

I thought you'd appreciate the planning, the strategy, and the execution. To do it at the fog bridge added a sense of drama I thought you might appreciate, too. I wanted my

*last few minutes to be a party, with you. A proper teenage
send-off.*

*Did you notice my backpack was laden with weights
before I went in the water? I hope not.*

*All the elements in place like a finely played chess game,
no?*

*Please don't be sad about it, or guilty. I'm sorry to bring
you into it for the sad things it'll make you feel, but please
try to get over that and think of it as a thing that bonds us,
even after I'm gone. I would like that.*

Thanks for everything.

Your best friend forever, Noah.

When Abdi finishes reading, he thinks: *You used me. You
intended to die on Monday night.*

That's when his tears finally come. It's a release of sorts.

A few hours later he asks to speak to Detective Inspector
Clemo. He's ready to tell the whole story, in his own
words.

Fiona Sadler hears the metal slap of the letterbox.

She walks slowly through the hall where the family
grandfather clock ticks steadily. There's an envelope on the
mat in the porch and on it a sticky note explaining that Sofia
picked it up by mistake when she fetched Abdi's things. Fiona
peels the note away and sees Noah's handwriting. She calls Ed.

Her fingers shake as she tears the envelope open, ever
so carefully, and unfolds the letter. The sight of her son's
handwriting is as painful as if the words were lines that
have been carved into her own skin.

370

Noah's explanation is short: he decided to take his own life because he wanted to spare them the steep decline that he knew was imminent. He didn't want to diminish in front of them. His words tear at Fiona. She and Ed knew that Noah didn't have long to live, but she'd wanted every nanosecond of that time. She was accustomed to the pain of watching Noah's struggle with his illness. She'd felt as if she had it in her to help him to the end, that she was as ready as anybody ever could be to face such a thing.

Noah's letter ends with a thank you to his parents for everything they've done, and some heartfelt words of love that will help sustain Fiona and Ed as they grieve for their loss, though his choice to take his own life in this way is something they'll struggle to get over.

A short time after reading the letter, Ed Sadler calls DI Clemo. 'Noah went out on Monday night intending to take his own life,' he says. 'Abdi Mahad was not responsible for his death.'

Fiona herself picks up the phone to call Emma Zhang. She forbids her to publish any of the material from their interview. She threatens legal action if Emma goes against her wishes. She knows that this appeal to Emma's better nature is probably hopeless, but she gives it her best shot.

When Emma puts the phone down, she's irritated but not surprised. There's no dilemma for her here, though. She's been working hard on the material and it's nearly ready for publication. It's a terrific story, and there's no way she's going to drop it.

Fiona Sadler's call has piqued her interest, rather than dampened it. She wonders if there's more to this. She can't call Jim, but there's somebody else who might be able to give her the inside story. If there's a lot more to this story than she first thought, she could act on her idea to develop it into something that could be published in a few parts. A state of the nation piece on the racial situation in Bristol, perhaps, anchored by a gripping personal story. Surely the editor would bite her arm off for that.

She leaves a message on the voicemail of an officer she used to work with, giving the name that they've agreed on. It's not her own. She wonders how long it will take for him to call her back. While she waits – he doesn't usually take long – she returns to the document on her laptop. It's a work in progress, a report of the botched police shooting from yesterday, specifically an in-depth commentary from an ex-insider on how something like this could happen. When that's written she's going to continue her work on the main story, of the boys, but also follow up on any other angles she can think of: the witness, Janet Pritchard, for one.

She brings up a search engine and looks her up. Emma thought she'd seemed familiar when they met, but didn't put the pieces together until she'd done an internet search and found the woman's Facebook page. There, deep down in the photographs, was the link: Ian Shawcross. He's associated by a previous marriage with a fairly well-known Bristol crime family that Emma encountered when she was working her first ever case, right after joining CID. She thinks she must have met or seen a photograph of Ian at some point in the course of that investigation, though she doesn't remember exactly when.

On her notepad, she writes down his name beside that of Janet Pritchard, and circles them both.

Days pass before Fiona and Ed Sadler are able to talk to each other properly.

When the news comes that Noah's body has been released for burial by the coroner, Ed says very carefully, not wanting to push his luck: 'We could invite Abdi and his family to the funeral.'

'Yes,' Fiona says. 'And we could ask Abdi to do a reading, but only if he wants to.'

Her words sound strange to both of them. They're so reasonable. She's unsure whether she means them or not.

When I wake up on the morning after we find Abdi Mahad, my alarm clock tells me that I've slept for a six-hour stretch. It's the first time for as long as I can remember. Abdi Mahad is safe, but there are many details of the case that still need my attention, not least whether we'll be charging him with anything. I head to HQ.

Sunday morning in the office is deadly quiet. Only a couple of us are in. Otherwise it's like the *Mary Celeste*. Some new evidence has arrived: Noah Sadler's backpack, pulled from the canal yesterday afternoon. It's in the evidence room, not yet fully dried out. It contains two large bottles of beer, a sodden pack of cigarettes, a lighter and a full set of kitchen weights, the type you'd use on old-fashioned scales.

The DC on duty and I are coming to our own conclusions about what that means when we get a call from Ed Sadler telling us about a suicide note that Noah left and, a little bit later, a call from the hospital saying that Abdi Mahad is ready to talk, and that he's in possession of a letter from Noah, too.

On the way to the hospital I think through the case. I don't like loose ends, but I'm aware we have one in Janet Pritchard. I'm in agreement with Woodley that there's probably more going on there than meets the eye. Jason Wright, the security guard, came in as arranged yesterday morning and gave a statement that varied significantly from Janet Pritchard's. Apparently he asked if helping us out might make us look more leniently on his benefit cheating habit. Between him and Pritchard I don't know who's telling the truth, but I will unpick it. I make a note to speak to Fraser about it first thing on Monday morning. With her permission, I plan to dig a little more deeply.

When I arrive at the hospital, I find Abdi in a small room that the nurses have cleared for us. He's with Nur Mahad, who sits close to him and lays a reassuring hand on his arm as we talk. The boy looks drawn and tearful.

I sit down on a chair that's set at a right angle to his. I want this conversation to feel informal.

'I didn't know he meant to kill himself,' Abdi says. 'I thought going out was just another crazy Noah idea, because he was always trying to prove himself. The cancer made him feel like a freak. It gave him a massive inferiority complex. I didn't even know he was dying.'

We wait while he mops up his tears.

'We can do this another time,' I say.

'No! I want to now. I want to say it all.'

He talks. The tale he tells is of a night where he found out a devastating truth about his own origins. It continues with a journey through the city centre where he felt vulnerable and confused about what he and Noah were doing at first, and then increasingly frightened. Everything he says fits with the CCTV images we have, and with the evidence: the sodden backpack, the letters. He's extremely articulate, but I'm continually reminded by words he uses, and gestures he makes, that he's just a boy, and that all of this is far too big for him to have to carry on his shoulders alone.

'It's my fault he's dead,' he says, when he's finished talking us through it all.

'It's not your fault, Abdi. Noah intended to take his life.'

'None of it's your fault,' says his father.

'I didn't believe him. I thought he was lying when he said he was dying. If I'd believed him, maybe I could have stopped him.'

'It was always Noah's intention to take his own life on Monday night. Even if you'd tried, I'm not sure you could have prevented him. And if you'd stopped him then, he would probably have found another way on another day.'

'But I pushed him. He shoved me first, but I shouldn't have pushed him back. I had so much going on in my head, though, I couldn't deal with his stuff. So I didn't think, I just did it.'

'Did you intend to push him into the water?'

'No. He tripped, and then it was like he let himself fall. He spread his arms out before he hit the water, and it covered him up so quickly. But I should have tried to save him.'

'No,' I say. 'You shouldn't. Not if you can't swim. You would have risked your own life.'

'I thought that my own life was over that night. It was doing my head in.'

'It's not over,' Nur says. He gently cups the boy's face in his hands and looks into his eyes. 'Your life's not over, Abdi. It's only just beginning.'

Shortly after that, I take my leave.

Ultimately, it's not my call, but I hope we won't be charging Abdi with anything, and I shall be arguing strongly against it unless there's clear evidence to support it. A criminal charge wouldn't be a just outcome for a kid who got sucked into somebody else's world so very deeply, and who's dealing with the fact that his own world is a far more difficult and complicated place than he thought it was, by miles.

When I get home, I have a quick phone call with Fraser. When she pulled Abdi from the scene in St Werburgh's, she fell badly and broke her wrist. She's home and in a cast. I hear opera playing in the background. She lets me know that she's pleased with the outcome of the case and pleased with my work, but also that she's got a new understanding of painkiller addiction.

'Off my bloody head, Jim, that's how I feel. There's no way I can be on these while I'm working. Anyway, in case you hadn't noticed, it's still the weekend and my husband is cooking me a roast that I'd like to go and partake of, if you don't mind.'

Regardless of the good outcome of my first case back, it occurs to me that next week's unlikely to be much fun if Fraser's working with a broken wrist and no painkillers. No matter. I'm fired up for whatever the week brings. In the meantime, there are a lot of hours to get through before tomorrow. I feel my adrenalin crashing. I want to talk to somebody else about the case, but there's nobody here.

I call Woodley. It goes to voicemail and I leave him a message congratulating him on his work on the case. 'It was good to work with you again,' I tell him. It's definitely easier to say in message than in person.

Perhaps it's a streak of masochism that makes my finger hover over Emma's name on my contact list, but I decide that it would be a very bad idea to call her. I don't even know what I'd say.

I put my work clothes on to wash.

I turn on the TV and turn it off again.

I notice the message light flashing on my landline answering machine. I press PLAY.

'Hi Jim. It's Francesca Manelli. Dr Manelli. I noticed you called on Friday evening and hung up. I wondered if you're OK. I'm in the office for a few hours today if you want to call back. I'm glad you called. I'm always here if you want to talk.' She leaves me her mobile number before saying goodbye.

I replay the message and note the time stamp. She left it yesterday. I wonder if I'm imagining that her tone sounds warmer than it perhaps should if she was being strictly professional. I replay it again. I don't think I am imagining it, and I don't think it's usual for therapists to give clients their mobile phone numbers.

I don't call back right away, but I think I might, maybe next week.

I relax a little bit, but I still don't know what to do with myself.

Late on Sunday, as afternoon fades into evening, I'm back outside, perched on my parapet under a patchy sky, smoking a cigarette and watching the weekend walkers on Brandon Hill start to head home as the city darkens, when Becky lets herself into the flat. She says nothing, but makes us each a cup of tea and climbs out to join me. She takes a cigarette from my pack and I light it for her. There's a strong smell of Sunday dinner from one of the neighbouring flats. Becky's huddled inside a big parka, but I can see that her wrist has been clumsily bandaged. I don't mention it.

The blossom on one of the trees on Brandon Hill has burst. As the street lights brighten against the dying light and paint the blooms with an orange haze, they start to look artificial.

'It's a pretty view,' Becky says. Her voice sounds rough.

'You can stay as long as you like.'

'Thank you.'

'But he doesn't come near this building or even this street.'

'It's properly over this time.'

'I hope so.'

We smoke.

'Why do we want the people who hurt us?' Becky says when the ash on her cigarette's long enough to droop.

She looks at me as if she actually wants an answer. A tear slips down her cheek.

'Because we're afraid of being alone.'

*

378

Noah Sadler's funeral is held at a crematorium on the outskirts of Bristol two weeks later. The non-denominational chapel sits in the middle of generous and well-tended grounds, where carefully tended spring planting has been allowed to gently brush and frame the memorial stones of the dead.

Noah's mourners arrive in large numbers. The car park fills quickly, and the overspill vehicles stack up along the edge of the long driveway, most of them taking care not to track onto the closely cut grass. Jim Clemo notices this as he arrives on his bike. It's a late morning service and he's come straight from work. At the side of the chapel he hastily ties a black necktie around his neck and removes his cycle clips from his suit trousers. When he enters the chapel, he accepts an Order of Service from a man whom he assumes to be a family friend, and finds an unobtrusive spot near the back. From where he's sitting he notices the headmistress and some of the staff from Noah's school. It looks as if a fair few of the students have turned out, too.

Jim doesn't notice Emma Zhang, who's found a seat that's even more discreet than his. She sees him, though, and leans backwards to ensure that his view of her is obscured by another member of the congregation.

One of the last cars to arrive is Nur Mahad's taxi. It travels down the drive and circles around the crematorium. Abdi, Sofia and Maryam Mahad get out of the car near the entrance, while Nur finds a spot to park in. The only spaces left are a few minutes' walk away, at the far end of the driveway. He arrives back at the crematorium just in time. His wife and children have been shown to seats near the front of the chapel, reserved for those contributing to the service.

The music playing is a classical piece that Noah chose because he knows his mother loves it. It's a Dvořák piano trio, spare and beautiful. The guests talk quietly; some already weeping. The chapel is packed to capacity.

Abdi Mahad declined to do a reading at the funeral, in spite of Noah's request that he do so in the notes he prepared with his father. Instead, in agreement with Ed and Fiona Sadler, Abdi will be delivering some of the eulogy. The bulk of it will be given by a family friend of the Sadlers, but they also wanted a young voice to speak for their son. They asked Abdi to talk for a few minutes, no more, and only if he felt happy to.

According to Noah's wishes, the mourners hear a reading from *The Little Prince*, and a performance by some of the Medes College students of Abba's 'Super Trooper', chosen because Ed used to sing it in the car to make Noah and Fiona laugh.

After that, it's Abdi's turn to speak. He stands up, steps carefully past his father, who's on the end of the row, and walks to his place at the lectern, head bowed. He touches the microphone and clears his throat. Somebody in the congregation is crying audibly. A few coughs punctuate the silence between sobs. Abdi takes a piece of paper from his pocket and unfolds it, spreading it out flat on the lectern. His handwriting covers the page. He wrote this speech with Sofia's help. It doesn't say everything he wants to say, and it's not as nuanced as he would like it to be, because this is not the time or place. But there's truth in it. In most of it.

Dear Noah,

You wrote me a letter just before you died, and this is my reply.

I feel angry with you for taking your own life, but I understand why you did it.

You did it because you spent years suffering from your disease, and you didn't want to suffer any more. You did it because you wanted to save yourself and your family and your friends from seeing and feeling some horrible things in your last few weeks. You did it because you were tired of the disease that had owned you for more than half your life.

I never knew you without your disease. When I met you, it was already part of you, and I saw that you had to get up every day and deal with the fact that there was something destructive inside you. It must have been hard to live like that.

But I wish you hadn't ended your life early, because it means you stole from the people who loved you and the people who cared for you. You stole time, and you stole our goodbyes. We would have liked to have spent your last weeks with you, whatever it was like, and we would have liked to have been able to say a proper goodbye.

This is my goodbye. These are things that I would have said to you if I'd had the chance.

You were a good friend to me because you were funny. You were my favourite chess partner, even if you were impossible to beat sometimes. You helped me out sometimes. When I felt stupid, you told me I was smart. When I felt like I didn't belong, you told me that I did. When I felt like I couldn't do something, you told me I could. You judged me on my inside, not my outside. You drove me nuts sometimes, but you made up for it at other times.

I believe that you were a better person than you thought you were.

I will miss you.

Rest now.

Your friend, Abdi

ACKNOWLEDGEMENTS

This story owes thanks to many. Enormous amounts of gratitude must go to the following people, without whose support, talent and hard work this book and my career would be far lesser things: Helen Heller, Emma Beswetherick, Emily Krump, Liate Stehlik, Amanda Bergeron, Tim Whiting, Cath Burke, Jen Hart, Molly Waxman, Lauren Truskowski, Elle Keck, Julia Elliot, Aimee Kitson, Stephanie Melrose, Dom Wakeford, Thalia Proctor, PFD agency, Camilla Ferrier, Jemma McDonagh, and the team at the Marsh Agency, the publishers and editors of my translated editions, and the wonderful sales teams who get my books out into the world.

Special thanks to Elsie Lyons for the stunning cover design.

My research would be sorely lacking if it wasn't for the two retired detectives who very kindly advise me on police procedure and other related things. Thank you both. Thanks must also go to Frank Hemsworth, who patiently fielded my questions about IT. Any mistakes made in the novel are mine alone!

On the home front, thanks go to my writing partner,

Abbie Ross, and to all my wonderful friends and family who prop me up and regularly lose me to my writing, but put up with both very gracefully. Biggest, warmest and most grateful thanks of all are reserved for Jules, Rose, Max and Louis, all of whom have no choice but to live through the writing process with me every single day, and somehow remain generously and unfailingly supportive throughout. I couldn't do it without you.

THE STORY BEHIND *ODD CHILD OUT*

A long time ago, one of my children was diagnosed with a rare cancer. He was a thirteen-month-old infant with grey-blue eyes and skin on his temples as soft as velvet. He had an infectious, mischievous laugh and perfect small hands that would grip yours hotly and tightly.

Early on in his gruelling treatment I left the hospital one morning to visit a local supermarket to buy some supplies. There was no shop or restaurant on-site for parents to use, even though we camped by our children's bedsides day and night.

The walk to the supermarket was a welcome break from the pediatric oncology ward and the institutional machine that is hospital life. The movement felt good, the fresh air felt good, the freedom felt good. For a few minutes.

As I walked the aisles of the supermarket, I experienced a numbing wave of disorientation at the sight of the other shoppers moving purposefully between the rows of products packaged in hues that were oversaturated and overstimulating to my ward-worn eyes. I was acutely aware that these people didn't know where I had been ten minutes before or what I had seen. As I stood – probably reeking of despair, as my hair and my clothes had surely absorbed the smells of the hospital – I realized that my son's illness and treatment had comprehensively destabilised me. But if you had glanced at me, you'd have seen nothing more than an ordinary youngish woman contemplating the sweet-smelling shelves of bakery goods. You would never have known how the fear I felt silted my mouth, coursed through my blood abrasively like grains of sand, and whitened the tips of my shaking fingers, which were well hidden under the cuffs of my coat.

I bought nothing. I left the store and returned to the hospital. I raced up the stairs and along the corridors to my son's room. I leaned into his crib and smoothed down the silken hair on his head. I traced the curve of his ear with my fingertip and watched the rise and fall of his chest while my husband went out instead of me.

After that, during all the months while my son was gravely ill and enduring treatment, I avoided public spaces where life's carousel kept turning so flagrantly and I fled the cheap sympathy offered by those who love a victim. I felt altered, as if I could never navigate my life by the same compass again. I felt wounded – whether mortally or not, I wasn't sure then.

I was drawn to safer places: family and friends who didn't judge, who didn't sugarcoat, who were extraordinary enough to have the stamina for us as we put on a brave face for them and fell apart in front of them in turns. People's compassion helped up to a point, but my emotional wounds were salved most gently and effectively by something unlikely.

By chance I came across a sculpture called the *Pazzi Madonna*. It was created by the Italian artist Donatello almost six hundred years ago. It's a carved marble relief depicting Mary and Jesus. The religious aspect did not matter to me. What mattered was the power of its portrayal of a mother and her child.

Seen in profile, the mother's forehead leans gently on her baby's. Their eyes connect, his hand reaches upward to clutch the scarf at her neck, her arms enfold him, and his body curves to hers. She is his protector. The relief is carved from unyielding marble, but it couldn't be more delicate or fluid in its expression. There is nothing else to it apart from a carved square frame, cutting her off at the waist, as if we glimpse them through a window. The baby's toes rest on the sill.

The image spoke volumes to me across the centuries. In its simplicity, it absolved me for feeling such grinding sorrow and it told me that my ferocious feelings for my son as he suffered were acceptable and appropriate and somehow true. It did so because it told me a story about fundamental things, about a common humanity that lies at the core of each of us.

The events of *Odd Child Out* play out in my home city of Bristol. My main characters live there, and it's where their worlds collide. They share a home city, but on the surface of it little else. Their disparate experiences and situations create tension as the story unfolds. As I wrote, I considered what else they might have in common. Their flaws were the first thing to spring to mind; these are the nuts and bolts of fiction, after all. Some of my characters also share a feeling of being outside the 'norm' of society, just as I did that day in the supermarket. I remembered Donatello's sculpture. I thought about how the fundamental emotional needs for my main characters in *Odd Child Out* are the same. These people may not always be compassionate or fair or even likable at times, but they love and are loved; they crave affection and deserve our understanding and empathy.

Every day as I sat down to write *Odd Child Out,* I thought about how crucial the quality of empathy is when writing fiction. Treating your characters with respect and humanity is essential to developing insight into their complexities, and this felt especially important as I wrote about the Mahad family, whose life experience is the furthest removed from my own or any characters I've written about before, and was therefore the most challenging to imagine. I hope I've done them and my other characters justice. You as reader will be the judge of that.

And if empathy is an important tool for writers, I firmly believe it should guide us in life also. In our messy modern-day society, it feels essential.

My son is well now. He is thriving. I shall always remember the mother and child in Donatello's sculpture and how they helped me through the dark days.

QUESTIONS FOR DISCUSSION

1. *Odd Child Out* paints a picture of the horrors refugees face in their native countries and the challenges they encounter when entering a new community. Has reading this book given you a new perspective on the struggles of refugees?

2. Even though Noah and Abdi came from entirely different worlds, they developed an extremely deep and trusting friendship. What do you think each boy needed from the other that made them so close?

3. Abdi was raised in the UK, yet his Somali heritage plays a strong role in how others perceive him and his actions. Discuss the roles of race, prejudice, and privilege during the investigation.

4. The Mahads and the Sadlers each try to protect their son in their own ways. Do you feel their actions were justified? When, if ever, do you think you should cease protecting someone you love?

5. Noah wanted to explore and experience the world before his sickness took him. If you were ill, what would your bucket list be?

6. Edward Sadler knows he isn't a perfect person. Did your feelings about him change as the novel progressed?

7. Detective Inspector Jim Clemo is tackling his own personal demons when he is brought onto the Noah Sadler case. How do you think Clemo's personal and professional lives affected each other?

8. Maryam, Nur, and Sofia each had secrets to keep about their pasts. Do you think they were right to bury their history as they did, or should they have been more open with Abdi? What would you have done in their situation?

9. The man with the cleft palate is a figure of mystery for most of the novel. Did you suspect who he was? Were you satisfied with his fate at the end of the novel?

10. There are several cases of the media presenting partial or skewed narratives throughout the novel, such as Edward Sadler's exhibition and Emma Zhang's article. Do you think the media can ever be completely non-partisan? Do you think the media has any obligations to its subject when exposing a story?

11. Were you surprised by the truth of what really happened to Noah? Do you think anyone is still to blame for Noah's untimely death?

12. What do you think is the significance of the title *Odd Child Out*?

ALSO BY GILLY MACMILLAN

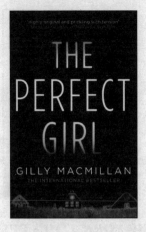

To everyone who knows her now, Zoe Maisey – child genius,
musical sensation – is perfect. Yet several years ago Zoe
caused the death of three teenagers. She served her time,
and now she's free.

Her story begins with her giving the performance
of her life.

By midnight, her mother is dead.

The Perfect Girl is an intricate exploration into the mind
of a teenager burdened by brilliance, and a past that she
cannot leave behind.

'**A wonderfully addictive book with virtuoso plotting
and characters – for anyone who loved *Girl on the Train*,
it's a must-read**' Rosamund Lupton

ALSO BY GILLY MACMILLAN

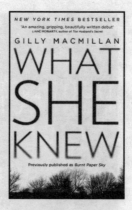

THE *NEW YORK TIMES* BESTSELLER

Rachel Jenner turned her back for a moment. Now her eight-year-old son Ben is missing.

But what really happened that fateful afternoon?

Caught between her personal tragedy and a public who have turned against her, there is nobody left who Rachel can trust. But can the nation trust Rachel?

The clock is ticking to find Ben alive.

WHOSE SIDE ARE YOU ON?

'One of the brightest debuts I have read this year – a visceral, emotionally charged story ... Heart-wrenchingly well told and expertly constructed, this deserves to stay on the bestseller list' *Daily Mail*